MW00788366

Stolen Knight

Knights of Kilbourne, 4

KEITH W. WILLIS

CHAMPAGNE BOOK GROUP

Stolen Knight

Published by Champagne Book Group
2373 NE Evergreen Avenue, Albany OR 97321 U.S.A.

~ ~ ~

First Edition 2022

pISBN: 978-1-957228-68-6

Cover Art by Melody Pond

www.champagnebooks.com

Version_1

*As always, to Patty—as beautiful
and as fierce as any dragon.*

Praise for Traitor Knight

SFF World (online magazine)
"...*a witty and action-packed page-turner that takes the classic fantasy land and adds depth, character, romance and political intrigue to brilliant effect.*"—http://www.sffworld.com/2016/05/traitor-knight-by-keith-w-willis/

Myths, Legends, Books & Coffee Pots (blog)
"*Medieval England meets fairy-tale. I soon felt at home there. All of the characters in this book had flesh on them—their individuality shone through. There was plenty of action, romance, suspense, a murder or two, a chase across the roof tops and a dragon—did I mention a dragon?*"—http://maryanneyarde.blogspot.com/2016/03/traitor-knight-by-keithwwillis.html

Praise for Desperate Knight

SFF World (online magazine)
If you haven't read Traitor Knight *and you enjoy swashbuckling, heroic fantasy with a light-hearted touch and a modern feel, go and read that – and then read* Desperate Knight. *Thoroughly enjoyable, and now with even more dragon!*—https://www.sffworld.com/2017/08/desperate-knight-by-keith-w-willis/

Dear Reader,

If you've purchased this book, there's a pretty good chance you're not a newcomer to Kilbourne. You've already made your way through the previous three adventures of Morgan and Marissa (and their friends and adversaries). You've spent an evening or two at the Sword and Crown, met face to face with a dragon, and cheered our heroes and (hopefully) hissed at the villains along the way.

And for this, I humbly thank you.

Because you're why I keep writing these stories. For people like you, who've read the previous books, come up to me at Renaissance Faires or other events, or send emails, and say, "When's the next book coming out? I can't wait!" Oh, my heart. It's that heady rush of your enjoyment as readers that makes me want to keep writing. The thought that someone out there is eager to dive into the tales I create drives me. And, I have to admit, there's a little bit of me that really wants to see what happens next too.

I hope you'll enjoy this latest outing. It is, as my granddad use to say, a "real rip-snorter", and it took me to some very surprising places. Get ready for new adventures, new locales, and a bunch of surprises—ones I never even saw coming.

When you're done reading, I hope you'll do me the favor of posting a review somewhere, whether Twitter or Facebook feeds or anywhere else you visit. And I hope you'll tell your friends if you enjoyed this book. Word of mouth is one of the best forms of advertising for an author.

And now, on to the story. That's the important bit...

Keith W. Willis

Chapter One

The cat stalked in an angry circle, lashing her tail like a small whip. "No!" she snarled. "It is not simply a book. It's dangerous."

Morgan discreetly moved his feet away from the cat's path. He glanced over at Marissa. She stared, wide-eyed, at the furry beast.

"But—" she began.

"Wrong," the cat remonstrated. "But me no buts, witch. It. Is. Dangerous. I should know."

Marissa's sharp intake of breath made Morgan's heart unexpectedly skip a beat. She swallowed, hard. "Yes." Her voice sounded raspy, almost unfamiliar. "You do, don't you? The—the binding spell. It's in the book. You created it. You told me."

Francesca bowed her head in apparent acknowledgement. "Yes."

Morgan was still getting used to the notion of a talking cat. This one, undeniably, talked. In fact, he'd come to realize over the last few days, she was rarely silent. Then, with a start, he understood what they were talking about. He cast a basilisk eye on Francesca and said coldly, "The binding spell? The one Kiara and Rhenn used? On me?"

"Well, yes," Francesca admitted. "That's the one."

The cat's expression, he thought, was rather hangdog. Which was a bit incongruous, all in all. Morgan rose from his seat to loom over Francesca. His breath came in a hiss mimicking the cat's own response. Marissa's head swiveled between them as she gaped at Morgan and her familiar. Francesca arched her back, her tail bristling, as they exchanged glares.

"Morgan, please," Marissa said. "Not now. We have other things to deal with. Go on, Francesca," she instructed the cat. "You were saying?"

"No, wait a minute," he protested. "Enlighten me, please. This thing, this book, was just lying about where anyone could pick it up?

Make use of such a dangerous spell?"

Francesca's ears were ears flat against her head. Her green eyes glittered. "No, it wasn't," she spat. "I mean, it shouldn't have been. There aren't even supposed to be any copies still in existence. They were said to have been destroyed ages ago. Well, all but one. That one was supposed to have been secured, under protective enchantments, in the archives of the Royal College of Wizards."

"Right. One copy, eh? Which somehow happened to fall into Kiara Northram's hands?"

"More likely the wizard's," Francesca opined. "Oh, I don't know. Anyway, what does it matter now? The point is, the blasted book should be destroyed. Before it can cause any more trouble."

"I'll second that," Morgan said. Marissa gave a less than enthusiastic nod. "What?" he asked.

"Nothing," she said. "No, I— Well, shouldn't we give it back to the wizards? To keep secure? I mean, destroying it sounds so… final."

"Keep it secure?" Francesca arched her back. "Like they did before?"

"Nooo," Marissa said. "But—"

The cat levitated into her lap and stared into her eyes. Marissa blinked and sat back.

"Oh, no you don't," Francesca said, her voice sharp. "You've felt the book's call, haven't you? It has power on its own, never mind the spells it contains. It's whispering to you, isn't it?"

"No!" she protested. "Don't be silly It's only a book."

"Is it?" Francesca purred. "Is it really? This is no laughing matter, witch. Books like this have serious magic. Deadly magic. I won't say they are aware, or alive, but they do have… desires."

Marissa shivered. "What kind of desires? I don't—"

"I don't think I really want to know," Morgan. Neither cat nor witch paid him any heed. He returned to his seat, anxious fingers drumming a nervous tattoo on his knee.

Francesca leapt up into Morgan's lap this time. He found himself giving her ear scritches. "No, I'm sure you don't," she said. "But you're going to. Because she—" the cat nodded toward Marissa, "—is in danger."

He blinked. Then he heaved a sigh. "All right. Tell us."

"Books of power—and make no mistake, this is a book of power—seek those who will make use of them. They want, no, need, this. Because then they absorb even more power, from those mages. As the wizard, and this Kiara woman, did."

Marissa's eyes widened. "So, you're saying the book wanted me to find it? Pick it up?"

Francesca flowed back down the floor again. She paced in a circle, then sat, with her tail curled around her paws, before she answered. "I won't say the book is alive. Still, because of the power contained within it...well, let's simply say I won't rule it out. Consider it like this. It has a certain awareness. So yes. When there was a choice between being stuck in that tower for ages, or coming along with you? No contest. You were the logical choice."

"And now I have the book," Marissa mused.

"Now you have the book. On the other hand, the book also has you. Which brings us back to my original point. I don't want my witch caught up in this. You need to destroy the book."

Marissa was silent for longer than Morgan thought called for. "Marissa?" he prompted.

"Yes, yes, I'm just—"

"Come on, let us destroy it." Francesca stared at her, unblinking.

"How?" Morgan asked. "Do we just...burn it or something?"

"No!"

Morgan could see Marissa's response was involuntary. She went ashen as the word sped from her and clapped her hand to her mouth.

Francesca eyes glittered with a fey light. "No?"

"Yes, all right. We'll...we'll burn it."

Even to Morgan's ears she didn't sound particularly convincing. "I'll build up the fire in the grate," he offered.

Francesca cocked her head, regarding Marissa. "I'm glad to hear you say it, even if only with reluctance. However, I fear attempting to burn the book won't work."

Marissa, Morgan noted, looked relieved. Which was not reassuring in the least. "It's just paper, isn't it?" he asked. "I'd think a nice hot fire... No?"

"No. If this were merely a normal book, certainly." Francesca glanced up at him, her green eyes glittering. "But it's not a normal book, is it? It is a magical artifact. A very powerful one to boot. It contains all manner of dark spells, woven into it by its crafters. Your little hearth blaze here? The book would snuff it out before you could blink twice. What's worse, the book would not be best pleased. There are tales, from ages long past, of just such attempts. Objects of power, like this, which the possessors attempted to destroy in such a manner. Things did not...go well."

"Umm. I see. At least I think I do." He considered this. "Drop it into the sea?" he suggested.

Marissa sighed. "No, it wouldn't be any better. Some big fish would just swallow it, get caught, and someone would end up with the book again. Someone who wouldn't be able to withstand its call."

The cat nodded approvingly. "You are learning, witch," she said.

"I'm learning the things we can't do," Marissa replied. "Very well, what can we do? How do we destroy it?"

The cat shrugged. "I wish I knew. Not, I realize, the least bit helpful. I shall have to consult."

Morgan glanced over at the hearth. "Francesca, you said our small fire wouldn't be able to do the job. What about something bigger? Much, much hotter?"

"You mean like a smithy's fire?" Francesca resumed her pacing again. "It's been tried. The attempt I mentioned before? The one which didn't go well? That time, it was a magical ring, if I remember correctly. It got a little…feisty, shall we say? Spread itself a bit." Her gaze went from Morgan to Marissa. "You do understand what I'm saying, don't you? The results, well, they're not something I even want to discuss."

"Actually," Morgan said, "I was thinking more along the lines of a dragon."

Francesca halted her pacing. Sitting back on her haunches, she stared up at Morgan, her eyes unblinking. The force of her gaze was so strong he only barely managed to not look away.

"You," she said at last, "are not as stupid as one might think."

Marissa choked out a laugh. Morgan merely nodded. "Thank you," he said. "I shall take that as a compliment."

"It was meant as one. Enjoy it; it's not likely you'll get another anytime soon. Hmm. I don't suppose it's ever been tried. A dragon's fire, I mean. Until now, there would have been no one who could have even asked. I wonder…"

"Should I speak to Wyvrndell?" Marissa asked.

"No, not yet. Let me do some research first. In the meantime, don't use the book." She turned her gaze on Marissa. "Don't even touch it."

Morgan rounded on the cat. "This book—this thing—is it somehow possessing her?" he asked. "Already? This soon?"

"Hello," Marissa said, waving at them. "I am here, you know."

Francesca ignored her, stalking in a small circle before she spoke. "No, I don't think so. She is rather reluctant, I'll admit. But she hasn't used the book, as far as I can tell. Which is to her benefit."

"Are you certain? I mean, certain she hasn't used it?"

"Still here," Marissa said, a bit louder this time. "And no, I haven't. Barely even opened it."

"Certain? No." Francesca was still focused on Morgan. "I

believe I'd be able to tell, although I offer no guarantee. Dark magic like this generally leaves traces. Auras, if you will. The witch shows no signs of it. We'll see. If she willingly gives it up. If she allows it to be destroyed. If the book allows itself to be destroyed."

Morgan shuddered. *If the book allows itself to be destroyed?* A most unsettling notion. Even more unsettling, he suddenly became aware of Marissa marching up to him, fire in her eyes.

"Morgan McRobbie, I do not appreciate being ignored," she snapped. "Or being talked around, like I'm not even here. This affects me, you know."

"Yes, we know," Francesca said. "That's the problem, isn't it?"

"Well, then, you'd be better served to include me in your discussions, instead of being rude. Otherwise, I shall have to get witchy about things."

"Marissa, I'm sorry," Morgan said. "I just wish you'd never picked up the blasted thing in the first place." He enfolded her in his embrace, but she jerked away and crossed her arms.

"Don't you think I feel the same way?" she demanded. "I never asked for this. For any of this. Learning out of the blue I'm a witch? Having to fight off Rhenn? Getting saddled with this stupid grimoire... I hate it."

"Yes, I imagine you do," said a voice from the doorway.

~ * ~

Marissa whirled to face the intruder. "Sebastien," she said. Her voice came out a hoarse mixture of exhaustion and relief. "I—"

"I tried to stop him, Your Ladyship." Briana, Marissa's maid, pursued the wizard into the room, indignation writ plainly across her face.

"It's all right, Briana," Marissa replied. "Always delighted to welcome Master Sebastien."

Briana retreated with a toss of her head and muttered imprecations.

"Apparently I've come at just the right time. I gather the grimoire is under discussion?"

"Got it in one," purred Francesca. "We've been discussing how to destroy it."

"Yes, well, I'm not sure you can." Sebastien eyed Marissa with an appraising gaze. "How do you feel about it, my lady?"

She heaved a gusty sigh. "Oh, I don't know. Francesca says she thinks the blasted thing will overwhelm me. Use me somehow. For something horrible, naturally."

"Of course." The wizard gave her a rueful smile. "What fun

would it be otherwise, eh?"

"I don't—oh, very well, have your little joke. Seriously, Sebastien, do you feel the same? Is this thing dangerous to me? To us? It's only a book, Sebastien. Isn't it?"

"Well, yes. And no. It's a book of magic, has magic woven into it. Dark magic, I fear. I think perhaps it might be best if we stored this thing somewhere a bit, well, safer. Where there's no likelihood it might do anything…suspect. Away from any temptations." He locked his eyes on Marissa's. She met his gaze at first, then hers faltered. She looked away. At the floor. At the cat. Anywhere but at the wizard.

"Lady Marissa," Sebastien said. "Please, don't fret. You did the right thing in agreeing to destroy the book. Happily enough, I feel it means the grimoire has no irreversible hold upon you."

Morgan exchanged glances with Francesca. Marissa cocked her head at them, then returned her attention to Sebastien. "Well," she said, "then that's all to the good, eh? Would you like tea, Master Sebastien?"

"Thank you, no. What I'd like, if you'll permit, is for me to take the grimoire away with me."

"Where?" she asked, as Morgan and Francesca both said, "Yes!"

The wizard smiled. "It's for the best, I believe, if the location remains secret. No offense intended."

Marissa considered his words. "Yes, I suppose you're right. Very well, I'll get it for you. It's upstairs. In my room." She headed toward the door, then turned back to add, "Where I have most assuredly not been perusing its contents. It's stuffed well away, in the back of a closet, behind a box of old boots."

"As good a place as any," Sebastien said. "Probably more secure there than it was in the wizards' archives. Please, fetch it down. I'll deal with it." He held up a hand. "Now, wait just a moment." Striding to the hearth, he caught up the tongs and brought them to Marissa. "Just to be certain, take these."

She took them, even as her brows rose. "Really? You feel it's necessary?"

"Let's just say I'm going under the theory of 'what could it hurt?' Humor me?"

"Of course." Taking the tongs, she strode from the room.

Mounting the stairs, she entered her bedroom. As she glanced over, she noticed her reflection in the glass and gave a harsh laugh. She was holding the tongs out before her, like a fencer ready to enter a fight.

"Hmph," she muttered, lowered them then opened the closet. As she did, an almost palpable sense of dark foreboding suffused the room.

"Ridiculous," she muttered, pushing aside gowns and chemises to reach the spot where the book lay hidden.

Shifting the box of boots to the floor, she finally uncovered the hat box where the grimoire reposed. She lugged the box into the room, set it on the bed, and opened it. A wave of nausea spilled over her, and she felt near to retching.

"Stop that," she ordered, both to the book and to her rebellious stomach.

The feeling passed. Marissa reached in with the fireplace tongs, lifting the grimoire from the hatbox. When she was certain it was well secured, she turned to go back downstairs. Just then, she caught sight of her reflection again. This time, the image shimmered and blurred, distorting her own appearance into something haggard and crone-like. The grimoire, caught in the teeth of the tongs, looked more like a writhing serpent. She gasped, nearly dropping the book.

A soft, sibilant whisper slithered into her ears. "Is this what your beloved sees, witch? When he looks at you, does he see the true witch you see in the glass? Or does he only see what you allow him to?"

"No!" she shouted. "You lie! I'm not like that."

"No?" The whispers were more strident. "Are you sure? There is a monster, deep within each of us. Some show more than others… Gaze into the glass, witch. See yourself as you are truly revealed."

Unwillingly, yet unable to resist, she stared into the mirror again. Her features blurred once more, until she was displayed as a distorted, repulsive old woman, bent with age and hatred.

With a harsh breath, Marissa rasped out the spell Sebastien had first taught her, when he'd discovered her magic. The spell allowed her to block out external forces. As the final word left her lips, the image in the mirror shifted again, back to her normal features. The hideous crone was banished.

"Damn you," she whispered.

Then, trembling, but resolute, she renewed her grasp on the handles of the tongs, to ensure she didn't drop the grimoire. The book appeared normal again, the serpent-like form banished as well. She squared her shoulders, marched into the hall then headed back down the stairs.

"Here," she said to Sebastien. "Take this. I never want to see it again."

The wizard regarded her with a thoughtful expression as he accepted the tongs into his gnarled hands. "It did something, eh?"

Not even daring to speak of the horror she'd just seen, Marissa simply nodded. Sebastien's smile was grim. "I wondered if it might. I'm happy to see you were strong enough to resist. Well done."

"I told you it was dangerous," put in Francesca.

"Yes, thank you for your kind concern," Marissa said. "Next time, you can deal with it."

"I wouldn't have picked it up," the cat replied.

"Yes, but that's only because you don't have any hands."

Francesca snorted. "Fair enough. Still, if you can joke about it, I supposed there's no lasting harm done you."

Sebastien held the book out before him, as she had. Marissa wondered, if only for a moment, if he could see it in its serpent form. She shuddered at the thought.

"My lady?" he said. His voice sounded strained, as if he was exerting a great effort. "If you'll bring me that little box?"

He gestured with his head. Marissa saw a small wooden casket on the table near the door. She fetched it over to the wizard. It was quite heavy for its size.

"Please open it," he said. She did so, observing the box was lined with some kind of metal. The wizard dropped the book neatly into the open box. "Now, close it, quickly."

She slammed the lid shut, uttering a low sigh. With a wan smile, Sebastien leaned the tongs against the hearth and picked up the box. Setting it back on the table he placed his hands over it and began to chant. His words rolled out, the power he poured into them infusing the very air. His voice grew stronger, the words unfamiliar, but redolent and filled with authority.

He grasped the little box as if it might try to escape. Casting his gaze to the heavens he cried, *"Fermiti signati!"*

She half expected an accompanying rumble of thunder. Instead, there was only a sound like a soft breeze caressing the leaves of an oak tree, and then a sharp click.

Stepping back, he swayed like a young tree in a stiff wind. Morgan hurried to take his arm. With a grateful nod, the wizard allowed himself to be helped to a seat. He drew a long breath and scrubbed a hand across his suddenly weary face.

"My, that took a lot out of me," he said in a tone of mild surprise.

Marissa frowned. "Are you all right?"

"Yes, yes, I'll be fine. Just some serious magic, like I haven't done in many years. I need to catch my breath for a few moments. Although I wouldn't say no to that cup of tea now."

"Of course. Wait right here." She hurried out, calling for Briana.

When she returned, Sebastien was leaning back in his chair, with Francesca curled up in his lap.

"Well, don't you two look cozy," she said.

He drooped one eye in a slow wink and chucked the cat under her chin. "I am endeavoring," he said, "to ensure I remain on good terms with Lady Francesca. One never knows when an ally might be useful."

Francesca purred. Finally, the cat stretched, then drifted to the floor. "For a wizard," she observed, "you're not so bad."

"High praise indeed," murmured Morgan. Marissa could see him struggling to keep a straight face.

"Wizard, be sure you keep the blasted book somewhere safe," Francesca added. She stared at Sebastien. "Very safe. We wouldn't want anything to happen to it."

"No, we certainly wouldn't," he agreed. "I shall do my best."

With a curt nod and a flick of her tail, Francesca stalked out. Marissa returned to her seat, making a wide detour around the table where the box stood. With the grimoire now secured, she felt lighter, somehow able to breathe easier.

As she sat, Morgan reached over to take her hand. His eyes held a question, and she nodded. "I'm fine. Still a witch, though." A mischievous smile danced across her face.

"Enchantress," he corrected.

Marissa shook her head. "Only in public. For you, I'm a witch, through and through."

"Casting spells upon your unsuspecting betrothed?"

"Hmph," said Sebastien. "Young love is all well and good, but where's my tea?"

Chapter Two

"Lady Marissa?"

"Good morning, Wyvrndell. You are early, are you not? I thought we were to begin today's lesson at ten."

"You are correct. At least to a degree," the dragon replied. *"Have you ever stopped to consider time? We dragons do not mark time as humans do. We do not, in fact, make use of clocks."*

"I—" Marissa pulled up short. "No, I suppose I haven't. I beg your pardon. I meant no offence."

"I have taken none. I merely mention this as illustrative of one of the myriad differences between our species."

"Like humans having—" She swallowed, as heat rose to her face. "Oh, I've done it again."

"You were about to say 'magic', were you not?"

"Well. Yes, I suppose I was."

"It is rather ironic, is it not?" said the dragon after a pause. *"You have something you really don't want. Yet it is the very thing I, along with a great many of my kin, desire above all else."*

"I'm sorry, Wyvrndell. I wish there was something I could do…"

The dragon's voice sounded a bit odd as he said, *"I'm glad to hear you express such a sentiment, Lady Marissa. Because in truth, I believe there may be something you can do."*

"Seriously? I will if I can, I assure you. But how? You've always told me dragons, as beings created from magic, can neither use it nor have it used against them."

"True. You have paid attention. What I have not yet said, is that there is a prophecy."

She clapped a hand to her face. "A prophecy? Another one? Really? I think I've had quite enough of those to last me a lifetime."

"This one," he said, undaunted, *foretells one who will not use*

magic against dragonkind. Instead, they will use it for the benefit of dragons. They will, in fact, aid dragons to achieve their dream of acquiring magic. I believe you, Lady Marissa, are the one who has been foretold."

She sighed, shaking her head. "It wouldn't surprise me in the least."

"Indeed." The dragon's voice rumbled in her head. *"Consider. Dwarves use magic, but they would never see fit to aid dragons. Even with the peace accord we now hold with them, it is a line King K'var'k would dare not venture beyond.*

"I see," was all she could manage.

"Historically, dragons' dealings with humans have likewise been fraught. Fear and mistrust have always existed on both sides. This has precluded any hope of fulfilling the prophecy."

"I just know you're about to say 'until now', aren't you?"

Wyvrndell gave a draconic chuckle. *"Yes, Lady Marissa. You and I—and Sir Morgan, of course— have ushered in a new era of relations between dragonkind and humans. It is the merest beginning, but I believe we will come to coexist peacefully."*

"How does this help dragons acquire magic?"

"I have researched this problem for a long, long time. In my opinion, only a human, one with powerful magic of their own, would be able to fulfill the prophecy. Until now, no human would have been willing to do so. Fear, suspicion, and legend run too deep."

"Yes," Marissa replied thoughtfully. "I suppose even if someone had been willing, the same fear and suspicion might have prevented dragons from accepting?"

"You are, as I have told my kin, an excellent pupil. Exactly right. But now, here you are, a human with powerful magic. Humans and dragons are not at enmity. And…"

"And so, I might be the one who can help you obtain magic?"

Wyvrndell was silent for so long, Marissa feared she had said something wrong. When he finally spoke, his voice was barely recognizable.

"That you would see this…would even contemplate such." He broke off, then seemed to collect himself. *"They sneered at me, the other dragons, when I told them I considered a human to be my friend. Well, not all. Petrandius, and Aireantha, they understood. But most jeered, or called for my exile, or worse. Even through their scorn, I held fast to the fact you were my friend. You, along with Morgan McRobbie."*

He paused, and Marissa waited for him to continue. At last, he said, *"Dragons do not have friends, Lady Marissa. We form alliances from necessity. We do not form friendships. It is an unknown concept among my kind."*

"That's terrible," she exclaimed. "How sad for you. For dragons, I mean. But for me, I am honored you consider me your friend. Thank you. I—"

He said, *"Lady Marissa, there is no need to declare anything you do not feel."*

"I was going to say, though I haven't given it a great deal of thought, you are indeed a good friend. Such is the way with humans. We often don't really think about friendships. They frequently just sort of happen, when we're not really paying attention."

Wyvrndell said nothing. She went on. "You saved my life. You did so at Morgan's request, but you did it out of friendship for him. You offered to teach me the arts of magic, in order that I wouldn't do something awful. You have been kind, considerate, and very, very patient. Believe me, humans, friends or no, are often lacking in those virtues. You have given me much, in friendship. If I can do something for you in return, why, what kind of friend would I be to say no?"

"Thank you," said the dragon. *"Before you make any rash promises, I would have you consult with Morgan McRobbie. With the wizard Sebastien. Perhaps even with your King Rhys. Seek their counsel in this matter. Then, if you are still resolved, we may discuss it further."*

"But—" she began.

Wyvrndell sighed. *"Lady Marissa, please do as I have suggested. Not all your kin will wish to see dragons gain magic. Speak with those whom you trust, learn their counsel, and then decide. We dragons have waited this long. A few more days or weeks is nothing."*

"Whereas we humans live such short, frenetic lives?" She smiled as she quoted his own words back to him.

"Exactly," chuckled Wyvrndell. *"Now, let us begin your lesson for today. I think perhaps we should discuss the costs of magic."*

"All right." She wrinkled her brow. "I guess I didn't realize magic came with costs. No one has mentioned it thus far."

"Of course, I cannot speak from direct knowledge. However, I believe if you consult the wizard Sebastien, he will tell you the same thing. The spells you cast are rooted in your own energy, your life force, if you will. Casting a minor spell only uses a tiny bit. A larger spell, naturally, will require more of your own energy."

She frowned. "I see. It's why I was so exhausted after my battle with Headmaster Rhenn. I used a lot of magic, so I used a lot of my energy."

"Yes, exactly right. Casting major spells, or several smaller

spells, one after another, requires a great deal of energy."

She considered this. "Are you saying I could potentially use too much magic? Harm myself somehow?"

"It is certainly possible," he replied. *"As you might tire after a strenuous activity, you also would become extremely weak after using a substantial amount of magic at one time. Any magic wielder would need to rest and restore themselves afterwards. You, especially, because you are not yet well practiced in your art, would need to restore yourself more than another who has practiced magic for a long time."*

"Well, that's good to know. Is there anything special I should do?"

"Rest, eat, and drink. The more you practice your magic, the stronger you will become. The less likely to exert yourself beyond any level of safety."

"Very well, I'll try. It's simply very difficult to find the time right now. I have so much to do…"

"Yet, there may come a time when this knowledge of your limitations becomes vital. Keep this in mind."

"Yes, I will. Thank you, Wyvrndell." Marissa smiled ruefully. "I'll try to get more practice in whenever I'm able."

"Good. Because I will say, if you do decide to assist in obtaining magic for dragons, it will require your utmost effort and skill."

"So, no pressure, then," she said.

"I'm afraid I do not understand."

"Never mind." She smiled to herself. "I'll work on it as much as I'm able."

Chapter Three

Kate Taggart, standing at the bar of The Mean Ewe, squeezed her eyes shut and uttered a low moan.

Donal, the barman, halted his cursory polishing of ale tankards. He glanced up to see what was wrong, then grinned as a sallow youth with a dyspeptic air staggered in, bearing what was, to Kate, an unwelcome cargo. It was, in fact, a large wicker basket, filled to overflowing with flowers. The wild variety and casual placement of said flowers gave the impression of their having been pilfered from some unsuspecting soul's back garden.

The youth grunted as he heaved his basket onto the bar with a thump that threatened to send the contents scattering to the ale-stained floor. "Flowers," he announced, perhaps in case his audience was too dim to recognize them. "For, um, uh," he searched his memory. "For Kate."

He glanced between Donal and Kate, evidently attempting to decide which of them might be Kate. She heaved a sigh, tipped the boy, and made a valiant effort to ignore her barman's knowing grin.

"Third lot this week," Donal observed.

Her only response was a fierce glare.

"Two last week," he continued, unfazed. "Can't be very many flowers left in the city, I reckon."

"Good," she muttered. "Then perhaps he'll stop sending them."

"I figured he'd stop after you blacked his eye," Donal mused. "Still, I have to admit, he seems right determined. I kinda maybe think," he went on, "he likes you."

"Ooooh, do you really think so?" She clasped her hands and fluttered her lashes. "Lucky me." She rounded on the barman, who dodged back with a guffaw. "Take these somewhere," she ordered. "Toss them in the river, why don't you? And yourself in with them."

Donal, still chuckling to himself, lugged the basket out. He wouldn't, Kate knew, dispose of the flowers. If history repeated itself, as it was often wont to do, she'd find the basket in her dressing room when she closed up The Mean Ewe and retired for the night.

Why was he tormenting her like this? Not Donal, she amended, although he was tormenting her too, albeit in a different way. No, she meant the sender of flowers. Her not-so-secret admirer. Her unrequited, unwanted swain. Captain Aartis Poldane.

She ought, Kate supposed, to be flattered by his attention. Aartis Poldane's reputation as a connoisseur of Caerfaen's womanhood was nothing if not the stuff of legend. He reputedly flitted from flower to flower like an extremely amiable bee.

He hadn't so much flitted in her direction as landed at her feet with a thump. Her mouth tilted into a reminiscent smile, squelched, as she recalled their first meeting. He'd been sprawled in the street before her, knocked ear over elbow by a fleeing drunk she'd ejected from The Ewe. He'd stared up at her, mouth agape, as if he'd just laid eyes on a rare treasure. He'd displayed none of his well-known aplomb, instead tripping over both his feet and his tongue.

As she and Aartis worked together to thwart the band of pirates infesting Caerfaen, he'd somehow managed to fall in love with her. In spite of her humble status and unsavory background.

Well, perhaps not so humble as that. She wasn't a mere barmaid but was in fact the owner of The Mean Ewe, along with several other thriving enterprises: a livery stable, a company of carters, and a couple of bustling dockside warehouses.

No, her heritage was the problem. Not an issue for her, necessarily, but certainly an obstacle to any hope of a relationship with Aartis. Something, she reminded herself, she was not interested in at all. But if she were—well, her father would be a problem.

Not because he disliked Aartis. On the contrary, they were friends. Kate had a sneaking feeling her father would approve such a match. Still, the fact remained: Aartis was a nobleman and a knight of the King's Legion, sworn to uphold justice. Her father was Ian Taggart, the man responsible for the majority of Caerfaen's criminal enterprise.

Aartis was one of the very, very few people who knew she was really Katherine Taggart. Perhaps the only one, since the pirate, Sharkey, had gotten himself killed trying to escape from a dungeon cell. To everyone else, she was simply Kate, the barmaid at The Mean Ewe.

Somehow Sharkey had managed to suss out her darkest secret. She'd never really understood how. Not that it mattered. What mattered was that Aartis learned of it when the pirate boasted about his plan to hold her for a ransom from her father. After he'd stormed into The Ewe to fight and vanquish Sharkey, Aartis had immediately confronted her with his knowledge of her connection to Ian Taggart and professed his love for her. She'd tried her best to dissuade him, but the blasted man was as stubborn as he was handsome. He'd simply smiled and said her parentage didn't matter in the least.

But it did matter. She'd refused his offers of marriage three times now, knowing it would never work. An honorable man like Aartis couldn't link his lot with the daughter of a criminal. It didn't matter if her father's enterprises were generally of the non-violent variety—it would still pull him down into the muck of her world, something she couldn't allow.

Yet there Aartis was again, sending her flowers. Not to mention, he'd vowed he was taking her to dinner tomorrow. To the Black Swan, of all places.

The Black Swan's reputation was nearly as legendary as her father's, if not quite so unsavory. It was a hotbed of seduction, a place no respectable girl would allow herself to be seen. Kate chuckled to herself. *Respectable?* The last thing anyone, at least in polite society, would call her. Then again, did she really care about polite society or their opinions?

Unbidden, a scene suddenly flooded her mind. In it, she wore a dazzling gown, her hair was coifed to perfection, while jewels glittered at her throat and ears. She stepped from a well-appointed carriage, sweeping into the Black Swan on the arm of the notorious, devilishly handsome Captain Poldane.

"Who is she?" ladies would ask one another. "I've no idea," would come the reply. "Never seen her before. She certainly is striking."

Then Aartis would escort her into one of the secluded, curtained booths the Swan was famous for. He would feed her dainty morsels, ply her with intoxicatingly rich wines, and then...

"Fool!" A raucous voice broke in. Kate's idyllic fantasy went scattering away like a morning mist before a stiff breeze. "Damned fool!" the voice said again.

Kate glared at Donal's parakeet, who strutted on his perch and squawked out one of his favorite epithets. In truth, she couldn't argue, even if the blasted bird wasn't actually referring to her. She was a fool to dare to dabble in such daydreams. Even if they'd been, well, quite delicious fancies.

She glanced round the tavern. Men cursed, and drank, and argued, and scuffled, and drank some more. What, she wondered, were their daydreams? Did they aspire to anything more than another round of drinks or a flirt with a sassy barmaid?

The smoke-filled room seemed to swirl around her. Kate staggered a bit, grabbing at the bar to keep from collapsing. When she opened her eyes again, Donal was gazing at her with fatherly concern.

"You all right?" he asked. "You looked a bit queer just now."

"I-I don't know," she replied. She took what should have been a steadying breath, and instead choked on the acrid air of the tavern. "Donal, can you handle things for a bit? I think I need to go—I don't know, go lie down, take a walk, something..." She gestured helplessly.

"Sure," he replied with a smile. "G'wan, scat. It's quiet. I can handle things. Maggie will be in soon, too. Go on, git!"

"Thanks, Donal. I owe you." He waved this away.

She walked out of the tavern into the fresh—well, fresher, anyway—air of the street, with no destination in mind. She just needed to walk. To think. To get her equilibrium back.

Heavy clouds hung in the sky, precursors to an oncoming storm. Kate felt uplifted by them. They matched her own mood, and she welcomed the oppressive atmosphere, reveling in it.

"Fool!" the bird had squawked. Was she a fool? Until now, she'd have responded with an emphatic "no". She was a prosperous woman, making her own way in a man's world. Her father had advanced her the funds she'd needed to buy The Mean Ewe, to be sure. She'd paid him back, every bit, plus interest. She'd made a go of the tavern and gone on from there. By any reckoning, she was successful.

So why shouldn't she be allowed to dream, even if only a little? Was it wrong? To dream of something a bit brighter than the smokey, ale-spattered life she led? Was it—?

As if in reply, the clouds broke open. A radiant beam of sunlight sliced down, illuminating the scene before her like a perfect painting. Suddenly Kate felt a genuine smile spread across her face. She breathed in, filling her lungs with air, and her heart with, perhaps, something more. With hope.

When she finally took stock of her surroundings, she found her wandering steps had led her, of all the places she could never have imagined, to the house where her parents once lived.

It was closed up, unlived in, and fallen into disrepair. Her father had for years made his home in his lodgings over The Fox and Hare. The house, he'd told her one day, after a bit too much to drink, simply brought back too many painful memories.

She'd been so young, only three or four, when she'd lived there, so the sight of the house didn't bring back any great flood of fond memories.. She did have a vague recollection of sneaking to the top of the grand staircase to watch her parents in the room below. They'd been dancing together, swaying to music only they could hear.

But then Mama had taken ill. The doctors, her father told Kate years later, had tried everything they could think of, to no avail. Mama had died, and her father closed up the house, taking both of them off to The Fox and Hare.

She didn't know if he'd ever been back. She'd once asked him why he didn't sell the place. He'd not answered, just shaken his head, a faraway look in his eyes, and poured himself another drink. She'd let the tears flow, just a little, once she was alone again. Her father was so strong, so commanding, so... in control. Except when he thought of the love he'd lost. Then he'd crumble a little bit. The brandy didn't seem to help.

Kate stood on the street and gazed at the house. It was set back from its neighbors, with its once-lush garden now overgrown with weeds and brambles. She shoved on the filigreed iron gate, now rusted with age and disuse. It creaked and protested, but she gave a heave and managed to get it open wide enough to slip through.

Navigating the broken, tipsy flagstones, she brushed aside clumps of tall grasses and encroaching lilac bushes gone to seed. A stout tree limb, fallen from a lightning-struck oak, lay across the path. She edged it to the side with her foot.

She had no idea why she'd ended up here, or why she was even going up toward the house. It was locked up tight, and she didn't have a key. Yet the compulsion to continue was too strong to resist.

A sound broke the silence. A squirrel, scampering through the undergrowth? She looked around but saw nothing unusual. Anyway, this noise had sounded much more human in nature.

"Damn!"

Kate froze. That was no squirrel. Unless, of course, it was taking speaking lessons from Donal's parakeet. She scanned the façade in an attempt to locate the intruder. There didn't appear to be anyone in the garden. Could there be someone in the house itself?

A sneeze rang out from inside the house. Kate's heart raced, but her ire rose even faster. How dare someone break into her family's home?

She considered beating a strategic retreat to summon a watchman. Another sneeze from inside the house put paid to this idea. Remembering the oak branch on the path, she smiled. A cudgel was a most effective weapon, a fact numerous rambunctious, bruised patrons of The Mean Ewe could attest to.

She gave the branch an experimental heft. With a satisfied nod, she advanced toward the house. The intruder sneezed a third time. The place was no doubt filled top to bottom with dust. *Ha!* Served him right, she thought.

Moving with caution, she made it to the marble steps leading up to the carved oak front door. The stones were cracked, and the steps canted drunkenly in every direction. One of them tried to tilt up under her feet, nearly sending her flying. Only a far from graceful leap saved her from crashing to the ground and alerting the intruder to her presence. For the rest of the way, Kate made sure to navigate them with a bit more care.

She gained the wide porch fronting the house. Another curse, accompanied by a hearty sneeze, assured her the burglar still lurked within. Tiptoeing to the door—well, as much as anyone could tiptoe while carrying a stout oak cudgel—Kate tried the door.

The latch lifted, and the door edged open. And, more importantly, it didn't raise a ruckus like a swan disturbed from its nest. For this, at least, she was grateful to her burglar. If he'd thought to lock the door, she'd have needed to break a window to get in. She narrowed her eyes and took a steadying breath. Then Kate slipped into the foyer. She paused a moment to allow her eyes to adjust to the dim interior.

The next sneeze came from—that way, she decided, following the sound. She crept toward the sniffling intruder.

Concentrated on the location of her prey, she wasn't focusing on her surroundings. The cudgel knocked against a small table someone had left in the hallway, and a china bowl crashed to the floor, smashing into shards with a sound to raise the dead.

Or at least to raise a burglar. Kate froze, realized this was silly, and hefted her cudgel. The intruder, now on high alert, was heading toward her, muttering, "What the devil?"

She froze now, her shock overriding any thoughts of attack or flight. She knew that voice. She…

"Who's there?" demanded the intruder. A shadowy figure lifted a guttering candle to survey the hallway.

"D-dad?" she managed to stammer, lowering her club. "What are you doing here?"

Chapter Four

Ian Taggart stared at her. "Katie? I-I might well ask you the same thing"

Kate raised her head in an attempt to look down her nose at him. Which was difficult, since he topped her own height by a good eight inches. "I asked first," she said in her haughtiest tone.

He chuckled, a liquid warble that always filled her with a surprising, comforting warmth. "That you did, that you did." He eyed the cudgel. "You wouldn't care to divest yourself of your weapon, perhaps? You wouldn't thump your old dad, would you now?"

She dropped the club. It landed, with dazzling accuracy, on her foot. Hopping, uttering a fierce curse, she made for her father, flinging her arms around him. "I should thump you, scaring me like this." She released him from her embrace and stepped back to glare at him again.

"I, scaring you? 'Tis you who's come sneaking around, scaring me out of a good couple of years I'll never see now."

"Hmph. You'd have just squandered them anyway," she teased. "Now tell me, Dad, for real. Why are you here? You've never come back to this house."

He shrugged, huffing a little sigh. "Ah, I really don't know, Katie. I got this strange urge, a feeling out of the blue, telling me I ought to come visit the ol' place, and well… here I am."

She knew her father's "feelings." He lived by whim and instinct, and for the most part they'd served him well. If they'd told him to visit his old home, he would have obeyed those instincts without question.

"It's odd, though," she mused. "Your feelings sent you here at the exact time I, for no reason at all, also decided to show up."

"Is a funny ol' world," replied her father. "That's how I met—" He stopped, swallowed, and shook his head.

"Mama?" Kate suggested, her voice gentle.

"Aye, lass." His eyes assumed a faraway look, as if he were

seeing something from a dim and distant past. "Ah well, no sense dwelling on it. So, tell me, Katie, why are you here?"

"No idea," she said. "I needed to get away from The Ewe for a bit, to think a few things out. I decided to go for a walk, and somehow I ended up here. I was standing outside, heard someone in the house, and figured it was robbers. I came in to deal with them."

He eyed the stout oak branch askance. "You have a right forceful way of dealing with things, don't you?"

"And who did I learn my lessons from?"

He barked out a laugh "Well enough. So, since we're both here, what do we do now?"

Kate quirked a grin. "Give the place a rousing dusting?"

"Ach, to be sure. It's a disgrace, ain't it? No, I'll have someone come in and give the place a good airing." He took her hand, something he'd not done since she was a little girl. "I know. Let's go up and visit your old nursery."

She opened her mouth to protest. When she saw the eager expression in her father's eyes she said, "Lead on, Dad." He beamed, and she knew she'd made the right decision.

Hand in hand, they went up the stairs. There was the landing where she'd peeked down at her parents, dancing in the salon below. She almost blurted out the memory, then decided this might not be the right time to bring up Mama again.

The nursery, when they surveyed it, didn't really bring back any great flood of memories. Until— "Bun-Bun!" Kate cried, pointing to a ragged stuffed rabbit which sat forlorn on a shelf. "I'd all but forgotten him, Dad. I loved him so."

"He was a faithful friend," her father observed stoutly as she hurried to pick up the toy.

It began to disintegrate under her touch. One of the rabbit's ears fell off, an arm dropped to the floor, and his little overalls crumbled into dust. A sob welled up, and she choked it back as best she could.

Her father wrapped a comforting arm around her. "Perhaps this was a mistake, Katie," he murmured. "I reckon sometimes it's best to let the past stay...well, in the past. Not to try and stir up old memories."

Kate felt an unexpected pang of sorrow for her father. "It's all right, Dad, don't fret. It was just a silly old toy. Didn't mean a thing." She flashed him a brave smile, hoping to forestall his maudlin musings.

"Ah, you're a good girl, an' no mistake. Yer ma would have been sae proud o' ye." His highland lilt was prominent, a sure sign he was feeling his past.

"Thanks, Dad," she said. "Come on, let's go."

She led him out of the nursery. As she made for the staircase he hesitated. "Hang on a bit. I want to show you something."

She eyed him warily. "Is it going to get you upset again?"

He laughed. "No, I don't think so, lass. C'mon." He led her down the hall and pushed on a door. The hinges creaked, but the door swung open to reveal a dim, dusty room she didn't remember.

"This was your ma's room," he said, gesturing around the room.

"Dad," she protested, certain he was going to be overwhelmed with emotions again. She wasn't sure she could handle seeing her father break down into tears.

"No, you'll like to see this," he said. He strode into the room and threw open the curtain.

A shower of ancient dust filled the air. She waved her hands in a futile effort to keep from choking on it.

"Ach, I have let this ol' place go," her father said. He sneezed, then flashed her a wry grin.

"All right, what did you want to show me?"

He gave another sneeze as he looked around the room. "Ah, exactly what I wanted," he crowed, strolling over to a vanity table. A candle rested in a stand. He found a flint on the table top. Striking it a couple of times, he managed to ignite a spark, and lit the wick.

"Now I'm ready," he said. He picked up the candle in its base. He led the way to a door and pulled it open. Stepping back to let Kate see, he held the candelabra high.

It was a cedar closet. The warm scent of the wood chased away the musty smell of the bedchamber. "'Twas sealed up nice an' tight," he observed.

She peered into the closet and caught her breath. "Are these…are these Ma's gowns?" She gasped.

Silk and satin and velvet, in a panoply of blues and greens and burgundies, lined the closet, shoulder to shoulder in dizzying array. There was no dust there. The door had been sealed tight against the depredations of time and moth.

"Beautiful, ain't they?" he said.

He studied her with a critical eye while she stood in the center of the closet, fondling the rich fabrics.

"They're splendid," she breathed, awestruck. Her father must have spent a fortune on this lot.

"I-I want you to have 'em, Katie," he said. His voice was husky with emotion. "You're just about the same size she was. I think your ma would like the notion."

"Dad, no!" Kate whirled to face him. "You don't mean it."

"Not doing any good hanging about in here, now are they?" he pointed out with unarguable logic. "You could use some nice things, eh? I don't imagine you've had time or inclination to be about getting' much of this kind of thing on your own."

"Noooo, not so's you'd notice," she said, casting a covetous glance at the gowns again. Her "best" dress was a patched, tattered affair which should have been consigned to the rag bin ages ago. "But Dad, these—"

"I mean it," he said. "I want to you to take them. Well, at least take a few. They're just going to waste in here, and," he spread his arms, "well, you're a grown-up lady now, Katie-me-lass, and should have some nice things."

She threw her arms around him in a ferocious hug. "Thanks, Dad," she murmured.

"I know I've not been much in the way of a father for ya," he said, hugging her back. "Maybe this'll make amends, at least a little."

"Pooh," she said. "I've no complaints."

"Well, maybe you should have," he said. "Anyway, pick yourself a couple, for now. You never know when you might decide to make a night on the town. Ah, you'll knock their eyes out, like yer ma did…"

"Well, if you're going to insist," she said.

She examined the gowns in the candle's flickering light. A rich green brocade caught her eye, along with a marvelous burgundy velvet which beckoned to her. She pulled them from the long rod. They might fit, at that. She shook her head in bemusement. What did she need with fancy gowns? It wasn't like…

She stopped, catching her breath.

"What is it, Katie?" her father asked, his brow furrowed.

"Nothing, Dad," she replied, holding the green one up against herself. "It's just a bit funny, is all. A fellow asked me to dinner. I told him no. Said I didn't have a thing suitable to wear."

"Ah, did he, now? And who is this feller?" He loomed in fatherly concern, and she stifled a giggle.

"Who is he?" he repeated. He was breathing hard, and she glanced at him in surprise.

"Rein in, Dad. It—well, if you must know, 'twas Aartis Poldane." She watched for his reaction from under lowered lashes. This should be interesting.

He stopped in mid gesture. "Aartis, eh?" he said, his glower softening a bit. "And how—? Oh. The pirates."

"Yes, the pirates. You sent him to me in the first place, if you recall. We were working together, trying to figure what they were up to, and how to stop whatever it was. Well, I guess he kinda took a fancy to me."

Her father's face would have put any thundercloud to shame. She hastened to set him straight. "He's been naught but a gentleman, Dad. I told him it wouldn't work, him and me. Still, it didn't put him off one bit. He's been sending me flowers, and comin' round to see me at The Ewe…"

"Oh, Lord, 'tis all my fault," he moaned. "I should never ha' done."

"Why? He's sweet, really, a right baa-lamb, in spite of how they talk about him. Still, there is one thing, Dad."

He stared at her, his eyes hard and mouth set in a thin line. He scanned her, then said, "All right, tell me the worst. Did he—"

She could tell where his thoughts had gone and cut him off before he could get it out. "No, it's not what you're thinking." It was worse, she reflected. Much worse. Might as well out with it. She said, "It's… well, he knows. I mean, he knows who I am."

"You told him?" His expression was shocked, mortified, and furious, all in one. "Katie, how could you?"

"No, steady on. Of course not. I didn't tell him a thing. Truly, I didn't. I've never told a soul. I promised you I wouldn't, and I've kept my word."

"Then how'd he find out?"

She shrugged. "Somehow, though I've no notion how, one of those damned pirates figured out who I was. Am. About me being your daughter. He came for me at The Ewe. Was going to take me captive and make you pay a ransom."

If her father's expression had been thunderous before, it was nothing to the one creasing his face now. Still, there was nothing for it. She went on, "Aartis came tearing in, fire in his eye, and fought him up and down The Ewe. I can't believe you never heard about the brawl. It was magnificent. Anyway, he managed to best the pirate and save me. Afterward, he told me he knew who I was. The pirate had let on what he planned. Aartis says he doesn't care. And—and he says he wants to marry me."

She regarded at her father, waiting for the storm to break. "I told him he was mad as a hedgehog in moonlight. Told him he couldn't marry someone like me, with him a nobleman an' all. And me a mere barmaid, and…"

"And the daughter of Ian Taggart," he finished. "Still, come now. A mere barmaid? I think not, Katie, me lass."

"Oh, he knows that bit too."

"Hmph. I think Aartis knows too damned much, and more than's good for him."

"Now get that look out of your eye, Dad."

"Look? What look? Me?" he protested, but she could see a grin threatening to spread across his face.

A feeling of relief washed through her, like a fresh breeze on a spring day. He wasn't about to throw a fit after all. "Yes, you. That look, the one that means someone's about to come up against it, and things are about to get messy. This is my concern, not yours. I'm a grown woman. I can take care of myself."

He drew a breath to argue, then let it out again. "Aye, ye are. All right, I'll not interfere. Aartis is a good lad and has always been square with me." He eyed her again. "So, he's asked you to dinner, eh? And you've nothin' to wear? Well, I think we've solved your problem then, haven't we, now?"

She laughed. "Perhaps," she ventured. "I haven't said yes, you know. To be honest, I've said no."

"Ah, our Aartis, he's a persistent feller. If he wants somethin', or someone, he goes after it."

"Kind of like someone else I know," Kate said.

"Hmph," he replied, but she could tell his heart wasn't in it. Despite his earlier agitation, he almost sounded pleased. "You've got yer ma's eyes, and her spirit too. Might as well have a gown or three to go with it, eh? If anyone deserves to be squired about and spoiled a bit, Katie, it's you."

She hung the green gown back on the rack and gave him a fierce hug. "Thanks, Dad. Now, what do you think? The green one, or the red?"

"Ah, the green was yer ma's favorite. You'll be smashing in it."

"The green it is, then," she said. "If it's all right, I'll take them both."

"Take them all," he said with a wave. "I should've cleared this place out and sold it ages ago."

"Why didn't you?"

"Ach, just sentiment, I reckon. I-I guess I had this crazy notion we'd come back here someday, you an' me. Nothing but moonshine, I guess. I've trod a dicey road, Katie, and no mistake. After yer ma died, I reckon I didn't care. Then, by the time I came to me senses, I was in too deep, and things were hummin' along. I was coinin' money, lass, and for what?"

She remained silent.

At last, he said, "Look at me now. Sure, I've got all the gold any one man would ever want. Which doesn't mean a thing, when my own sweet girl can't even acknowledge her dad or be seen in polite society. Ah, I reckon I've made a right mess o' things."

"Polite society? Pooh for them," she scoffed, snapping her fingers. "It's just a chance to get a good dinner into me, for once."

"As you should. You take those gowns and have a good time. Forget you're stuck with this ol' reprobate for a father."

"Like I'd forget you. Don't you go getting all maudlin on me. You're my dad, and I love you. Even if you are an old reprobate." She flashed him a brilliant grin. "Takes one to know one, eh?"

He started to object, but she laid a finger across his lips. "Let's go," she said. "I want to try this on and see if it needs to be altered. And I've got to let Aartis know I'll accept his offer. Of dinner," she added, lest he misinterpret which offer she meant.

There was a distant look in her father's eyes as she led him out of the house. She knew it well. It meant he was planning something. She just had no idea what it might be.

Chapter Five

Marissa woke to find Francesca curled up on the quilt next to her in a puddle of sunlight. She slipped from under the warmth of the covering, careful not to disturb the cat. Not careful enough, evidently; Francesca opened one green eye, impaling her with a basilisk stare.

"And good morning to you too, Francesca," Marissa said over her shoulder as she hurried off to the garderobe. The cat's only reply was a throaty growl.

When she returned, Francesca had roused herself and was engaged in an elaborate toilette. As Marissa yawned, the cat said, "You have an engagement."

"I…see," she replied, though she didn't in the least. "Might I ask with whom? And when? Perhaps even where?"

"You are to present yourself at The Gray Dove. At the stroke of two," Francesca replied, scrubbing a paw across her face. "Please be prompt."

Marissa sighed. "Don't be so blasted mysterious. What's this about? Tell me, or I shan't go."

"I can't tell you any more than I have," Francesca said, "because I don't know any more. Well, I do know one thing. It is witch business. But in this instance, I am merely the messenger."

"Oh." There wasn't much else to reply to this statement. Marissa heaved an aggrieved sigh. "Very well. Gray Dove, at two." Then she brightened. "At least, with any luck, I'll get a decent pot of tea out of it."

"Hope," said the cat with a philosophical air, "is what keeps us going. That, and breakfast," she added, as Briana came bustling in with a cart laden with comestibles and coffee. "Is this a pitcher of cream I see before me? Mrwow."

"Your breakfast, m'lady," Briana announced, pouring coffee while managing to ignore the cat. Marissa smothered a smile. Briana's opinion of talking familiars ranked with her opinion of root vegetables.

Francesca, for her part, made no effort to cultivate favor with the maid, despite the fact she brought the cat's meals along with her mistress's.

Francesca jumped from the bed to the floor in time to pounce on a plate of fish. Marissa sipped her coffee and slathered jam onto a hunk of warm bread. "You won't tell me anything more?"

Briana's mouth opened and closed in confusion. At last she managed to say, "Tell you what, m'lady?"

"I'm sorry, Briana. I was speaking to Lady Francesca," Marissa said.

Briana rolled her eyes and departed at speed.

Francesca watched her go, swallowed a morsel of fish, and said, "I don't know any more. I gave you all the information I possess. You'll simply have to go and see. Think of the tea."

"Hmph. Thank you for nothing. It's not like I have anything else to do." Marissa gestured with the hand laden with bread and jam, nearly dropping it to the floor. "Just a very involved wedding to plan, taking place before the bloody king and queen. Nothing, no not much at all."

"Sarcasm," Francesca said, "does not become a witch. In particular, not the Royal Enchantress."

There was either too little, or way too much, one could reply to this. Choking back a laugh, Marissa turned her attention to her breakfast. She did, in fact, have a lot to do today. The wedding was only a few days hence, and her parents would be arriving tomorrow from Vynfold. It would be wonderful to see them, she mused. She'd left them in a mad rush several weeks ago, via a magical portal with Sebastien, off to save king and kingdom. Of course, she'd sent letters, but it wasn't the same.

After attending to the myriad responsibilities requiring her attention, Marissa presented herself at The Gray Dove Tea Shoppe just when the bells sounded the hour of two.

Stepping inside, she found the air suffused with the welcoming aroma of fragrant tea and fresh-baked buns. Not, Marissa said to herself with a slight chuckle, the atmosphere for clandestine meetings and "witch business". No, The Gray Dove was exactly what it purported itself to be: a rather genteel tea shop catering to ladies of good breeding. The cups were clean and unmarred by cracks, the tea first rate, and the buns—well, more than one debutante had been forced to forgo a scheduled ball due to consuming too many of the addictive buns, then not being able to have her gown altered in time.

Marissa scanned the room, searching for her mysterious host. Or, more likely, hostess, since this was "witch business", according to Francesca. Every head in the place turned at her entrance, A good number of the ladies present commenced whispering excitedly to one another behind spread fans. She quirked her mouth in annoyance. Was this what Morgan went through all the time? The sidewise glances, the overt stares, the constant whispers? Probably so, she reckoned. It was, in fact, the price of notoriety.

Was this why she'd been summoned there? In order for someone to claim renown by association with the Witch of Caerfaen? Her mouth tightened into a fierce frown at this notion. The whispers died off for a moment, then increased in pitch and fervor. Dismissing the chattering chits, she returned to her scan of the room.

There, in the rear. A lone woman, clad in a dusky black gown, stared back and dipped her head. Marissa threaded her way through the staring, prattling women, sizing up this stranger while she maneuvered.

The woman in black—unusual enough for daytime wear to be remarkable—was dark herself, with sleek hair the color of a raven's wing and piercing, coal black eyes. Her face was well formed, although her nose was a bit too long to be considered beautiful. What she was, Marissa acknowledged, was striking.

As she approached, the woman smiled. Marissa caught her breath in surprise. The simple act of smiling transformed this woman's face into something a sculptor or a painter would give his left arm to capture. It was classically radiant.

"Welcome, Lady Marissa," the woman in black said. She gestured to the chair opposite her. "Please, join me. I've taken the liberty of ordering refreshments to be brought the moment you arrived."

As she slid into the chair, Marissa regarded her companion with a quizzical gaze. "Who are you?" She asked. "I've never seen you in Caerfaen before. And I'm sure I would have noticed you."

The woman flashed Marissa another dazzling smile. Any reply was forestalled by the arrival of their hostess, bearing a tray groaning with tea and buns. Once the buns were equitably distributed and the tea poured, the woman in black took up her cup, blew on the steaming beverage, and said, "My name is Catoya Alford."

Marissa raised one brow. "To what do I owe the honor of your kind invitation, um, Lady Catoya?" she ventured.

Then, succumbing to irresistible temptation she gathered up one of the buns before her and took a large and unladylike bite. And gave a sigh of exquisite pleasure.

"Whatever the reason," she murmured around her mouthful of pastry, "I must thank you. I've not been here in quite some time, and I'd forgotten quite how good these were."

"They are divine, aren't they?" Her companion munched her own bun with every evidence of satisfaction. Once the bun had been disposed of in the best possible manner, she went on. "Miss Alford will do. I claim no honorific and have no need of one. I invited you here because I needed to speak with you."

"Well, I gathered that much. I didn't presume you brought me here merely to ply me with wonderful buns." She took another bite, savored it for a moment, then asked, "What are we to speak about?"

Miss Alford took a sip of tea to keep her bun company. She leaned back in her chair and regarded Marissa with a thoughtful look. When she spoke, it wasn't with an explanation, but with a question of her own. "How much do you know about witches, Lady Marissa?"

To hide her bafflement, Marissa picked up her own cup and tasted the tea. It was excellent, yet the strangeness of this question left her failing to appreciate its finer qualities. She looked into Miss Alford's dark eyes for a moment, found it hard to meet her steady gaze, and regarded the next bun instead. "Very little, I'm afraid. Although, thanks to my tutor, I am learning a bit. Why do you ask? And what business have you to do so?

Miss Alford smiled. This time Marissa found it more enigmatic than appealing. "I ask," Miss Alford replied, "because I am myself a witch. I make it my business because I happen to be the duly elected leader of COVEN." At Marissa blank stare, she explained, "Council of Venerable Enchantresses."

Marissa blinked. "Umm. I see. Shouldn't it be COVE?"

Miss Alford shrugged, but her eyes crinkled with mirth. "We use the 'e' and 'en' from 'enchantresses'. It felt more…appropriate. Especially since the only word anyone could come up with beginning with 'n' was necromancers. Well, we certainly didn't want any of them hanging about."

"No, of course not," Marissa said. "Exactly what does your council do? And what does it have to do with me? Oh, wait, this must be the council Francesca was going on about."

"No doubt." Miss Alford's mouth quirked a half-smile. "Yes, I know who Francesca is, Lady Marissa. I must say, I don't envy you in that respect. She can be a bit…vexing at times. But she means well. At any rate, COVEN is the governing body for witchcraft in Kilbourne. Rather like the Royal College of Wizards is for wizardry. Our sisterhood was affiliated with the College; we decided quite some time ago to strike out on our own. The wizards," she said by way of explanation, "are not at all gracious to those they consider their inferiors. Which includes pretty much anyone who can't grow a beard. Although old Mistress Agatea, up in Cormaine, has some fairly robust chin whiskers. She might still be allowed in the old boys' club."

Marissa took another bite of bun. She'd gotten to the chocolate filling on this one and decided she could keep listening as long as the buns and tea held out. After that, well... She flapped her free hand, the one not engaged in the aid of bun consumption, for the other woman to continue.

Miss Alford nodded, seeming to understand Marissa's reticence. "This has to do with you because of the prophecy," she said, and took on a cargo of chocolate laden pastry herself.

"Prop'cy?" Marissa swallowed, cleared her throat, and repeated herself. "Prophecy? What prophecy?"

"Oh, it's been handed down for ages and ages. It concerns"— here Miss Alford lowered her voice into a raspy, if theatrical, whisper— "the Witch of Caerfaen."

Marissa threw up her hands. Realizing she was about to cast away a perfectly good bun, she brought them down again with an aggrieved sigh. "Really, Miss Alford. You too? Am I really to be the subject of every blasted prophecy ever made? This is getting a bit ridiculous." She glared at Miss Alford, then transferred the glare to the bit of bun still in her hand. Since the bun had done nothing to deserve her disapproval, she popped it into her mouth.

Miss Alford's mouth opened and closed, but no words were forthcoming. Marissa took a sip of tea to help the bun along to its final resting place. Then she said, "You may have exactly one minute to tell me why I should not simply thank you for the buns and tea and walk out. Proceed, if you feel you must."

"Very well." The other woman's voice was compelling. Marissa found herself hesitating, despite her determination to leave. "I beg you, listen for a moment. Please. We need you."

Marissa narrowed her eyes. "Exactly who is 'we'?"

"The witches. Well, not just the witches. Really everyone in Kilbourne who doesn't want to be in thrall to the wizards. You're the only one who has a hope of stopping them."

"According to your precious prophecy?"

"Yes, according to my precious prophecy." Miss Alford's words were cold enough to have been chipped from January ice. "Mock if you wish, Lady Marissa. You can't escape this fate."

"Perhaps not," Marissa agreed. "Still, which fate? Lucky me, I'm subject to more than one prophecy. The wizards claim to have their own version." *Not to mention the dragons*, she added to herself.

Miss Alford snorted. "Of course they do. They may be covetous, ambitious, and have insatiable appetites for power, but they're not fools. They know you pose a danger to their plans. A bit of judicious prophecy, to their way of thinking, should be sufficient to cloud the mind of a mere woman."

Marissa did her best to assess how much to trust the woman's words. Finally, she said, "Very well, Miss Alford. You have, at the least, managed to pique my interest. Continue, if you wish. I'll listen."

The other woman, who'd been still as a marble statue, relaxed. "Thank you," she murmured. Picking up her cup of tea, she downed the contents, then took the pot and poured herself another helping. As the pot was nearly empty, she only got a little in the bottom of the cup, along with a dark shower of tea leaves.

Miss Alford gave the pot a reproachful glance, then turned her attention to the cup. She swirled the last of her tea, then set her cup down and regarded it with a thoughtful expression. "Well. When life gives one tea leaves," she remarked, "one uses them for divination. This opportunity may be unexpected, but not unwelcome."

Marissa watched while Miss Alford studied the contents of her mug. At length, the cup was returned to its saucer and Miss Alford raised gleaming dark eyes to meet Marissa's.

"Well?" Marissa inquired. "What did you see?"

"An encouraging future," her companion replied with a grin. "A future in which another pot of tea and more buns feature." As the words left her mouth their hostess appeared, bearing a tray laden with another steaming pot and a fragrant cargo of pastry. Miss Alford breathed a blissful sigh.

"Well done." Marissa was unable to completely squelch the chuckle threatening to infuse her words. The other woman gave her an insouciant grin. Then her expression grew somber once again.

"Perhaps, if this gets sorted out, we might be friends, Lady Marissa. I think you would be a lovely person to enjoy an afternoon with, in more pleasant circumstances. Unfortunately, we have much to do first." She glanced back at her teacup. Suddenly her eyes flew open in a horrified stare, her body going rigid.

"What is it?" Marissa asked, her voice tinged with concern.

What in heaven's name is wrong? Miss Alford sat still as an ogre turned to stone by the dawn's morning sunshine. Her eyes, dark and penetrating and alive only moments before, now seemed vacant, practically hollow. Marissa waved a hand in front of her face, but there was no reaction.

"Miss Alford," she said, grasping the woman's arm and giving her a quick shake. "Miss Alford! Buns!"

Whether it was the shake, or the tone of Marissa's voice, or the prospect of buns, Miss Alford finally stirred, emerging from her trancelike state. With a sharp intake of breath, she sat back, blinking in surprise. Her gaze darted around, as if verifying where she was.

When she looked at Marissa, she relaxed, and her lips twisted into a rueful smile. "I'm sorry. I…something just came over me."

"So I gathered." Marissa gestured toward the offending teacup. "What on earth did you see? It certainly wasn't any encouraging future."

"No, not exactly. The tea leaves shifted, showing an entirely different prospect. Not a promising one, I'm afraid. You were on the roof of a building. It was grand, like a palace, but not like any I've ever seen. You were in the midst of a storm, with unseen dangers besetting you from every side. I… I've never seen anything like it. I don't normally read the leaves. This was…" She gave a little shiver.

"If I hadn't seen your face go white," Marissa said, "I might have believed you made this up to scare me. To convince me to do whatever it is you want me to do." She grimaced. "I think you really did see something, didn't you?"

Miss Alford nodded. "I'll admit, I would do almost anything to convince you to support our cause, Lady Marissa. But this?" She shook her head. "I've never seen anything like this. So I have to believe the prophecy is true, and you are the one it refers to."

"All right, Miss Alford." Marissa heaved a reluctant sigh. "Tell me about this prophecy."

Chapter Six

Miss Alford caught up the last bit of bun on her plate, popped it into her mouth, and flashed a satisfied smile. Once the bun had been dispatched in the appropriate manner, she said, "Please, call me Catoya."

"Very well, Catoya," Marissa agreed. "The prophecy?"

Catoya sipped tea, then assumed a grave expression. Leaning toward Marissa, she lowered her voice. "The prophecy has been handed down for generations. It was given by Mistress Ephebra Attlesby, a highly regarded witch in her day. She was reputed to be a first-class diviner. This was ages ago, I believe. Around the year 1080 or thereabouts. The prophecy has been entrusted to each of the succeeding heads of what has now become COVEN."

Marissa flapped an impatient hand. "I really don't need the history lesson," she said. "I get enough of those from my tutor."

"The dragon," Catoya breathed. "How lucky you are."

"You haven't had to deal with him," Marissa muttered. "Anyway, exactly what does this prophecy prophesy?"

"I do believe you are mocking me," Catoya said, her eyes narrowing.

"Not you," Marissa assured her. "Perhaps this mysterious prophecy, a little bit. It just feels so…ridiculous."

"Yes, I suppose it might. Please believe me, it is deadly serious." Catoya glanced around, seemed to decide no one was paying them any close attention, and went on in a low voice, "The fate of Kilbourne may rest on this. Here is what the prophecy says." She closed her eyes for a moment, then opened them wide to regard Marissa as she spoke.

"'Dark daughter of magic, long hidden, long awaited. Arise now, Witch of Caerfaen. Take your rightful place. Shepherd your sisters when all languish in hopelessness. With power and mercy, scour the land of evil, and uproot the tree of the usurpers of true power, who seek to grind the witch beneath their boots. Thus shall a new era of peace and jubilation reign.'"

Marissa stared. "Good heavens. Isn't that a bit...um... vague?"

Catoya shrugged. "Prophecies do tend to be quite vague. The nature of the beast, I'm afraid."

Marissa tilted her head. "What in the world makes you believe all this vagary has anything to do with me?"

"Well." Catoya took a sip of tea and cocked her head. "The fact you have managed to earn the title 'Witch of Caerfaen' seems to me a pretty good start."

With a fierce scowl Marissa said, "Bah. It doesn't count. People being people is all. Besides, I'm still a very novice witch, you know. I don't really know how to do anything even the tiniest bit...um...witchy."

"Haven't taken up cackling lessons yet?"

Catoya's grin was infectious. Marissa found her earlier scowl give way to an answering smile.. "I'm pretty sure cackling is not on Wyvrndell's curriculum. But no matter, I'm about as unskilled as I can be. I can't imagine this prophecy refers to me."

Miss Alford leaned forward, her arms on the table and her gaze steady. "One may have great power, yet not be trained in how to use it. The lack of training does not diminish the power lying within. I can sense the magic in you, Lady Marissa. It is like a banked fire, ready to be called forth. I am certain you are the one of whom the prophecy speaks. Just as I have every confidence you will one day take my place."

"Catoya, I have no wish to take your place. Please, believe me."

"Oh, I know. I didn't mean you would attempt to usurp me. I meant I believe your rightful place is as COVEN's leader. As with many things, only time will reveal the truth."

Marissa said nothing. There was really nothing she could say. Catoya went on, "Another telling bit, for me, is the wizards' interest in you. We witches are, not to put too fine a point on it, less than the dandruff beneath their pointy hats to them. For a wizard like Augustus Rhenn to take such a personal interest, to the extreme of violating one of the laws of magic, is most intriguing. And if Rhenn was concerning himself with you, you may be sure other eyes are turning your way too."

"To what purpose? What's this all about?"

Catoya shrugged. "I can only hazard a guess. You might be perceived as a pawn in some power struggle within the Wizards' Council. From what little I know, it's simply rife with them. Or it might be some scheme is afoot, one the wizards, or at least a faction of them, fear you might use your powers to oppose. It's hard to say. Might even be a combination of the two."

Marissa sipped at the last of her tea as she considered Catoya's words. Finally, she said, "All right, you've made your case. It is not, I reckon, without its merits. Assuming I accept the notion that I am..." She hesitated.

"The Chosen One?" suggested her companion.

"No!" Marissa half rose from her seat as a sudden wave of heat rushed through her. She glared at Catoya, who rocked back from the force of it. Marissa took a deep breath, in an effort to steady her emotions. She glanced around, saw a number of the other ladies in the shoppe staring, and sank back into her seat.

"No," she said again, with less heat this time. "Not 'The Chosen One.' If I do whatever it is I am to do, it will be because I chose to do so. Because I think it a worthy cause. Not because it is something I 'must' do."

"My dear Marissa, is there really such a difference?"

Marissa nodded. "To me, at least, there is. The difference is, I'm the one doing the choosing. Not some vague, ancient prophecy. Not some random fate. Not you, or your council. I choose. And if I choose to do this thing, whatever it may be, I will do it to the best of my skills and my power."

Catoya folded her hands together and inclined her head. "I understand. No better oath could I have hoped from you."

"Oath? I've sworn no oath." Marissa felt a surge of panic flash through her.

"Oh, certainly you have. You've sworn by your power. For a witch, there is no stronger oath."

"Bother. That wasn't my intent. I don't think it really counts."

Catoya smiled. Despite her air of smug satisfaction, Marissa couldn't find it in herself to be angry. Instead, she said, "Regardless, here's the question. What is it I'm supposed to do?"

"I've no idea. The prophecy is..."

"Vague, I know," finished Marissa. "A bit too blasted vague, if you ask me. Why on earth don't the people who make these pronouncements add in at least a dash of specifics? It would be more than a little helpful and make life easier for all concerned."

Her companion's mouth quirked up into a rueful smile. "Mistress Attlesby did make this one about three hundred years ago. Rather hard to be too specific, don't you think?"

"What I think," Marissa replied, "is we're out of both tea and buns. Did she mention anything about that?"

Chapter Seven

Wyvrndell shook his massive head, heaving a steam-laden sigh. "I don't know," he admitted.

Petrandius, king of the dragons, raised one bony brow ridge.

Wyvrndell hastened to clarify. "It is not Lady Marissa I'm concerned about, Your Majesty. She will aid us if she is able, I'm certain. I am concerned about King Rhys. Even more, I am anxious about the wizards. Mostly the wizards, in truth, for I think they will try to prevent her from assisting us, if they can manage it."

"I would not doubt it for an instant. Have they such sway?" Petrandius asked.

"Your Majesty, this business falls into the realm of the magical. No doubt, the wizards will try to claim jurisdiction."

"Wizards have no jurisdiction over dragons." The king was adamant.

"No, Your Majesty, of course not. Yet they might presume to claim authority over Lady Marissa. Even though she is not of their order, they may well argue they have the final say on such matters."

"As if it's any of their affair," grumbled Petrandius. "It's not like there is a finite amount of magic in the world, where if one gains some, another will lose a bit of his."

Wyvrndell considered this. "Yet isn't it less about the amount of magic? More about the amount of power and influence that magic gives the user? If dragons have magic, the wizards will still have theirs, of course. Yet they may perceive, rightly or not, they will then have less power to influence events in the world."

Petrandius nodded his hoary head. "Well done, young one. I'd wondered if you would see this aspect of the problem. Many older, supposedly wiser, dragons would not have done so. You are learning, Wyvrndell, scion of Wyzandar. So, tell me: how would you endeavor to resolve such a problem?"

Was the king testing him for some reason? If so, Wyvrndell couldn't discern why. Still, he resolved to rise to the challenge. "Your Majesty, in truth, I can only see one solution. We would need to negotiate some form of covenant with the humans. Similar to the one you recently made with King K'var'k. A pact of mutual non-aggression and aid at need. It is far from a perfect resolution, but it is the only one I can conceive of."

"Indeed, young one. You have gained wisdom beyond your years. What you have put forth is the only solution I can envision. Now, what problems do you foresee? A breach of trust, on the part of the humans? Or rather, by those pesky wizards?"

"It is, of course, a possibility," Wyvrndell replied, even as his mind worked rapidly. "The wizards are wily, cunning, and avaricious, to be sure. Yet their conduct would not be my main cause for concern."

"Then what?"

"Our own," he said bluntly. "I would worry about the dragons. I fear one or more might breach such an accord and thus begin a needless and costly war."

Petrandius stared at him with such intensity Wyvrndell feared he had misspoken, angering the king. Then he realized the old dragon was gazing at him with an expression of something near to respect. Wyvrndell maintained a judicious silence.

At length Petrandius shook his head. "Sadly, I fear you are correct in your assessment. For if wizards are cunning and greedy, they have naught on dragonkind."

Wyvrndell remained silent in the face of this pronouncement. Finally, the king went on, "Still, unless some more elegant solution presents itself, I think we must enter into such a covenant. And once again, young one, you shall be my emissary."

Wyvrndell's head shot up at Petrandius's words. Recalling his mission to the Dwarf king, he nearly raised a protest. In the same instant, he checked his thoughts. Petrandius was the most cunning of all the cunning dragons. He did nothing without deliberation and reason. If he wanted Wyvrndell to act as emissary, so be it.

"Yes, you shall be my envoy again. Not to the wizards, I think. You shall treat with Rhys Gwynfallis, King of Kilbourne. He knows you, and in addition you will likely have the support of this Sir Morgan, the consort of the enchantress. It is with Rhys we shall make our covenant. Then, it will fall to him to keep some measure of control upon the wizards of Kilbourne. As it will fall upon me to keep rein upon the dragons of my kingdom."

"I see, Your Majesty," Wyvrndell said.

"I will, of course, assign Aireantha to assist in this endeavor. I am not yet ready, however. I will need some time to draw up my terms and conditions. This agreement will be even more difficult than the one we negotiated with the Dwarves. I must consider carefully before I commit my honor, and my dragons, to it."

"I am at your command," Wyvrndell said, arching his neck as a flush of pride coursed through him.

"Speak to no one of our discussion," the king directed. "I do not wish news of what we have planned to get out before I am ready. After the recent treaty with the Dwarves, I fear my dragons might not look favorably on a similar course of action with the humans. I wish to lay a bit of groundwork behind the scenes."

"Of course, Your Majesty." Wyvrndell preened, if only a little bit. "What we have planned," the king had said.

Then Wyvrndell shook himself back to reality. He had played no part in the plan, no matter how generously Petrandius put it. Still, he would have the honor to serve as Petrandius's agent in the negotiations with Rhys. That was something.

And Wyvrndell would have Aireantha to accompany him. This knowledge made him want to caper like a hatchling. He jerked to attention as Petrandius said, "Go now, and inform your sire I desire his counsel. Tell him no more."

"At once, Your Majesty." Wyvrndell bowed his head in respect, then hurried out of the king's chambers. He hastened up the passage, in search of his sire, Wyzandar.

He found Wyzandar sometime later, sunning himself on a rocky ledge overlooking the valley below. The elder dragon's eyes were half closed, his wings extended to catch the warmth of the afternoon sun beating down. Wyvrndell had rarely seen him this peaceful.

Although, if he was honest, a good deal of Wyzandar's normal state of agitation no doubt was caused by, or directed at, his offspring. Wyvrndell hesitate for a few moments. Then, plucking up his courage, he spoke. "Greetings, Father."

Instead of the rebuke he half expected, his father folded his wings and rumbled, "Greetings, my son. Come, join me, and enjoy the sunshine for a bit. Soon enough it will be cold winter. We shall find ourselves missing these days."

Wyvrndell blinked. Was this his sire? "Thank you, Father," he said, stepping onto the ledge to join him. The sunshine did feel luxurious, and he wriggled in blissful pleasure as its warmth caressed him.

At length Wyzandar heaved a sigh and shook himself. Turning his head to regard Wyvrndell, he said, "All right, I suppose I'm ready now. What has brought you here?"

"Petrandius sent me to fetch you. He has need of your counsel. He awaits you in his chambers."

"Why didn't you—" Wyzandar rose up in wroth, then subsided. "No, I am wrong. I invited you to join me. I am at fault, not you. Very well, I will go. Do you know what he wishes?"

"I am not at liberty to disclose it," Wyvrndell told him.

"Indeed? Then I suppose I'd best hurry and find out." Wyzandar rose from his prone position.

To Wyvrndell's amazement, he sounded as if he was chuckling to himself. Before he could inquire why, the elder dragon departed.

Chapter Eight

"Chief Wizard Foxwent," Sebastien mused, "will not like this idea."

The wizard leaned back in the chair he had placed in the pool of bright morning sunshine streaming in through the sitting room window. He sighed, placed his feet up on a hassock, and cocked his head, waiting for Marissa's response.

"Oh, I've no doubt he'll hate it." She favored her friend with a brilliant smile. "Of course, being Chief Wizard, he does have a great many important matters with which to concern himself., I see no reason to burden him with this trifle. Do you?"

"Trifle? My lady," the old wizard said, "you are incorrigible."

"No, merely practical. I don't see how Wizard Foxwent's likes or dislikes figure into the thing. He has no authority over me and certainly none over the dragons. If I choose to assist Wyvrndell in his efforts to obtain magic for his kin… Well, it's my concern, not theirs."

Sebastien sat with an unreadable expression on his face. He sipped his tea, appearing to contemplate her words. Marissa watched him for several moments. At last, she asked, "What do you think, Sebastien?"

"Mmm," he replied, his expression pensive. He took another sip of tea.

She curbed the impulse to urge him on. This was something which couldn't be rushed. Not to mention, she really did want his opinion. Even though there was no guarantee she'd abide by it.

He set his cup down, sending it clattering in its saucer. "All right," he said. "Here's what I think. The universe," he spread his hands wide, "is a funny place."

When he didn't continue, she asked, "Was that supposed to be helpful?"

He laughed. "Don't worry, I'm getting to it. So, here's the point. When something needs to happen, a way will be found. Not always the one you'd expect, or even think practical, mind you. Still, a way is found. Thus, it strikes me the universe, or fate, or whatever you'd care to label it, has decided it's high time the dragons have magic."

She waited. He went on. "Between the two of you, you and Morgan McRobbie have managed to befriend a dragon. This has never happened before, at least according to everything I've discovered in my research about the subject." He held up a finger. "This, in conjunction with your possession of a not inconsiderable font of magic, has led to your being named the first ever Royal Enchantress. Finally, there is your public pledge to use those powers for good, on behalf of the kingdom."

"Good," Marissa interpreted, "in this instance meaning aiding the dragons in their quest for magic?"

"You could certainly make a good case for it. No doubt Foxwent, and perhaps Rhys as well, will argue giving the dragons access to magic would be the equivalent of an army handing over its weapons to the enemy."

"Sebastien, the dragons aren't our enemies," she protested.

He waggled a hand. "Wyvrndell is not your enemy, of course. However, he's the only dragon you've interacted with. He might not be representative of the true nature of dragonkind."

"Oh." Marissa scrunched up her nose. "Well, I suppose..."

"On the other hand, one must factor in the recent accord reached between dragons and Dwarves. They have been at odds since time immemorial. The notion of these two races coming to a peace agreement, after so long and contentious a conflict, might be indicative of their willingness to live in peace with men as well."

"Yes, I see what you mean," she said. "I hadn't really considered it in that light. It does make sense. So, you think I should do it?"

"Well, I don't know if I'd go quite that far. Not yet."

"But—"

The wizard held up a hand. "Lady Marissa. You said Wizard Foxwent holds no authority over you. Consider this: who does?"

"What do you mean?"

"As Royal Enchantress..."

"Oh. The king." She nodded. "Yes, you're quite right. I should have thought of it. Wyvrndell himself even told me to consult the king"

"Did he, now? Well, to me, this in itself is another indication of his good faith in this matter."

"It is, isn't it? All right, I'll discuss it with Rhys as soon as possible. Will you come with me?"

"If you like. My arguments won't matter a whit. You'll have to be the one to convince him. You and McRobbie."

"Um. Yes. About that…"

Sebastien's brows rose. "You haven't told him either, have you? My, my, keeping secrets already? Not an auspicious beginning to your marriage, is it?"

She laughed. "All right, you've caught me out. If you want the truth, the only reason I haven't said anything to Morgan is because I wanted to speak with you first. This way I could get my thoughts in order and weigh your counsel. Now I have. I'll tell him straight away."

"Good. You'll need him on your side if you're to persuade the king. McRobbie's word will carry a lot of weight. Much more than mine ever would. And marshalling your arguments for your betrothed will be excellent practice for your attempts to convince the king of the soundness of this course of action. If you're set on it, of course."

"Yes, I suppose so." She squeezed her eyes shut for a moment. Then she asked, "Sebastien, do you think whatever it is the dragons have in mind will be dangerous? For me, I mean. Because…"

"Because the duke will be ill-inclined to allow you to put yourself at risk again, no matter how noble or desirable the cause?"

She heaved a sigh. "You do have a way of cutting right to the heart of the problem, don't you?"

He chuckled. "My lady, would you expect any different of him? He loves you and wishes to protect you. So, I'm afraid my answer to your question is, yes."

"Oh." She sagged a bit.

"Lady Marissa, all magic is dangerous. At least to some extent. Even the simplest spell, if not applied with care, may go awry, with unforeseen consequences."

"Those small furry creatures Morgan's always prattling on about?"

"Exactly. Oh, things would have to go quite bad for something like that to happen. But yes, even small spells can go wrong. A working like what Wyvrndell has in mind? Whatever it is, you can rest assured it'll be no small undertaking. In its very nature, it will be dangerous, if only by virtue of the sheer amount of magic required. If something were to go amiss? Well, I reckon we'd need pretty large broom."

"A—a broom? You mean like a witch's broom?"

Sebastien laughed. "No, I mean something to sweep up the pieces."

"Oh," she said in a small voice.

"What pieces?"

"Ack!" Marissa's hand flew to her mouth. She spun to find Morgan leaning against the door frame.

"What pieces?" he repeated.

"You weren't supposed to hear. How long have you been skulking there?"

"Me?" He assumed an air of injured innocence. "I've skulked nary a skulk. I haven't even lurked. Not much, anyway. What pieces?"

"Hmph. You're worse than a dog worrying an old bone. Very well, since you'll give me no peace, I'll tell you."

"I'm simply agog." He was still leaning casually against the wall, a gentle smile on his lips. Well, she'd shift him out of his comfort in a moment. She exchanged a glance with Sebastien, who nodded encouragement. "Wyvrndell," she said, "has asked me to consider assisting him with something."

Morgan nodded. "Tips on how to capture the fancy of a lady dragon?" He grinned. "I gather he's somewhat enamored of...what's her name?"

"Aireantha," Marissa replied. "Nooo, he hasn't asked me for any help with his love life. If dragons even have such a concept." She shivered. "Something I reckon doesn't even bear thinking about."

"What, then?" He looked from Marissa to Sebastien and back. A wary expression crossed Morgan's face. "Umm. Perhaps I'd better sit down for this."

"An excellent suggestion," put in Sebastien.

Marissa bestowed a glower on him. He was simply no help whatsoever.

Morgan leaned back in the chair he'd commandeered, lacing his fingers behind his head. His hazel eyes, bright and curious, belied his casual air, even as he announced, "All right, I'm braced for the worst. Tell me your darkest secrets."

"Wyvrndell thinks I can use my powers to help the dragons have magic." She blurted it out in a rush. It didn't really help to make the statement any more palatable.

He blinked. Crossed his legs. Scrubbed a hand across his face. This last, Marissa knew, was a sure sign of extreme agitation.

"Magic," he said at last. "You're to give magic to...dragons."

"Well, yes. That does seem to be Wyvrndell's intent."

"Dragons. With magic." He rolled the words over on his tongue, as if trying to make sense of them. "Somehow it just sounds... well, dangerous." He looked up at Marissa. "Don't you think?"

She stood in silence, watching Morgan. Finally, he said, "Perhaps I'd like this better if you told it from the beginning." He squeezed his eyes shut. "I doubt it, but let's give it a try, eh?"

So, she told him. About the dragons' prophecy. About how

Wyvrndell was certain she was the one who could bring magic to dragonkind. About her conversation with Sebastien and how he thought it might be possible. About her own mounting sense that, perhaps, this was why she'd been blessed—or cursed—with such an awesome abundance of magic.

Morgan listened, his eyes wide open now, watching her face while she spoke. When she finished, he rubbed his forehead, as if it ached. She flashed him a smile, knowing it lacked some of its normal brilliance.

He took a deep breath, then let it out again. "All right, what aren't you telling me?"

She bit her lip. Blast the man, he already knew her too well. With a wry smile, she said, "Sebastien feels it might be dangerous. Whatever it is the dragons are planning to do to accomplish this."

"I'd be amazed if it weren't," he replied. "Sebastien?"

The wizard said, "Of course, all magic is risky, to some degree. The spell required to do this, though, would be one of massive proportions."

"So, massively risky," Morgan extrapolated. He turned back to Marissa. "And if, as your husband, I forbid it?"

"Well, I'd rather hoped it wouldn't come to that. After all, when Rhys installed me as Royal Enchantress, I pledged to use my powers for good. So…" She waved a hand.

"Mmm, yes, I see. Speaking of Rhys, am I correct in assuming you haven't told him about this little endeavor yet?"

She shook her head. "I wanted to talk to Sebastien first and hear his thoughts. Then discuss it with you and hear your objections."

Morgan scowled. "My main objection, oh light of my life, is that I'd like to have you around for a bit. We haven't even had the wedding yet." His eyes glinted with anticipation. "This sounds like a surefire way to risk your pretty neck."

"And if Rhys favors the notion?"

"Well, I do have some small bit of influence at court…" He favored her with a lazy smile.

"Morgan McRobbie, don't you dare. I think I've shown over the past months I'm no shrinking violet. I—"

He raised his hands in surrender. "You're right, of course. You've taken on dragons, assassins, and pirates. Not to mentions mad wizards. And you've bested 'em all. I just worry your luck will run out someday."

"Luck?" Marissa felt a surge of righteous indignation at this. "Was it luck when I trapped Lord Ramis, saving you from the executioner? Or luck when I rescued you from Kiara Northram and that horrible Augustus Rhenn? Hmph! Luck, indeed…"

Morgan's mouth opened and closed, but no words emerged. She narrowed her eyes at him. Then an unexpected laugh bubbled up within her, and she relented. "Oh, all right. Perhaps a bit of it was due to luck. Only a tiny bit, mind you."

"As you say, my dear," he replied. His mouth twitched. Then he, too, was laughing, He stood up and took her into his arms. Still chuckling, he said, "I couldn't bear the thought of something happening to you. Of losing you."

"I couldn't bear the thought of something happening to me either. I feel it's a much better and happier world with me in it."

Morgan pulled her closer, crushing her against his chest. She continued, if a bit muffled, "But you know how it goes. We do what needs to be done."

He went rigid, his breath coming quick and harsh. "That's—"

"Not fair? It's the McRobbie motto, isn't it? And soon, assuming my luck holds, I'll be part of the family, so…"

He held her at arm's length now, staring into her eyes. He chewed on his bottom lip for a moment, then seemed to come to a decision. He gave a slow nod. "You are correct, my lady. I was in the wrong in this instance. Forgive me the error of my ways."

"Oh, Morgan, of course. Believe me, I don't want to get involved in something that could turn into a disaster. I'll be very clear about it with Wyvrndell. But if I can help them…"

"How could you refuse? We both owe a debt to Wyvrndell, at the very least."

"And Sebastien will help me decide if it's too risky. Won't you?"

"I will try my best, my lady."

"You see," she said, beaming. "So what could possibly go—"

"Don't even say it," Morgan interrupted. "Just don't."

Chapter Nine

Rhys Gwynfallis, king of Kilbourne and monarch of the outlying provinces, set down his goblet of wine. "I...see," he said, in the voice of a man who's been informed the headsman awaits his custom.

He picked the goblet up again, blinked as if wondering how it had gotten into his hand, and gulped down the rest of the wine. "Magic," he mused. "Dragons. With magic."

Marissa exchanged a glance with Morgan, who quirked a wan smile in her direction. Inclining his head toward Rhys, he mouthed, "Get on."

Oh. Right. She was supposed to be pleading the dragons' case. Before she could begin Rhys asked, "Do you think this is a good idea?"

Well, what had she expected? For him to welcome the notion with glad cries of glee? She had work to do if she was to convince him.

"Your Majesty," she said. "In my capacity as your Royal Enchantress, I do. Think it's a good idea, I mean." She wilted a bit under his skeptical gaze, then took a breath and prepared to soldier—or would it be witch?—on.

Rhys gave her a noncommittal smile. She wasn't being very convincing, Marissa realized. She said, "We have magic. The Dwarves have magic, or so I've been led to believe. Why should the dragons, oldest of the races, be prevented from obtaining it, too?"

"Well," he ventured. "Because then they'd have all the advantages. Size, armor, fire, flight. Add magic too? We humans wouldn't stand a chance. It sounds like a recipe for complete disaster, if you ask me."

"I don't see why it should," she said. "On a transactional basis, we—well, I, but you know what I mean—would be giving the dragons something they've desired their entire existence. I'd think they would be quite grateful."

"Mmmm," said the king, raising a brow. "Go on."

"They haven't bothered humans for over three hundred years," Marissa said. "And they've pretty much had the upper hand right along, haven't they? Even without magic?"

"Well, yessss."

"And not long ago they sealed a peace agreement with their ancient foes, the Dwarves. If they can do it, I'm sure we could some to some formal accord between Kilbourne and the dragon kingdom. Wyvrndell tells me their king, Petrandius, is very a practical, and most astute, dragon."

"You mean, something on the order of, we'll give you magic if you promise not to eat us?"

"Exactly. Oh, I know you're making a joke of it. Still, why shouldn't we have a treaty with them?"

"Treaties," Rhys said in a quelling tone, "can be broken. Have been, over and over. Witness our treaty with Rhuddlan, as a prime example. I've no doubt King Petrandius is quite as cunning as Jarik Varsil ever was. Probably much more so, come to think of it."

"Rhys, it's not at all the same," Morgan interjected. Marissa favored him with a grateful smile. "Varsil wants what we have. Land, and resources, for the most part. The dragons don't need, or want, anything we have. Well, except magic, and if Marissa can do what they want, they'd have it."

"So, you agree with the Royal Enchantress, Knight-Commander? You think giving magic to the dragons would be a wise decision?"

Morgan grinned. "At first, I thought it was a horrible idea. I expressed pretty much the same objections you have. In much stronger terms, if you want to know the truth. Since for me it's more personal. After all, it would be my wife risking her neck to do this."

"But now?"

"If King K'var'k trusts the dragons to keep their bargain after the hostility they've endured from one another over the centuries? Well, I see no reason to think we couldn't also enter into a treaty of some sort."

Rhys nodded slowly. "All right, you do make a good point."

"Also," Morgan went on, "I think Marissa is correct in her estimation about the dragons being grateful for our assistance. It might serve us in good stead one day."

"Perhaps. I wonder what the wizards will say about this. Nothing good, I'm sure."

"Begging your pardon," Marissa said. "What does it matter what the wizards think?"

Cocking his head, Rhys said, "Go on."

"If the dragons obtain magic, it will be because I've helped them. Wyvrndell says he's certain I'm the only one who can manage it. So, it's my choice. With your agreement, of course," she temporized. "The wizards don't figure into the thing at all."

A hint of a smile tinged the king's lips. Taking this as license to continue, Marissa said, "The wizards have no sway over me. I'm not a wizard and certainly no part of their order. I'd have to grow a beard, and I don't think Morgan would approve. Anyway, what I choose to do with my powers is of no concern to them. Or it shouldn't be."

"Mmm. Augustus Rhenn made it his concern," Rhys pointed out.

She shuddered. "A different thing altogether. That was greed, and hubris. This is politics."

"You don't think there's greed and hubris in politics, my dear?" Rhys asked, a twinkle lighting his eye.

"Of course there is. But we're talking about something else entirely. This is me, as your Royal Enchantress, making use of my power on behalf of Kilbourne, to aid another sovereign nation. Who will, in their turn, be duly appreciative of Kilbourne's efforts on their behalf. Oh, and to be fair, it was Wyvrndell's suggestion for me to consult you before making any commitments."

Chuckling, he held up his hands in capitulation. "I don't say I'm convinced, Lady Marissa. However, you've given me some food for thought. Allow me a chance to digest this before I make any decision."

"Of course, Your Majesty." She inclined her head in obeisance. "Please, take your time and consider what we've said. There's no hurry. I've already told Wyvrndell not to expect any decision until after the wedding."

"Which is fast approaching," Rhys noted. "At any rate, your points are well taken. I simply need to consider and perhaps seek some additional counsel."

"Thank you for hearing me out, Your Majesty," Marissa said, dipping a curtsey. "We'll not trouble you further."

"My lady," he replied with a nod. Their audience concluded, Marissa made for the door "Commander," Rhys said as Morgan rose. "A moment, if you please. I won't keep him long, Lady Marissa."

Dismissed from the royal presence, she took her leave. She wondered if Rhys was instructing his Knight-Commander to quell his betrothed. Surely not, but—

"What have you been up to?" said a voice at her elbow. She gasped, whirling to face Queen Gwyndolyn.

"Gwyn, you startled the wits out of me," Marissa said. "Don't sneak up on me like that."

"How should I sneak—" Gwyn laughed as Marissa skewered her with a ferocious glare. "All right, all right, I'll stop. Come join me for lunch. You can tell me why you and Morgan have been closeted with Rhys for over an hour."

Marissa considered. Lunch with Gwyn could range anywhere from bread and cheese to a lengthy, sumptuous repast. "I'd love to," she said. "I can't stay too long. I have a hundred things to attend to this afternoon. Wedding things."

"Tea and scones?" offered Gwyn.

"Perfect. In large quantities, if you please. I'm famished. It's hard work, this Royal Enchantress business."

The queen laughed, tossing her head like she used to do when they'd been at St. Marguerite's together. "Come along, then, oh Royal Enchantress, and tell me about it."

They strolled the palace halls together, to the sunny solar Gwyn favored. Marissa filled her oldest friend in on both the situation with the dragons and her final preparations for the wedding.

Once seated in the solar, under the warm embrace of a pleasant sunbeam, with tea, scones, and jam at hand, Gwyn pursed her lips. Slathering a scone with raspberry jam, she said, "I see Rhys's point, of course, but I think you have the right of it."

As she swallowed a bit of scone and washed it down with strong tea, Marissa blessed her good fortune. This was better than she could have hoped.

Gwyn, for all her exuberance and outward flightiness, was quite practical, with an eye to the main chance. It was one of the reasons she made an excellent queen for Rhys.

Marissa continued to make silent inroads on the scone supply, waiting for Gwyn to continue her thought.

She sipped tea, then put the cup down with a clatter. "If the Dwarves and dragons have a treaty, it only makes sense for us to have one as well. We already have an accord with the Dwarves, thanks to you and Morgan. Establishing an accord with the dragons would give us two sets of allies. It only makes sense. I think you're quite right: the dragons will be so grateful we've given them access to the magic they've hungered for all these many years, they'll be more than happy to live in peace with us."

Marissa drank tea, watching her friend over the rim of her cup.

Gwyn pursed her lips again, then said, "I think I'll speak to Rhys about this. I'm sure I can make him see the benefits."

"It would be lovely if you could," Marissa said, licking the last of the jam from her fingers. "Thank you. And thank you for lunch. Now, I've got to run, or I'll be late."

Rising, she embraced Gwen and hurried out.

Chapter Ten

"Shall I draw the curtain closed?" Morgan asked, reaching up to suit word to action.

Marissa considered as she sipped her wine. "No, leave it for now. I'm having fun watching the people here."

"Here" was a table in one of the private alcoves at the notorious Black Swan Inn. The only time she'd been there before had been the fateful night Morgan kidnapped her. He'd whisked her away to the Oak Tree Inn, as part of his mad plan to unmask the traitor on Rhys's council.

She'd been so annoyed with him at the time, she hadn't really paid much attention to the Black Swan itself or to the food. She did remember flinging a piece of squab at Morgan in frustration when he refused to answer her questions.

Then she'd stalked off in high dudgeon, demanding he take her straight home. Instead, he'd been attacked by an assassin and still managed to carry her off in his carriage to…

She dragged herself back to the present. "Hmm?" she said.

"I asked," Morgan said, "if you'd like some more wine"

She held her glass out to him. "What in the world possessed you to come back here, of all places?" she inquired. "Of course, I'm not complaining, mind."

He shrugged. Then his face broke into a devilish grin, one which could still make her insides feel warm and gooey, like a jammy tart. "Perhaps I just wanted to carry you off again," he suggested. "Forget about the wedding. We could just run off and—"

"Ooooh, no you don't." She almost choked on her wine. "Not a chance, Morgan McRobbie. Not after the work I've put into this. Besides, it wouldn't reflect well on Kilbourne's newest duke, now, would it?"

"Perhaps I'm not feeling ducal at the moment," he groused. "I'm feeling—oh, I don't know. Thwarted, I guess."

"Thwarted? How so?"

"Well, for starters, at the moment the only thing I want to do is pull the curtain closed and kiss you. At length. Instead, you want to keep it open and watch the other denizens of this place."

"Mmm, that does sound interesting," she said, , not paying his words much attention. A familiar, if unexpected, figure had caught her eye, sending thoughts of kisses fleeing, if only for a moment. "Hello, here's Captain Poldane."

"Oh?" Morgan craned around. "Who's the damsel du jour?"

"I've no idea." Marissa cast an interested gaze at Aartis's companion. "I don't recall ever seeing her at court. Do you?"

Morgan turned again, then shook his head. "No. I've never seen her before."

"She's striking," Marissa observed. "Quite different from the girls he normally favors. She's more...well, I don't know, but more something."

He chuckled. "Less, if you ask me."

"Less? Less what? Not less attractive. She's quite lovely. Although her gown is by no means the latest style. I recall my mother had one like it."

"No, I didn't mean less attractive. I guess I meant less flighty. The girls Aartis fancies are long on appearance and short on wits. This one somehow doesn't strike me the same way. She looks, well, rather competent, I suppose."

"Mmm. Perhaps. I'm not sure how you can leap to such a conclusion by one quick glance. I thought only the ladies at court had such talents. But who am I to argue? Let's have them over, and we'll find out."

He opened his mouth to protest. She sent him a quelling look and he subsided. She called out, "Why, Captain Poldane, how nice to see you."

Aartis shied like a startled stag. Marissa raised her glass in greeting. Morgan gave a half-hearted wave. "Come, join us for a few moments, and introduce us to your charming companion," Marissa went on.

She noted with some interest the wary glance Captain Poldane exchanged with the girl. He seemed nervous, clasping and unclasping his hands, something counter to everything Marissa knew, or had heard, about the man considered the most notorious rake in Caerfaen. Plus the surrounding countryside.

With a resigned expression, he led his companion over to their alcove. "Lady Marissa. Commander," he said, giving a slight bow.

"Good evening. Quite a surprise to find you here."

Morgan rose. "Captain. A pleasure to see you."

Feeling awkward, as the only one still seated, Marissa scrambled up from her seat. "Hello," she said to Aartis's companion. "I'm Marissa duBerry."

"This is Ka—um, Lady, um," Aartis mumbled

"Plain miss," said the girl, rolling her eyes at Aartis's mangled attempts at introduction. "Katherine Taggart. My friends call me Kate." She smiled at Marissa. "I hope you will too."

Marissa reached over to take her hand. "Kate, I'm delighted to meet you. Are you new to Caerfaen? I don't think I've seen you before."

"Oh, no, I've lived here my whole life. I'm afraid we don't travel in the same circles.

"Taggart," Morgan repeated, his brow furrowing. "Not relation to…?"

Kate flashed him a fetching smile. "He's my father."

As conversational stoppers went, this was right up near the top, Marissa thought with an internal giggle. Morgan's face went shuttered. Aartis's mouth dropped open. Did he know, she wondered. He must have.

It didn't matter. She fell a strong flash of insight: Kate Taggart, no matter her parentage, or perhaps because of it, was feeling out of her element here. Her nervous demeanor, the vintage gown—a hand-me-down, perhaps? Her gaze darted back and forth between Morgan and Marissa, as if seeking approbation. As if, she realized, Kate was ready to take flight at the merest hint of censure. Which Morgan was providing in abundance, by virtue of his forbidding expression. Stepping on his foot, Marissa beamed at Kate Taggart.

"Don't mind him," she said with a jerk of her head toward Morgan. "He's gotten all stuffy since he was made a duke."

"Hey!" he protested, but his mouth quirked up a bit at one corner. Good, at least she'd routed his snit.

She drew Kate closer. "I understand, at least a little," she said in an undertone. "I've been rather *de trop* myself, ever since I learned I'm a witch. People do tend to look askance. I imagine it's similar."

Kate gestured helplessly. "I-I wouldn't really know. I've always stayed pretty much in the shadows. My father wanted it that way. To protect me, I suppose, from people who might try to get at him through me. So, I've never been exposed to polite society."

"Well, you haven't missed much, in all honesty," Marissa said. "I don't see why you should have any problem. You have beauty and charm going for you, and you seem to have your wits about you.

Something fewer than half the ladies of 'polite society' can lay claim to, I'm afraid. So I'd say you're off to a rousing start."

Kate gasped, then choked out a laugh. "Thank you," she said. "You're really more than kind."

"Nonsense. Simply being honest. It's a fault of mine; ask Morgan. But here, you came to have dinner with the dashing Captain Poldane, and we're keeping you. Unless you'd care to join us?"

"Thank you," Kate said, with a sideways glance at Aartis. He gave an infinitesimal shake of his head. "It's nice of you to offer. Perhaps not this time."

Marissa nodded in understanding. "Very well," she said, "I'd be delighted if you'd call on me soon. For lunch, perhaps? Cook makes a splendid roast and peas. I think we might be friends, you and I."

"I—you don't mean it."

"I wouldn't have said it if I didn't mean it," Marissa said. "I would like you to come."

"All right," Kate said, looking bemused. "I will."

"Good. Now, go enjoy your dinner. I think they're bringing ours now."

Aartis bowed and led Kate off to find their table. In another one of the private alcoves, Marissa was certain. She smiled in approval, then turned back to Morgan, who was still staring after them.

"Hello, Morgan," she said, waving a hand in front of his face.

"Taggart's daughter," he muttered. "Good lord."

"She's marvelous," Marissa told him. "She could be the making of Captain Poldane. She has spirit. To just announce it like she did. My, my. I like her."

Morgan stared at her in astonishment.

"You may close the curtain now," she informed him with a dazzling smile.

Chapter Eleven

The next morning, Marissa was engaged in a review of the list of things she needed to do to prepare for the wedding. It grew larger by the day, no matter how many tasks she managed to accomplish. As she made a note to speak with the seamstresses about final adjustments to her gown, the bell rang.

"Who on earth?" she muttered.

Her parents weren't due to arrive until the next day, and Clarise was supposed to call later in the afternoon. Morgan? Perhaps, but he'd made no mention of coming round when they'd parted the previous evening.

She heard Rose at the door say, "Oh, Your Grace, good morn. Please, come in." In a moment, Morgan entered into the morning room.

"Good morning," he said, bending to brush a kiss against Marissa's cheek. "Are you ready? You don't look particularly ready."

She gaped at him, bemused. "Ready? What are you on about? Did you tell me we had plans today? Because if so, I certainly don't recall it."

"Well, I thought I'd done." He shrugged apologetically. "What with one thing and another, it might have slipped my mind. Still, you're not in the middle of anything urgent, are you?"

She managed, barely, to stop herself from acerbically informing him that no, she wasn't doing anything important at all. Merely planning their wedding day. Instead, she said, "Where are we going?"

"You told me in no uncertain terms I needed to find us a place to live. Well, I've taken your command to heart. Would you like to come see it?"

"Really? You found something here in Caerfaen?"

"We dukes get things done," he said, sweeping a courtly bow.

"Well done, oh mighty duke. Very well, let us venture forth to see this humble abode. I'm afraid I'm envisioning something with three crumbling walls, no roof, and a pigsty in the yard. Still, one can hope."

"Hmph. Pigsties, indeed. I like that. You wound me, my dear, simply wound me. Care for a walk? It's not too far."

"Do dukes walk? I was under the impression they only rode about in well-appointed carriages, drawn by a team of matched bays. Perhaps I was misinformed."

"Some dukes," he replied, "even deign to wed sarcastic witches." A mischievous twinkle lit his eye as he said it.

Marissa found herself grinning with him. "Some witches are luckier than others."

"I'm delighted you recognize your good fortune in landing such a magnificent catch." He swept her into his arms and kissed her soundly.

"Well, at least you are a good kisser," she observed after a brief interval. "I suppose between that and a title, I shall count myself fortunate."

Hand in hand, they left the house. Morgan led her along the bustling streets of Caerfaen. Finally he stopped and pointed. "There is it."

"The one with the blue door?"

"Right. What do you think?"

The house was set well back from the street, rather than standing shoulder to shoulder with its neighbors. Towering oaks provided ample shade, while low hedgerows of holly, allowed to run wild, rimmed the perimeter. Despite its impressive size, the house presented an aspect of...well, coziness, Marissa decided. It was rather like a charming little cottage, suddenly taken with an unexpected growth spurt.

"I think I like it," she ventured. "Although when I said we needed something a bit larger than your lodgings... Well, this is three times as large." She peered at the house. "At least."

"As was patiently explained to your humble servant, the number of available homes in Caerfaen is next thing to non-existent. It was this or move you into my place. Which didn't really seem the solution. I've taken it, contingent on the approval of the future duchess."

"Future duchess," she mused. "You know, I rather like the sound of that."

"So do I." He squeezed her hand in affection.

"I believe you're coming over romantic," she teased.

"And whose fault is it?"

"Point taken. Very well, the future duchess approves. Well, of the outside, at least. Are we allowed to go inside and poke around a bit? I'd like to see what it's like before I say yes or no."

Morgan produced a key. "The owner, who's something in

shipping, decided to remove himself to his place in Cormaine. The house is empty. Well, except for the ghost."

"A ghost? Oh, how lovely! A friend for Uncle Harold." Raising one brow, she asked, "Morgan, are you serious or merely having fun at my expense?"

"I'm reporting the facts as related to me. The ghost, if indeed there is one, is the specter of the home's first owner. Military fellow, a sergeant in the Queen's Guard, ages ago, from what I gather. The chap I spoke to says he's only been seen on rare occasions and is completely harmless. Having had a session with your Uncle Harold, I figured it might be acceptable."

Marissa considered. "Well, I suppose if my parents put up with it, it must rather run in the family. All right, let's go see your haunted house."

Their tour proceeded apace. No spirits were encountered, with the exception of some of the liquid variety discovered in the owner's study. She pronounced the kitchen suitable and the main suite of bedrooms on the upper floor spacious and airy. "These windows are marvelous. Look at the light in here. I shall have to recommend to Papa he consider windows like this for their townhouse."

"Won't they also let in the winter's chill?" Morgan asked dubiously.

"No, see here, this glass is thick as anything. With proper drapes..." She cast an appraising gaze about the room. "Perhaps a new carpet, as well. This one is definitely showing its age, and there's a merchant in the bazaar who has some simply lovely Parthanian carpets."

Morgan grinned. "So, I reckon this means we're taking it?"

"We're taking it," she agreed. "Ghost and all. Oh, Morgan, it's perfect."

"Well, that's good, since it's pretty much the only thing available suitable for a new duchess. But I'm glad you like the place. I'll have my solicitor push through the required paperwork at once. I shall leave draperies and carpets and such fripperies in your capable hands."

"Good try. You're not wriggling out of it that easily. You shall accompany me in my search for the proper fripperies, as you so tactfully put it, to furnish this place. After all, it's to be our home, so you deserve to have your opinion heard. And likely ignored, but that's beside the point."

"Hmm. Is it too late to—?"

"If you even think of saying 'cry off,' I shall have to revert to my old self. I'm warning you."

"You mean the girl who used to slap me cross-eyed at every

opportunity?"

"Yes, her. I've been on my best behavior of late, in case you haven't noticed. Don't try me." She raised a warning hand and bestowed a fierce glower upon her betrothed.

Morgan cowered appropriately, but he chuckled as he did. "Yes, my love."

"That was the correct response. Now run along and chivvy your solicitor into action. I must go tell Briana to start packing."

Morgan caught her arm. "You do know we can't move in until we're married?"

"I know. Still, Parthane wasn't packed in a day, to butcher an already ridiculous aphorism. And the wedding is only a couple of days away. What day is this, Tuesday? Oh, my word, I've got a fitting this afternoon, then Clarise is coming, and…"

"Then I'll push off to see about acquiring us a house." Morgan closed the gate behind them, bestowed a kiss on her cheek, then strode off down the street.

Marissa took a final look at the house. It would be her home as Duchess of Westdale. She smiled in contentment at that thought. One of the curtains in an upper window fluttered, almost as if the house were tipping her a wink.

"Hmmm," she muttered as she eyed the place curiously. Nothing else stirred. No spectral faces showed themselves at the window. Shaking her head, she hurried on her way.

Chapter Twelve

Late the next morning, a dusty coach halted outside the duBerry's townhome. Marissa threw open the front door and hurried down the stairs. Her father emerged from the coach.

"Papa!" she cried, flinging her arms around his neck. "Oh, it's wonderful to see you."

"My heavens." Marcus duBerry laughed. "You'd think you'd not seen us for years, instead of only a few weeks."

"And you too, Mamma," she said as her mother stepped out the coach. She helped her mother down the coach steps, then hugged her tightly.

Annalysse duBerry returned her fierce embrace. "Marissa, you look radiant, my dear."

"I'm happy," Marissa said. "Happy to be marrying Morgan. And truly happy to have you both here. Let's go in, I have so much to tell you."

"You two go along," her father said. "I'll be in after I see to the trunks."

"All right, Papa." Taking her mother by the hand, Marissa led her into the house, chattering away. As they entered the morning room, Marissa asked, "Would you like tea, Mamma? Or something else to drink? Cook will have lunch ready soon, I believe."

"Nothing right now, Marissa. I'm going to go up to my room and change out of these dusty clothes. I feel like I have half the road stuck to me."

"Of course. I'm afraid I was thoughtless. I'll come with you. Papa and the coachmen should be in with your trunks any moment." Together, they walked up the stairs to the upper floor.

"Which room are you sleeping in?" her mother inquired. "I would hope you've been in ours. It's much the nicest."

"I was," Marissa admitted. "I changed yesterday since you and

Papa should have it. Almost all my things are packed anyway."

"Packed?" her mother glanced at her in surprise. "Wh—Oh. Yes, of course. I take it you've found a new place to live?"

"Morgan found it. I have to say, it's simply charming. You're going to adore it. It even has a resident ghost."

"Oh, lovely, a friend for Uncle Harold."

"Exactly what I said." Marissa giggled. "I don't know if it's true, about the ghost, but I rather think it's fun. As long as he comports himself in a gentlemanly manner, of course."

"One can hope for no less. I can't wait to see your new home and meet your ghost as well."

A tap on the door heralded the advent of Marcus and the porters. Trunks were distributed, lavish tips were handed round, and the porters returned to the coach. Her father glanced around. "You've kept the place well, daughter," he said. "Well done, you."

Marissa laughed. "None of my doing, Papa. I'm afraid the credit must go to Briana and Rose. They keep things, including me, quite tidy." She paused, then said, "Well, perhaps not me, truth be told. I seem to find myself pursued by assassins, or doing battle with mad wizards, or consorting with dragons. It does take a bit of a toll on my wardrobe. I think Briana despairs of me. I'm sure she keeps a couple of seamstresses on the payroll, just to keep me from appearing in public in tattered rags."

"Your letters," her father said, eyeing her with an air of curiosity, "have obviously not been quite as informative as one might hope." He rubbed his chin. "On second thought, perhaps, they've been quite pertinent enough. I'm not quite sure I'm ready to know all the grisly details of your rather chaotic existence." He smiled. "However, you seem to be in good health and good spirits, so I reckon it's for the best, eh?" He patted her on the shoulder.

Marissa grinned at him. "I'm the Royal Enchantress, Papa, and about to wed the Knight-Commander of the Legion. What could possibly stand against the two of us?"

"Mmmm," was all her father replied.

"Marcus, could you open up those trunks?" her mother asked. "I'd really like to freshen up before we go down to lunch."

"Speaking of which, I'd better go let Cook know you'll soon be ready. She's thrilled to be able to do a meal for someone besides just me. I've no doubt she's spreading herself in preparing luncheon."

"Fine, fine," her mother said, rummaging through a trunk. "We'll be down in about twenty minutes."

Marissa left them to change and hurried downstairs to check on luncheon. When they convened in the dining room sometime later, and

Cook brought in the roast and peas and potatoes to the admiration of all parties, her mother said, "She's a gem, Marissa. Will she come with you to your new home?"

"Yes, she, Rose, and Briana have all agreed to stay on at McRobbie House. At least I think that's the name Morgan will give it."

"So, tell me all about the wedding," her mother commanded. Marissa was happy to oblige, showering her parents with myriad details, from flowers to her dress to the enormous guest list necessitated by a wedding attended by the king and queen.

"Speaking of invitations," her mother said, a twinkle lighting her eye, "I was interested to learn you sent one to Lady Hermione."

"Oh, dear. I do hope she didn't give you grief, Mamma."

A grin spread across her mother's face. "Grief? Good heavens, I've never seen her so beside herself. What was I thinking, to allow you to marry some half-caste foreigner who's no better than he should be, when you could have had Henry? And on, and on. I thought she'd never run down."

"I'm sorry, Mamma. I know I was a bit of a cat, I couldn't help myself."

"Sorry? My dear, I'd have paid good money to see Hermione in such a state. I sent her away with a flea in her ear, I can assure you. I told her my daughter was to wed a duke who's a close friend of the king, and I was as pleased as could be about the whole thing. She went such a magnificent shade of purple, I thought she might have a conniption fit right there in the morning room. It was all too marvelous."

"How is Henry?" Marissa asked.

"Same as always," her mother replied as she sipped her wine. "Still chasing anything in a skirt."

"Oh, Henry's not so bad," her father said. "He'll settle down eventually, I'm sure."

Mamma rolled her eyes. "Men," she muttered.

"I'm happy to hear you're solid on Morgan, Mamma," Marissa said.

"Oh, I am indeed and not merely because he's a duke. I like that man. I said as much when you brought him to visit, if you recall."

The details of that visit, along with its aftermath, were etched in Marissa's memory. She shivered but managed to cover it with a cough. "Sorry, must have swallowed wrong. By the way, Morgan has offered to stand us dinner tonight, if that meets with your approval."

"Excellent," her father put in. "I like your young man, Marissa. I think you've done well for yourself. Even better, he's done well for himself too."

"Oh, Papa, you're sweet," Marissa said. "One thing, though. He asked if it would be all right if his mother joins the party. She's eager to meet you."

"Of course," her mother said. "It will be lovely to see her again."

"Oh, yes, I'd forgotten you know her," Marissa said.

"Not well, I'm afraid. She's a charming woman."

"Who carries a sword parasol," Marissa confided. She decided it might be best if she didn't mention just how well she and Lady Sybil had become acquainted when they'd been taken prisoner by Captain Fanshawe aboard the *Mad Maudie*.

"Really? How splendid," her mother crowed.

"She's giving me several, in assorted colors," Marissa said. "As a wedding gift."

Her mother chuckled. "What more could a bride ask for?"

~ * ~

Morgan arrived in his coach promptly at eight bells, to whisk them away to the Inn of Tyree. Marissa, at her mother's insistence, had allowed Briana to perform arcane rituals on her hair. Examining her reflection in the glass, she had to admit the results were rather stunning. Clad in her best gown, Marissa and her parents went outside to meet her betrothed.

Morgan waited beside the coach and greeted her parents with obvious pleasure. Lady Annalysse beamed as her future son bestowed a kiss to her hand.

Lord Marcus shook Morgan's hand warmly. "Good to see you, m'boy," he said. "Although I suppose I'd best be on good behavior and address you in proper fashion as 'Your Grace'."

"Pah." Morgan waved this away. "We're family or will be in two days. I hope you won't hold to the title, Marcus, or I shall have to refer to you as Baron duBerry on every possible occasion. I know neither of us would care for it."

Her father barked a laugh. "Quite right, Morgan, quite right. Besides, if I addressed you by your title, I suppose then I'd end up referring to Marissa as 'Your Grace' as well, and I don't think I could quite bring myself to it."

"You'd best not," she warned. She assumed a scowl, but soon allowed it to morph into a grin. "Come on, let's go. I'm famished."

Morgan opened the door to the coach, ushering them inside, where Lady Sybil McRobbie, the dowager viscountess of Westdale, waited. Marissa's parents fell on her with glad cries of welcome, sitting beside her to catch up, while Morgan and Marissa sat together opposite them.

"Well done, bringing Lady Sybil," she murmured as the coach rocked into motion.

"As if I could have kept her away with anything short of a squad of soldiers," he replied, squeezing her hand. "It's nice they get along, isn't it?"

She nodded. "Yes, it is nice." She leaned over to give him a kiss on the cheek.

"Stop canoodling, you two," Lady Sybil said. Marissa jerked back, and Lady Sybil chuckled. "Tell me the news about your pirate friend, Fanshawe. What's he up to now?"

"Pirate?" asked Marissa's mother. "What's this about a pirate? How do you know him, Marissa?"

The coach came to a halt, as did conversations about pirates, and the knowing thereof, for which Marissa was grateful. Of course, it was doubtful her mother would give her any respite from her keen questioning. There was no one more persistent, like a dog with a bone, than Lady Annalysse when she wanted to know something.

Morgan herded them into the inn, where the owner himself appeared, leading them to a large table near the windows. In daylight, there would have been a lovely prospect of the well-appointed grounds. Even now, the light from strategically placed torches gave hints of the garden's delights.

The wine steward materialized. He bowed slightly to Morgan, who shook his head. "Here's your man," he said, with a gesture toward her father. "I know my limits, although Marissa is trying to school me a bit. I will absolutely defer to your choices, Marcus."

He acknowledged this accolade with a nod and was soon deep in conference with the steward. Her mother said, "Now, Marissa, tell me about this pirate. Although I'm not at all sure I want to know."

Lady Sybil's brows arched. "Ah, you've not told them about your latest adventures, eh? Our latest adventures, should I say?"

"Well, no... I was rather busy, and..."

"And didn't want to worry them, right?" Lady Sybil grinned. "Most thoughtful. I'll spin the tale, then. I was there. Well, for most of it, anyway, and got the rest from Morgan." She grinned at Marissa's parents, her eyes alight with mischief.

"It all started because Morgan here managed to get himself kidnapped by this mad girl who felt he'd rejected her many years ago and wanted revenge."

"My word," said her father.

"She'd teamed up with an even madder wizard, who also had plans, necessitating getting both Morgan and Marissa out of the way.

Permanently."

Her father looked from Lady Sybil to Marissa. "I see."

Marissa squeezed her eyes shut. When she opened them again, her parents and Lady Sybil were still there. Morgan's mother grinned good-naturedly at her.

"Well, Morgan disappeared, and we none the wiser. Marissa and I decided to set off to hunt for him. We'd barely left the house when we got taken prisoner by this fellow Fanshawe, the pirate in question. He'd devised some wild scheme to use Marissa as bait to lure the dragon away from his hoard."

"I...see." Her mother sent a piercing gaze in Marissa's direction.

Marissa just knew she'd be hearing much on the subject of consorting with dragons, not to mention pirates, later in the evening. Not a comforting thought.

Lady Sybil went on, relishing her tale. "Then, he figured, the pirates could swoop in and carry off the treasure. He took us out on the Thundermist Sea. It is the last place anyone should want to visit, believe you me. He dosed her with something to keep her from using her magic—"

"Witchbane," breathed Marissa's mother.

"That's the stuff. When we entered the Thundermist—which is more thunder, and more mist, than you'd ever imagine—it somehow infused Marissa, restored her powers and evidently gave her a bit extra to be getting on with."

Both her parents stared at Marissa, who found it difficult to meet their gaze. "I begin to see why we didn't get this story in a letter," her mother said darkly. "Go on, Sybil."

"Well, the upshot was, the dragon never showed up. Turned out he was off someplace else entirely and had no notion Marissa had been taken captive. The joke was on the pirates, though, because the dragon didn't have any treasure stored away. Evidently he doesn't go in for that sort of thing."

"A rugged individualist," her father said with a grin.

"As you say." Lady Sybil paused for a moment, glanced around, and muttered, "I hope that lad shows up with more wine soon. I'm getting parched here."

A waiter indeed appeared with the bottle her father had requested, along with crystal goblets. Once the wine was opened and duly tasted by her father, who nodded his approval, glasses were poured all around.

Lady Sybil took a sip. "Ah, much better, Now I can go on."

"I'm not sure I can," her mother said under her breath. Marissa winced. She was definitely going to get a hearty mother-daughter "chat" later.

"Anyway, Marissa managed to convince this Fanshawe fellow to take us to where we thought Morgan was being held prisoner. He even did one better and went with her. I couldn't go, blast it, much as I wanted to. Bunged up my ankle something fierce. I couldn't walk more than two steps without keeling over.

"So off they went to this black tower or whatever it was. Morgan was there, trussed up like a Christmas goose. This Fanshawe, who's not such a bad lot for a pirate, held off the wizard while Marissa dealt with the girl, Kiara. I don't know all the gruesome details. Morgan did mumble something about a magical flaming sword. I gather Marissa used it to deal with the wizard."

"Flaming sword, eh? How…quaint." Her mother said, eyeing Marissa darkly. She gave her a weak smile.

"So Fanshawe lugged my son down the tower. I reckon he would have had to haul Morgan all the way back to the ship, but just then a band of Tzigani showed up. They knew Marissa, had met her in Caerfaen, and offered their assistance to get back to Fanshawe's ship. As it turned out, the pirate wasn't really a pirate after all. He was a privateer, operating under a Letter of Marque from the king himself. Morgan's supposed to be getting him back into proper society, for whatever it's worth."

"I have kept my word on that," Morgan said. "I've given him letters of introduction to quite a number of people and expressed my good opinion of him all over Caerfaen. It may take some time, but he'll be fine."

"He was," Marissa said, "a most gentlemanly pirate."

"Hmph," sniffed Lady Sybil. "He wasn't so bad, I suppose. For a pirate."

"Let's talk about the wedding," Marissa chirped brightly, eager to change the subject. "What do you think of my dress, Mama?"

The look her mother gave her announced loud and clear the subject of pirates was not yet relegated to the dustbin of memory. Still, the conversation did turn to the upcoming wedding, and soon lackeys arrived bearing platters of food.

"I gather you've not heard the last of this incident with Fanshawe?" Morgan whispered in her ear once everyone was intent on their dinner.

"I wouldn't bet on it," she replied, but her attention had been drawn elsewhere. She was more focused on the people a couple of tables away. They'd been glancing over, faces dark and foreboding, for most of the evening. Marissa had caught one of the men's imprecations about "allowing Orskans in the place."

The bite of fowl in her mouth crumbled to ashes. She washed it down with a large sip of wine, then turned to her betrothed. "Would you excuse me for one moment, my lord? I have something I need to attend to."

"Marissa, no," he said. "Just let it go."

She shook her head fiercely. "I'm sorry, Morgan, I can't."

She stood, composed herself, and stalked over to the other table. She knew her parents, as well as Lady Sybil, were staring after her in confusion. It didn't matter. Marissa's ire was roused, and there was nothing for it but to storm the castle, as it were.

"Good evening," she said, as she loomed over their table. There were two men and two women, about her parents' age. They regarded her intrusion with a haughty superciliousness. Marissa, undaunted, pressed on. "I couldn't help overhearing just now, as I'm sure was your intent, your comment about Orskans. And I wondered, just where you think anyone from Orsk should get his dinner?"

"Back in Orsk," growled one of the men.

She rounded on him, skewering him with a glare. "Do you know," she asked, "just who this Orskan is? No, you probably don't care in the least, do you? Allow me to educate you. This particular Orskan," she pointed to Morgan, who she noticed winced, "is Duke Morgan McRobbie. Knight-Commander of the King's Legion. A close personal friend of His Majesty, King Rhys. Friend to dragons. And the man," she announced, "whom I will be wedding on the day after tomorrow, with the king and queen in attendance."

Marissa stared into the man's eyes, until he broke his gaze and looked down at the floor. "This means," she continued, "I am the king's Royal Enchantress and capable of wreaking all manner of magical havoc. Not that I intend to do anything the least bit magical." She gave the man a grim stare. "At the moment."

After a slight pause, she went on, "I've no doubt Morgan was good enough for you when he risked his life in defense of Kilbourne. When he led the Legion in repelling the Rhuddlani invasion. He's just not good enough to eat in the same inn as you. Is that it?" She glared, even as she felt a sudden swell of power rise in her. Tamping down the urge to do something dire, like turn this jackass into a real one, she gave the man a smile, all teeth and no humor whatsoever. "Where were you, I wonder, during the Rhuddlani invasion? Were you there, helping to protect Kilbourne? Or were you back here, cowering, in hopes this Orskan would manage to hold them back and save your sorry hide? It seems to me you're the one not fit to be eating in the same inn as he. I hope you enjoy the rest of your dinner. Good night."

A deafening silence stole across the room. Marissa saw several people nod, although others directed scowls in her direction. Whether because she'd disturbed the enjoyment of their dinner, or because they too wished Orskans banned from the Inn, she didn't know and didn't care to delve into it. She ignored the glares from the group she'd reproached, spun on her heel, then strode back to join her party.

"Marissa, you didn't have to do that," Morgan said. "I don't need you—"

She cut him off. "To fight your battles for you? No, I know you don't. Not the normal kind. But this is a battle you won't fight yourself. You just brush it off. Well, I can't, Morgan. I'll not have snobs like those looking down their noses at you, simply because of who and what you are. You're a good man, and I love you, and I'm going to marry you, if you'll still have me."

"No better champion could I ask for," he said, and kissed her soundly. "On with the wedding."

Chapter Thirteen

A beam of sunlight, sharp as a shard of glass, arced through the window, scattering refracted rainbows across the cathedral's inlaid tile floor. It fell directly into the path of the processing bride.

There were those, Morgan knew, who maintained no witch should ever be allowed to defile the cathedral with her presence. She would, they believed, be destroyed by just such a light, sent from heaven to scour abominations from the face of the earth.

Of course, it was all moonshine. Superstition, coupled with ancient prejudice. This knowledge didn't help a bit when these superstitions and prejudices were leveled at the woman he was about to wed. It was maddening.

In time with the swelling music of the cathedral's majestic organ, Marissa walked slowly, as befitted a processing bride, arm in arm with her beaming father. Step by agonizing step, she neared the pool of light. Hardly daring to breathe, his boots rooted to the floor, Morgan watched helplessly as she stepped into its radiance.

A low collective gasp from the spectators in the packed cathedral seemed to suck every bit of air from the enormous chamber. The light swelled to bathe her fully in its embrace, the colors from the stained glass somehow infusing Marissa's gown and painting it with rainbows. A sign of favor, perhaps, rather than condemnation?

She made her way slowly out of the sunbeam, unharmed. A soft susurration of relief (or disappointment) soared toward the rafters as Morgan moved forward to meet his betrothed.

Marcus duBerry, his face wreathed in a smile, turned to take his daughter's hand in his and bestow a fond kiss on her cheek. He stepped to the side, still holding her hand. Morgan bowed to his lady, trying desperately to hide the foolishly happy grin which threatened to spread across his face. She dipped a graceful curtsey in return, and Morgan could see her eyes dancing with her own obvious delight.

Marcus beamed when he gave Marissa's hand from his keeping into Morgan's. It was more than a merely symbolic gesture. He was now charged with his lady's care and protection. It was a responsibility he'd never truly imagined he'd have, but one he was ready and eager to take on.

Marcus retreated a few paces, nodding acknowledgement of Morgan's acceptance. Morgan was forced to suppress a laugh as Marcus's eye drooped in a slow wink. Taking Marissa's arm, Morgan faced forward toward where the fidgeting company of attendants, outriders, and priest waited.

He said quietly, "Shall we?"

"I can't wait," she whispered back.

Together they stepped forward to where their attendants waited patiently. Well, perhaps not so patiently in the case of Sir Byron, who was standing up for Morgan. He looked rather uncomfortable in a silk tunic, elaborate waterfall cravat, and tight-fitting trousers. He kept tugging on his cravat, as if it were choking him, and his expression clearly said, "Let's get on with it."

Clarise Rochford, who was standing up for Marissa, was quite resplendent in a gown of burgundy brocade. Marissa, however, was simply radiant, as if the sunbeam had filled her and lit her from within. Her eyes shone, her snowy white gown gleamed, and the ducal coronet in her hair added a golden luster to the ringlets cascading about her face. He escorted the woman who was to share his life up the two steps to where Bishop Randolph MacFarlane waited with a faint smile tugging at the corners of his mouth.

"Your Majesties," intoned the bishop. "Lords and ladies. Good citizens of Kilbourne. We gather here, under the protection and blessing of our Heavenly God, to witness the marriage of Morgan McRobbie and Marissa duBerry.

"If there be anyone present," Randolph continued, "who knows any reason why these two should not be joined in holy matrimony, let him speak now, or forever hold his peace."

Morgan's hand moved to his sword hilt. Granted, the weapon was ceremonial in nature, intended chiefly for show. Still, it would do the job in a pinch. He cast a baleful eye over the assembled throng, daring any one of them to utter a peep.

A man among the crowd cleared his throat. His eyes widened as Morgan's glare fell on him, and he sank down into his seat. Hopefully to continue right on into some horrible netherworld. Morgan felt the force of Marissa's gaze and placed his sword hand back to a neutral, less threatening position. She bestowed a somewhat frosty smile.

"Sorry," he mouthed.

Her smile foretold future discussions of uncouth behavior unbecoming a duke of the realm. He gave an infinitesimal shrug. Well, no one had spoken up, had they? Which, by and large, was quite the point.

"Hearing no objection," Randolph boomed, "let us continue." He turned to Morgan.

"Morgan James McRobbie, Duke of Westdale, Knight-Commander of the King's Legion, Baron..." He listed off an interminable catalog of Morgan's titles, holdings, and honorifics. "Do you take Marissa to be your wife? To have and to hold from this day on, to love, honor and cherish, come whatever may chance, so long as you both shall live?"

"I do."

Randolph now faced Marissa. A fond smile spread over his face. "Marissa Marie duBerry, Royal Enchantress of Kilbourne..."

Morgan noted a brief resigned, if slightly amused, expression on his beloved's face. Randolph's mouth turned up at one corner for a mere instant. He was not one to let an opportunity pass, and his championing of her elevation to the exalted position of Royal Enchantress had been a brilliant stroke. It was, she had grumbled, a better sobriquet than Witch of Caerfaen, although not by much.

"Do you," continued Randolph, not missing a beat, "take Morgan..."

"I do," she replied, when he finally ground to a halt.

"Then by the power bestowed upon me, here in the presence of God, Their Majesties, and this vast company, I now pronounce you man and wife. You may," he instructed Morgan, "kiss your bride."

Morgan needed no encouragement. All else faded into distant oblivion as he took Marissa into his arms and kissed her soundly. A dull roar finally penetrated his consciousness. He realized it was the sound thunderous applause from the wedding guests.

"You may now," muttered Randolph with a basilisk stare, "stop kissing the bride."

Morgan grinned at his oldest friend. He extended his arm to his bride. His new duchess, he amended. "Shall we process, my love?"

She smiled up at him. A genuine smile this time, one indicating past transgressions were, at least for now, held in abeyance, with no trademark slaps in the offing. She placed a hand on his arm, and he covered her fingers with his hand. He could feel the warmth of the McRobbie betrothal ring on her finger.

Together, while the music swelled to fill the cathedral and spiral up toward heaven, the Duke and Duchess of Westdale walked with stately tread to the rear of the church, into the slanting sunlight of a late September afternoon.

Chapter Fourteen

The celebratory banquet, held in the great hall of the palace, was a grand gesture from King Rhys to fête his newest duke and his bride. Morgan was acutely aware of the honor Rhys bestowed on him. On them: Knight-Commander of the Legion and Royal Enchantress.

They were a pair, he and Marissa. Oddities and curiosities, each thrust into the glare of public attention. Each coming to the other's defense against the forces arrayed against them. Taking turns rescuing one another from one dire peril after another.

As if sensing his thoughts—something she did entirely too often and much too easily—Marissa gave his hand a squeeze. Morgan forced aside his ruminations on this most joyous day, focusing on his bride. "I love you," he said.

"I know," she replied, in a maddeningly matter-of-fact tone. Then her face creased into a broad smile. "Oh, Morgan, I'm so happy. I can't believe it's real. We're married at last."

"Well, since most of Caerfaen, along with a good bit of both Westdale and Vynfold to boot, have turned out to witness the proceedings, I reckon we must be. And now—" he inclined his head toward the line of people stretched endlessly before them— "we have to greet every last one of them." He indicated Hugh Wollingford, the Lord High Chancellor, who was beckoning them over to receive the congratulations of the multitudes.

"I don't suppose there's any way we could simply sneak off?"

Morgan shook his head. "I'm afraid we're in for it," he said. At the same time, a familiar voice rang in his mind.

"I could fly you off somewhere private," Wyvrndell offered.

Morgan and Marissa both glanced over to where the dragon's head protruded through a set of open double doors. The bulk of him remained outside, but Morgan had been adamant in his assertion: the dragon should be part of the festivities.

Wyvrndell's eyes gleamed with interest as he watched the milling throngs of well-wishers. He politely ignored the wide berth most of them afforded him.

"Thank you, no. We should probably stay and accept everyone's congratulations," Marissa demurred. "It is only polite."

"As you will," replied the dragon.

Lord Hugh's frowns and gestures were becoming more insistent. Morgan led his duchess to where the chancellor waited, his foot tapping impatiently.

"If we don't get started," Hugh said, "we'll never get done in time for the banquet." He signaled to a liveried attendant who, in time honored tradition, blew a teeth-jarringly off-key fanfare on his trumpet to startle the crowd into a ragged semblance of silence.

Lord Hugh inhaled, swelling up to impressive proportions, and bellowed out, "Your Royal Majesties. Distinguished nobles. Welcome guests. I give you now the Duke and Duchess of Westdale."

After this proclamation, it was simply sheer chaos. The line of guests eager to congratulate, or ogle, or sniff disdainfully, as suited their natures, stretched on toward eternity. Morgan was beginning to wish they'd accepted Wyvrndell's offer when he spied a man in wizard's robes stepping forward.

"McRobbie," the man said.

"Foxwent," Morgan replied, struggling to maintain an even temperament.

His recent adventure—no, make it near murder—at the hands of a rogue wizard, had given him a rather jaundiced view of the cadre of magic wielders as a whole. Well, with the exception of his bride. And possibly Master Sebastien.

Marissa piped up. "Chief Wizard Foxwent. What a surprise. Especially since I'm certain your name was not on the guest list."

"An oversight, I'm sure," Foxwent replied. "Though I believe if you look, you'll find my name is there." He waved a hand. "It really doesn't matter."

"No?" Marissa glared. Her opinion of wizards—well, most wizards, anyway—was no doubt even more scathing than Morgan's.

"I came to offer my felicitations to you both," Foxwent continued, either unaware or unconcerned by the hostility she was exuding. "And also my apologies to the, um, Royal Enchantress, is it? On behalf of the College of Wizards. For what happened with Headmaster Rhenn. Sad, quite sad. Poor deluded fellow, led astray by that monstrous madwoman into threatening you both. Simply terrible."

Morgan opened his mouth to protest this inaccurate assessment of recent events. He was halted by the pressure of Marissa's foot on his.

"Chief Wizard," she said through clenched teeth.

Morgan spotted an extremely dangerous glint in her eyes. Now, he reckoned, would be a good time for anyone on the receiving end of said look to crawl into a convenient hole and hide.

"I will consider your apology in exactly the same spirit it was offered. Now, if you'll excuse us, we have a great many other invited guests to greet. Good day, sir."

The wizard narrowed his eyes. Marissa met his gaze, unblinking, and Morgan sensed the power swelling within her, infused with her anger. Evidently Foxwent did as well, for he turned on his heel without another word and stalked off through the crowd.

She glared after him for a moment, then pasted on a gracious smile and turned to greet their next guest.

"What on earth was he on about?" Morgan wondered quietly.

"I could eat him," offered Wyvrndell, crunching down noisily on the roast ox provided especially for him at the king's direction. A ring of guests watched with a mix of awe and horror.

"Not today," Morgan replied. "Should it become necessary, I will give you the heartiest encouragement."

~ * ~

When the banquet was finally underway, Marissa sat at the high table, to Gwyn's left, while Morgan sat to Rhys's right. Marissa listlessly chased a pea around her plate with her fork.

"Mmm?" She glanced over at Gwyn, realizing she'd been lost in thought and had not heard a word her friend said. She idly picked up an unwanted chicken leg.

"I said, what's wrong?" Gwyn scrutinized Marissa with a mixture of curiosity and concern. "I'd have thought you'd be happy, excited, and chattering away. Instead, you've been sitting here brooding and gnawing that empty bone like an old dog. You've also been muttering into your wine glass."

Heat rushed to her face. She hastily dropped the bone back onto her plate. "Oh." She glanced around, wondering if anyone else, like Morgan for instance, had noticed.. "Have I really?"

"Yes, you have. Now tell me what's troubling you. Wedding night jitters?"

Laughing, Marissa shook her head. "Heavens no, nothing like that. It's honestly nothing to do with Morgan. No, I'm ecstatically happy we're finally married."

"Then what is it?"

"That wizard." She glowered at the chicken bone she'd

unconsciously picked up again.

"Rhenn?" Gwyn's eyes widened in surprise. "He's—"

"Dead." Marissa glowered. "No, not him. Well, not exactly. It's the Chief Wizard, Foxwent. He somehow managed to wrangle his way in here, even though I know he was not on the guest list. He tried to offer up some lame excuses and apologies for 'poor deluded Headmaster Rhenn, led astray by that woman'."

"But he—Rhenn—tried to kill you. And Morgan. Didn't he?"

Marissa sipped her wine. It was an excellent vintage—Rhys had certainly spared no expense. "Evidently this trifling issue was entirely beside the point. Oooh, I wanted to spit in his eye. However, good breeding told. I'm a duchess now, after all. I suppose I have to act like one, despite extreme provocation. I reckoned it might cause comment, so I graciously refrained."

Gwyn giggled. "I'd wondered why he stormed off in such a foul mood. What on earth do you think he was after?"

Marissa waved a hand, realized she'd picked up the chicken leg again, and dropped it with a clatter back onto her plate. "I have no idea. It might be he's interested in somehow molding the story to protect Rhenn's reputation, by putting the blame for what happened on Kiara Northram."

"And you don't agree?"

Marissa shrugged. "I suppose we'll never really know the whole truth. From what I saw, Rhenn would have been quite content to murder both Morgan and me. I've a strong suspicion if their scheme had worked as planned, he'd have somehow done away with Kiara Northram as well. Then there would have been no one able to claim he had any involvement in what happened."

"How horrible."

She grimaced, realized she was being watched closely by several hundred people, and schooled her expression into one of pleasant placidity. "Yes, isn't it?"

Chapter Fifteen

"Where are you taking me?"

"If I told you, it wouldn't be a surprise, now would it?" Morgan grinned at her. His smiles, once a thing of legendary scarcity, were becoming much more frequent. At least it seemed where she was concerned. It felt rather nice.

"Hmph. Very well, oh man of mystery. Keep your little secrets." She scrunched over closer to him. "Unless you can be persuaded..."

He slid his arm around her, drawing her into a fierce embrace. "Try me."

The coach rattled on through the night. They'd finally managed to escape the banquet and the myriad well-wishers, but the whole affair had taken much longer than Marissa had hoped. It had required the combined efforts of Sir Byron and Sir Aartis to clear a path for them to the door. Those sturdy bulwarks had served as sentries, guarding their retreat until Morgan had Marissa ensconced in the coach and on their way at last.

"Well," he said some moments later, after she'd done her best at persuasion. "I suppose I can tell..."

His words were halted, as was the coach. "I shan't have to tell you," he said. "You can see for yourself. I believe we have arrived."

The curtains were drawn closed on the coach windows, so she couldn't see where he'd brought them. Morgan opened the door and kicked the steps down, then hopped down to the ground to help Marissa descend.

She stepped out, then stopped still on the top step, staring. "I should have guessed," she said.

"Welcome to the Oaktree Inn. Again," he said as he handed her down to the ground. "I imagine Master Sansbury is up making a final inspection of the suite I reserved."

"The suite you reserved?" she demanded, parroting own her

words from what seemed ages ago. "Do I strike you as the kind of girl to go flitting off for a night of dalliance with the first man to rescue her from a dragon?"

"Well, I certainly hope so." He cocked a sardonic brow. "Otherwise, I reckon I've gone to a good deal of bother and expense for nothing."

She tried desperately to control her mirth. It was no use. She burst out in a delighted peal of laughter. "Morgan, you're an idiot, and a hopeless romantic, and I love it. It's perfect."

"Thank you. I'm glad you approve my choice. I figured since we didn't really get to enjoy the place the last time we were here, this might serve to make amends."

"You mean since you're not bleeding all over the carpets, and we're not interrupted by murderous spies?"

"Just so." He chuckled then proffered his arm. "Shall we?"

She took it, and together they walked up the graveled path toward the entrance to the inn. Torchieres lit the way, their flames sending wild shadows dancing through the trees like agitated spirits.

"You can't imagine how much I've looked forward to this moment," he said.

"Really?" Marissa shivered, and Morgan put an arm around her bare shoulders.

"Yes, indeed," he replied.

He opened the carved wooden door and led her through. As on their previous visit, no one was visible as they walked into the entrance hall. Marissa gazed around. When Morgan had brought her there before, she'd been too furious to really take it in. Now, she could appreciate the warm wood gleaming with light reflected from the fire in the huge central hearth.

Several comfortable chairs and settees, placed in cozy groups around the room, simply begged for one to sink into them with a cup of tea and a good book. Green plants and flower pots added splashes of color. She strolled over to stand by the fire. The flames leapt and danced in counterpoint to her own feelings of joy and of love for her husband.

Husband. Such a prosaic word. Her duke. Her champion. Her love. She smiled to herself, then glanced over her shoulder as footsteps sounded on the stairs. An elderly man, neat and well-dressed, was descending from the upper floor.

He pushed wisps of hair out of his eyes and called out, "Ah, Your Grace, there you are. My most hearty felicitations on your nuptials. Both of you, I meant." He swept an elegant bow to Marissa. "Your suite is prepared."

"Thank you, Sansbury," Morgan replied. She noticed his eyes, suddenly filled with stars, never left her. "We'll go up now."

The old man chuckled, his face wreathed in a broad grin. "No need for bandages this time, Your Grace?"

Marissa bit down on a most unladylike snort. Morgan didn't even bother. Throwing back his head in a laugh, he said, "No, not this time, Master Sansbury. By some miracle, I managed to make it through unscathed."

The innkeeper, still chuckling to himself, handed over a key. "If you need anything at all, please let me know. Anything at all."

"Thank you," Morgan replied, and took her hand again.

Her mind brought up the memory of her previous visit to this inn. On that occasion, she stalked up the stairs sounding more like a company of soldiers than a demure duchess. This time, she allowed Morgan to escort her up. At the top lay a hallway running off in both directions, paneled in the same golden wood as in the entrance below. Candles glowed in sconces along the walls.

"This way," he said, heading toward the left-hand passage. An anticipatory shiver ran through her. She gazed up into his eyes. She'd waited so very long for this moment. She curved her lips into a smile. "Lead on, my lord," she said.

When they reached the end of the hallway, he used the key and pushed open the door to reveal the suite. A cheerful fire crackled in the grate. A table laden with food and drink beckoned. An open window presented a prospect of the gardens below, now shrouded in darkness, but offering fragrant hints of their daytime beauties. Some of those same flowers reposed in crystal vases about the room.

Marissa stepped lightly onto the luxurious carpet gracing the floor, its soft floral pattern reflected in the window hangings and the furniture's upholstery. An elegant settee was placed strategically before the fire, with other comfortable chairs spaced about the room. A large, lavish four-posted bed, laid with a patchwork quilt, invited from the adjoining room. She smiled, remembering its canopied hangings and the soft embrace of the bed when she'd slept—albeit fitfully—in it before, with him on the floor in the sitting room.

"Marissa? My love?"

She faced her husband. He had poured two glasses of wine and held one out to her. She took it, and he tilted his own glass toward her slightly. She touched the rim with her glass. The tiny *"ting"* that reverberated from the contact sent a shiver coursing through her body.

"To us," he said. "I can't believe we actually managed it."

"To us," she replied. "And to many, many years of happiness

together." They drank in celebration.

Morgan led her to the settee. She lifted her brows as she settled herself, and she regarded the wine glass curiously. "Morgan, wherever did you get this?"

He smiled lazily. "From your father. I asked him which was your favorite. He was kind enough to present me with a bottle. With several, in fact."

She stretched her legs toward the fire, snuggling against him. "You're sweet," she murmured.

Morgan slid his arm around her shoulders, pulling her even closer. "The wine is delectable," he said. "But not half as delectable as you."

"Are you trying to charm me? Because it's working."

"Good." He set his glass down. Then he leaned in to kiss her. His lips tasted like the wine, sweet and tart. A shiver ran through her as they kissed again, deeper, more urgent now…

Bam. Bam. Bam.

Marissa's eyes flew open wide, and she pulled away. Morgan reluctantly released her, as she came to the distinctly unwelcome realization the pounding wasn't merely her own thumping heart.

Some thrice-damned idiot was beating on the door.

"Ignore it," he said. "They'll go away."

The pounding continued. Marissa gave him a doubtful look. "I don't think they're going away."

Bam.

Morgan leaned toward the door. "Go. Away!" he bellowed. She giggled. Morgan rolled his eyes.

"Duke Morgan?" came a voice through the door. "Open up."

"That sounds like Mr. Barlbent," she said.

"I shall speak most sharply to Master Sansbury about this," he groused. "Letting riff-raff in here like this to disturb a chap on his wedding night. It's just not right."

"Duke Morgan!" Another voice, even more urgent. "Please open the door."

"Isn't that…" she began.

"Holman Barzak," Morgan finished. "I said go away," he repeated to the door. "There's no one here."

She giggled again. The pounding continued. "What on earth could they want?"

He shrugged. "I don't know, I honestly don't care, and I have no interest whatsoever in finding out."

Another voice, deeper and more resonant, bawled, "Open this

door, in the name of the king."

Morgan's head jerked around. "Good Lord! It's Rhys." His brow furrowed. "Blast. I suppose I have to let them in."

"Well, at least we'll be able to provide refreshments," she said, waving an expansive hand toward the table piled with food.

"Somehow I don't think this is a social call." To the men outside he called, "All right, all right, curse you, I'm coming." He released Marissa from his grasp and rose from the settee. "Damn it all." he muttered, as he strode to the door and flung it open.

"What the devil do you mean, barging in here like this?" he demanded.

Rhys shrugged apologetically. "Sorry, Morgan. Duchess." He bowed courteously to Marissa.

Barzak, his clerk Barlbent, and another man filed in behind him. Marissa drew in a sharp breath. The fourth man was Chief Wizard Foxwent.

Morgan returned to stand by Marissa as their guests—if one wanted to be charitable, which she didn't in the least—ranged themselves in a semi-circle facing them. "This," he growled, "had better be good."

"Morgan, I'm sorry," Rhys repeated. "I wouldn't have allowed this intrusion if I didn't think it urgent…"

Morgan sighed, ran a hand through his hair, and glowered. "All right," he said. "What's so blasted urgent?"

"The Demon's Fire has been stolen," Foxwent blurted.

Morgan looked as baffled and beset as Marissa felt. "Well, he's probably better off without it, don't you think? Thanks for letting us know. Now you have, I'm sure you have many other things to do. Off you go, then."

"The Demon's Fire," Foxwent said, obviously struggling to control himself in the face of Morgan's levity, "is a priceless ruby."

"Oh. Well, I didn't take it," Morgan growled. "I'm pretty sure Marissa didn't either." He turned to her. "Have you taken up jewel thievery as a new career, my dear? Something to support us in our old age, perhaps? Well done, if so."

He fielded the cushion she flung at him, tossing it onto the settee. "The only jewel I've managed to acquire lately," she said loftily, holding up her left hand, "is this one." She displayed the McRobbie betrothal ring, whose emerald winked in the candlelight.

"So, there you have it," he said. "Neither of us took it. Seek the culprit elsewhere. Good evening, nice of you to have dropped by, sorry to see you go."

Foxwent's face took on a thunderous expression. Barzak appeared amused, while Mr. Barlbent allowed himself a broad grin. Rhys, Marissa could tell, was having a difficult time holding back his laughter.

"This is serious," the wizard declared. "I demand—"

"Chief Wizard." Rhys laid a restraining hand on the wizard's arm. "A bit less demanding, and a good deal more pleading, might serve your cause better."

Morgan grinned as Foxwent swallowed whatever he'd been about to demand. Barzak spoke up. "No one is here because they think you've stolen the jewel. We're here because we need your help in recovering it."

"Our help?" She felt completely bewildered. "I don't— No." She shook her head. "Surely the Watch would be much better suited to such a task."

Foxwent, who appeared to have gotten himself under control, said, "The Demon's Fire is not merely a jewel. It is also a tremendously powerful magical artifact. It was kept in a highly secured vault in the lowest levels of the Royal College of Wizards and was guarded by strong protective spells. No one should have been able to get anywhere near it, much less steal it."

"And yet despite these eldritch protections," Barlbent observed with a laconic air, "someone waltzed right in and nipped the blasted thing."

Morgan glanced at Marissa. She shrugged helplessly. "All right, someone scarpered with the...whatever ruby," he said.

"The Demon's Fire," supplied Rhys. He rolled his eyes, although not where Foxwent could see him.

"The Demon's Fire," agreed Morgan. "What does this have to do with us? We have, as you may have noticed, only today gotten married. We have other things planned. The Watch, as Marissa has indicated, would seem your best choice to recover this stolen jewel."

The Chief Wizard snorted. "The Watch? Bah! This is beyond the Watch."

"If this jewel is a magical artifact, why don't you simply dispatch a wizard to find and retrieve it?" Marissa asked.

"Because Prince Azim would be on guard if a wizard came looking for it," Foxwent said. "And there would be...trouble."

She glanced at Morgan. He shrugged, no doubt steeling himself to ask the question she knew they were both thinking. She really didn't want to know the answer, but was certain if he didn't ask, she would. "Prince Azim?"

"Prince Azim of Parthane," Barlbent supplied. "The Chief Wizard is certain he's behind the ruby's theft."

"I see," she said, although she didn't in the least. She closed her eyes for a moment, finally realizing where this was going. Blast. She didn't like it. Not one bit. "All right, you can't send a wizard. So, your plan is…what?"

"The 'Royal Enchantress' will go and retrieve the ruby." Foxwent's expression was pained as he said it.

Marissa didn't blame him. She felt pained hearing it.

"The Royal Enchantress," Morgan said fiercely, "isn't going anywhere. Not today. Not tomorrow. Not—"

Rhys held up a hand. "I understand completely how you feel, Morgan. Unfortunately, this is more than simply the theft of a ruby. Otherwise, I wouldn't be here. Wouldn't be a party to this interruption."

"I heard him," Morgan said. "It's a magical geegaw. It…" With a frustrated growl, he said, "All right, tell us. Why is it vital for Marissa to drop everything to go after this ruby?"

"Because in the wrong hands, the Demon's Fire could cause a catastrophe," Foxwent said. "It—well, essentially it contains a large number of demons, trapped within it. If they should be released…"

"Um. Demons." Marissa shuddered. "How many demons?"

"Hundreds. Perhaps as many as a thousand. I don't think anyone's counted in a while."

"A thousand? How big is this thing? It must be enormous," she blurted. Her curiosity got the better of her.

Even so, she really had no interest in magical, demon-housing rubies. At the moment, she only wanted Morgan to sweep her up into his arms and…

"It's not all that large. Maybe half the size of a man's fist. It's— well, I suppose you could say it's bigger on the inside than on the outside."

"A thousand demons?" Morgan sounded incredulous. She didn't blame him in the least. The whole idea was preposterous. "Exactly what happens if this Prince Azim should manage to release them?"

"If they were released all at once?" Foxwent winced. "Total destruction, I would imagine."

"Of Parthane," Morgan said.

"I said 'total' destruction. Yes, Parthane would be first, obviously. Then they'd find their way back here soon enough. They'd destroy everything. The entire world."

"Oh," Marissa trembling like a little girl who's just been told a tale of monsters. "That's pretty total."

Morgan refilled the two empty wine glasses, then lowered himself heavily onto the settee. He wordlessly handed one to Marissa. She took a large sip. It didn't help. Foxwent, Barzak, Barlbent, and Rhys were still there. This wasn't merely a figment of her imagination.

"As much as this goes against my better judgement," Morgan said, "you'd better sit down and tell us everything."

Chapter Sixteen

Rhys pulled up chairs for himself and the other three men. Morgan pointedly did not pour them any wine. Marissa noticed the king snag a ripe peach from the overflowing bowl of fruit and bite into it. He licked his lips in appreciation, then slowly lowered one eyelid to wink at her.

Bemused, she turned her attention back to Foxwent, who was speaking again. "The ruby," he said, "has been the primary containment method for captured demons for many years."

"You don't simply banish them back to the demon realms?" she asked.

The wizard evinced annoyance at the interruption. "No, Lady...Duchess. They don't tend to stay banished. They come back again, bigger, scalier, and meaner than ever. Better to capture them and keep them in the ruby."

"You think this prince from Parthane stole it. Why?"

"Why do I think it, or why did he steal it?"

"Well... Both, I suppose."

"Only an extraordinarily powerful mage could have breached the defenses in place around the ruby. Prince Azim is such a mage."

"Why fix on him?" Morgan asked. "It sounds like you're saying there are a number of wizards who could have done it."

"Because he was seen in Caerfaen. None of the others were."

"I find your logic rather faulty, Chief Wizard," Marissa said. "I think if I were to steal a ruby rife with demons, I'd be sure not to be seen. Do you have valid reasons for ruling out the other possible suspects?"

"I detected Prince Azim's magical signature—his essence, if you will— near the vault."

She held up her hands. "Very well. We'll take it as read this Prince Azim did the deed. Why?"

"He's a collector," Foxwent said, evidently by way of

explanations. For Marissa, this didn't explain anything at all.

"Of demons?" she asked.

He blanched. "No, not of demons. One does not simply collect demons. Not unless one has a desire for a very short lifespan. No, Prince Azim collects...well, I suppose you could say he collects magical curiosities."

Morgan raised a brow. "When you say 'collects', you mean he steals them?"

"Frequently." Foxwent grimaced. "He is a bit...obsessed."

Morgan leaned forward, interposing himself between Marissa and Foxwent. "And you want Marissa to go up against this extremely powerful, obsessive mage? Are you crazy?"

"Perhaps," Barzak responded, before the wizard could reply. "What he is, is desperate."

"Why me, Chief Wizard?" Marissa asked. "Although the king has most generously bestowed the title of Royal Enchantress on me, it's no great secret I have yet to earn it. I'm still only a student of the magical arts. Of late, as I'm certain my tutor will attest, I've been a pretty poor student. Other things have rather taken precedence." She smiled up at Morgan, whose scowl softened, if only for a moment.

"As well they should," Barlbent acknowledged.

She favored him with a smile. She'd always likes Mr. Barlbent, who seemed to have a habit of turning up when least expected but most needed. Returning her attention to Foxwent, she said, "I repeat, Chief Wizard: why me? I'm sure you have lots of wizards who would simply jump at the chance to tackle a job like this."

Foxwent inclined his head slightly in acknowledgement. "True. But none possess something you do."

Marissa waited silently for him to elaborate. Foxwent, evidently realizing his build-up had fallen a bit flat, finally said, "The grimoire."

She blinked in surprise. "The...what? Grimoire? I'm afraid you've lost me."

It was the wizard's turn to blink. "The grimoire," he repeated, as if this explained anything. "The...the book you, um, acquired from Master Rhenn."

Marissa smiled, all teeth, and said, "Oh, you mean the one I found after Rhenn tried to murder Morgan and me? Is that the one you're referring to?" Her words poured out, harsh and cutting. She really didn't care. Who did this wizard think he was, to come in here and...?

Morgan said, "Just one problem, I'm afraid. We don't have the book anymore."

The wizard's mouth opened and closed silently. From the corner of her eye Marissa saw Lord Holman stifle a grin.

Foxwent finally found his voice. "What do you mean you don't have it anymore? What the blazes did you do with it? The book is pric— I mean, it's dangerous."

"So we discovered," Marissa said. "Francesca was adamant. She was certain it would try to subsume me."

"And Francesca would be…?" he inquired, distain written across his face. Whoever this Francesca was, his expression said clearly she was nothing compared to the great and powerful Foxwent.

"My familiar," Marissa said, enjoying for a moment watching him wince. "She says she was once a very powerful witch. Now she's a cat, which from her perspective tends to put a crimp in things. Although she is an excellent mouser."

He bit down on whatever he'd been about to say. Lord Holman came to his rescue. "What has happened to the grimoire, Duchess?"

She still wasn't used to the honorific yet and nearly glanced around to see who Barzak was speaking to. Then it hit her—she was the duchess. Morgan's duchess. She blinked and tried to focus on their unwanted guests. "I'm afraid Master Sebastien took it. He used a spell to seal it into a lead-lined box. He said he would keep it somewhere safe. Extremely kind, I thought. Sebastien," she aimed a dark glance at Foxwent, "is a very thoughtful wizard."

He said nothing, though his face was thunderous. Barzak said smoothly, "Evidently the copy the duchess, um, acquired from Master Rhenn was the one thought to have been secured in the archives."

"I see." Morgan scowled at Foxwent. "You lot aren't very good at security, are you? Losing dangerous books. Losing a demon-infested jewel… Anything else gone missing lately?"

She was sure she heard Barzak mutter, "Only my mind." It was so soft she couldn't be sure she hadn't imagined it. When Rhys flashed the little spymaster a grin, she knew she'd been right.

The wizard, however, was near to apoplectic. "Duke Morgan," he said from between clenched teeth. "We are not in the habit of 'losing things', as you cavalierly put it. Security in both the vaults and the archives is of the very highest standard. Still, a determined thief with his own magic? And with enough money to bribe an archivist?" He paused, took a breath and rubbed a hand across his face. A bit sheepishly, he admitted, "No, we didn't plan for either of those eventualities."

"The bribed archivist obtained the grimoire?" Marissa asked.

"Yes, for the Northram woman. I only learned about it when we realized the ruby was missing and I questioned everyone."

"All right, we'll leave it for another time," she said. "Supposing

I still had the blasted book in my possession, what would it gain anyone? Does it have some demon-jewel recovery spell or something clever like that? And don't look so indignant. If anyone should be indignant it's me. Well, and Morgan. You are interrupting our wedding night, you know."

Rhys said, "She's quite right, Foxwent. You are here to seek a favor. Best get on with it, eh?"

The wizard opened his mouth as if ready to argue. Finally, sanity seemed to prevail, Subsiding, he addressed Marissa, "Duchess, I humbly request your assistance in recovering the Demon's Fire Ruby. And, in all likelihood, saving the world."

Marissa flashed him a brilliant smile. Then she said distinctly, "No."

Foxwent's eyes went wide. His hands clenched into sudden fists. "No?" he demanded.

"Not on those terms. Chief Wizard, you want something from me. It sounds like it will be both difficult and dangerous. What's in this for me? Well, besides the world-saving bit, I mean."

"I—" The wizard appeared to be thinking hard. "I, that is, we, the Royal College of Wizards, will officially acknowledge you as Royal Enchantress?" he ventured.

Marissa raised a brow. It was something she'd practiced for simply ages before the mirror. From Foxwent's expression, she'd gotten it exactly right. "Chief Wizard, as I heard Morgan put it quite pithily not long ago, your recognition, along with a shilling, would get me a rotten cup of tea just about anywhere in Caerfaen."

He sighed. "All right, what do you require?"

"Nothing too onerous, I assure you. First, I want you—and the Royal College—to acknowledge what happened with Headmaster Rhenn. How he tried to murder Morgan and me. I imagine he would have killed Kiara Northram as well, but that bit's only speculation on my part. I won't insist on it."

His eyes went shuttered, like a house prepared for a storm. He sucked in a breath, then slowly let it out again. Finally, he gave one curt nod. "Very well. Now…"

Marissa held up a hand to stop him. She furrowed her brow, then cocked her head and smiled at the wizard. "There is one other small matter."

Foxwent heaved another sigh. "And what might this 'small matter' be?"

Marissa glanced at Rhys, a question in her eyes. He hesitated for a moment, then inclined his head in the merest hint of a nod. She smiled. "I'm afraid you're not the only one seeking something from me. You see, the dragons also want a favor from me. They feel I might be able to help them gain access to magic."

"What?" Foxwent bellowed. His eyes bulged, and his face went crimson.

"Magic," she repeated helpfully.

"No, impossible." The wizard appealed to Rhys. "Your Majesty, you cannot allow this. I forbid it."

Rhys fixed Foxwent with a tight smile. "What was that, Chief Wizard? I don't believe I heard you correctly."

Foxwent deflated slightly, as he realized his overreach. One did not just make demands on the king, no matter how toplofty one might be. "I beg pardon, Your Majesty, but... Giving magic to dragons? Not only is it ridiculous, it's impossible. Quite literally."

She caught the king's slight nod in her direction. She decided it was her cue to forge ahead. "The dragons don't think so, Chief Wizard," she said. "Wyvrndell, with whom I have established an excellent relationship, is quite certain such an outcome might be achieved. If, that is, I'm willing and allowed, to help them. While I'm not yet acquainted with the details, I see no reason to doubt his assumption. The dragons, from what I understand, have put a great deal of study into the subject. As one might expect."

Foxwent's eyes narrowed dangerously, but he remained silent.

Rhys took over now. "Chief Wizard, I have discussed this matter at some length with the Royal Enchantress. I'll admit I was not convinced at first. However, upon consideration, I've come to the conclusion it will benefit Kilbourne in the long run."

Foxwent opened his mouth, appeared to think better, and closed it again.

Rhys went on, "If you have compelling reasons why the Royal Enchantress should not perform this task, I will listen to your arguments. Otherwise, I think I shall encourage her to move ahead, in her own time."

"I shall consult the Royal College on this matter, Your Majesty," Foxwent said stiffly. "This is not the time and place to debate such a monumental issue, I see."

"No, it's not," Morgan put in.

"Consider this, as well, Chief Wizard," Marissa said. "You have come to me, requesting me to carry out a rather onerous task for you. It is one I am ill-suited for, and ill-inclined to undertake. Unless you agree to not interfere in whatever the king and I, as his enchantress, agree to do with regards to the dragons, then I fear my answer to your request will have to be a most emphatic no."

His eyes narrowed again. "You drive a hard bargain, Duchess."

"Really? I thought I was letting you off fairly easily. I could come up with something else, I suppose."

"No, no," the wizard said, somehow managing, barely, not to glower. "I agree to your terms. And you have," he glanced around at the other men in the room, "impeccable witnesses."

"Yes, I thought so. Well, now we've gotten it settled, perhaps you can explain exactly what the grimoire has to do with this…mess."

Rhys spoke up. "It's bait."

"Because this prince would want to get his hands on it?" Morgan asked.

"That's the theory, yes."

A little ran through her as she recalled the last time she'd served as bait. Captain Fanshawe had taken her captive in hopes Wyvrndell would come to rescue her, while his men made off with the dragon's hoard. It hadn't been a particularly jolly outing. This probably wouldn't be a marked improvement.

To Foxwent she said, "What am I supposed to do? Approach this Prince Azim and offer to trade the book for the ruby? I'm not sure why you'd need me. I'd think anyone could do it."

He shuddered visibly. "Good heavens, no. We don't want him in possession of the grimoire any more than we want him mucking about with the ruby. The grimoire would simply help provide an entrée into Azim's court. It would then be necessary to locate the jewel and steal it back."

Marissa choked out a laugh. "It sounds so simple when you say it. There's one slight problem. Well, a host of them, I imagine, but I see one right off the bat. I'm afraid I've even less experience as a thief than I do as a witch. I really don't see how I can help you."

Barzak spoke up now. "Thieves we have in abundance," he said. "Perhaps someone inserted within your retinue? We also have one additional asset who might be of some value."

She regarded him with a thoughtful expression. "One of your agents, in Azim's court?"

"Ah, well spotted, m'lady. Yes indeed. A young chap who's an archivist for the prince. His name is Alain. I think he might be useful to you in this endeavor."

"Why not have him grab the blasted ruby? I'd think it would save everyone a lot of time and bother," Morgan asked.

"He is not a magician," Barlbent pointed out. "Prince Azim will undoubtedly have magical guards on the ruby, as he does his other 'treasures'. No, Alain will be able to provide you with information and assistance, but this task would be quite beyond his scope."

Morgan nodded. "Yes, I see your point. All right. Marissa? What do you think? Are you game for this?"

She suppressed a strong urge to make a face at him. Did he really think she was game for this? It was the last thing she wanted to do. Still, needs must.

"I suppose," she said, albeit reluctantly.

Foxwent heaved a mighty sigh. "Excellent. It's settled. Come then, you'll leave at once."

She goggled at him. "Leave at once? It that supposed to be a joke?"

Before the wizard could reply, Morgan took him by the arm and was leading him to the door. Rhys followed, a grin tinging his lips.

"Leave this to me, Foxwent," Morgan said. "Lord Holman, Mr. Barlbent, and I have worked together before. We'll get things settled. I have a plan."

"But—" Foxwent protested. Holman Barzak swirled his cloak around his shoulders as he stepped toward the door.

"If Duke Morgan says he has a plan," Barzak said, "you may rely on it being a good one. Let's go and leave these folks be. I don't think the world will end tonight, no matter what we do or don't do."

Morgan ushered their guests out, then closed and locked the door behind them. Placing the key upon the mantle, he turned to his bride.

"Well done, m'lord," she told him. "So, what's your brilliant plan?

"Ha!" He grinned from ear to ear. "To get rid of those pests and continue where we left off."

"I see." She gave him a blazing smile. Its effect was somewhat spoiled by an anticipatory shiver. "In that case, my lord, pray do carry on."

Chapter Seventeen

Morgan straightened to greet Captain Tobias Fanshawe. Former Royal Navy, and more recently, former privateer. Fanshawe snapped off a crisp salute. "You wanted to see me, Commander?"

"Less of it, Fanshawe." Morgan waved him to a seat. "I'm not your commanding officer. Not even the right branch of service."

Fanshawe quirked a wry smile. "My loss, perhaps. Even so, I'm most grateful for all you've done on my behalf. Maybe one day I'll even be counted an acceptable dinner companion again."

"Remind me to tell you about my stint as a traitor to the Crown. Believe me, I understand what it's like to be considered anathema. However, it's I who should be grateful, if you want to know, and I am. Very much so. If not for you, it's quite probable neither Marissa nor I would even be here right now."

Fanshawe shrugged. "I did what needed to be done, Commander. They were lives worth saving. By the way, allow me to extend my congratulations on your marriage."

"Thank you," Morgan said. "Care for a drink?" He indicated a wine bottle on the table nearby. "I'm having a hard time believing it's real."

Fanshawe waved away the offered wine. "Leading me to wonder why you're here with me and not off with your new bride."

"No offense, but I'd much rather it was she. Unfortunately, there are…" Morgan hesitated, then said with a scowl, "complications."

"Already?"

Morgan laughed. "Marissa and I are fine." He scowled. "No, something has managed to intrude on our wedded bliss. The wizards, curse the lot of them, have mislaid a valuable artifact. Evidently, they feel she is the only one who can get it back for them. We have to get to Parthane as soon as possible to retrieve the missing whatsis. This means I need a man I can count on to get us there and back again. You fit the bill, especially since there will be a bit of skullduggery involved."

"Skullduggery, a specialty." Fanshawe grinned. "All right. I don't have any pressing engagements at the moment. Certainly nothing to keep me from accepting the job, at any rate. On the other hand," he spread his hands, "I also don't have a ship."

"So I heard," Morgan said.

If the stories were to be believed, Fanshawe had handed his ship, the *Mad Maudie*, over to his former crew, on the condition they continue exclusively raiding Rhuddlani merchant vessels.

Morgan said, "I have a vessel available. A three-masted schooner that belonged to my father. I reckon it's mine now. She hasn't sailed in quite some time, but she should serve. How long will it take you to get her seaworthy and whistle up a crew?"

Fanshawe shrugged. "It mainly depends on the shape she's in. How long do I have?"

"Well, it matters who you talk to. The wizards think we should have left yesterday. They, however, have no notion what it takes to plan an operation like this. At any rate, I figure we can sail on the tide day after tomorrow. Is that sufficient time for you to prepare?"

"I reckon it'll have to be. I'll make it work, Commander, don't worry. By the way, what is it we're after, if I'm allowed to ask?"

"I'll tell you once we're under way. You've got a lot to do, and I don't need you distracted with unnecessary details. Also, I don't want to have to go over it more than once, and I have other people I need to line up. You concentrate on getting the *Lady Sybil*—it's named for my mother, I'm going to have to change the name, I reckon—ready to sail. We'll discuss the horrid details later."

"Fair enough," Fanshawe agreed. "One thing, though I hate to ask. I'll need funds to supply the ship and hire on a crew. For something that size I won't need many men, but…"

"Of course," Morgan said. He tossed Fanshawe a purse. "Here's a hundred crowns. If you need more, let me know. Do keep track, if you would. Not for me. I'm going to want to present a detailed accounting to the Chief Wizard. He's going to pay for this little venture."

Fanshawe hefted the purse. "If you'll tell me where to find the *Lady Sybil*, I'll be on my way."

Morgan told him.

~ * ~

Sebastien stalked into the drawing room of McRobbie House, his robes flapping behind in a vain attempt to keep up. "I thought we agreed the grimoire was dangerous," he snapped.

"And good day to you, Sebastien." Marissa eyed him from her

seat on a needlepoint-worked chaise. "Would you care for tea?"

"What I'd care for is an explanation," the wizard said with a scowl.

"You'd best take the tea," put in Francesca from her place by Marissa's feet. "It won't help, but it might make you feel better."

His scowl grew, if such a thing were possible, even more dire. "As bad as that, eh?" he murmured to the cat. Returning his attention to his hostess, he said, "Yes, I suppose I'd better. Thank you."

Marissa rang the bell. Briana soon bustled in with the tea trolley, which groaned under its cargo of teapot, cups, iced cakes, and a heaping plate of ginger biscuits.

"Cook has been busy," Marissa noted as she rose to pour two steaming cups. "I gather she likes her new kitchens. Please, sit down, Sebastien, and stop pacing about like a caged bear. You're making me dizzy, and you've nearly trod on poor Francesca's tail."

"Yes, do," put in the cat acerbically. "My tail isn't much, but it's the only one I have. I'd like to keep it a bit longer, if you don't mind."

"My apologies, Lady Francesca." Sebastien seated himself in a dark leather armchair, although not before snagging a handful of ginger biscuits. He munched one, washed it down with tea, then cocked his head. "All right, I suppose I'm as ready as I'll ever be." He bit into another biscuit. "Tell me the worst."

"We've encountered a situation," Marissa said. Francesca snorted as only a cat can manage. Marissa sent her a quelling glare.

"What?" asked the cat, the picture of feline innocence.

Marissa frowned. "Not a situation of our own making," she continued. "Morgan and me, I mean. Neither of us really wants any part of it. However, Rhys was most insistent."

Sebastien popped the remainder of a biscuit into his mouth and chewed. Slowly and deliberately. In silence, he took another, raised a shaggy brow, and waited for her to continue.

So, she poured out the whole story, with Francesca offering snide commentary on the habits of wizards, present company generally excluded, and the foolishness of housing demons in rubies in the first place.

"Hmph," Sebastien said when they'd finished. "Foxwent has cheek to spare, doesn't he?"

"Morgan certainly thought so." She smiled reminiscently. "He was quite eager to toss them out on their ears."

Sebastien grinned. "As well he might."

He munched another biscuit and stared up at the ceiling. Finally, he said, "So, Foxwent wants you two to go haring off to Parthane to try to recover his missing jewel. Why?"

"Why us, you mean?"

"Mmm, yes, exactly."

"He said if wizards showed up at Prince Azim's palace, he'd suspect why they were there and keep the jewel too well guarded. Or simply toss them right out. Whereas, Morgan and I wouldn't arouse as much suspicion."

"Perhaps," he allowed. "However, I'm by nature a nasty, suspicious type. There's more to it, I'm certain. I wish I knew what his real motive was." He frowned. "Tell me, how does the grimoire enter into this whole mess?"

Francesca hissed and swished her tail. "The chief wizard, in his infinite wisdom," she said, her voice dripping with sarcasm, "has determined the grimoire will be bait for the prince."

"Bait, eh?" Sebastien's expression cast him as skeptical as the cat. "That seems..."

"Risky?" Marissa suggested.

"At the very least. Mad, would be more like it."

She grimaced. "If we should fail to find and scarper with the jewel, and this Prince Azim manages to get hold of the book... Well, it's not exactly an ideal outcome, is it?"

"No, not at all. I don't like it, Lady Marissa." He paused, then said, "Oh, sorry, I meant, Your Grace."

She waved this away. "Lady Marissa is fine. I'm not used to a title, and it feels a bit weighty, if you know what I mean."

Nodding, Sebastien helped himself to another biscuit. Marissa snagged one for herself before he finished off the lot. Cook had outdone herself with this batch, and she wasn't prepared to let them all go without a struggle.

"I'm also not quite sure how I go about it. Letting Prince Azim know I have the book, I mean. It does strike me as a bit silly to suddenly mention, 'Oh, by the bye, I happen to have an extremely powerful and dangerous grimoire amongst my things. It's all the rage, just what every new bride takes along on her wedding trip'."

"Ha!" Sebastien reached for the final biscuit. She grasped his wrist.

"No, you don't," she said. "As hostess, I claim the right to the last one. You've eaten ten, and I've only had one. Hands off."

"My apologies, my lady. Thoughtless of me." He smacked his lips and shook crumbs from his robe. "They are, in point of fact, most excellent biscuits."

"That's as may be," said Francesca, leaping lightly into the wizard's lap. "But all this talk of biscuits isn't getting us any forwarder. Can we get on?"

"Of course, Lady Francesca," he said, scratching her ears. The cat closed her eyes in contented bliss. "Where were we? Oh, yes, how to let this felonious prince know Lady Marissa has the grimoire. I shouldn't worry overmuch about it. If he's any kind of magician at all, he'll know you have it. He'll be able to sense its presence. It is not," he said with a scowl, "a particularly subtle thing. You'll positively reek of it."

"Mmm, I see. Is that what happened before?"

His eyes grew serious. "Yes, it was. Your own aura was becoming quite infused with it. Very dark, it was, felt almost like a stagnant pond, where something evil resides."

She shivered at this pithy description. "Hmm. I'm not sure I really want any more to do with it."

He nodded in approval. "The very words I wanted to hear. If you'd been eager to get your hands on the book again, I'd have been concerned. I feel better now. Well, a little, anyway."

"I'm glad you do," Francesca said. "I'm not sure I do. That thing is evil." She regarded Marissa, and her green eyes glittered dangerously. "You shouldn't muck about with it."

"I have no desire to muck about with it, as you put it. If I never saw the blasted book again, it would be fine with me. I'm just not sure I have any choice," Marissa said. "Rhys was quite vehement. The chief wizard has him convinced this ruby will bring about a full-scale disaster if we don't get it back."

"I'm afraid he might well be right," Sebastien said. "If what he says about the ruby is true. I have to confess, I've never heard of such a thing. Of course, I don't exactly have much knowledge about what goes on in the Royal College of Wizards. I only get bits and pieces on occasion from my, umm, spies. If he is… All those demons on the loose? Decidedly bad."

"So, you're willing to entrust the dratted grimoire into my keeping again?"

"No, I'm not. No offense, but I don't think you're strong enough. While you have power to spare, you still lack both control and discernment. You're doing quite well, overall, but those things take years to acquire. However, in light of the stakes, I suppose I don't have much choice, do I?"

Marissa waited in silence. Francesca purred loudly under the wizard's hands. Finally, he tugged on his beard. "All right. At least this time you'll know what you're dealing with. If you're careful, you might come out of this whole thing relatively unscathed."

"Relatively unscathed," Marissa repeated, the words tasting sour on her tongue. "I don't think I'd much care to be scathed." She cocked her head. "Um, can one be scathed?"

Sebastien threw back his head, bellowing a laugh. Francesca leapt indignantly from his lap, landing several feet away, her back arched. "You?" he said at last. "Probably not. To help make sure, I'll consult with your tutor. Between us, perhaps we can come up with some plan to help keep you from being... scathed. In the meantime, I'll fetch the grimoire. Even though it's a terrible, awful, horrible idea, it might work."

"The chief wizard says Prince Azim is a collector of magical curiosities," Marissa said.

The wizard shrugged. "I know nothing about him, to be honest. One point you might wish to keep in mind, though, my lady."

"What's that?"

Sebastien said, "Don't forget: you yourself are a magical curiosity."

"Oh." It was all she could manage to say.

He chuckled. "Don't worry. I'm sure the duke would have some quite pointed things to say, not to mention do, should such an instance arise. But often, an awareness of potential danger is the best remedy."

She nodded. "Forewarned being forearmed, I believe the expression goes?"

"Exactly." The old wizard leaned back in his chair and gazed wistfully at the empty biscuit plate.

"No," Marissa said firmly. "There are more, but I'm saving the rest for Morgan. He's not any happier than you about this whole mess. I need something to bribe him with."

Sebastien chuckled. "Oh, very well. Back to the matter at hand, since ginger biscuits are no longer in the offing. You said Foxwent evinced extreme reluctance to send a wizard to retrieve the ruby. I suppose his arguments make sense. However, it's my considered opinion you should have a wizard in your party. Clandestinely, of course."

"Oh, Sebastien, I was hoping you'd come!" Marissa could hardly contain her mix of relief and excitement.

"No, no, not me. I'm too old and set in my ways to go adventuring with you young folk. Besides, I don't know I'd have the necessary skills for such a task. No, I was thinking young Nardis Cardione might suit. He's quite a talented lad. Well, you've seen him at work."

She considered this. "Yes, he might do. Do you think he'd be willing to go along with us?"

"I think he might. We can ask. There's another thing, too, with having him along. He'll be someone Foxwent won't be aware of. I believe Nardis is one wizard you can trust implicitly. You may well need such on this mission."

"Perhaps disguised as a valet for Morgan?"

"Perfect," Sebastien agreed. "He's young enough to pass unnoticed in such a role, unless someone were to take a strong interest. Shall I speak with him?"

Marissa exchanged a glance with Francesca, who gave a brief nod. "Yes, Sebastien, thank you," she said. "It would be most helpful."

Chapter Eighteen

Morgan leaned back in his chair. Rain spattered noisily against the mullioned windows. A small fire crackled cheerfully in the grate, and a brandy decanter, with two glasses as outriders, stood at the ready on a small table nearby. He gave a faint smile. For once, he was going to enjoy this encounter.

"Come," he called, when a knock sounded on the door of what Marissa had designated as his study.

Morgan surveyed the wood-panel walls, where a small painting of his favorite horse, Arnicus, hung. Near it was a larger portrait of his parents. An open space on the wall lay ready to receive the portrait of Marissa he'd commissioned.

Kevin, his trusty valet, opened the door and ushered in a tall, lean, older man. "Taggart," Morgan said, not rising. "Thank you for coming."

Ian Taggart's eyes held a mixture of amusement and wariness. "Commander, how could I ever refuse your kind invitation?" He grinned ruefully. "After all, 'tis only fair, eh?"

"A drink?" Morgan suggested, rising to take up the decanter. Taggart nodded, his eyes watchful now. He was, Morgan was certain, recalling their two previous encounters. As he had done only a few minutes before.

"A wee dram would be welcome," he said. "The weather's taken a turn. This rain is downright chilly."

Morgan grimaced. The storm wasn't making things any easier for the plans he needed to implement. Well, he'd just have to worry about the weather another time. Right now, there were other matters at hand. "Please, take a seat." He handed Taggart a drink, snagged his own glass, then returned to his chair.

Taggart sipped, watching Morgan over the rim of his glass. "So, Commander—or should I say Your Grace? To what to I owe the pleasure?"

Shrugging, Morgan said, "I'm certainly not a stickler for the title. Either of 'em, for this conversation. My name will do fine." He leaned back once more, clasping his hands behind his head. "We go back and forth, you and I, trading favors."

Taggart said nothing. He sat, still as a cat watching a mousehole, his eyes bright and alert. And, Morgan thought with a suppressed grin, no doubt with his mind racing. "I find myself in need of another favor from you, Taggart. A small matter, but of some importance."

Taggart waited.

"I need," Morgan went on, "a thief."

He had the small satisfaction of seeing Ian Taggart blink. Whatever he'd expected, this certainly wasn't it. Morgan allowed himself another internal grin.

"A...a thief?" Taggart sounded puzzled now, as if he couldn't wrap his mind around the concept. "A thief," he repeated, shaking his head. "You'd not be referrin' to meself, now would you?"

Morgan laughed. "No, not at all. I merely thought you might, well, know someone. Not any old, run-of-the-mill, smash-and-grab type either. I need someone good. Someone—" he narrowed his eyes, "professional."

His guest raised a brow. "Am I allowed to inquire to whom this most professional thief might be paying his attentions?"

Morgan waved a lazy hand. "Oh, Prince Azim of Arvindir."

Taggart didn't blink this time. Instead, Morgan thought, the older man went a bit pale. Morgan went on. "The prince has, or so I've been led to believe, recently acquired an object to which he does not have right of possession."

"Wouldn't be the first time," muttered Taggart.

Morgan smiled. "Yes, that seems to be the general consensus. This time, he's managed to scarper with something belonging to the wizards."

"He's reputed to have a fancy for that kind o' thing."

"The wizards, as you might well imagine, are not best pleased. The wizards have, in fact, registered a formal complaint with King Rhys. Or at least Chief Wizard Foxwent has. Rhys, for his part, has come to me. On my wedding night, I might add, curse him. He has instructed the Royal Enchantress—my bride, if you will—to retrieve it."

Taggart's lips pursed. "I presume, from the purloined item's origin, that it's magical in nature?"

Morgan nodded. "Best I not go into any details, but yes, you may definitely assume so."

"Good Lord, no, I don't want to know. I am curious about one thing."

Lifting a brow, Morgan said, "Go on. With the understanding I may not be able to give you an answer."

It was Taggart's turn to smile now. "Why? I mean, why you two? Not really your line of country. Certainly not for your new duchess. My felicitations, by the way."

"Thank you. You were sent an invitation, you know."

Taggart shrugged. "You didn't really want me at your wedding, an' we both know it. I will admit, I was rather touched by the gesture. Quite kind, indeed. But we're getting a bit away from the point here. Why you two?"

"Because Foxwent, may his robes grow moldy, has decided this Prince Azim would suspect any wizards who came snooping about for ill-gotten gains. Whereas Marissa and I, at least in theory, would appear to be the very innocents we really are."

"Innocents, eh?" Taggart snorted. "Well, if you say so, laddie. I've seen and heard enough to know better. Now, about this favor—well, there is one small problem."

It was Morgan's turn to maintain a patient silence. His guest nodded in approval. "You're learnin', you're learnin'. So, here's the thing. I'm after getting out of my—well, my business, ye might call it."

"What?" Morgan sat up straight, nearly toppling over his drink. "I –well—"

"I know." Taggart shrugged. "But there 'tis."

His mind raced as he considered Taggart's statement. Then, in a flash, dawning struck. Taking a sip of the brandy to stimulate his thought processes, Morgan ventured, "Would this by any chance have something to do with a certain young lady, recently seen in the company of Captain Aartis Poldane?"

Taggart looked thunderstruck. Morgan soldiered on. "We saw them at the Black Swan a few evenings ago. She introduced herself as Miss Katherine Taggart."

Taggart closed his eyes. Morgan said, "My wife found her to be quite charming. She has, in fact, invited Miss Taggart to join her for lunch one day soon. I have to admit, once I got over the initial shock, I rather liked her myself."

"Ach, yer jist sayin' that." Taggart was reverting to his highland lilt. His eyes remained closed, as if he didn't want to face Morgan.

"No," he said, "she honestly seemed quite nice."

"For a Taggart, ye mean?"

Morgan shook his head in emphatic negation, then realized it was wasted, since the older man's eyes were still squeezed shut. "No, Taggart, I meant for the type of girl Aartis usually gets himself entangled with. She came across as charming, intelligent, and quite able to hold her own, even under a rather stressful situation. A refreshing change from the empty-headed title seekers he normally squires about."

"Ah, she's a good girl, even if I do say it. Yes, she's me daughter, though few enough know it. 'Twas safer that way, ye see."

"Yes, I do see. A wise move, all things considered."

"And now, I suppose unless I agree to help you, you'll tell everyone about her?"

"Whoa, Taggart, rein in." Morgan held up his hands. "I've no such notion. I don't deal in blackmail. My only reason for mentioning it was to let you know I understood your reasoning for, as you say, getting out of your, um, business."

Taggart inclined his head. "Please accept my apologies, McRobbie. I get a bit tetchy where Katie's concerned."

"Of course." Morgan thought for a moment. "Taggart, you've always played more than fair with me. You've made a bargain, stuck to it, and never tried to leverage it into any advantage for yourself. I also have Aartis's solemn word your dealings with him have been on the same footing."

Taggart stilled. He was no fool; he knew something was coming. Morgan was certain he could never envision what he was about to say. He could barely believe it himself. "With that thought in mind, and especially since you're retiring, you might be interested to know Rhys has authorized me to extend an offer to you."

Taggart's only reaction was to arch one eyebrow.

"To wit," Morgan continued, "for past and current services to the Crown—"

"Current services being the provision of one thief, as specified earlier?"

"Exactly. For past and current services to the Crown, His Majesty is prepared to offer you the rank and title of Baron Swansea. A small demesne in the north country."

If Taggart had looked thunderstruck before, it was nothing compared to his expression at this news. Finally, drawing in a deep breath, he brought the brandy to his lips and drank deeply.

"So," he said at last. "What you're offering me, and by extension my Katie, is a bit of respectability?"

"What the king is offering," Morgan corrected. "I'm merely the messenger. But I've spoken at some length with Rhys about your assistance with the d'Eastmond mess. Also, about your concern for the city during our recent pirate infestation." He forbore to mention how he'd recently recruited the pirate captain to be part of the team dispatched to retrieve the ruby. "Rhys feels, despite your, um, various other enterprises, your assistance in the matter at hand would warrant certain considerations."

Taggart chuckled. "Laddie, now you sound like you've been consorting with lawyers. 'Matter at hand.' 'Certain considerations.' Indeed."

"Consorting with lawyers? Me? Sir, I'll have you know I've called out men for less an insult than this. If you blaspheme me so, I might have to do the same with you."

"That's the spirit. Keep far away from 'em. They even make me seem downright saintly, if you can believe such a thing possible."

Morgan raised his glass. "So, are you willing to forgo your imminent retirement, at least long enough to find me an appropriate— hmm, what should we call him?"

"Retriever of stolen goods?" Taggart suggested.

"Perfect."

"Aye, I think I've got the fellow for you. Toniq is his name. Like a ghost, he is. In an' out, and no one ever the wiser. Even better, he has a certain affinity for magical items. He's your man, all right."

"You think you can get him?"

"Oh, I'll get him. You tell me when and where you want him."

"We sail on the tide, day after tomorrow. My schooner, *Lady Sybil*. She'll be in Caerfaen harbor. Tell this Toniq to pack whatever he needs for a sea voyage and for the job at hand."

"Very well. I know you're under orders. But can you give me any idea how large an item he'll be after retrievin'?"

Morgan held up a clenched fist. "About half this size, from what I've been told."

Taggart gave him an appraising gaze. "I see. Well, McRobbie, let's drink to the success of your mission. Your marriage, as well."

Morgan smiled. "Thank you. Also to your retirement and new life as Baron Swansea."

He and Taggart clinked glasses.

Chapter Nineteen

"When this is over," Morgan began.

His wife—his duchess—glanced up at him. They stood side by side at the rail of the *Lady Sybil*, her hand clasped firmly in his, gazing out at the panorama of the Thundermist Sea. At the moment, there was neither thunder nor mist, for which he was grateful.

"When this is over?"

He quirked a rueful smile. "Assuming we manage to pull this off and aren't up to our necks in ornery demons."

She shivered. "Sorry," he said. "In my line of work, there's always a better than even chance things don't go as planned. Anyway, when this is all over, perhaps we really should go to Orsk. You've never been, have you?"

"Me? Morgan, I've never been anywhere. Vynfold to Caerfaen and back has been the utmost limit of my worldly travels."

He slipped his arm round her waist, pulling her close. The sea was fairly calm, under clear sky, although the air was a touch chilly, redolent of salt and spray.

"Mmm, you feel wonderful," she said, snuggling closer into his embrace. "And yes, I'd love to visit Orsk. I've lived a pretty sheltered life, you know. The thought of exotic places, like Orsk or Parthane, seems something like a dream."

Morgan nodded. "All my travels, if you can call them such, have been to less than exotic places. Generally to where men were intent on doing their best to slaughter me and my mates."

"Boring for you, eh?" she said, squeezing his hand.

He laughed. "Only place I've traveled to for anything besides battle was to Orsk. Mama's sister, my aunt Emilee, is still there, with her family. And her father, the old admiral."

"Your grandfather? Does your aunt have children? Do you have cousins?"

Morgan considered. "Well, yes."

She pulled away from his embrace long enough to give him a sharp poke in the ribs.

"Ow!" he protested. "What was that for?"

"Why didn't we invite any of your people to our wedding? They're your family."

He encircled her with his arm again. "They were invited. Don't you recall the list you got from my mother?"

Marissa's brow furrowed. "Vaguely. Clarise and I divvied them all up. My word, there were so many. Those must have been in her lot. But...none came."

"Honestly, I'm not in the least surprised they didn't. The admiral is quite elderly, and not really fit to travel any more. Aunt Emilee spends most of her time caring for him. As for my cousins, well, I haven't seen them in donkey's years. Not since we were kids. Mama would drag us to Orsk on occasion. The last time, I was probably twelve or so. Wouldn't know any of 'em if I fell over them, to be honest. Nor they me, I'm sure."

"Hmph. We shall have to remedy this appalling situation at our earliest opportunity. After all, they're your family. We can't have our children growing up not knowing their cousins. Assuming, of course, your cousins have children of their own."

"Children," he murmured.

"Well, yes, I should think. Would you mind terribly?"

"Mind? No, I wouldn't mind. I rather like the idea."

"Oh, good. It's only, we've never really discussed it. I wanted to be sure how you felt about the notion."

"It's a splendid idea," he assured her with enthusiasm. "Perhaps we should go below and discuss it in more, um, intimate detail?"

She swatted his arm. "Incorrigible," she said, but her voice was tinged with affection and laughter. And, if he read the signs correctly, also with a certain amount of longing.

The sun, which had been descending precipitously toward the sea, chose this moment to illumine the horizon with a sudden suffusion of orange and gold. Beams of light streaked the sea toward them, while others clawed their way toward the heavens.

"Mmm," Marissa said dreamily, tucking herself closer into Morgan's arm. This swiftly changed to "Oh!" as he swung her around and pressed his lips to hers in a passionate kiss. His hand threaded its way into the silken mass of her hair, those tantalizing ringlets beckoning his fingers to tangle amongst them. His other hand traced the contours of her back.

The sun dropped below the horizon, the last shafts of light

flaring like Morgan's heart within his chest. She uttered a little moan against his mouth. When they parted at last, her eyes were wide and glittered with a fey light.

Her voice, when she spoke, was strangely husky. "Perhaps we might retire below after all."

Morgan needed no further encouragement.

~ * ~

The sea writhed and roiled, tossing the ship in what felt like six directions at once. Morgan, his arm wrapped protectively around Marissa to keep her from flying off the bed, gripped a ring set on the bulkhead to keep himself from following.

"This," she said from between clenched teeth, "is merely a small sample of what I went through when Captain Fanshawe took us into the Thundermist. Keep in mind, this is merely a normal, everyday storm. No Thundermist involved."

"How can you possibly tell?" Morgan asked, intrigued.

"I don't exactly know. But I can definitely sense the energy in the Thundermist. I told you, I think it did something to me. I could feel it, filling me somehow, and enhancing my magic."

"Magic which needed little enhancement," he noted.

"Perhaps not. At the time, with me captured by pirates and you heavens knew where, plus your injured mother to watch over, I wasn't about to turn my nose up at it. Not that I had much say in the matter. But I think the Mist may have been what gave me the ability to do the whole flaming sword thing."

"Which," he said, with a slight shudder, "is what enabled you to defeat Augustus Rhenn. Yes, I see your point." He thought for a moment. "What did Wyvrndell say about it?"

"He—oof!" She broke off as they went bouncing about again, like ducks in a storm-tossed pond. "He didn't make too much of it. Although he did say something recently about how much clearer my focus was and how my spell work was sharper. Honestly, I'd been practicing really hard, so I chalked it up to that."

"So, you think it might have been the effects of whatever the Thundermist did?"

"Well, when you consider Captain Fanshawe dosed me with witchbane to prevent me from using any magic. Once the Thundermist took hold, I had my magic back again. Stronger than before. And…, this will likely sound completely daft, I imagine. Afterwards, whenever there was Thundermist nearby, I could sense it. Felt a strange connection to it."

"Interesting," Morgan said. "I wonder if the wizards know about this? The effects of Thundermist, I mean."

The boat rocked violently for a moment. When it settled again, Marissa said, "I doubt it. If they did, I'd think they'd be organizing regular tours into the Mist. And it's not something anyone in their right mind would do willingly. Well, except Captain Fanshawe, when he was playing at pirates."

The ship capered through another swell. "The man must be mad."

"Oh, he is. The thing is, he kept us afloat, so I can't fault him there. I—" They crashed into another trough, hard enough to rattle Morgan's teeth. "There's no one I'd rather have pilot a boat through a storm."

"The one good thing, if there is one, is this: the storm certainly gives us a perfect excuse to end up off course and find ourselves in Parthane. I don't think Fanshawe will have to do anything dodgy to the ship. The storm looks like managing it for him."

As if eager to help out, the storm roared with a renewed vigor. Morgan made a valiant effort to keep his stomach under control, but he wasn't sure how much longer he could keep it up. Or down, as the case might be. He reckoned it was a good thing the cabin was dark. At least that way his bride couldn't see quite how green he was. He'd never been a particularly good sailor, even as a lad on his father's cutter, *The Raven.* It was the primary reason Morgan had opted for land-based military service, rather than adhering to the McRobbie tradition and entering the Royal Navy.

A sharp "*crack!*" resounded above the storm's clamor. The ship veered sharply to port. Or starboard; Morgan had long since forgotten which was which. "Tops'l's down!" came a cry from one of Fanshawe's crew.

Morgan could hear the captain bawling orders as he tried to keep the ship afloat and under way. Fanshawe was a good man in a storm, Morgan had to admit. Literally. The *Lady Sybil* felt like she was coming back under control. The captain continued to exhort his crew to greater efforts.

After several lifetimes, the storm finally slackened its assault. Morgan swallowed bile and sent up a fervent thankful prayer. The ship appeared to still be on top of the sea rather than under it, even though he'd doubted this outcome only a short time before. A moment later, a rap sounded on the cabin's door.

Morgan straightened, helped Marissa to sit up, and called, "Come." The door opened, and Fanshawe stuck his head in.

"We're still in one piece, Commander. Well, relatively. We're going to be limping into the nearest harbor. We've lost the main mast, or at least a good chunk of it. The others will serve to get us there, but we'll definitely need to effect repairs before we can continue on our way."

"Well done, Captain," Morgan said. "Where have we ended up?"

"You wanted to go to Arvindir, didn't you?" Fanshawe grinned. "Well, Arvindir it is."

"Well done indeed, Captain," said Marissa. "Even through this storm. Impressive."

"Oh, that little blow was nothing,"

"Easy for you to say," Morgan muttered under his breath. Aloud, he said, "How long before we dock?"

"Well, docking's not in the cards. The rudder's fouled as well, so we've lost some maneuverability. We'll anchor in the harbor, then take the jolly boats in to get you ashore. It'll be several hours, I imagine. I'll send someone down to let you know once we're ready to drop anchor."

"Well done, Fanshawe," Morgan said again. "And thanks, for keeping us afloat."

"No problem, Commander. The *Sybil's* a nice craft, by the way. A pleasure to captain her."

~ * ~

Morgan stretched out a hand to steady Marissa as she emerged from the hatch onto the *Lady Sybil*'s deck. Clouds scudded across the sky, and a few patches of blue peeked down on them as the storm fled eastwards. An undefinable fragrance suffused the air, redolent of exotic spices and flowers. Marissa breathed in and gave a heady sigh.

The ship rocked gently in the harbor's swells. Arvindir's domes and spires rose over the mist-shrouded outline of the city, soaring up as if trying to pierce the heavens.

"It's so different from Caerfaen," she said. "It's lovely. Like something from a fairy tale."

Morgan eyed the city with a critical eye. "Not bad, I suppose," he allowed. "A bit showy."

"Hmph. I think it's lovely. I never thought I'd see Parthane, even though I read loads about it in school."

"Yes, but keep in mind, we're not here to admire Arvindir's wonders, marvelous as they may be. We have a job to do. Or at least you do. I'm merely a supernumerary."

"I know," she said, placing a hand on his arm. "I can still appreciate it while we're here, can't I?"

He grunted in reply. This garnered him a sharp look from his bride. "What's the matter?"

He scowled. "Nothing."

"Morgan James McRobbie, what's wrong?"

Her use of his full name surprised a chuckle from him. Before he could speak, she said, "You should know I have permission—encouragement, actually—from Lady Sybil, to use that name as necessary. So, don't come over moody on me, or I'll use it again."

He laughed again and pulled her into an embrace. "What did I do to deserve you?"

"I don't know, I'm sure. It must have been something pretty awful. Are you done sulking now?"

"Yes, I suppose. I'm sorry. I'd simply prefer to be anywhere but here. Doing anything but what we're doing."

"You mean, you'd prefer not to be taking your new duchess on a grand tour?"

"A low blow, my dear. Not what I meant, and you know it. Don't go trying to twist my words. I can manage just fine on my own."

"Well, I'd rather not be here either, if you want the honest truth. At least not for the reason we're here. Since we are, we might as well make the best of it, shouldn't we? I mean, how many people do you know who can say they've visited Parthane? I don't know anyone who has. It'll be something to tell our children someday."

Morgan found his good humor restored by her chatter. "You're assuming we'll manage to get away with this and get back home in one piece."

"Assuming? Pooh. The Knight-Commander of Kilbourne's Legion and the Royal Enchantress? These Parthanians don't stand a chance."

"Well then, let's get on with it." He gave her a smoldering glance. "So we can get home and get started on the necessities for children."

She returned his gaze with one equally fiery. Then spoiled it by bursting out laughing. "You are incorrigible."

Morgan held up his hands. "All right, you win. Here comes Fanshawe. I reckon he has the boat ready to take us ashore."

"Good," she said. "I'm ready to get on with this mission. And to see Arvindir," she added quickly, flashing him a brilliant smile.

Morgan lifted a brow, but Fanshawe was there before he could reply.

"Captain," Marissa said.

"Your Grace," Fanshawe replied, sketching a bow. "Duke Morgan. If you would care to clamber down into the jolly boat, we're ready to take you ashore."

"Thank you, Captain." Morgan cocked his head in silent inquiry. Fanshawe's mouth quirked into a tight smile.

"There have been glasses trained on us for the last hour," he reported. "They're quite curious. To tell you the truth, I'm astonished no one has ventured out yet to see what in the world we're doing here."

"Well, hopefully their lack of action means they don't regard us as a threat."

"Not as yet." Fanshawe waggled a hand. "Now, shall we go ashore?"

"After you, Captain." Marissa sounded a bit less eager, now that they were about to embark on the task they'd been sent to do.

Fanshawe led the way to the rope ladder dangling over the rail, leading down to the tender.

Morgan went first at Marissa's insistence. "You can cushion my fall," she grinned.

With a wry grin, he descended, keeping right below her, ready to catch her if she did indeed slip. He needn't have worried. She was as nimble as a cat, making her way down the swaying ropes with ease. As her foot reached the last rung, he placed his hands about her waist and swung her down into the boat.

"Thank you, my good man," she said, plunking down onto the seat.

Morgan sat next to her. One of Fanshawe's sailors untied the lines, then nipped back up the ladder. The sailors assigned to the jolly boat took up their oars and rowed toward the docks.

Morgan gazed back to where the *Lady Sybil* rested at anchor. The schooner was ostensibly their only means to escape Arvindir when the job was done. Right now, she looked in pretty sad condition. Hopefully, he'd be able to negotiate to effect the necessary repairs.

She squeezed his hand. He captured her small fingers in his, holding them in what he hoped was a reassuring manner. Then he rolled his eyes slightly. Like she needed reassurance. His bride possessed all the bravado and swaggering confidence of a trained Legion soldier. Plus, she had magic on call. More than was normal, even for her, if her notions about the Thundermist were correct.

The oarsmen soon held the boat alongside the main dock. A fixed, wooden-rung ladder led upwards. This was fine with Morgan. It was imminently more secure than the wavering, tenuous rope they'd used to descend from the *Lady Sybil*. One of the sailors held the boat steady, and Morgan assisted his lady onto the ladder. Once she was on her way, he hauled himself up after her.

Even with the wooden ladder, the ascent took several minutes. The tide was on its way out, so they began from the very lowest rungs, which at high tide would have been well covered with water. As they neared the top, Morgan saw an arm reach down to assist Marissa up onto the dock. He clambered up after her.

Planting his boots on firm ground for the first time in several days, Morgan took stock of their welcoming committee. This consisted of several burly chaps in dark robes and turbans, each bearing a short, curved sword in his sash. A guard detail, no doubt. The fellow in charge appeared to be a palace official—probably a low-ranking functionary, dispatched to go learn what these strangers were about. His skin was swarthy, nearly dark as Morgan's, and his robes were a riot of colorful silks resplendent in orange, green, and purple. A red turban crowned his head, and his eyes were bright with interest.

"Welcome to Arvindir," he said. "You are travelers from Kilbourne?"

"We are," Morgan acknowledged. "Travelers in a bit of distress, I'm afraid. Our blasted boat didn't weather the last storm very well. We were blown off course, and here we are."

"I see." The man's gaze went from Morgan to Marissa to the *Lady Sybil,* lying out in the harbor. "I am most distressed at your misfortune. Still, you have arrived in one piece."

"It could have been much worse," Morgan agreed. "Whom do I have the honor of addressing?"

The man gave a tight smile. "I am Orzani, khatib to Vizir Azarat. And you…?"

"Morgan McRobbie, Duke of Westdale, and Knight-Commander of Kilbourne's King's Legion, at your service. This is my bride. Marissa, Duchess McRobbie."

Marissa favored the man with a fetching smile.

Orzani's eyes widened. He'd no doubt figured on having to deal with a mere ship's captain. The duke of a foreign realm was well above his pay grade, Morgan reckoned. Evidently Orzani was quick on the uptake and arrived at a similar conclusion. He beckoned over one of the guards and whispered something to him. The guard nodded brusquely, then hustled off up the dock.

Morgan went on, pretending not to notice the exchange. "We were on our wedding tour when our ship was disabled. We'd planned to travel about a bit and end up in Orsk before we returned home. My captain says the main mast was split clean in two. We were lucky to make it into your harbor."

"Felicitations upon your blessed nuptials," murmured Orzani.

"And upon your safe arrival here in Parthane. I have sent for Vizir Azarat to come greet you properly. If you will come with me to somewhere," he looked around and shrugged, "a bit more comfortable until he arrives?"

"Lead on," Morgan said. He glanced at Marissa. "We're extremely fortunate to be here, eh?"

Chapter Twenty

As Orzani led them away from the docks, Morgan cast a final glance back toward the *Lady Sybil*. "Do not worry, Your Grace," said the Parthanian. "We have most excellent craftsman who can help to repair your vessel."

Morgan proffered a slight bow. "Thank you, Khatib Orzani. Parthane's hospitality is well known." His words were no less than the truth.

In general, Kilbourne maintained an excellent relationship with the Parthanian nation, especially in matters of commerce and trade. Of course, there were always diplomatic squabbles over some trifle or other. Rhys and his ministers always managed to resolve those issues before they got to the point where Morgan and the Legion needed to become involved. Although, he mused, a conflict with Parthane would fall more under the purview of the Kilbourne Navy, under Lord Admiral Watkins.

Hopefully what they were about to do wouldn't create the need for any such intervention. Their plan was to get in, get the jewel, and get out again, with no one the wiser. Morgan had his doubts on this score. Plans, whether on the battlefield or in life, rarely came off as originally envisioned.

Before Orzani could bring them to wherever he'd intended, an entourage headed toward them at speed. Vizir Azarat, complete with outriders, no doubt.

"Company," Morgan murmured to Marissa, with a nod toward the hurrying men.

"Remember, be charming," she replied.

"Right. Charming, charming... Hmm, where did I leave my charm? Blast, I think it's still on the ship."

"Don't be an idiot," she muttered as the new arrivals halted before them.

Orzani genuflected to a Parthanian of impressive girth, who

sported a purple turban and enough sashes to outfit an entire band of Tzigani. "Vizir Azarat," the khatib cried. "These are the stranded travelers I sent word of, newly arrived to Arvindir."

Vizir Azarat glowered at Orzani. Morgan got the distinct impression their arrival had interrupted something important. He glanced up toward the sun, stifling a grin. In all likelihood, he thought, they'd cut short Azarat's luncheon. Unless Morgan missed his guess, the vizir was a man who didn't miss many meals.

The vizir took in a good bushel of air, composing himself to the task of welcoming strange nobles to the kingdom. He managed an infinitesimal bow and intoned, "Welcome, Duke of Westdale. Your fame precedes you."

Which, Morgan thought with an internal chuckle, was probably a bald-faced lie. He doubted this fellow had ever even heard his name. The vizir studiously ignored Marissa. An attitude not exactly destined to endear him to the new duchess.

Before she could speak, Morgan said, "Thank you, Vizir Azarat. Allow me to present my bride, the Duchess Marissa. Just married, you know, and on our wedding tour when we landed unexpectedly on your doorstep. Your gracious hospitality is much appreciated."

Azarat's lips pursed momentarily. Then, seeming resigned to his fate, he pasted on a smile of dubious origin, gave an even slighter bow to Marissa, murmured something indecipherable and returned his attention to Morgan.

Morgan, exuding charm from every pore, asked diffidently, "Do you suppose there's an inn where we might stay for a few days, while our vessel is repaired?"

The vizir sucked in more air, considered this, and shook his head.

"No inns here?" Morgan ventured.

"Inns, we have many. But not for the likes of you."

Morgan opened his mouth to protest that he bathed regularly and could even use a fork when required. Marissa, evidently sensing his indignation, stepped on his foot.

He closed his mouth again as Azarat went on. "My master, the prince, will no doubt wish to accommodate you in the palace."

"Oh, right," Morgan said. "Most kind, I'm sure. Let us proceed then, with all due haste. My lady is fatigued. It has been a bit of an ordeal."

With a curt nod, Azarat began barking orders in his own tongue to Orzani and several minions. Then he beckoned for Morgan and Marissa to follow. They fell in behind him.

The palace's spires glowed pink and gold in the bright sunshine, as banners snapped and waved gaily from them. A wide cobbled courtyard fronted the palace, dotted here and there with thin, leafy trees like nothing he had ever seen.

"Date trees," the vizir replied tersely when Morgan inquired.

Off to the left lay the bazaar, where he could see row upon row of tents jammed together in a fractious, merry hodgepodge. Some sported gay silks and exotic fruits, while others exuded enticing aromas of spices and roasting meat. Still others were dark and mysterious, where men murmured quietly while coins changed hands, in purchase of some unseen ephemera.

All too soon, his brief glimpse of the market stalls was cut short. He was certain Marissa would have loved to wander and browse through them. Honestly, he wouldn't have minded himself. Instead, Azarat led them briskly on to the great doors of the prince's palace.

From Lord Holman, Morgan had received a brief tutorial on Parthane. The kingdom was ruled by King Radagav, who had given over Arvindir's three major cities into the control of his three sons. Arbin, the youngest, oversaw Qbaan, a smaller city in the North. Fraazi, the middle son, held Gaazbar, in the East. Azim, the eldest, ruled in the South in Arvindir, the largest. Lord Holman had noted that when Azim wasn't flexing his power in Arvindir, he was busily acquiring ever more magical curiosities for his collection. Sometimes he even purchased them, although according to Holman this was the exception rather than the rule.

Azarat approached the great wooden doors leading into the palace. Intricate designs and reliefs were carved into them, jumbled together so the eye didn't know which way to look first. Most depicted battle scenes: men striving against other men or against monsters of some sort. Morgan noted a many-legged sea creature wreaking havoc on a pair of ships. Giving silent thanks they hadn't run afoul of this particular specimen during their voyage, he held Marissa's hand in his as Azarat came to a halt before the portal. The vizir tugged vigorously on a rope pull.

The doors, each easily six feet wide and twice as tall, formed an impressive arch set into the palace's fortress-like façade. From within, a bell tolled, deep and resonant, similar in tone to the one atop St. Basil's Cathedral in Caerfaen. The doors began to swing open inch by inch.

An elderly Parthanian, bewhiskered, be-robed, and be-turbaned, tottered out to confront the intruders at the gate. He was hardly an impressive figure for a door warden. Morgan was quite certain there were plenty of burly guards with those short, curved swords at his beck and call should the need arise.

The door warden genuflected, touching his hand to his heart, and ushered the vizir and his party inside. Beyond the doorway lay a courtyard like a tropical oasis. Flowering shrubs vied for space with fruit trees. Fountains sparkled and tinkled, pools glistened, and bright colored birds swooped and darted overhead. A large green snake slithered up one of the trees and lay coiled along a branch. Morgan pulled Marissa a bit closer.

"The prince's pleasure garden," Azarat informed them, brushing past the old door warden. "Come. I will present you to His Highness."

The vizir, Morgan reckoned, was eager to rid himself of these pesky travelers who had interrupted his luncheon. Azarat hastened though the garden area, sandals slapping against the cobbled pathway. His pace was quick for a man his size, and Morgan began to wonder if the vizir wasn't about to chivvy his charges into a trot.

Beyond the garden, another set of carved doors stood open. Azarat strode through them, gesturing to a brace of guards with suddenly drawn swords to stand down. "Where is His Highness?" he demanded.

"The prince is contemplating his mongoose," a sentry reported. "He has instructed us he is not to be disturbed, most worshipful Vizir."

"Bah. I bring noble travelers for him to contemplate," Azarat snapped. "His Highness's mongoose must wait. Where is he?"

"This way, revered one," the guard replied, in the tones of one who hopes it would be the vizir, rather than himself, who incurred the prince's wrath for disobeying orders.

"Contemplating his what?" Marissa whispered into Morgan's ear.

He could only shrug. Whatever a mongoose was, he wished it the joy of Azim's steadfast contemplation. Meanwhile, Morgan noted the palace was simply rife with guards. All things considered, this was not designed to make their task of burglary any easier. He didn't doubt that Azim, who evidently enjoyed making off with other people's valuables, would guard his own with extreme vigor.

As if reading Morgan's thoughts, something she did all too often and too well, Marissa said, "Vizir Azarat, the prince certainly has a lot of guards, doesn't he?"

"The prince," Azarat replied, "is beloved by all his people."

"Of course." Marissa smiled sweetly. "No doubt these are loyal family retainers, kept employed simply from His Highness's magnificent benevolence."

A strangled sound, which seemed as if it wanted to be a snort when it grew up, issued from the guard. Morgan had never heard eyes roll audibly before, but he was pretty sure he just had.

Azarat, who either didn't hear, or chose to ignore it, merely echoed, "Of course."

"Javin, you may go," Azarat told their guide. "I myself will announce these visitors." The guard sloped off, obviously delighted to be spared the task of interrupting mongoose contemplation. Azarat rapped on a door, then thrust it open, announcing, "Your Highness, I bring noble guests."

A bolt of sizzling green lightning struck the wall next to the vizir's head. Morgan was impressed—the man didn't even flinch. "Royal travelers, stranded upon our shores, oh mighty prince," he continued. "From Kilbourne they come, cast up here by storm and sea, wind and wave."

"Bother!" said a snappish voice from somewhere in the room.

It was dark inside, except for a single candle. Morgan could barely discern a man seated on a cushion on the floor. A lithe creature—which he assumed was the aforementioned contemplated mongoose—wrenched itself from the prince's grasp and darted between the vizir's legs to scamper off down the passageway. Morgan got the impression of something akin to a badger, if a bit smaller and quicker.

Prince Azim rose, extinguishing the candle. He strode to where Azarat waited with his charges. "Most revered Vizir Azarat," he said, "I left strict orders I was not to be disturbed."

"Yes, Your Reverence, but see—travelers from Kilbourne." He stood aside.

Morgan stepped forward. "Morgan McRobbie, Duke Westdale, from Kilbourne. Sorry to be a bother, Your Highness. Our vessel has suffered a slight mishap, and we're rather stranded here."

Azim eyed Morgan unenthusiastically. "Duke," he said by way of acknowledgement.

"And this is my bride, Marissa, Duchess Westdale." Morgan allowed Marissa to emerge from his ducal shadow.

At the sight of Marissa, Azim emerged from his sulk. Eyes alight, he allowed his countenance to transform into a beaming smile. With his thin, angular face and pointed beard, his appearance called to mind the more sinister denizens of the demon dimensions. Or at least what Morgan imagined such a creature would look like. He wouldn't have been surprised to see the prince suddenly begin to smoke and gibber. No doubt this was mere prejudice on his part.

Azim caught Marissa's hand in his, pressing a rather too-moist kiss to it as he flourished an elegant bow. "Vizir Azarat, you did not say you came bearing lovely flowers from the west. Duchess Marissa, welcome. You must consider yourself a treasured guest, a jewel, here in this, my most humble palace."

"Thank you, Prince Azim," Marissa replied, managing to retrieve her hand from his clutches. "Hardly humble, from what we've seen. And thank you. We," she placed emphasis on the word, just so there was no doubt in anyone's mind, "would be honored to be your guests. Just until our captain is able to effect repairs."

"Yes, yes, well, these things often take simply ages," Azim said, grabbing her hand again and leading her off. "In the meantime, you will grace us with your lovely presence. Come, let me show you my pleasure garden."

"Forgive me, Your Highness, I'm afraid I have a strong aversion to snakes."

"Ah, Vapir is quite harmless, I assure you. Besides, I will be right beside you, to protect you."

"Thank you all the same. I'm sure the duke's protection will be quite sufficient. Perhaps some other time? It has been a rather trying day, and I feel the need for rest. Also, we do need to make arrangements to have your most excellent craftsmen help repair our poor boat."

"Azarat, see to it," the prince commanded, with a wave of the hand not engaged in attempting to capture Marissa's again.

Morgan stalked forward, exuding bonhomie and teeth. He stepped between Marissa and the fawning prince. "Thank you for your generous hospitality, Your Highness. Most kind of you. I'm sure your workmen will soon have the *Lady Sybil* put to rights." He took Marissa's hand in his and felt a grateful squeeze.

"Yes, yes, no doubt." Azim regarded his supplanter with disfavor.

Morgan found himself glad, for once, to be a duke. His being zapped by one of Azim's green lightning bolts would cause more political turmoil than the prince would likely care to risk. At least, he hoped so.

"Nice place you've got here," Morgan went on. "Your vizir mentioned we might be able to cadge a room for a few nights?"

This comment perked Azim up again. "Yes, certainly, stay as long as you wish. While you're busy with your repairs, I shall be delighted to show the duchess the wonders contained here in Arvindir."

I'll bet you will, Morgan said to himself. Aloud, he laughed. "Oh, that's what I pay my captain for. But we'd love to see the sights a bit while we're here. Thanks for the kind offer."

If looks were green lightning, Morgan was pretty sure he'd have been instantly reduced to a sizzling pile of goo. Fortunately, a distraction presented itself.

"Azim, who are these people?" A woman's voice, soft and redolent of warm breezes, inquired.

"Saia." Azim's voice sounded suddenly weary. "Duchess Marissa. Oh, yes, and Duke Morgan, from Kilbourne. Allow me to present my sister, Princess Saia."

Marissa hastened forward to greet the princess, taking her by the hand. "So lovely to meet you, Princess Saia. Your brother didn't mention you. We're on our wedding tour and were stranded here when our boat was disabled by last night's storm. This is my husband—well, of only a week—Duke Morgan McRobbie. Won't you please join us while your brother shows us the palace?"

Saia's laugh was warm and liquid. "My brother often forgets he has a sister. Welcome, Duchess Marissa, I would love to join you. We get so few visitors here in Arvindir. Azim, will you also display your treasures for them?"

The prince scowled. "Perhaps some other time, Saia. For now, we must get the duchess and her husband installed in a suitable suite."

"What about the Rose Suite, in the tower," Saia suggested. "It provides such a marvelous view of the city."

"Oh, that sounds simply lovely," Marissa enthused.

And thus, the first part of their mission was completed. They were installed in Azim's palace. Now, all they needed to do was locate the Demon's Fire, somehow manage to steal it, and escape Arvindir with their skins intact. Simple.

Morgan scowled.

Chapter Twenty-One

Marissa flopped down on an ornate settee and rubbed her eyes. "Well. That was interesting."

Morgan gave a low growl, like a bear whose dinner has just unexpectedly slipped away. She glanced up to watch him as he paced the floor near the large windows. "Why Morgan McRobbie, I do believe you're jealous."

"Jealous? Me? Why ever should I be jealous? Simply because Azim was pawing at you like a love-starved youth?"

"I didn't encourage him one bit. You know I didn't."

"Of course you didn't. He didn't need any encouragement. Good heavens, he practically drooled on you."

"Blech. Thank you for a most enchanting picture." She shuddered.

Morgan grinned, his humor evidently restored. "You are quite welcome, my love. Always happy to be of service."

"Yes, no doubt. Anyhow, I'm proud of you."

He quirked a brow. "Oh? Why, if I may ask?"

"Because even though I know you longed to, you refrained from ripping Azim's arm off and beating him with it."

"Well, you did tell me to be on my best behavior," he pointed out.

"Good boy. Well done, you."

"There was also his green lightning to consider," Morgan judiciously allowed. "And I suppose it might have created a bit of a problem for us if you'd hauled off and slapped him silly."

"Well, yes, that too. We do need to stay somewhat in Azim's good graces if we're to do what we came here to do."

"Hmph." Morgan's face assumed a dour expression. "If staying in Azim's good graces means allowing him to put his hands all over you, I think Foxwent can go hang. Ruby or no ruby."

"Yes, I've been thinking about that. Not about the Chief Wizard and his ruby. About Azim's reaction, I mean. I wonder if it was less about me personally and more because he sensed the dratted book."

He halted in mid-pace. "Hmm. Do you think so?"

She held up her hands. "Sebastien said it can leave an aura on anyone who has it. One a wizard would be able to sense. So I suppose it's entirely possible. Also, he said Azim might consider me to be—well, something of a magical curiosity."

Morgan started pacing again. He scrubbed a hand across his face. "You," he said in an ominous tone, "are most definitely not going to be added to his collection. You're mine."

"Oooh, you have a collection of witches? Funny, I had no idea. Wherever do you keep them?"

"One witch," he replied in quelling tones, "is plenty enough, and then some."

"Oh, you say the sweetest things." She feigned a swoon.

He snorted. "All right. Seriously, Marissa, I don't like the way he hangs all over you, oozing what I suppose he imagines is charm. However, I reckon I—and you, more to the point—will have to put up with it a bit for the sake of what we're here to do. Which doesn't mean I like it any better."

"No more do I," she said. "But yes, I suppose we'll have to endure and make the best of it."

There was a soft knock on the door. Morgan went to open it and was soon lost amidst a phalanx of servants, bearing their luggage. Marissa watched, bemused, as they unpacked the trunks and stowed the contents in drawers. Gowns were shaken out and hung up in an extravagantly ornate wardrobe. Morgan's spare boots received a brisk polishing before they were relegated to a separate closet. The blur of activity was almost dizzying.

She closed her eyes for a moment, reaching to close a hand around her reticule. Within, she felt the dark presence of the little grimoire. It was…not comforting, exactly, but there was a sense of connectedness—

Marissa's eyes flew open. She drew in a sharp breath and forced her hand open, allowing the reticule to drop to the floor. An observant minion swooped in to retrieve it. She waved him away. Morgan hadn't noticed, thank goodness. He was still busy dealing with the porters.

She sent a fierce glare toward the reticule and its contents. She'd decided it best to keep the book close by, in order to protect it. Now she wondered if this had been such a smart idea after all. The blasted thing was trying to exert its influence over her again. She had thought perhaps when she'd tried to burn it, the book would take umbrage and be done with her. Evidently it held no grudge and was as eager as ever to assimilate her. And her power.

To what end? This was a question she really didn't want to know the answer to. She was going to have to do something to keep Azim from getting his hands on the book, while keeping herself from being swept any further under its influence. Perhaps now, since he had sensed the book's aura about her, she could return it to the box Sebastien provided for it.

The mere speculation produced a wave of nausea, to the point she felt she might retch. She glared at the book again. *"Stop it!"* she told it sternly. *"I am in charge here, not you."*

Was she? Since she now knew the book for what it truly was, she wasn't so certain. Well, once the servants departed, she'd pop the cursed thing back into the security of its little casket. Sebastien had taught her the spell, in order for her to be able to seal it away from prying princes. And, hopefully, keep herself away from its influence. Out of its clutches? Did the blasted book have clutches? Not a thought which wanted thinking.

She shivered, even as she fought down another wave of nausea. Closing her eyes again, Marissa centered her mind. She was stronger than the book. She was stronger than the book. She was...

"Are you all right?"

Marissa's eyes flew open. Morgan was watching her, his expression concerned. She gave him a wan smile. "I'm fine," she said, hedging just a bit. "It's just been a long day."

"If you say so," he replied, though he didn't look convinced "I told Azim we were too tired to do anything besides eat quietly in our room tonight. I hope this meets with your approval."

"Brilliant," she replied. "I don't think I could have handled a banquet, much less people, this night. I really am worn out. I know you're used to things like this, being on the go all the time. I'm not, and it's frankly exhausting."

"We'll have to see about getting you into training," he said.

She skewered him with a glare. "Morning runs with the Legion? Thank you, but I think not."

"Good practice for getting way from spies and assassins," he countered. "You never know, it might come in handy."

"I'll take my chances."

Morgan grinned. "As you wish. Hopefully our dinner isn't in the too distant future. In the meantime, I'm going to step into what appears to be the servants' quarters to make sure Nardis and Toniq are situated."

"If I'm asleep when you come back," she said, only half joking, "don't bother to wake me."

He stroked her hair for a few moments, bent down and kissed the top of her head. "Sleep well, my love," he murmured.

She gave a contented smile.

Chapter Twenty-Two

Aartis strolled through the doors of The Mean Ewe. It was only two bells, which meant the crowd was still fairly small. There were only a few dock workers and sailors, enjoying a restorative pint or three after a hard day's labors.

Donal, the barman, flashed a grin when he noticed Aartis enter. "Pint?" he asked, holding up a mug.

"I'd not be one to say no," Aartis said. "Thanks." He took a pull of the ale. He cocked his head, regarding the mug. "Is there something different in this? Apple, maybe?"

"Aye, you've guessed it. Something new we're tryin' out," the barman admitted. "Herself decided it might catch on. What d'ya think?"

"Different," Aartis said, and took another sip. "I think I like it."

"Good, good. Be sure to let her know."

"Speaking of Herself..." Aartis gestured toward the stairs. "Is she here?"

"Aye, she's here. An' grouchy as ever, like an ol' she-bear woke from her nap. Go on up, if ya want. It's your neck."

He laughed and raised his pint in a salute. "I reckon I'll need this, eh?" Draining it, he tossed a few coins onto the bar, then headed for the stairs up to Kate's rooms.

As he reached the landing outside her door, he paused for a moment. Not normally one to assess his own feelings, he realized this moment warranted it. He felt, he decided, rather like he did right before entering into a battle. The same heady rush of adrenaline pumping through his veins, the same heightened senses of hearing, scent, and sight. Shaking his head in bemusement, he raised his hand and rapped gently on the door.

"What?" came a snarl from inside, along with what sounded like a chair overturning. "I said I didn't want to be bothered!" The door was precipitously yanked open. Kate, mouth open to continue her diatribe, deflated. "Oh. It's you," she muttered.

He flashed a grin. "Come, now, my lady, is this any way to greet your most ardent admirer?"

She eyed him up and down, frowning as if she found nothing to recommend itself.

Aartis unaccountably felt as if someone just slapped him with a cold, wet fish. "Do I have a smudge on my nose, or what?" he inquired.

She sighed, rolled her eyes, and stepped back. "You might as well come in," she said. "We need to talk."

"Words no man likes to hear," he said cheerfully, following her into the room. As usual, it was a jumble: clothing, books, and half-filled wine bottles littered every surface. And flowers. He grinned at those, then schooled his features and asked, "What's wrong?"

Her expression was stricken. Aartis's heart clenched. "It's my father," she said.

"Ian? What's wrong? What's he done?"

She glanced around, shrugged, and cleared off a chair by the simple expedient of sweeping the dress and stockings on it over onto the bed. "Sit down," she ordered.

He did. To his surprise, she plopped herself onto his lap. "Nowhere else to sit," she said.

He wasn't about to argue. Instead, he wrapped his arms around her, holding her tightly, reveling in the feel of her body against him. "All right, tell me all about it."

"Dad's decided…" She hesitated, then said, "He's decided to become an honest man."

"What?" He would have jumped up, if not for the woman currently occupying his lap. "Well…how does he propose to manage such a thing? I mean—"

"I know." She heaved a sigh. "He told me not to worry about it. I think it started a few days ago. You remember, I told you I met him at our old house?"

"Yes, I do. You said he was a bit mawkish."

"I think it was difficult for him, going back there after all these years. Thinking about Ma and the life he left behind after she passed away."

Aartis held her tighter. "It must have been hard. For you too, I reckon."

"Maybe a bit. Not so much for me, I was too young to remember much. And Dad was always good to me when I was growing up. I know I didn't have what you might call a normal childhood. Still, all in all, I've no complaints. I told him so too."

"But to up and decide to give up his…well, his business?"

"His life of crime, you mean?"

Aartis shrugged, nearly dislodging his delectable cargo. Settling her again, he said, "Well, yes, I suppose I do. I mean, I know Ian is involved in some dodgy things. Truth be told, I've never really seen that side of him. We mostly play cards, or drink, or both when we get together. Which isn't very frequently, I'm afraid. He never talks about…well, the things he's involved in."

She shook her head. "He never really discusses it with me, either. He's always been very firm about keeping me away from the dodgy side of his life, as you decorously term it. He said it was bad enough he was involved and better all-around for me to not ask."

"Mmm." Aartis snuggled her a bit closer. She relaxed into him at first, then drew away.

"Focus," she said. "What am I going to do?"

"What do you mean, what are you going to do? I don't see why you need do anything. It's Ian's decision, isn't it?"

"Well…yes. But he's only doing it for me. And it's your fault."

"My fault? Why my fault? I haven't even spoken to Ian in weeks."

"Yes, but if you hadn't become my most ardent admirer, this wouldn't have happened."

Aartis gaped at her, and in his agitation half rose up in protest, spilling her from his lap. She landed on her feet, cat-like. She bristled like an angry cat as well.

"Now wait a minute, Kate," he said. "The fact I'm in love with you in no way involves your father." He almost said, "Let him get his own girl," realized just in time how awful this would sound and managed to curb his tongue before he let fly. He ended up saying, "This is between us. Ian has nothing to do with it."

"Doesn't he?" She paced about the room, gesturing in frustration. "Aartis, I'm his only daughter. The only family he has. Do you seriously think he would simply stand back and not care?"

"Well, if he cares about you, isn't that a good thing?"

"Of course it is, idiot. But he's about to throw in everything he's ever done, become respectable, so he won't be what he sees as a hindrance to my happiness."

"This is bad, how exactly? I mean, if anyone can pull off a transformation like this, it's Ian Taggart. Well done him, I say."

"But I'll feel awful. Guilty. I mean, I don't want to cause him to be unhappy, for me to have a chance to be happy. It—"

"Ah, so I do make you happy." He beamed at her, then flinched as she punched his arm. "Yes, I see," he went on, putting his arms around her again, then pulling her to his chest. She sniffled into it. "You'd rather suffer than see your father renounce his 'life of crime', as you put it. Cut his ties with his old life, to take a chance at becoming someone people might invite to their homes? Is this what you're saying."

"Oooooh, you're twisting my words around, damn you!" She struggled a bit.

He held her tight. "No, I'm trying to understand," he said mildly.

She choked back what might have been a sob if allowed to grow. "I don't want him to do something he doesn't really want to do," she said at last. "Not just for me."

He stroked her hair. It was particularly nice hair, and his hand tingled at its touch. "Kate," he said quietly. "Ian is a grown man, and no one's fool. He's never done anything in his life he didn't want to do. If I know anything about him, I know this to be true. If he's turning over a new leaf, changing his course, it's because it's what he feels is best. For him, and also for you. Let him take the opportunity. It might be that this will make him happy, you know."

"I hate it when you're logical," she snuffled.

"When I'm right, you mean," he said with a grin.

"Hmmph. Well, perhaps. Don't let it happen too often, mind you."

"Yes, my love," he replied. "How about this. What if I go speak to Ian, sound him out a bit? I need to ask his blessing on our engagement anyhow."

"What?" She rounded on him, hands on her hips, and fire in her eye. "What do you mean, engagement? I've not said I'll marry you, Aartis Poldane. Don't you dare ask my father for my hand."

"I wouldn't dream of it," he said. "Good heavens, what kind of fool do you take me for? He'd laugh me out of Caerfaen. Ask him for your hand, forsooth! It's you I'm asking, Kate. But I want Ian to be happy with the arrangement, and I think he will be." Aartis caught her hand, pressed a kiss to it, and sank down to his knees. "Kate Taggart, will you make me the happiest man in the world and consent to be my wife?"

"I— Oooooh, get up from there." She looked wildly around the room, as if expecting to see an audience. She turned back to Aartis, who remained where he was, kneeling at her feet. "You're mad, you know," she groused. "Adorable, but mad. I suppose I'll have to, if only to stop you sending urchins in here with more stolen flowers. Where do you get them all, anyway?"

"The urchins? Oh, they're all over, eager to earn a penny or two." He rose, then cowered back in mock terror from the ferocious glare she sent his way. "I've faced entire armies who weren't nearly as grim as you," he said. "Is the prospect really as awful as that?"

"Well, one thing's for sure," she said, coming to him. "It will likely never be dull. Kiss me, you fool."

He did. At great length, while his heart leapt within his chest.

Chapter Twenty-Three

The next morning, Morgan left early, to see to getting repairs begun on the *Lady Sybil*. Marissa, left to her own devices, decided to act on her notion of sealing away the grimoire into its protective box, at least for the time being. It wasn't something she needed to carry about, since the prince was now aware of its presence. Having it close to hand might prove taxing on her own strength. Not to mention too much a temptation for Azim.

She'd just completed the spell and listened to the satisfying "click" of the box sealing closed, when there was a soft rap at the door. Hastily stashing the box in a handy trunk, she called, "Come in."

Nardis, in his role as valet, opened the door. "The Princess Saia," he intoned, sweeping a low bow.

Azim's sister bustled past him. "Good morning," she said. "I hope you slept well. Have you had anything to eat yet? I wondered if perhaps you might like to come back to my rooms and break your fast with me. I seldom get to talk to another woman."

Marissa beamed. "Thank you, Princess, that would be lovely. Nardis, will you tell the duke where I've gone, when he returns?"

"Of course, Your Grace." Nardis was playing his part to perfection.

She hoped she could do half as well. She hated to deceive Saia, who seemed simply starved for someone to talk to. Still, Marissa was here to do a job, not to make friends with strange princesses. Well, it never hurt to be kind, no matter what. A lesson her mother had taught her from an early age, and it had stuck.

So. pasting on a pleasant smile, she said, "I'm truly glad you've come, Princess." Which was no lie. "The duke has gone off and left me alone in this strange palace. I could use some coffee and a good chat."

Saia was practically dancing with excitement. "Excellent. We will go now."

Taking Marissa by the hand, Saia led her into the corridor, through a baffling maze of stairways and long halls lined with portraits, mosaics, and displays of assorted weaponry. Saia chattered nonstop until Marissa's head was practically swimming by the time they arrived at the princess's suite. The princess bustled about, chivvying servants, plumping cushions for Marissa, and generally behaving more like a nervous schoolgirl than a poised princess.

Once the servants had provided refreshment—coffee and sticky pastries oozing with honey and nuts—and they'd conversed for a bit more, Marissa turned to her hostess. Widening her eyes ingenuously, she said, "Princess Saia, I've heard so much about Arvindir's wonderful archives." She sipped her very dark coffee tentatively then asked, "Do you think I might be allowed to visit them?"

"The archives?" Saia asked. Her expression brightened measurably, seeming to indicate she found the subject of archives extremely interesting. Which was, Marissa mused silently, a bit surprising.

"You like to pore through old books and scrolls, then?" the princess asked.

"Oh, yes indeed. I do love books, and history. The collection here is said to be first rate. A quick look, perhaps?"

"Of course. You are an honored guest in this house. If an expedition to the archives is what you wish, then an expedition to the archives is what you shall have." She set her tiny coffee cup on a nearby table, then rose gracefully. Her silken garments shimmered in the morning light suffusing the cozy solar.

If I were to wear something like this, Marissa mused to herself, *I'd be even more notorious than I already am. Although Morgan would no doubt love it.* Rising, she said, "Hurray!" She grasped Saia's hand. "We shall have such fun."

"Yes, I believe we shall." Saia's eyes were bright and eager.

Marissa wondered what possible attraction the undoubtedly dusty archives held for her.

"Are you also interested in history and books?" she asked. Not that it really mattered, so long as the princess was amenable to escorting her there. She and Morgan had determined Saia was their best option for gaining access to the archives. Azim might become suspicious at the request, and they had to recruit Alain, the archivist, if their mission was to have any chance of success.

"Mmm," was Saia's only reply. They traversed several long flights of stairs, descending into the palace's nether deeps. "I find certain," she smiled like a cat made free of the cream pitcher, "attractions there," she said at last.

Well, that was cryptic. Marissa supposed she'd simply have to be patient. Hopefully Saia would reveal why the archives were of such great interest. Of course, there was certainly nothing wrong with an interest in archives, though it felt very out of character for the princess.

They descended yet more stairs. Candles flickered in sconces along the walls, throwing their shadows dancing as Saia led them ever downward. "This is such a huge palace," Marissa exclaimed. "Much, much larger than King Rhys's in Caerfaen."

"Really? Tell me about the palace there."

Marissa obliged with descriptions of the great hall, Rhys and Gwyn's personal apartment, and the marvelous views from the turrets. Marissa regaled the princess with stories of grand balls and festivals, of dancing and the court ladies' splendid gowns, and some snippets of court gossip and scandal.

"And you, you are the grand lady of the balls?" asked Saia.

"Hardly." Marissa laughed. "I'll confess, before I met Morgan, I only rarely attended such events. Most ladies go seeking husbands. Honestly, such was the farthest thing from my mind."

"Yet," Saia pointed out, "you have landed yourself a most attractive husband and a duke to boot."

"Yesss," Marissa said. "I suppose I have. I really hadn't thought about it that way."

"Now, since you are a duchess, a person of great importance, all the other ladies will have to defer to you, will they not?"

"Perhaps," Marissa replied, although she thought this outcome highly unlikely, not to mention wholly unwelcome. "I didn't marry Morgan for his title. Just for himself. Since we've been wed for such a short time, I'm afraid I really haven't had much opportunity to find out."

"I suppose." Saia sighed. A slight pout of her lips seemed to indicate the princess was frustrated with Marissa's evident lack of ambition. Well, it couldn't be helped.

"What about you?" Marissa asked. "You're a princess, after all. You outrank me by oodles."

"Oodles? What a funny word." Saia giggled, her humor at least somewhat restored. "Ah, here are the archives. Behold."

She threw open a door to reveal the room beyond, lit by scores of small lamps which seemed to glow without any flame. At low tables, men sat cross-legged on cushions on the floor, bent over pages as they copied, transcribed, or illuminated, or whatever men did in archives. Marissa wasn't quite sure.

Beyond the tables, shelves rose, rank upon rank, toward the high ceiling. They bulged and shuddered and writhed with books and scrolls and ledgers. The sheer weight of so many words, gathered together in one place, was both awe inspiring and, truth be told, a little overwhelming. Marissa's hand went to her mouth.

"I-I had no idea," she managed weakly.

Saia waved a hand toward the shelves. "There are," she observed matter-of-factly, "a great many books."

"More than one could ever read in a lifetime," Marissa breathed in reverent awe. "In ten lifetimes. Maybe a hundred."

Saia eyed her with amusement. "You would read them, then, all these many books? And your husband... he would not object?"

"Morgan? Heavens, no, he loves to read too. He, like me, is quite interested in history. We both love to explore the past through books, to learn about the great—and sometimes awful—things done by those who came before us. I read a good deal of history in school, and—"

"School? You were allowed to go to school? A girl?"

"Oh, yes. My parents were adamant about my receiving a good education. Are girls not allowed to go to school here? How terrible."

"Education is only for men and boys in Arvindir. In all Parthane, in truth. Although, there are a few villages that provide their girls at least enough schooling for them to know how to read and write a little. It is not really accepted, however, and the elders frown upon it, even if they sometimes look the other way."

Any comments Marissa might have made regarding the inequity and foolishness of such rules were forestalled by the sudden advent of a young man hurrying toward them. His robes flapped around him as he hastened to greet them. A clerk or archivist, Marissa assumed, noticing with a smile a series of ink splatters, both on his robes and his hands, along with one delightfully irreverent splotch right on the tip of his nose.

"Your Highness," the man gasped as he reined to a halt and bowed low before Saia. From his almost prone position, he said, "You do us great honor."

"Get up, you silly boy," Saia said. Her tone was more indulgent than censorious. "I bring you a guest, who wishes to admire your moldy books and ancient scrolls."

The cleric rose, shaking out his robes. "Then, fortune indeed smiles upon us, here in our dusty archive. For you bring splendor and light, as does the sun after a rain." He bowed again, though Marissa noted with interest how his gaze never left the princess's face.

"Pah. Flatterer. You have been reading too many of your own scrolls of poetry. Now: here is the Duchess McRobbie, come by fate and fortune from Caerfaen, across the sea."

The young man straightened, wary interest now filling his eyes. "Caerfaen, eh?" he said. "So very far, indeed. Your Grace, I am your humble servant. Alain I am named. I hold the honor to be head under-archivist here. May I show you our treasures? With Her Highness's permission, of course."

Without waiting for her to agree, Alain led Marissa, with the princess tagging behind, all about the vast library. He pointed out the ancient texts being copied at one table and the intricate illuminations being painted at another. He led them among the shelves, highlighting centuries-old scrolls of poems, including a work by Arvindir the Great himself. Alain fairly danced with excitement, though Marissa was uncertain if his eagerness was less about the presence of a guest to whom he could display the archives, and more about the presence of the Princess Saia.

If this boy isn't besotted with her, I'm a dragon, Marissa said to herself, even as Alain displayed yet another treasured tome.

After an hour or so, Saia said with a throaty laugh, "Alain, enough. My poor head will fly off into the heavens if you show us any more wonders."

"I'm sorry, Your Highness. Please, I meant no offense. It's only we rarely receive visitors, except for hoary old scribes and priests, who mutter in their beards and leave books and scrolls scattered like grains of sand in the desert. To have such flowers, such—"

"Yes, yes." Saia cut him off, but Marissa noted she favored him with a smile nonetheless. "Another day, perhaps, if the duchess desires. We will go now, I think."

Marissa beamed at the archivist. "Alain, thank you for your time. Your archive indeed does you credit." She glanced at Saia. "If I might ask one small boon?"

The princess nodded. Marissa said, "I wondered if you might have a book I've been unable to locate in Caerfaen's archive. Your collection is so vast, I'm sure you must have a copy."

"Of course," he said. "I will try. What is it you seek?"

She stared directly into his eyes. "It is titled *A Treatise on Activation*, by Barzak." She smiled. "If you think you might find it?"

Alain's expression remained bland, but she caught the swift flash of comprehension in his eyes, along with a soft intake of breath as she uttered the code phrase given to her by Holman Barzak. Bowing again, he said, "I believe I might be able to locate this text for you, though it may take me some time. Perhaps I might deliver it to you later?"

"That would be lovely. Thank you. His Highness has installed us in…" She turned to Saia. "You can likely tell him better than I."

"The Rose Suite, in the West Tower," Saia told the archivist. "Do not fail, Alain, or my wrath will be merciless."

The flutter of her lashes, Marissa noted, belied the severity of her words.

He's not the only one besotted. She grinned to herself.

Chapter Twenty-Four

"Of course he understood." Marissa held her breath while Morgan did up the last laces on the back of her gown. "He caught on right away. If you'd seen his face... Well, not really, he was very controlled, didn't give away a thing. Saia didn't have any notion we were discussing anything besides some dry old tome. But he knew. By the way, should you ever decide to give up your commission in the Legion, you might have a flourishing career as a ladies' maid. You do excellent work. I—ack!"

He stopped her chatter by the simple expedient of whirling her round and sealing her lips with his.

"You were saying?" he asked, several minutes later.

"Um... I forget?"

"Excellent. Nice to know I've still got the old McRobbie touch."

"Hmph!" she said, even though her eyes were shining.

Morgan extended an arm. "Shall we venture forth and attempt to find where we're supposed to eat dinner? I'm famished."

"Saia told me there would be someone to guide us. Morgan, this place is massive. We'll never find our way around, much less find the ruby."

"All the more reason we need this chap, Alain. He should be able—" He stopped at a discreet knock on the door. "Come."

Nardis opened the door a bit. "A servant is here to lead you to the hall where dinner will be served," he intoned.

Morgan inclined his head to Marissa. "Shall we go?"

Their guide led them through myriad passageways, to what Prince Azim labeled "the small banquet hall." Small was evidently a relative term here in Arvindir. Fully occupied, the hall could have easily seated a hundred or more guests. The presence of Azim, Saia, and a dozen or so nobles and dignitaries led Morgan to suppose this was to be a more intimate affair. There would, Azim had informed them earlier, be a grand state banquet laid on in the great hall on the morrow, with a multitude of guests.

Morgan found himself in a place of honor, on Azim's right. Marissa was placed on his left. While Saia sat next to her, Morgan's nearest companion appeared to be an ancient beard—probably there was a man in there somewhere, although Morgan couldn't have proved it—who maintained an aloof silence to any conversational sorties.

The beard did appear to enjoy the service of a pair of disembodied hands, floating from under the sleeves of a voluminous robe and shoveling food into the beard at a prodigious rate. Morgan politely refrained from inquiring if the beard had recently undergone a seven-day fast and was making up for lost time. Still, he had his suspicions.

The lack of congenial conversation was not offset by his host. Azim only turned in Morgan's direction when he wanted his wine goblet. Otherwise, he focused his attention fully on Marissa. Morgan noted the prince's eyes boring into Marissa's, who smiled and nodded noncommittally.

Though the beard maintained its stoic silence, Morgan couldn't manage to overhear what Azim was saying to her through the chatter at the table. With nothing else to distract him, Morgan gave his attention to some really excellent lamb kofta and lentils. Not his usual fare, to be sure, though no less delicious for being exotic.

Glancing up, he noticed the fellow across the table smiling in his direction. Munching another kofta, he nodded amiably and finally swallowed enough to speak. "Delicious."

"Azim has his faults, but he does keep an excellent table," the man allowed. Inclining his head toward the bearded wonder on Morgan's right, he said, "Don't mind him. Uncle Darvin probably hasn't spoken more than twenty words in the last dozen years. Most of those were when he dropped a stone tablet on his foot."

Morgan chuckled. The beard quivered in indignation. It rose, followed by robes flapping like an animated scarecrow, then stalked off.

"I thought perhaps it was because he didn't care for foreigners," Morgan said to his new friend.

The man waved a lazy hand. "No, Uncle Darvin hates everyone. You're in good company." He popped a kofta into his mouth. "I'm Nadiz Rashan, Azim's cousin. Well, second cousin, twice removed, or some such. Close enough."

Morgan laughed. "I'm afraid I always get lost after the first round."

Nadiz grinned conspiratorially. "Me too. Whatever the relationship, it gets me invited to a banquet now and then, so I don't make an issue of it. Rumor has it you and your most charming duchess were washed up here by the storm."

He nodded. "We were making for Orsk, to visit my people. No doubt second cousins twice or thrice removed, all over the shop. The blasted storm blew up from nowhere and put us way off course. The mast got broken, the rudder fouled, and we were never more excited than when we spotted land. Not the way one wishes to take one's bride on a sea voyage, I can assure you. I figured it would end up being some deserted island with no food or drink for miles. Never expected we'd been blown this far off course. We were extremely fortunate, actually, and Azim has been most gracious."

"Yess," Nadiz said thoughtfully. "Orsk, eh? You really were tossed about, weren't you? So very far. I've never heard such a thing, and I spend a good bit of time on the Thundermist Sea. You were indeed most fortunate."

Nadiz was a bit too sharp, Morgan decided. Time to change the subject before he could give the matter much more cogitation. "Azim tells me there's to be a grand banquet tomorrow."

"Mmm, yess." Nadiz's brow was furrowed, and he didn't seem to be paying Morgan much heed. "Orsk," he repeated. "All the way from Orsk and with a broken mast…"

Cursing himself for not sticking with the bearded, silent Uncle Darvin, Morgan went back to his food. He found it no longer as enjoyable.

Dinner finally completed, they endured an interminable series of jugglers, dancers, sword wavers —nothing on the Tzigani, Morgan noted idly—before he could finally retrieve his duchess from Azim's clutches and retreat to their suite.

Nardis entered from the door of the servant's quarters. "Good, you're back. There's a rather itchy lad here, bearing a scroll and saying he must deliver it personally to the duchess."

"Ah, good," she said. "Our archivist, no doubt. Show him in in, please, Nardis."

The young wizard stepped out, returning moments later with Alain. "Thank you for coming, Alain," she said.

"Here is the text you requested, Your Grace." He bowed, but when he straightened, Morgan could see his eyes were filled with questions.

"Can we be overheard?" Morgan asked.

Alain nodded, pointing to a grate high on the wall. Morgan called Nardis over. "Can you do anything to make sure no one is able to hear us?"

Nardis smiled, concentrated for a moment, then flicked his thumb and forefinger. "All anyone listening will be able to hear is a muddled hubbub," he said. "It will sound like several people are talking at once, but nothing with be distinguishable."

"Handy." To the archivist Morgan said, "Since you responded to the code phrase, you know who sent us."

"Yes, Your Grace. Lord Holman Barzak."

"Right. We're actually here on orders from King Rhys. Barzak has given leave for us to request some assistance from you."

"Of course. May I inquire why you're here?"

Marissa answered, "Prince Azim came to Caerfaen and stole something—a ruby—from the wizards. We've been sent to fetch it back."

"A ruby. As important as all that?"

"He stole it from the wizards," Marissa reminded him.

"Ah, of course. Wait a moment, ruby, ruby—oh, my lord, not the Demon's Fire?"

"That's the one," she said.

"It...it's used to..." Alain stared, aghast. "Very well, I see why you're here. What do you need from me?"

"Well, the ruby's location would be an excellent start," Morgan said. "Or, if you don't know, any maps or plans of the palace would also be very helpful. Perhaps any security measures in place? Details like that."

"Plans I can provide. The jewel's location? I could make some educated guesses. Nothing more, I'm afraid."

"Thank you," Marissa said. "We'll be very grateful for whatever you can share with us."

"How soon can you manage to get the plans?" Morgan asked. "We don't have a lot of time. Only as long as it takes our captain to effect repairs on the ship. He can stall a bit, but we've probably only got a couple of days, at most."

Alain's forehead wrinkled, and he appeared to be calculating.. "Normally, I'd make a copy, but it would take ages. I'll have to extract the originals. It shouldn't be a problem. No one has looked at them in decades, probably. I believe the plans do contain some of the palace's original security measures. Most of those are likely still in effect. No doubt Prince Azim will have added his own, but I don't have any records for those."

"About those educated guesses," Marissa prompted.

"I'll show you on the plans when I bring them. Of course, I can't mark anything, since they're the originals. Still, I can give you a fairly good idea."

"No, best not to mark anything up," Morgan agreed. "It would be the one time Azim would decide to take a look at them. Alain, I hate to pressure you, but how soon?"

"The archive is closed for the night," he replied. "Not until tomorrow, I'm afraid."

"That'll do fine," Morgan said. "And thank you."

Once Alain had taken his leave, Morgan asked Nardis, "Where's Toniq?"

The wizard shrugged. "No idea, Your Grace. I can't keep track of him. Here one moment, gone the next. A regular will-o-the-wisp, our Toniq."

"All right, no matter. We can't do anything until we have those plans, at any rate. We won't need you any more tonight."

"Shall I remove the spell on the listening grate?"

Morgan glanced at his bride, who flashed him a dazzling smile. He said, "Why don't you leave it be..."

Chapter Twenty-Five

Toniq's face, when he entered the room where Morgan was waiting for him the next morning, was a mask of inscrutability. "You wanted me?" he asked.

A bit sullenly, Morgan thought. "Yes, I did. I do. Where were you last night?"

"What's it to you?" The thief's tone was just this side of belligerent.

This didn't faze Morgan in the least. He'd stood under roars and rantings from some of the hardest, toughest men the Legion could offer. This lad had nothing on them. Morgan's old sergeant could have given him a ten-minute head start and still bested him ninety-nine times out of a hundred.

So, Morgan merely assumed a bland expression—the one he used when forced to deal with boors and buffoons—and said, "What it is to me is this: I'm tasked with our mission's success. You are a member of the—well, squad's as good a word as any, I suppose. If someone raises a ruckus because they've missed something valuable, and it's traced back to you, it jeopardizes what we're here to do. And," he raised his voice to near parade-ground bawl, "I can't have that!"

Toniq didn't flinch. Morgan gave him full marks for this. Better men than this young thief had cowered under his tongue-lashings. He modulated his tone and continued, "I'll ask you once more. What were you up to last night?"

"Exploring, if you must know." Toniq grinned. "That'd be recon, to you."

Nodding slowly, Morgan said, "All right, fair enough. Was it at all helpful?"

Toniq shrugged. "Gave me a chance to get the lay of the land, so to speak. I can find my way to the kitchens and back again. In terms of being useful to the mission, not particularly, since"—he assumed a milder version of Morgan's bawl— "No one's bothered to tell me what the hell we're doing here."

"True," Morgan said, stepping to the door, "And you're about to learn." He opened the door and called, "Come in, everyone."

Nardis, Fanshawe, Marissa, and Alain filed into the room. Marissa commandeered a comfortable wing chair. Nardis took a seat on an ornately embroidered settee and, after a moment's hesitation, Toniq joined him there. Fanshawe snagged one of a pair of wooden chairs flanking a small table and turned it backward, settling himself onto it. Alain, in Parthanian fashion, sank cross-legged onto a large cushion on the floor.

Morgan stood, surveying his team. A novice witch; a thief of unknown capabilities and caprices; a journeyman wizard; an archivist-cum-spy with no field experience; a reformed pirate; and a soldier, himself. As ragtag a band of adventurers as ever there was. Well, they were what he and Marissa had to work with. They'd simply have to hope for the best.

"All right, everyone, I reckon it's time you learned exactly why we've been sent here, as Toniq has reminded me. It's quite simple. Prince Azim has stolen something from the wizards of Caerfaen. We've been sent to find it and fetch it back."

All gazes were focused on him now. Marissa and Nardis both knew the score; the others only had bits and pieces. Morgan went on, "What he stole is a ruby. It's about half this large," he held up his fist, "according to what I've been told. And it's extremely valuable."

"A ruby that size," Toniq observed, his eyes alight with keen interest, "would be worth a small—no, make it a substantial—fortune."

"Oh, I'm sure it's worth quite a bit," Morgan said. "However, it's not the stone's value itself that's has brought us here under false pretenses. The ruby has another side."

He paused, more for dramatic effect than anything else. "The wizards have, for centuries, used the Demon's Fire, as this particular stone is called, as a repository for captured demons."

Alain nodded, while Fanshawe blanched. Nardis, privy to wizard's ways, remained silent. Toniq held up his hands in negation. "Wait a minute. No one said anything about demons. I'm only a simple thief. I don't do demons."

Morgan raised a brow. "Oh? Well, perhaps not demons. Still, Ian Taggart told me you have a certain affinity for 'items of a magical nature.' Anyway, assuming we do the job correctly, demons shouldn't enter into the thing."

He didn't appear convinced. Morgan couldn't honestly say he

blamed the thief. He wasn't too keen on the idea of a jewel loaded with deadly demons either. Still, they couldn't allow Azim to keep the thing and risk a cataclysm.

"Alain here," Morgan gestured to the archivist, "has managed to provide us with plans of the palace. They're not necessarily up-to-date. Still, they're the best we've got. Certainly better than nothing." He spread the plans on the table. Toniq shot up from his seat to come study them.

Morgan continued, "Alain has suggested the jewel may be secured in what Azim terms his 'treasure chamber.' Alain?"

The archivist rose to join Toniq at the table. "The prince has a secret, hidden chamber where he displays the items he collects from all over the world. I'm afraid I don't know its exact location. I do know it's somewhere in this area." He tapped a section of the plans with one finger.

"Hmmm," Toniq murmured, his gaze darting to where Alain pointed. "Are we allowed to keep this? It would be very useful."

Alain shuddered. "Good heavens, no, they're the original plans. I have to return them tonight."

Toniq sighed. "All right, then I'd best get busy, eh? Have we parchment? Quill and ink? I need to make at least a rough copy of this. While I do, perhaps you can explain these markings? I assume they indicate defensive measures? Traps and such?"

Alain produced the required items from his satchel. "I'd wondered if one of you might wish to attempt this. I'm terrible at copying, and obviously I couldn't very well instruct one of the copyists in the archives to do it. Yes, this indicates some sort of trap. And this…"

Morgan left them to it.

Chapter Twenty-Six

From the parapet at the top of one of the palace towers, Azim swept an expansive arm in a half circle toward the city below. Domed temples and soaring towers jostled for primacy in a confusion of space. Silk banners and washing flapped in the evening breeze. As the late afternoon sun sent its golden rays on the scene, the roseate stones that pervaded Arvindir began to glow various shades of pink and rose.

"How splendid," Marissa breathed.

"This is my favorite moment of the day," Azim said, taking her arm in his. "The city laid out in all its splendor. And yet," he squeezed her arm in an overly familiar manner, "it still could not match your own beauty."

Morgan, standing with Saia several paces along the parapet, stiffened. His hand reached for a weapon he wasn't actually bearing at the moment. *Steady on, leave it to Marissa.* "No, the view is much nicer," she said in a tone intended to quell Azim's ardor a bit. "What is that tallest spire there?" She pulled her arm free to be able to point. "The one glowing so brightly now."

Azim tossed a glance in the direction indicated. "Ah, yes. It is the temple of Intharia. Intharia is the goddess of love," he murmured soulfully, pawing her arm again.

Good heavens. Goddess of love, forsooth. Morgan rolled his eyes.

"Really?" Marissa exclaimed. "Oh, Morgan, come see this." As he hastened to join her, she twisted away before Azim could capture her arm again. "Ah, there you are," she said.

"Sorry, darling," he said, placing a protective arm around her shoulders and smiling brightly at Azim. "Ah, charming view, Your Highness. How very... pink."

"The soul of a poet," Marissa muttered. Morgan could tell she was making a valiant attempt to keep from laughing at Azim's indignant expression. Even Princess Saia's mouth turned up in amusement.

"The pink stones," the princess said, "are enchanted. The ancient Djinn created them for our forefathers."

"Enchanted?" Marissa exclaimed, intrigued. "How?"

Saia opened her mouth to reply. Azim cut her off. "Arvindir's enchanted stones serve as protection against all manner of dangers. Dragons, for example."

"Dragons, eh?" Marissa said.

"Dragons. Indeed." Morgan exchanged a swift glance with her.

"And more mundane dangers, like fire," Azim added.

"And have dragons ever given you problems?" Morgan asked.

"Never," Saia replied with a laugh. "So I suppose these enchanted stones must be working."

Marissa ran her hand t along the parapet's stones. "Is the palace constructed from these enchanted stones as well?"

"Of course." Azim smirked. "It was the first to be built with them."

"And you say the Djinn enchanted them?" Morgan asked. "Why? If you don't mind my asking."

"A bargain," Saia said, before Azim could answer. "Made by our great-great-great-grandsire. The enchanted stones in exchange for their freedom."

"I...see," was the only response Marissa could manage.

Morgan felt less constrained. "You have Djinn running about loose?"

"Not loose, exactly," Saia said. "The bargain, as I understand it, was freedom for the Djinn. In exchange, they agreed to do no harm to humans. The bargain was made, and thus all are bound."

"Correct," Azim said. "We have never had problems with the Djinn in the long centuries of their freedom. Here, enough grim talk. Saia, shall we show our guests the city from the air?"

"Very well, brother," the princess replied. She sounded, Morgan noticed, more resigned than excited by this suggestion. "I will fetch the carpets."

"May I assist you, princess?" Morgan inquired, trailing in her wake even while he kept a watchful eye on her brother. It rankled no end to allow Azim to fawn over Marissa like this. There were limits to his tolerance, and this mission was testing them to the extreme.

Saia smiled up at him. "Thank you, some help would be most welcome. When no servants are handy, I am an easy substitute, at least in Azim's mind."

She led the way to the opposite side of the tower. What at first glance appeared to be intricately carved wooden benches, each about eight feet in length, opened to reveal storage areas within. Reaching into the first one, she struggled to pull something out. He hastened to help her, and together they withdrew a rolled carpet.

"We will need both carpets," she said, wrinkling her nose.

"Allow me." He hauled the second carpet from its hiding place. "You don't appear to be thrilled with this... well, whatever it is Azim is planning to do with these." He gestured at the carpets.

She shook her head. "He only does it to impress your—to impress our noble guests."

Morgan didn't even bother to suppress his scowl. So, it was blatantly obvious to Saia as well. Was this normal behavior for Prince Azim? Or was his interest in Marissa due to her magic, and her possession of the grimoire?

All in all, it wasn't exactly a question he could put to the princess. Choosing to ignore her slip of the tongue, he said, "What is he planning for us, if you don't mind me asking?"

She hefted one of the carpets and slung it over her shoulder. Morgan did the same with its mate. He almost dropped it again when Saia said blandly, "Azim uses his magic to enchant the carpets. Then, he can fly above the city, looking down at all the pretty lights and the little people, scurrying about like ants."

Well, he supposed he shouldn't have been surprised. Still, it felt rather risky. "And no one falls off?"

"Not off Azim's carpet," she said. Her voice was quieter now, as they approached the prince, who kept Marissa's arm locked in his own. "Although he does sometimes forget there is a second carpet to keep track of."

"Like tonight." Morgan didn't bother to hide his scowl this time.

"Do not worry," the princess said, chuckling softly. "I will see you do not fall."

"Ye gods," he muttered. "*Sicut necessitas...*"

When they reached Azim and Marissa, the princess shrugged her carpet onto the tower's stone floor. Morgan dumped his beside it. Tearing his gaze from Marissa for only a moment, Azim snapped, "Well, what are you waiting for? Unroll them." He flapped an impatient hand at his sister.

Saia huffed out an aggrieved breath and bent to remove the ties holding the first carpet rolled neatly. Morgan interposed himself, saying, "Allow me, Your Highness." With deft fingers, he undid the ties, spreading the first tasseled carpet open on the cobblestones.

He stepped back and stared in awe. There were many fine

carpets, most of Parthanian design, throughout the palace at Caerfaen. None could hold a candle to this. Vibrant crimsons, blues, and golds, woven into intricate floral patterns, were so vivid one might believe this beautiful object had been completed only moments before.

He allowed his gaze to travel further. At the head of the carpet, a rampant peacock's image glared back with a supercilious air. How appropriate, Morgan thought with a suppressed grin. He glanced at their host, whom the peacock resembled most magnificently.

"This is incredible," he said, more to Saia than to her brother. "You toss this into a storage bin up on the roof? It should be on display, hanging on a wall in the palace, at the very least."

"This?" Azim stepped close, regarding the carpet with disdain. "Adequate, I suppose. Nothing special, I assure you. It suits the purpose I intend it for, no more."

"As you say." Morgan knelt to untie the second rug. He gave it a push, the woven fabric unrolling in a second dazzling display of color, even more striking than the first. He sucked in a breath.

Marissa stared, saying only, "Oh. My."

Saia, however, was at no loss for words. "Azim, you pig. This is the carpet from Father's chamber. How could you?"

"It is old and worn," he replied. "It is of little value."

She snorted. "I'm glad I'm not the one who will have to explain it to Father."

"Pah!" Azim said in an irritated tone. "Enough, Saia. This is not the time for such discussions. Now is the time to soar, like the great hawks of the desert."

"Very well, oh great hawk." Scorn dripped from her tongue. "Soar away, if you will."

If the prince took offense at his sister's words, he made no show of it. Instead, he ushered Marissa onto the first carpet, directing her to sit. Morgan went to join her, but Azim caught his arm. "No, no, you will be with Saia," he said with a grin.

Morgan itched to smack it off his face. Azim practically dragged Morgan to the second carpet and bade him sit.

Saia joined him, sitting cross-legged. "Try it like this," she advised. "You'll have much better balance."

Morgan, who'd had his legs straight out, felt dubious. Still, Saia seemed confident, so he drew his legs up and made the attempt. "I'm afraid I don't fold quite as gracefully as you," he said, squirming into a relatively—if entirely awkward—similar position.

On the carpet ahead, Azim sank down next to Marissa. Taking her hand, he said grandly, "I shall keep you safe, Duchess." Morgan glared daggers at the back of his head. Azim waved his free hand.

"*Abba el adimbe*," he said. The carpets trembled, their edges jerking to send the tassels dancing gaily. "*Abba el adimbe*," he repeated.

The carpet Azim and Marissa sat on rose gracefully into the air, where it hovered several feet above the tower. The second carpet bucked like an angry stallion, threatening to send Morgan tumbling overboard.

"Azim, you idiot, pay attention," Saia yelped, grasping at the carpet's edges to keep from being launched into the air.

"Yes, yes, very well." The prince flapped a dismissive hand, instead focusing his attention on Marissa again. Still, Morgan and Saia's carpet settled a bit, rising into the air until it nearly matched the first.

"Hang on," Saia advised.

Morgan scrabbled for purchase. He could find little to latch onto unless he resorted to clutching at Saia. Since this didn't seem either smart or helpful, he finally settled for gripping a small fold in the carpet with his right hand and the tasseled edge with his left.

Right in the nick of time. The carpet, until now hovering gently in place, shot forward like a missile fired from a trebuchet. He gripped harder, his knuckles white with strain.

"Ack!" Marissa gasped from ahead.

"Azim, you fool, slow down," bawled Saia. "You'll kill us all."

Both carpets had been angling skyward. Now they leveled off. Azim's settled into a smooth glide. Morgan and Saia's followed, their carpet's progress punctuated by a series of fits, starts, jounces, and sudden, unexpected veers to the right or left.

Morgan turned his head enough to inquire, "You do this willingly? For fun?"

"It is... hmm...an acquired taste."

"I'm surprised it's not used to torture prisoners."

"Hmmph. Don't give my esteemed brother any bright ideas," she muttered.

Still, Azim heeded his sister's entreaties. The carpets now glided gracefully over the city, laid out below in rose-hued splendor. They banked around an up-thrusting minaret spire, then soared over the bazaar. Below, land-bound observers pointed up and shouted. Azim paid them no attention, although Morgan noted Saia waving as they passed overhead.

The carpets angled in unison, so they faced back toward the palace again. Beyond, the sun neared the horizon, far out to sea. As they watched from their high vantage point, it flared down into the Thundermist Sea, its light slowly fading.

"That," Morgan said reverently, "was almost worth it. Almost," he repeated, glaring at Azim, who appeared to be bending toward Marissa, seemingly intent on kissing her.

"Damn it," Morgan growled.

Saia murmured something under her breath. Their carpet surged forward, and they caromed into Azim's.

"Blast you, Saia," Azim sputtered, rocking on his suddenly unstable conveyance. Marissa, eyes wide, scrabbled furiously for something besides Azim to cling to.

"Me?" Saia inquired, her tone all syrupy sweetness. "You're the one who controls these things, brother. Perhaps if you paid more attention to what you should be doing..." Her eyes glinted with unsuppressed malice.

"I think I've seen quite enough," Marissa said. "May we go back now? Slowly? I quite enjoyed my lunch, and I'd like to keep it a little bit longer."

Morgan grinned fondly at her. She returned the grin, tossing him a slow wink for good measure.

"Hmph," Azim said. He waved a hand, and the carpets commenced a gentle descent back toward the palace's high tower.

Once they'd landed on the tower, Morgan rose on shaky legs and reclaimed his duchess. As the city fell into shadow below them, they descended the stairway, back down to the main part of the palace. If Marissa kept casting curious glances at the pink stones, Morgan couldn't exactly blame her.

Chapter Twenty-Seven

Morgan stripped off his shirt and tossed it onto a nearby chair. They were back in their suite in the Rose Tower, with an hour to wash and dress for the evening's banquet. Marissa eyed him appreciatively.

He kicked off his boots. "I'll be more than happy to pinch the blasted jewel back. If only to give Azim a severe case of indigestion." The muscles in Morgan's shoulders rippled in a most appealing manner when he moved. Marissa caught her lower lip in her teeth as she watched him.

He must have felt the intensity of her gaze, for he looked up and grinned at her. "We have at least an hour before we have to leave for the banquet," he murmured as he stalked toward her.

"Yes, and I'll need every minute to get ready," she said, a bit regretfully. "I'm not about to make an entrance at what's effectively a state banquet—at least it would be in Rhys's court—in a tousled mess. Which, if you had your way, is exactly what would happen."

He affected a pout. "Poor thing," she said unsympathetically. "Get along and make yourself presentable. I have to make do with a borrowed maid, and lord only knows what she'll try to do to my hair. Now, scat. Running your fingers through it won't help matters in the least. Go, before I forget myself." She eyed him again. "Well, perhaps one kiss before you go. Only one, mind."

Several minutes later, her lips swollen and hair mussed, Marissa rang for the maid. If her eyes glittered a bit more golden than usual, only her husband might have noticed.

When Morgan returned, nearly an hour later, he was clad in a dusky maroon tunic and well-fitted leather trousers and sported a snowy white cravat. His boots were shined to perfection.

"If Nardis ever decides to retire from wizardry, he might have a nice future as a gentleman's valet," she said, eyeing him appreciatively.

Morgan, however, seemed to have been rendered speechless. He gazed at her, mouth slightly open and eyes wide. She gave a graceful pirouette. "Do you approve?"

"It's… I… Marissa, you look amazing," he finally managed. "I've never seen this gown before, have I?"

"No, it's new. Although you did pay for it." She favored him with an impish grin. "I didn't think you'd wish your new duchess to be seen about in old rags. I was fairly certain we might be required to dress for a formal occasion while we were here."

She twirled again. "I'm normally not one for fancy clothes, but I do think this is quite nice."

Morgan stepped toward her, his hand outstretched. He took her hand in his and pressed a kiss to her palm. "Marvelous!" he said. "I'll be the envy of every man there tonight."

She quirked a brow. "Do you think so? I don't know; some of these Parthanian girls are quite beautiful. Get them outfitted in exotic silks, and I don't think I'd really compare."

"Ha," was all he said. On the whole, Marissa found this quite satisfactory.

"You're looking quite dapper yourself," she said. "Are you planning to wear a jacket?"

He grimaced. "Nardis told me I must. It's lurking over on the chair."

"At least he allowed you to wear your sword," she pointed out.

"Oh, he was fine with the sword. Although he did give me a rather frosty look when I tucked a knife into my boot. 'Ceremonial weapons are fine, Your Grace,'" Morgan mimicked, "'but daggers are for killing people.'"

"Well, please try not to kill anyone tonight. I'd rather not get blood on this gown if I can possibly avoid it. At least not on its first outing."

"I shall endeavor to maintain a strict decorum, my lady. If I have to kill anyone, I'll make sure to do it somewhere else."

She patted him on the head. "Good boy." As she sent the gown's hem in a swirl about her legs, Morgan's eyes followed her movements like a cat watching a particularly delectable mouse. "You," she added," are having improper thoughts again, aren't you?"

"Not in the least, my love. We're married now, don't forget. Any thoughts I have about your delightful self are entirely proper."

"A fair point," she conceded. "Hold onto them for later. They won't spoil for waiting, I don't imagine."

"Minx," he said. "I suppose we'd best get going, eh?" He took her hand in his.

"Hang on a moment," she said. "I need to do one thing before we go."

Morgan brightened, and she swatted his arm. "Not that, you fiend. I want to make sure the blasted book is still warded properly. I don't like to leave it about, even if it is secured in Sebastien's little box. Not with Nardis and Toniq in the next room."

"Especially with Toniq in the next room," Morgan said.

"Toniq? Why? Don't you trust him?"

"I trust him to do the job he's paid to do. The thing is, he is a thief. According to Taggart, he's attracted to items of a magical nature. Can't get much more magical than the book."

"I suppose," she said. "Although, I can't say I find him the type to steal from his employer. Especially since we're his only way out of Arvindir once the job is done."

"True. Nevertheless, I'll rest a lot easier when the book is no longer our hands—well, your hands—and Sebastien has it hidden away once more. Come to think of it, perhaps it would be for the best if Toniq did pinch it."

"No, it wouldn't. There's no telling who might end up with it, or what might happen if it got into the wrong hands." She ran her hands over the lacquered box. "The wards are intact. We can go now."

Morgan gave the box a parting glower. As he went to don his jacket, a little shiver ran through Marissa. The book, warded or not, was calling to her. She could feel its dark pull, the insistent urge for her to unlock its secrets.

Tearing herself away, she followed Morgan and pasted on a smile. "Shall we go?"

Chapter Twenty-Eight

Marissa allowed herself to be led astray.

Away from the banquet hall's noise and light and crowd. Away from Morgan. Away from...sanity? Was she daft to let Azim drag her off to heavens knew where? "Is it much farther?" she asked.

"No, only a little way. It's right down here," he replied.

As they walked down the dimly lit corridor, his fingers rested gently on her arm. She didn't think it would be possible to turn tail and flee, tempted at the prospect as she might be. Back to lights, and music, and people, and the security of Morgan's arms.

She opened her mouth to say, "I think I've made a terrible mistake." The words caught in her throat as Azim uttered a low incantation and made a gesture with the hand not holding her arm.

A panel in the wall snicked open to reveal a door. Another low word from Azim caused candles in the room beyond to flare into life. "Welcome," he said genially, "to my hall of treasures." He ushered her inside.

The candles in their sconces lit a six-sided chamber, paneled in lacquered wood so dark it almost swallowed the light they gave off. Shelves on each wall held his collection. Golden chalices glinted, a jeweled scepter shone, and a dizzying assortment of figurines, of men and creatures of every type, caught her eye. She spun in a slow circle in a futile attempt to take it all in. She realized her mouth hung open and closed it with a conscious effort.

"It's breathtaking," she said. "Also a bit...overwhelming." Azim's mouth curved into a smug smile.

Then it hit her. It wasn't simply the objects themselves that caused her to feel dizzy. No, what she felt was something much more. It was the force of their combined magic. That much power, confined into this one room, pressed against her senses like an almost physical pressure.

"Oh," was all she could manage to say. The magic pounded against her from every side, making it hard to even catch her breath. The candles flickered wildly. Or perhaps her vision clouded as she came near to collapse.

At that moment, she recalled one of Wyvrndell's first lessons. He'd taught her a way to block external stimuli. She'd used it to protect herself from Rhenn in their first encounter. From the depths of her muddled brain, she dredged up the spell and set it to work.

Too late, she realized, as she strained in vain to pour more power into the protective spell. The accumulated magic in the room was too much for her, her spell too late, and she was falling, falling into a blackness so dark…

When she was able to open her eyes, she found Azim bent over her. He patted her hand and called, "Duchess. Duchess Marissa, return."

She blinked at him muzzily. "Water, she croaked.

"Into which a good bit of strong spirits has been added," he said, releasing her hand. "Can you sit up?"

With a dawning horror, she realized she was nearly prone on the stone flagstones. *Good heavens.* Her dress, bunched up around her knees, provided him with an unrestricted view of her legs. With more effort than she'd dreamed possible she sat up and levered herself off the floor, collapsing onto a conveniently placed settee. She hastily tugged down the hem of her dress to a reasonable level of propriety and tried to keep the room from dancing a sprightly reel.

"I'm sorry," she said as she accepted the glass he handed her. "I don't know what—gack!" If blazing fire suddenly became liquid and could be bottled, this would be the result. She managed not to spit it out, barely, but would definitely be in need of new plumbing, from her throat down.

"It is called Zevinia," Azim said. "A local brew, renowned for its restorative properties."

Marissa was forced to admit it possessed those in abundance. Feeling almost normal again, she silently completed her protective spell. The pressure of the magical artifacts around her lessened to a much more tolerable level.

"I'm sorry," she said again.

"Think nothing of it. The accumulation of magic in this room can sometimes be oppressive to one so sensitive as yourself. I have laid on a protective enchantment."

Ah, he didn't know about her own spell. She released it and felt no ill effects. Still, she kept it at the ready to call up again should the need arise. "Thank you," she murmured. "It was just so sudden."

"Perhaps some food will help restore you?" He gestured to a nearby table, groaning under a cargo of sumptuous golden grapes, sticky sweet figs, delicate pastries, ripe peaches, and dark cherries.

A platter of sweetmeats and another of cheeses jockeyed for position on the crowded table. Marissa smiled to herself, as she recalled the feast Morgan had arranged for their wedding night. Funny, she didn't remember eating a bit of that one.

Even as her attention focused on the offered food—she'd hardly had time to take more than a bite or two before Azim spirited her away from the banquet—she saw something that made any thoughts of mere comestibles fade to naught. It lay, shimmering darkly, right beyond the piled-high table

How, she wondered, had she not noticed it straight away? Near the center of the chamber stood a dark marble plinth, about four feet in height. The base, carved into the shape of lions' paws, claws extended menacingly, rose into a mass of writhing serpents stretching upwards toward their goal: the top of the plinth, which bore a simple marble top. Resting on it lay an enormous ruby, winking evilly under the candles' light.

"Food, yes," she said absently, moving toward the table. Her gaze never left the jewel on its plinth, even as she took a fig and bit into it, the juices coating her lips with sticky sweetness.

"This one has a place of honor," she said. She gestured with her fig toward the ruby. "A prized possession?"

"Bah, it is only a trifle. It simply fit nicely in this spot. It has little real value, except as an attractive bauble. Rather like you."

Good grief. Rather like you, indeed. Marissa rolled her eyes at this. Still, even had she not already known the jewel's true nature, the timbre of Azim's voice would have proved him a liar. Was this a test to determine if she was interested in the ruby? Bringing up her defensive spell once more, she examined the jewel more closely.

"Yes, I see what you mean," she said, adopting a bored tone. "Oh, yes. Doesn't it have a rather large flaw?"

"What?" His reply was sharp as he stepped forward to examine the ruby. "I...I see no flaws." He peered anxiously into its vermillion depths

"Ah, my mistake then. It must have been a trick of the light." She made sure to modulate her voice to sound completely careless. "I think I'll have a bit more Zevinia, if you please."

With a final, suspicious glance divided between the ruby and Marissa, Azim hastened to refill her glass. Fill being the operative word, the fiery Zevinia practically sloshing over the rim. Was he trying to get her intoxicated? If so, for what motive? This secluded room, the opulent banquet, the weight of magic pressing upon her...

The Parthanians, rumor had it, were much less concerned with marriage vows than were her own people. She probably came across quite staid and stodgy to someone like Azim. This was, all in all, perfectly fine with her.

Did it make her more a challenge to be conquered? While she knew Morgan found her beautiful, she was realist enough to be aware she didn't possess the charms that drove men like Azim, so worldly and decadent, to howl at the moon or set schemes of seduction in train.

If not, then what did the prince have in mind? Why bring her there, of all places? Why display the ruby to her?

She took another sip of the Zevinia. This time she was prepared for it, and the drink brought an unexpected mental clarity, even as her legs suddenly felt treacherously wobbly.

"Yes, my dear," Azim said. "Why do you not recline upon the settee? Allow me to assist you..."

Marissa made a valiant attempt to marshal her senses, to bring her powers to bear. With an effort of will, she tried to conjure the flaming sword she'd used to defeat Augustus Rhenn. All that appeared was a tiny blip of light, promptly extinguished again. The walls were no doubt thick enough to muffle the loudest cries for aid.

And Azim, blast him, had put something besides Zevinia in her drink.

"Help," she mumbled as strong hands pushed her down onto the settee.

Chapter Twenty-Nine

Morgan seethed.

Glowering into his nearly empty wine glass, he fumed silently. Around him music played, people chattered, and everyone made merry. Except Morgan McRobbie. Where the devil was Marissa? He scanned the hall once more, hoping to catch a glimpse of her head, familiar to him now as his own features in the glass, somewhere among the cacophony of revelers.

She wasn't in the room. Neither, for that matter, was their host, Prince Azim. Morgan's brows rose, even as his mood lowered. This didn't bode well.

Under normal circumstances, he'd bet on Marissa against all comers. This situation was far from normal. Azim was a mage of extraordinary power and few scruples. Combined with what Morgan knew of the Parthanians casual disregard for the sanctity of another man's wife, Morgan was reduced to gnashing his teeth while an excellent vintage turned to ashes on his tongue.

If she wasn't back at this side by the time the orchestra finished the next song, he would start taking Azim's palace apart, stone by bloody pink stone, until he found her.

An incessant, annoying buzz finally resolved itself into a voice by his ear. Blinking, he found himself confronted with Princess Saia.

"Come," she said. She tugged urgently on his sleeve. "We must hurry."

Morgan stared at her, not comprehending her words.

"Come on!" She tugged harder. "There's no time to waste. If you want to save your duchess from Azim, we must hurry."

Morgan shot up from his seat like he'd been launched from a catapult. "Where?"

"Follow me. It's not too far. I imagine he has spirited her away to his treasure chamber. Such is his habit."

He followed in her wake. She padded swiftly down a dimly lit passageway. Her slippers slapped softly against the marble floor, in counterpoint to the clatter of his boots. Saia halted.

"Take off those noisy boots," she ordered. "Azim will hear us."

He complied at once, asking, "Why are you doing this?" The princess merely shook her head and placed a finger to her lips.

Finally, after a myriad of twists and turns which he reckoned took them to a remote part of the palace, she stopped. The walls were identical to the rest of their route: dark, forbidding, and exceptionally solid. Still, when she directed him to stand in a particular spot, he was not about to argue.

Once he was in position, she raised her small fist and pounded on a section of the wall. Nothing happened.

She pounded again, more forcefully this time. "Azim!" she cried.

A crack appeared in the paneling, and light streamed through to dispel the gloom. The crack widened, and a door became visible, set seamlessly into the wall's wooden panels.

The door opened outwards, toward Morgan, effectively concealing him from the view of anyone—presumably Prince Azim—in the room. "The palace had better be on fire," growled Azim, his voice cold with fury. "Because it's the only reason—"

"Azim, you must come at once," Saia blurted. "That old fool Vinticus has challenged Avir to a duel of spells, right in the great hall."

"What? Curse them both! All right, all right, I'll come."

"Hurry!" She grabbed Azim's hand and dragged him along the passage, giving him no time to close the secret door.

Morgan wrapped his fingers around the door's edge to prevent it from closing on its own. When Saia and her brother were gone from sight, Morgan darted into the room. He paused only a moment to prop the door open with one of his boots. He was certain if it closed, he might never find it again. Or get it open, even if he should manage to locate the appropriate panel.

He spared only a quick glance around the room. His attention was focused on the figure which lay motionless on a plush settee. With a low growl he sprang forward, cradling her in his arms.

As nice as this was, he knew he only had a few moments to make an escape before Azim came storming back to finish whatever he'd been about. Morgan lifted one of Marissa's hands. It was completely limp. She was either drugged or under some sort of spell. It didn't matter at the moment. What mattered was getting her—both of them—away from this room.

He bent and hefted her up onto his shoulder. Awkward, but it would have to do. He staggered to the door, retrieving his boot. There was no need to leave such a blatant calling card to announce he'd been in this chamber. Stamping his feet securely into his boots again, he lugged Marissa into the passageway.

Now, which way to go? If he went back the way Saia had led him—assuming he could even find his way—there was a better than even chance he'd meet Azim on his way back to his secret lair.

If Morgan went the other way, there was no way to know where he'd end up. Still, there was really no choice.

"Hsst!"

He started like a colt at the sound, almost dropping his precious cargo.

"Your Grace!" A diminutive maidservant beckoned to him from down the passageway. "My mistress sent me to guide you. Hurry, before the prince returns."

He needed no encouragement. Settling Marissa more securely on his shoulder, he followed.

His guide was either navigating an extremely circuitous course or Azim's palace had been designed by a frustrated maze maker. Morgan lost count of the turns they took after the first dozen. There were no windows in this section, nor even any arrow embrasures to give any sense of direction. He simply had to trust the girl knew where she was heading.

And hope it wasn't much further. Marissa wasn't particularly heavy, nor did Morgan lack in strength. But carrying a limp body, even a child, for any length of time takes its toll. It was no little relief to hear his guide whisper, "Quiet now. We're almost there."

She unlatched a panel in the wall, opened the door a crack, and peered out. Evidently satisfied, she pushed open the door and led Morgan back into a well-lit passageway. Marissa stirred on his shoulder and uttered a soft moan.

"Keep her quiet a bit longer. It's only down here," cautioned the maid.

He realized they were back in familiar territory, at last He recognizing a couple of the smugly supercilious portraits which hung on the walls. Another half minute and the maid opened the door of their suite.

Laying Marissa on the bed, he stretched his aching back, then turned to offer thanks to the servant. She was already gone, the door shut softly behind her.

Marissa stirred restlessly. Morgan spied a water pitcher and went to pour a glass when he noticed a much better choice. A bottle of Vynfold wine, brought amongst their belongings, stood on a side table.

With a grin he poured a glass. He arranged pillows into position against the headboard and propped her into an upright position. She moaned again, and her eyes fluttered. He put the glass to her lips.

Her reaction was as instantaneous as it was unexpected. With a swipe of her hand, she knocked the glass away, and wine splattered onto the carpet like drops of crimson blood. "No!" she said, her voice strangely harsh. "No."

"Easy, my love, it's me," he said in tones he'd use to calm a frightened child. "It's all right now. You're safe."

Her eyes opened, closed, opened again. She blinked and tried to focus. He could see she was still fighting the effects of whatever Azim had done to her. Her eyes were cloudy, and she looked in danger of sliding off the stack of pillows.

As he watched, she ran a hand over her face and muttered something he couldn't catch. Then she straightened and uttered a gasping sob. "Morgan? It is really you?"

"In the flesh," he confirmed. "Are you all right?"

"Just…need to rest," she said.

"And a restorative drink, I think. Water, or wine?"

"Water," she said. With a shudder, she added, "I may never drink wine again."

Morgan's brows rose in surprise, but he managed to hold his tongue. Fetching the water pitcher, he poured a glass and placed it into her hand. There would be time enough for explanations later. But…no more wine? This was almost inconceivable.

She downed the water and held out the glass for more. As he refilled it, she said, "I saw it!"

He handed her the glass. "Saw what?"

"The ruby. I saw it. Azim has it on display, in his treasure room. Alain was right, Morgan. It was right there. I could have picked it up and walked right off with it."

"Is that why Azim did…blast it, Marissa, what did he do?"

"No, it's not. I didn't let on I was interested in the ruby. At least I don't think I did. No, he was up to something else. I thought at first he'd drugged me—by the way, if Azim ever offers you something called Zevinia don't touch it—because he intended to—well, you know…"

"He what?" Morgan exploded. "I'll—"

"No, no, he didn't do anything."

"Are you sure?"

"Yes, Morgan. I'm sure."

"Thank God," he muttered. "Then what?"

"I don't know, at least not for certain. If I had to guess, I think he planned to somehow try to steal my magic from me."

"Marissa, that's impossible." He met her worried eyes. "Isn't it?"

"Until tonight, I'd have said yes. Now, I'm not so sure. I want to find out. Nardis should know."

"But he didn't succeed." It was a statement, not a question.

"No, I don't think he had time. Now it's your turn. How did you ever find me? This place is a regular rabbits' warren. And, what happened to Azim?"

"It was completely thanks to Azim's sister. I was ready to make a nuisance of myself with strenuous inquiries as to where you'd been taken. It felt like you'd been gone for ages. Suddenly Saia showed up and led me straight to where you were. She lured Azim away with some cock-and-bull story about a duel he needed to stop. I popped in and scooped you up. Slung you over my shoulder and lugged you back here. Led all the way, uphill and down, by one of Saia's handmaidens, who conveniently appeared to show me the way."

"My hero."

"Sarcasm," he pointed out, "does not become a duchess."

"I was serious. Thank you for coming to rescue me from …well, from Azim's clutches, anyway. Hmm. I wonder why Saia interfered in whatever her brother was up to. I mean, she seems awfully nice, and it must be simply rotten for her to be stuck with Azim as a brother. Still, why help us?"

Morgan shrugged. "Why, indeed? I've no idea. I'm certainly glad she did. I'd have never found you own my own, and I really didn't want to call in reinforcements quite yet."

"No," Marissa agreed. "Only as a last resort. I think we can manage this. Now we know where the ruby is, all we have to do is nip in and steal it."

He threw back his head and roared with laughter. She shot him a baleful look.

"I don't know what you find quite so amusing," she said tartly.

"I'm sorry," he said, stifling his mirth. "Your optimism cheers me, that's all."

"Hmph. Oh, I know, we can't simply waltz into Azim's treasure chamber and scarper with the jewel. He'll no doubt have set all manner of booby traps and alarms to protect the things in that room."

"Right. So, how do we get around them?"

Marissa gave him helpless shrug. "I'm foxed if I know. I wish I did. No matter. I've no doubt some scheme or another will present itself. In the meantime, I want to talk to Nardis."

Chapter Thirty

Nardis frowned. "In theory," he said slowly, "I suppose it's possible. I couldn't do it. No one I know could do it. Perhaps Chief Wizard Foxwent, but…" He shrugged one shoulder.

"So I'm being silly?" Marissa asked, even as she attempted to tamp down the hopeful note that threatened to seep through.

"I didn't say that." He tugged on his collar as if it choked him.

She was certain he found it much less comfortable than his normal wizard's robes. The uniform of a footman of Morgan's household, however, provided an excellent disguise. She was certain no one would ever suspect him of being anything besides a servant.

"These Parthanian wizards are an odd bunch," Nardis said. "There are stories, certainly. There are always stories. We wizards in Caerfaen really don't know what these fellows get up to or what they're really capable of. So, when I say 'in theory,' it doesn't mean they couldn't do it."

"Why would he do such a thing?" Morgan asked. "I mean, if you have magic, does it really benefit you to have more? I thought you either have it or you don't. No degrees."

Nardis clasped his hands behind his back, for all the world like a schoolboy about to recite his lessons. "It's not really quite so simple, Your Grace. There are indeed varying degrees of magic. From the country hedge witch, with her sometimes effective charms and potions, to someone like myself or Sebastien, who have been trained and have pretty wide capabilities. To someone like Foxwent, or even the duchess here. Sebastien tells me your abilities," he nodded to Marissa, "with the right training, could be almost limitless."

He went on. "With power comes responsibility—one of the first things they try to teach us at the Academy. What they don't mention, the problematic bit, is with more power also comes greater influence, prestige, and the ability to do pretty much anything you want. Because few others will have the power to hold you in check."

"Yes, I see what you mean," Morgan said.

"So, if Azim were to add my reputedly limitless magic to his own store?" She winced. "He would be—"

"Unstoppable, if he were a mind to really cut loose," finished Nardis.

"Mmmm." Marissa considered this. "Two things. First, is there a way I can protect myself? Second, do you think the ruby somehow has a part in this?"

The wizard cocked his head. At length he said, "As far as protection goes, there's nothing I'm aware of. Remember, I said all this is theoretical." But a distant look came into his eyes, and he trembled slightly.

"What?" she asked. "You've thought of something."

The young wizard dragged himself back to attention. "Yes. Well, no. I mean yes, but it's…well, drastic is putting it mildly."

"Tell me," she ordered. Then, with a smile, "In the spirit of theory."

He sighed, then scrubbed a hand across his face. To Morgan, he asked, "Your Grace?"

"Don't ask me," Morgan said. "I'm merely an innocent bystander among you magical types. She's the Royal Enchantress. You'd best tell her."

Nardis swallowed. Hard. "All right. There is a way—in theory, mind—to…well, to seal off your magic. No one would be able to touch it." His eyes turned dark as he finished, "Not even you."

"How very dramatic." She glanced around. "I fully expected a convenient rumble of thunder just then."

She felt more than saw Morgan roll his eyes. Nardis was stone-faced. "It's not a matter for jest, Duchess. It would be very dangerous to attempt. Fortunately, you can't, because I, thank all the saints, have no idea how to go about it. If you were to attempt such a thing, there's a good probability you couldn't reverse it. You would lose your magic. Forever."

Marissa sniffed. "I did quite well without it for twenty-five odd years. I don't think I'd really miss it very much. And it might be better than the alternative of allowing Prince Azim to co-opt it. Who knows what havoc he might cause?"

"I'm afraid I haven't been clear," Nardis said. "You haven't 'done without' your magic until now. You simply weren't aware of it. But it was, and is, a part of you. An integral part, like your heart, or your brain. Imagine what would happen if you suddenly removed one of those. It would be the same if you were to take away your magic."

Marissa stared at him, her eyes wide. "Oh," was all she could manage.

"Oh, indeed," he replied grimly.

Morgan said, "Nardis, tell me this, for the sake of argument. If Azim were somehow able to steal Marissa's magic, would the same apply?"

He waggled a hand. "First, please understand this: we're way, way off into the realm of the unknown. I'm not even sure I know what I'm talking about. My gut says no. I don't think it would be possible to take another person's magic in its entirety. There should be some left, hopefully..."

"In theory," prompted Marissa.

"In theory," he said with a rueful smile, "this would prevent as drastic an outcome as sealing off your magic entirely."

"Mmph. Well, since we don't know how to do it anyway, I reckon I shan't fret about it. What about my second question?"

"The ruby?" He rubbed his chin. "Well, you said Azim told you the items in that room were all magical in nature?"

She nodded. Vigorously. "It wasn't only what he told me. I could feel it. The force of those magical things, gathered in one place... It was frightening. It was almost like it all pressed in on me, like a really heavy weight."

Nardis's face grew pale. "This sounds bad. I mean, if he's collected these magical items and is seeking to gather magic from other magicians as well... It sounds to me like Azim plans to attempt something on a grand scale. Magically speaking, of course."

"This," Morgan said, "does not bode well. What are we talking about here? A power play so he can rule over all Parthane? Grab control from his brothers and his father?"

"With all due respect, Your Grace, I fear you're thinking in small terms. With such power at his disposal, Azim would literally be unstoppable. There would be no one strong enough to counter him. He might start with Parthane. Yet power breeds the desire for more power, doesn't it? Once he got started, I don't think he'd be satisfied with one little kingdom."

"You're saying he might be able to...take over?" Marissa shuddered. "Everything?"

Nardis voice was flat as he said, "Everything."

She suddenly felt very small and very afraid.

"But there's something worrying me," he said.

"Um. Something worrying you? Taking over the world isn't

bloody well enough to worry you?" She barked out a harsh laugh.

"No, I mean besides that. You said you could feel the force of all the magical energy in that chamber, right?

"Yes, I could. It was awful." She shivered at the memory.

He grimaced. "If you could feel the magic's presence as strongly as you say, well, it might mean Azim has begun to lose control of it. If he has…"

"Let me take a guess," she said. "Lots and lots of wild, stray magic flying around. Which would be just as bad."

"Maybe even worse. At least Azim presumably is trying to control it. Without anyone to channel it?" He shrugged. "Well, it doesn't bear contemplation."

"Especially with the blasted ruby in the mix," Morgan pointed out. "Uncontrollable magic, in great amounts, coupled with a horde of hungry demons suddenly released from their prison? It sounds like a recipe for disaster if I ever heard one."

Chapter Thirty-One

Marisa sat in the comforting warmth of a pool of morning sunlight as she sipped her coffee.

Morgan sprawled across a settee, his coffee all but forgotten. "I don't like this," he muttered.

"No more do I," she replied equably. "I don't see we have much choice."

"We could forget the whole thing," he growled.

"And leave the ruby to Azim? What happens if he somehow releases a ruby filled with demons? Either accidentally, or with—what's the term? Malice aforethought? You heard Foxwent. It doesn't matter either way; they'll overrun the entire world."

"I wonder how much we can trust Foxwent." He scowled. "No one else really knows much about this demon-imprisoning ruby."

"By no one else, you mean Sebastien?"

Before Morgan could reply, a knock sounded at the door. Nardis went to answer it. He returned a moment later to announce, "Her Highness, the Princess Saia." He needn't have bothered, for Saia was practically on his heels.

"Princess Saia," Morgan said. He flourished a bow. "Thank you for your timely and unexpected assistance last evening."

The princess gave him a distracted nod, but her attention was focused on Marissa, who came to a quick decision. "Morgan," she said, "Why don't you leave us girls alone? Take Nardis with you. Go…check on the boat, or something manly."

Thankfully, Morgan was quick to catch her intent. With a word to Nardis and a bow to the ladies, he departed at speed.

Marissa watched him until the door was closed and they were alone. She smiled at her visitor. "If you are here for my thanks as well, you have them. Although I'll admit, I'm curious why you would interfere with your brother's scheme, whatever it was."

Saia's lip curled. "Azim? He always schemes. Ever he seeks more power for himself. He gathers up all his so-called treasures in that room."

"What is he after?" Marissa inquired quietly, wondering if she would get an answer. "And what did he want with me?"

"Him? Bah. He wishes to have everyone bow before him. To be Azim the Great. To have sway over all. To have men fawn over him, to have women throw themselves at his feet."

"This is why he wanted to steal my magic? That is what he planned to do, wasn't it?"

"Of course. You are a woman; you should not have such power. Any power! It is anathema to him, to think a woman might also have strong magic."

"But you, you have—" Marissa began.

Saia sneered. "Me? Have magic? No, no, I have none. It is impossible. No woman in Parthane holds magic. The few who do possess any, they soon find it ripped from them. It is the law."

"You're not serious?"

"Oh, yes. And you, you would have ended up like them, an empty husk, mumbling and staring into nothing…"

Marissa stared. "Good heavens. How awful! This might have happened to me?"

Saia nodded vigorously. Marissa said, "This is your law? Hmph. A law made by greedy men for their own benefit. It's always the same, isn't it? The strong seek to oppress the weak. And it's much easier when it's women you're trampling on, isn't it?"

The princess's eyes were cold and hard as she said, "Azim would think, 'Why should a woman, a mere nothing, have such power when it could as easily be mine?' Once he took your magic, he would also have your little book. Ah, there is much strong magic there, to put the things in his collection of trinkets to shame."

"If you have no magic," wondered Marissa aloud, "how do you know about the book's power? Surely Azim didn't tell you."

"Him? Ha. He tells me nothing, except I am to marry some old mage with bad teeth and a smelly beard. No, I know about your book because I can feel it. Feel its power. Like I can feel the power of Azim's collection. Like I can sense the strong magic in you."

"I…see." Somehow, Saia's explanation didn't ring true. She needed to talk to someone with more knowledge to confirm her suspicions. She merely said, "Again, I thank you most sincerely for saving me from your brother. Didn't he suspect something when he found there was no duel?"

"Ah, but there was." Saia grinned. "Or there would have been, had Azim not arrived when he did to stop it. I told Vinticus what Avir said about him. And I told Avir what Vinticus called him."

"So each was ready to call out the other? That was brilliant, Saia."

Saia smiled wolfishly. "These mages; they are like little boys sometimes. They'll believe anything, and they get their feelings hurt by less than nothing."

"So, Azim thinks I simply got up and left on my own, while he was gone?"

"I would imagine so. Why should he think otherwise? He will be sure your magic is even stronger than he thought, as you were able to resist his efforts. Be wary, Duchess Marissa. Do not wander the palace alone. Do not let Azim give you any food or drink meant for you alone."

"Oh, you'd best believe I shall be on my guard. But here, I'm being a terrible hostess. Come have some tea and let us speak of more pleasant things."

The princess looked suddenly nervous. Very young, and very alone. I'll bet she has no one to talk to, Marissa said to herself. *No friends at all, thanks to her rotten brother.*

Cautiously, like a doe stepping out of the forest's protection, Saia perched on the edge of a chair. Marissa bustled about to distract her a bit. She poured tea and piled a plate with biscuits. The ginger ones, Morgan's favorite, she explained to Saia. This, at least, elicited a shy smile.

"The duke, he is so very handsome," Saia said. "A man with substance and influence."

Marissa smiled fondly. "He's a dear. I've just started to get him properly trained up."

Saia laughed. "I could not believe it. You are his wife, but you said 'go', and he went. If a woman in Arvindir tried such with her husband, she would sleep standing up for a week."

"How terrible," exclaimed Marissa. "I'll admit, there are a few men who have similar ideas where we come from. Morgan and I...well, we've been through enough things together. He respects me for who I am."

"Really?" Her eyes were wide. "Who arranged your marriage?"

"Arranged our marriage? No one, Saia. Well, I suppose you could say we arranged it ourselves. When we fell in love, I mean." She laughed. "Of course, when I first met Morgan, I couldn't stand him. But he grows on you."

Her companion sighed. "Such freedom. Oh, to have even a taste of freedom as you have. To do what you wish, to love who you want. It's almost more than I can bear."

"Your parents?" Marissa asked. "They feel the same as your brother?"

"My father, of a certainty. It is his law, after all. My mother, for all she is Parthane's queen, would never gainsay him. Women here, even a 'princess' such as I, are little more than cattle, to be bartered at need, to enhance a bloodline or solidify an alliance. It's...oooh!" Saia growled.

"Do you have any sisters?"

"No. Only three brothers. Fraazi is not bad, except when he has too much Zevinia. He only wants to be left alone with his books, not be bothered with the oversight of a principality. Arbin is almost as bad as Azim. Azim is by far the worst of them, though. And he grows worse all the time."

"Yes, I think you may be right," Marissa said. "I wonder what he's really up to..."

"What do you mean?"

"Oh, nothing. It's merely a bit strange he would attempt such a thing with me. I mean, I am the wife of an influential duke from Kilbourne. Did he think Morgan would stand by and do nothing? Let him rip my power from me and go on his merry way?"

"When Azim gets an idea into his head, he doesn't think about the consequences," Saia said. "He is Azim the Great, and thus can do whatever he wishes, with no one to tell him no. Including your husband. Azim thinks himself not only a man of power and influence, Arvindir's ruler, and the king's eldest son. He is also a most powerful mage, probably the most powerful in all Parthane. So, he never stops to wonder, 'Should I?' He just does it, because he is Azim."

"Well, the sooner we leave Arvindir, the better," Marissa said, crossing her fingers behind her back. "Mage or not, king's son or not, Morgan won't stand for any more nonsense from your brother."

Saia's expression became forlorn.

"What's wrong?" Marissa asked.

The princess sniffed. "You are right. You should leave this place as soon as you can. I just wish you could stay. I have so few people here I can talk to."

"I'm sorry, Saia," Marissa said and meant it. "Perhaps you can come to visit us some day."

"Truly? You would allow this?"

"Allow it? My dear girl, I think it would be splendid."

The princess sighed. "If only there was a way." She shook her head. "No, Azim and my father, they would never let me leave."

Marissa reached over to give the princess a hug. "You will figure out a way," she said. "I'm certain you will."

~ * ~

Morgan pulled the door closed as he left Marissa with Princess Saia. "Well, I reckon being a duke doesn't count for much. Tossed out right on my ear, eh?"

Nardis chuckled. "Don't worry, Your Grace. You do still command the Legion, at least."

"I suppose it counts for something." Morgan grinned. "Still, I reckon it's not such a bad idea to go check in with Fanshawe, to see how repairs are coming along. Care for a stroll down to the docks?"

"No, Your Grace, I have a few things I should attend to. If you'll excuse me?"

Morgan shrugged. "Suit yourself."

He headed down the tower's stairs. He figured he stood a halfway decent chance of finding his way out, with only the single staircase to navigate. Even so, he still managed to get lost, descending one flight too many and startling a flock of scullery maids into excited chatter, giggles, and shrieks. He made a hasty exit and bolted back up the stairs again, finally locating the door to freedom and fresh air.

Shaking his head to clear his mental cobwebs, he set off at a brisk pace toward the docks. The problem was, he realized, that he was used to being the one in charge, the one responsible for everything. On this mission, he was little more than a supernumerary. He hadn't even managed to protect Marissa from whatever Azim tried to do last night. *Did the blasted fellow really think he could steal Marissa's magic?*

Morgan grunted in frustration. Marissa might as well have left him home and brought along the cat, for all the good he'd done. Francesca had wanted to come, in fact, and might have done a better job overall.

He managed to put aside this less than comforting thought as he dodged around the sailors and dockhands bustling about, intent on hauling unknown things from here to there. He made his way onto the wharf. It took a bit of doing to arrange with the harbormaster, who evidently only spoke Parthanian, to have someone ferry him across to the *Lady Sybil*.

Still, it wasn't long before he was able to bellow "Ahoy, the *Sybil!*" From the dingy, he saw Fanshawe at the rail above.

"Ah, Duke Morgan, welcome," Fanshawe called. "Hang on, will you? I'll toss down the ladder."

In a few moments the rope ladder tumbled over the side, unfurling as it dropped. Morgan grasped the ends, steadied himself, and made his way up.

Fanshawe leaned over the rail, hand extended to help him aboard. "Thanks," Morgan said, then wobbled a bit when a swell rocked the boat.

"I'm glad you came out," Fanshawe said. "Saves me having to come find you."

"How are the repairs progressing? Are there problems?"

"No, not at all. We'll have the new mast in place this afternoon, unless we run into problems, which I don't anticipate. It's a pretty straightforward job. No, I wanted to see you about a different matter."

"Oh?"

Fanshawe glanced around. "Why don't we go to my cabin. There are too many men here I can't vouch for. Parthanians, you know. I don't know how much they understand. They do brilliant work, mind. I just think what I have to say might be better done in private."

"Mmm. That doesn't bode well." Morgan frowned as he followed Fanshawe to his cabin.

Once they were seated, Fanshawe said, "There's been a local fellow, named Nadiz Rashan, snooping around out here."

"Nadiz, eh? Yes, I know who he is," Morgan said. "Snooping? How so? What was he after?"

"He asked a number of rather pointed questions about the storm that landed us here. Where we were, headings, that type of thing. I found it odd and thought you should be aware of it."

Morgan nodded. "I met him over dinner a couple of nights ago. I mentioned we were bound for Orsk when the storm hit. I could tell then he felt something was off about my story, but there was nothing I could do about it. What did you tell him?"

"Pretty much the same thing. We were taking a long-way-round route to head for Orsk, kind of meandering along, as the vessel's owner instructed. We got blown way off course by the storm. How we were lucky beyond belief to make it to the harbor here in Arvindir, especially since we had no notion where we'd ended up."

"Did he believe you?"

Fanshawe shrugged. "Hard to say. He seemed satisfied with my answers, but who knows? And even if he's certain it's lies, so what? I mean, what could he do about it?"

"I suppose," Morgan said slowly, "he could talk to his cousin, the prince. He might persuade Azim we're here under false pretenses. Perhaps get him asking some awkward questions before we're ready to act. He might even send us packing, before we've gotten a chance to do what we came here for."

"Yes, I see. Well, hopefully I managed to convince him not to pursue it any further. I figured you'd like to know."

"I certainly do. Well, I can't say I like it, but at least I know what we're up against. All right, now we've dealt with Nadiz, tell me about the *Lady Sybil*. When will she be ready to sail? Or will she?"

"Oh, she'll be seaworthy, right enough. We've already repaired the rudder. Once the mast is in place, we'll only need to hang the rigging again. We were lucky; we didn't lose any sails. We'll be ready by tonight."

"Could you stretch the work a bit if we needed? We still haven't decided quite how we're to get our hands on the ruby. Until we come up with a firm plan, we're a bit stymied. Extra time to complete repairs on the *Lady Sybil* might be the only way we can have a good excuse to stay."

Fanshawe grinned. "No problem there. Let me know, and I'll arrange it. It can take quite a while to hang rigging, you know."

"Good man. Come up to the tower tonight, and we'll discuss our plans a bit further. About nine bells?"

"All right, I'll be there. One thing, Commander."

Morgan raised his brows.

"I got a real bad feeling from Rashan," Fanshawe went on. "I don't know what his game is but watch your back. He's up to something. I don't think it's anything good."

"Thanks for the warning. I reckon I'd best get back before this Rashan causes any trouble. Let me know if you see him again."

"If I see him again," Fanshawe replied, "I won't let him come aboard."

Morgan considered this. "Nooo, best not do that. If you refuse to allow him on board, it will make him certain there's something dodgy going on. There is, of course. He just doesn't need to know it. If he comes back, show him around, sing the praises of the Parthanian workers, and send him on his way. Let him think we've nothing to hide."

He nodded. "Right, I see your point. Very well, if he comes back, he'll get the full tour. But if he happens to trip over a coil of rope and fall overboard, well, accidents can happen on a ship."

Morgan grinned. "Captain, I never heard you say those words."

With a nod, he took his leave. During the quick journey back to shore, his mind buzzed with questions he didn't have answers for. What the devil was Rashan after? How much time did they have left to steal the ruby? Would they even be able to penetrate Azim's security and get into the treasure chamber?

As usual, when Morgan was forced to deal with wizards, he felt completely out of his depth. Leading men into battle was much simpler.

All this conniving and skulking about just wasn't in his nature.

For conniving and skulking, he knew just where to go. It was, he decided, time to have a chat with Toniq.

Chapter Thirty-Two

Toniq, when Morgan found him, had the copy he'd sketched of the palace's plans spread across a table. The thief was totally absorbed in his work, muttering to himself and making little notes with a pencil. He paid no attention when Morgan entered the room.

He cleared his throat. Toniq made another mark on the plans, stuck the pencil behind his ear and faced him. With a nod toward the plans, Morgan asked, "Getting you anywhere?"

Toniq shrugged. "At least I have an idea where I'm going. Well, somewhat. I did a little trial run last night, just to get a feel for things. It won't be easy, but I think we'll at least be able get to the corridor leading into Azim's treasure room. Or at least the general vicinity. Once we're there, I'll be able to locate the hidden door, don't you worry."

"Once we're inside?"

The thief shrugged again. "Anyone's guess. There's no way to know what traps and defenses he's set up in the chamber itself. Based on what I've seen so far, I've no doubt they'll be nasty and tricky."

"Do you think you can get around them?"

"Only one way to find out, isn't there?" Toniq flashed an uncharacteristic grin. "If I can, we scarper the ruby and get out of here. If not, we'll probably all die a horrible death."

"Hmmm. Very comforting," Morgan muttered.

"Ah, don't fret, Commander. I'll manage it somehow. Then it'll be up to your lady witch to do her bit."

"Yes, her bit." Morgan chewed on his bottom hip, then gestured to the plans. "How much more time do you need? Any tools or supplies?"

"I brought my kit with me. I'm pretty well stocked with whatever I might need. As far as when? I can go anytime you say the word."

"Really?"

He grinned again. "You didn't think Taggart would saddle you with some halfwit amateur, now did you? You tell me to go, and I'll do my job, to the best of my abilities. Which, if I may boast a bit, are not inconsiderable."

"Fair enough." Morgan nodded. "All right, then. Keep your kit close and stick around. We may go sooner rather than later. I think the Parthanians are getting a bit suspicious about our little party. If we delay much longer, they may decide to do something about it."

Toniq smoothed down the plans, tracing his fingers lightly over them. "Tonight, you think?"

"I don't know. Stay ready. I'll give you as much advance notice as I can."

"I'll be ready." The thief reached under the table and drew forth a small pack. "I'm always ready."

And this, Morgan decided, was good enough.

An hour later, he'd finished listening to Marissa's account of her chat with Princess Saia.

"I don't like this place, Morgan," Marissa said. "I want to get this done and get away from here."

"The sooner, the better," he agreed. "You remember I told you about Azim's cousin, Nadiz Rashan? Well, he's begun to ask a few too many awkward questions about how we ended up here. Which might lead to him wondering just why we're here. He's been down to the *Lady Sybil* to try to pry information from Fanshawe. I'm not sure why he's developed such an interest, but I don't like it. He has the potential to become a problem for us."

She got up and walked to the window. Their tower room provided a panoramic view of the harbor. Storm clouds were gathering on the far horizon. She turned to face Morgan. "Why wait any longer?"

"Go on. I'm listening."

"Toniq says he's ready. Captain Fanshawe thinks the *Lady Sybil* will be seaworthy tonight. There's a storm on the way, which will give us cover for our escape. I've practiced my part until I can just about do it in my sleep, and both Nardis and I think I'm ready. It seems like all the pieces are in place. If we wait, well, your friend Nadiz may convince Azim we're up to something. If he manages to do so, Azim might decide to curtail our movements at best, or confine us at worst. I say we go tonight."

Morgan nodded. "You make a good case. Your points are spot on, and I agree. Very well. We go tonight. I'll go tell Toniq and Nardis. Fanshawe is supposed to come up at nine bells. We won't be able to go until much later, after the palace has gone to bed. It should give us plenty of time."

Marissa paced for a few moments. Finally, she said, "Before you rush off to alert the others, there's something I need to tell you."

"What's wrong? Are you all right? Has Azim done something?"

"No, no, I'm fine. Morgan, it's about the ruby."

"I'm beginning to wish," Morgan grumped, "I'd never heard about this blasted ruby."

"You and me both. But I got to wondering about some things. So I've been conferring with Wyvrndell. He and Sebastien have done some research and…"

He waited. She remained silent, still pacing. Finally, he asked, "What have you learned?"

"There's much more to this ruby than the Chief Wizard deigned to mention," she began. He listened with a growing sense of dread to what she, Wyvrndell, and Sebastien had managed to piece together. When she'd finished, Morgan McRobbie, who had faced death more times than he cared to remember, felt his blood run cold, for the first time ever.

With a little shudder, he stared at Marissa. "Good lord," he said quietly. "So, what do we do about it?"

Her eyes glittered with a fey light.

~ * ~

Morgan glanced around the room. His gaze was met by a phalanx of grim faces. "Any questions?"

Toby Fanshawe cocked his head. "What about me and my crew? We sail tonight?"

"The *Lady Sybil's* ready, isn't she?"

Fanshawe grinned. "Mast has been replaced. Good as new. Better, in fact. The rudder is fine. It only needed some new cabling. As for Azim's so-called navy? Bah! I've been watching them. There are no real sailors among his lot. They'd be lucky to even make it out of the harbor." His grin broadened. "If you give the word, I can make sure they don't."

"Mmm." Morgan considered. "It's tempting. Still, I'd rather not create any more problems for Rhys to have to deal with. If we were to sabotage their ships, it could be considered an act of war. Unless you feel it absolutely necessary, I say no."

"Oh, it won't be necessary," Fanshawe assured him. "We can outrun and outsail these lads going away. Besides, there's a storm brewing. It's still a couple of hours away, but it'll be here before you're ready to act. It'll help cover our departure. Even if they do come after us, they're not likely to make it very far in what's on the way."

"Thundermist?" Marissa asked.

Fanshawe nodded. A reckless gleam lit his eyes.

"You've no mist sails," she said.

"Well, Your Grace, it just so happens we do." Fanshawe flashed a piratical grin. "I nipped 'em off the *Mad Maudie*, right before she sailed. They are mine, after all. I paid for every yard of that canvas, along with the spells woven into them. They were stashed below decks on the *Lady Sybil,* in case we needed 'em. They're hung now, and we're ready to sail whenever you give the word."

Morgan leaned back and laced his fingers behind his head. Fanshawe raised a brow, and Morgan gave him a nod. "It sounds like you've got this under control, Captain. If you're certain you can get you and your crew out safely—"

"Commander, you're talking to the Scourge of the Thundermist Sea." The former pirate flashed a crooked grin. "If the Rhuddlanis couldn't catch me, good as they are... Well, this lot doesn't have a prayer."

"It would make our exit much easier," Marissa pointed out. "Fewer people to transport by, shall I say, less conventional means? It's not such a bad thing, don't you agree?"

"Nooo, it isn't," Morgan said. "Very well, Captain. Prepare the *Lady Sybil.* Quietly. We don't want the Parthanians to get the wind up if they see you getting ready to sail. They might start to ask questions I really don't want to answer quite yet."

"By your order, sir." Fanshawe tossed a casual salute. "I'll be ready to weigh anchor by midnight at the latest. Just give the word."

"Don't worry," Morgan said. "You'll know when."

Fanshawe flourished a bow to Marissa. "My lady," he murmured, and took his leave.

"You think he'll be all right?" she asked.

Morgan snorted. "Fanshawe? Are you joking? He loves this, can't you tell? He's still half pirate at heart. He'll wear the storm like a lady wears her cloak and leave the Parthanians so far in his wake they'll never be sure he was even there in the first place. I hope he gets home in one piece. If he manages, I've got plans for the *Lady Sybil.*"

"Do you, now? Well, enlighten me, oh man of mystery." She crinkled her nose.

Morgan found himself with a sudden urge to plant a kiss on its tip. Instead, he said, "She's going to get a new coat of paint, new fittings, and a new name."

Marissa raised a brow. "You've given this some consideration, I see. What's the new name? Dare I even ask?"

Suddenly mischievous, he grinned. "Well, for a while, I toyed with the notion of calling her *The Sea Witch...*" He cowered in mock terror as she skewered him with a fierce glare. "Then, I considered *The Royal Enchantress.*"

"Better," she muttered.

"In the end, I settled on *The Lady Marissa.*"

"Oh." She considered this, then beamed at him. "You are a romantic at heart, aren't you?" She bent to kiss him.

"Well, let's not get carried away," he said. "We still have to get out of here in one piece. With the blasted ruby."

"Pshaw. What could—"

He held up a hand. "Don't even say it. Let's not jinx things before we begin."

She sighed. "I suppose so. All right, it's getting late. Do you want to go over the plan again?"

"Probably wouldn't hurt," Morgan said.

"Good. While you're doing so, Nardis can help me practice my part one last time."

The young wizard, glanced up from where he'd been slouched in a deep armchair in the corner of the room. "Yes, let's."

Morgan halted his mental review of their plans to watch them. He hadn't seen her do much in the way of real magic, and he was curious. She closed her eyes in concentration, then took several deep, even breaths. She'd tried to explain about the need to center herself. He understood, at least a little bit. He often felt the same way before going into battle. To steady the nerves, reach inside, find the well of inner strength needed to do what must be done. He supposed it was similar.

Eyes still closed, she recited a series of arcane words. He didn't understand a bit of what she said. Honestly, he wasn't even sure what language she used. It didn't matter, at least not for him. What mattered was her. If she didn't get the incantation exactly right he knew, the whole operation would be for naught. He watched her with a mixture of pride and concern, willing the spell to work.

"Oh, look! I've done it," she exclaimed.

"Well done, my lady," Nardis said.

He sounded somewhat relieved. Morgan returned to his review. Over against the wall, a slight shimmer, like heat off a fire, caught his eye for an instant. He blinked, and it was gone again.

He smiled.

Chapter Thirty-Three

Thunder growled, distant but no less ominous for being so. "Thundermist?" Morgan wondered.

Marissa cocked her head to one side as she considered. "Yes," she said at last. "I can feel it. It's only a slight tingle, so it's still fairly far away. But yes, definitely Thundermist. All the better. For Captain Fanshawe, I mean."

"Oh, I'm not worried about him. The Scourge of the Thundermist Sea? He'll be fine. No, it's us I'm concerned about."

She shrugged one shoulder. "We'll manage somehow. Don't we always?"

"Your optimism," he said, as he wrapped Marissa in his arms, "is contagious."

"Well, good," she mumbled into his chest. "I just hope it isn't misplaced."

A jagged finger of lightning rent the sky, illuminating the darkened room. "It's almost time," he said. "Are you ready?"

She burrowed closer. "No. Well, yes, I am. As ready as I'll ever be, at any rate."

"As need requires," Morgan quoted. "It's your motto too, now. You've married into it, I'm afraid. We do the things that need to be done. And this, apparently, is one of the things that needs to be done. Bad luck for us, but there it is."

She flashed a wan smile. The storm had moved closer, and rain pelted against the window in a staccato tattoo. The clock tolled the hour: a single knell.

"We do what has to be done," she echoed. "Together?"

"Always," he assured her. "Shall we rouse the others and get started?"

She heaved a sigh from the vicinity of her boots. Squeezing his hand, she nodded. "Let's go."

He didn't move. "Before we do, I want to tell you…"

"Yes?" Her voice was a little breathless.

"…how very much I love you. Know this, no matter what happens tonight."

"Thank you," she said, smiling up at him. Her eyes were suspiciously moist. "I love you too, Morgan. There's no one I'd rather walk into danger with." She pulled him close and kissed him. Gently at first, then with an urgent ferocity. "That," she said finally, "is a promise. For later, when this is all over."

He grinned, his spirts suddenly buoyant. "Then let's get this job finished. I'm suddenly looking very much forward to later."

Hand in hand, they left the bed chamber. Morgan cast one last glance around. With luck, they'd never see this place again. Well, even if their luck ran sour, they wouldn't be returning to this room. They'd be in a dungeon cell, or dead.

Tearing his thoughts from this unhelpful and unpleasant reverie, he focused on the task ahead. In the sitting room, the rest of their little crew waited. Nardis, whose talents as a wizard might well come in handy. Alain, who would help guide them through the maze of the palace. Toniq, who would get them into the places they shouldn't be in. And, hopefully, out again.

All three men wore serious expressions. Keyed up and ready to go. Alain, though, appeared nervous. He kept picking up his pack, checking the contents, and setting it down again, only to catch it up once more. Well, he'd likely never done anything like this before.

Morgan gave the archivist a reassuring nod and a smile. The men stood and hefted their packs as another sizzle of lightning practically filled the room.

"Ready?" Morgan asked.

The three men nodded. He donned his own pack, then nodded to Marissa, who followed suit. They were only taking the bare essentials. In Marissa's case, this included the grimoire, in its little casket.

They were ready as they'd ever be to relieve Prince Azim of his illicit treasure. "Right, then. Let's be off."

Toniq held up a warning hand. "Wait a moment! Someone's coming," he hissed. "Guards."

Morgan sucked in a breath. "Toniq, you and Nardis go back to the servants' quarters. Marissa, you're in bed. Stuff Alain under the bed, or wherever you can. All of you, stash your packs out of sight. Move! Quietly."

They scattered. Morgan plopped himself in a chair just in time. Moments later, a sharp rap sounded on the door. "Wha?" he mumbled, giving himself the part of a man half in his cups. "Who's there?"

"Open this door at once." The voice from the other side gave the impression of brooking no nonsense or delays.

He stumbled to the door, managing to trip over a side table and send a decanter crashing to the floor.

"Open it now!" the voice commanded.

He fumbled with the latch, finally releasing it. He was nearly sent off his feet when the door was unceremoniously shoved open. Three burly guardsmen, scimitars drawn, strode into the room. Behind them, Nadiz Rashan strolled in, a lazy smile on his lips.

"Wha's all thish?" Morgan asked plaintively. "Tryin' to sleep, ya know. M'lady's abed. Keep it down, will ya, so's ya don' wake 'er."

"Duke McRobbie," Nadiz said. "I am here to place you under arrest for conspiracy against the sovereign city of Arvindir."

Morgan blinked muzzily. "Arrest? For trying to get some sleep? Silly bugger, come back in the morning."

"You can stop your games, McRobbie. I'm not sure exactly why you're here, but it's not by accident. You're up to something, I'm certain of it." Nadiz smiled wolfishly. "A few days in one of Azim's cells should encourage you to talk. They are most uncomfortable cells. Although they do have some, shall we say, 'creature' comforts."

"I've no idea what you're talking about," Morgan protested. "We're here by accident, blown up by the storm. You saw my ship. The mast was torn right off her."

"Yes, but now it's repaired, and your ship has sailed," Nadiz said. "In more ways than one."

"Sailed? What do you mean, sailed?"

"Gone, McRobbie. Now, come along quietly, I shouldn't like to get blood on the carpets. They can be so difficult to clean again. Take him," he instructed the guards.

Before they could act, the door to the bedchamber was flung open. Marissa strode out, clad in a voluminous dressing gown. It hid, if only barely, the hem of her long black traveling dress.

"Morgan, what on earth is going on out here?" she demanded. "You know I wanted to sleep, and here you're throwing a party. The nerve!"

She bore down on Morgan, fire in her eye. The guards edged away, seeming uncertain of their course without direction from Nadiz.

"And who the devil are these men?" she went on in full voice "Why on earth do they have swords? Is this to be another sword-dance or some such nonsense? Not at this time of night, gentlemen. I'll thank you all to leave right this minute."

Her voice and demeanor were so commanding, two of the guards put away their weapons and headed for the door before Nadiz could halt them. The third, evidently the leader, stood his ground, although his gaze darted back and forth between Marissa and Nadiz.

"Go back to bed, Duchess," Nadiz growled. "This does not concern you. I'm sure, once the duke is secured in a cell, Prince Azim will deal with you in a manner of his own choosing."

"Cell? Morgan in a cell? Are you mad?" She stared as she raised her hands to her mouth as if in shock.

As Morgan watched, she spoke a few quiet syllables, then spread her hands apart. A soft blue light flowed from them, directly toward Nadiz and the guards. Morgan dodged away from its path just in time to avoid being caught in the spell himself. When the light engulfed the four men, each gave a quiet sigh and slumped bonelessly to the floor.

She nodded in a mixture of surprise and satisfaction. "It worked."

Morgan laughed. "It did indeed. My love, you were magnificent. Most effective, as well. Four in one go. I'm impressed."

"Yes, well, I'm not sure how long they'll be out. We'd best get them sorted quickly."

"I hear and obey." He strode to the servants' quarters to fetch Nardis and Toniq back in. "Let's get this bunch trussed up and gagged," he said. "Use whatever you can find, but make sure they can't get loose, or cry out for help, for quite a while."

The two men, now joined by Alain, set to work to secure the sleeping prisoners.

"Well, now they've torn it," Morgan said to Marissa. "There's no way we can get away clean now. Not with four men tied up in our empty suite. Especially since one is the prince's cousin. Someone's bound to take notice. Not to mention umbrage."

"It might cause some comment," she agreed. "Although I never gave much credence to the notion we'd get away without anyone the wiser anyway."

"No," Morgan said. "Still, we should stick to the plan as much as possible. No need to alert anyone to exactly how we did—well, whatever we're going to do—and what our ultimate objective was. Agreed?"

"Agreed."

"We still have to get the jewel and get out of Arvindir. If we can do it before this lot gets free and sounds the alarm, I'll feel much better. I mean, even if Azim knows we took the ruby, he can't very well protest to Rhys, now can he? Not when he stole the damned thing in the first place."

"Where shall we stash the bodies?" Toniq asked.

"Um. They are still alive, aren't they?" Morgan asked.

"Oh, sure. I was merely speaking figuratively."

"How about in the bath chamber," Marissa suggested. "It's farthest from the doorway and pretty solid as well. Even if they manage to call out it might be a while before anyone hears them from in there."

"Do it," Morgan instructed his minions. He bent and grabbed Nadiz, who was bound hand and foot, then dragged him across the floor, making sure to bounce the Parthanian's head several times. Merely by accident, of course...

Once the four Parthanians were stored away in the bath chamber, Morgan rallied his team. "Grab your packs, take a deep breath, and let's move out."

When they were ready again, Toniq headed to the door. He listened for a moment, then opened it a scant inch and peered out. With a thumbs up gesture, he slipped into the passageway. Alain went next, then Nardis.

Marissa took a deep breath and followed after them. Morgan came last, pulling the door gently closed. He turned the key in the lock, then dropped it into the cover of a small, potted bush.

Candles in sconces, spaced along the walls, gave enough light to navigate the hall. From what Alain told them, there would be no such light once they left the residential wing.

Edgy but resolute, Alain led the way. Nardis strode next to him, back in his wizard's robe again, his staff in hand. Toniq followed a pace behind, out of Nardis's way in case the wizard needed to cast a defensive spell.

Marissa walked behind the thief. Her dress, so black it almost swallowed what light there was, swished gently over the rich carpets lining the passageway. Her soft soled boots, also black, made no noise as she walked. Morgan nodded in approval.

He brought up the rear, hand on his sword's hilt, ready to draw it at need. In his customary dusky black leathers, with a brace of daggers secreted on his person, he moved like a shadow. He checked behind them often. If anyone came up from behind, he'd have to silence them before an alarm could be raised.

A slight prickle on the back of his neck kept him scanning the rear. No one was visible. There was only a soft sigh, like a whisper of breeze through the leaves of a young tree. He smiled.

Chapter Thirty-Four

Steadily, they made their silent way through the palace's more populated sections. Due to the hour, no one else was abroad. After a seemingly endless series of twists and turns, Alain halted. They'd reached a cross passage, with darkened halls leading off both left and right. The archivist pointed left. Morgan nodded.

Nardis raised his left hand, uttered a soft word, and a little ball of light glowed softly in his hand. It was exactly like the ones Marissa practiced when she first started taking what she blithely termed "witching lessons" from Wyvrndell, Morgan noted with a quick smile. The light was faint, giving only enough illumination to guide their progress. The group tightened up as Nardis and Alain set off again.

Morgan prided himself on a healthy sense of direction, but after the seventh—or was it the eighth?—turn, he confessed himself completely lost. Without a map, or a guide, he could wander these twisty little passages forever and likely not find his way out.

Alain halted and held up his hand. He faced his companions. "We've reached the end of the unguarded halls," he whispered. "From here on, there are traps and wards in nearly every passage."

Toniq stepped forward now to join Nardis. "My turn," he said softly, as an eager light glinted in his eyes. "I've got the route pretty well memorized, and I know where the traps are lurking. Just remind me which way to go at the junctures, will you?"

He led the way, indicating to Nardis to keep back. Alain dropped back to walk beside Marissa. Morgan continued to bring up the rear, glancing behind every few moments.

Toniq paused when they reached the passage's halfway point and motioned for the others to remain still. Morgan watched the thief, whose feet moved with light, dancer's steps as he navigated his way around the first trap. Morgan tried to recall what they'd expected to encounter. *Oh yes, particular a stone set into the floor.* If stepped upon it would release a flight of deadly darts tipped with a particularly nasty poison.

Toniq signaled for more light. Nardis lifted his hand, to allow the ball of light to flare a bit brighter. Toniq studied the wall for a moment, pressed two stones at once, then nodded. He stepped quickly back to where Nardis waited, not bothering to watch where he placed his feet this time. No darts flew at him, and Toniq motioned for them to follow him.

He disarmed three more traps as they ventured deeper into the recesses of the palace. As he led them through another corridor, he suddenly stopped, flinging up a hand to halt the others. "No one move! There's a second trap here. This one wasn't on the plans. They added it afterwards."

"How can you tell?" asked Nardis, gazing around the dim corridor. "I don't see anything."

"I just know," Toniq said. "I've got a sense for these things. Trust me. Now stay back and let me figure this out."

The others clustered together, several paces behind Toniq, who carefully inspected the corridor ahead. Finally, he focused on a small section of the floor. "All right, see here," he said quietly. "Make sure to stay well away from this bit of stone." He pointed. "If you step on it, bad things will happen. Trust me, you don't want them to happen to you."

They each took turns edging around Toniq's dodgy bit of floor. When everyone was past it, he scanned ahead. "All right, we can move on," he said.

As they approached the corridor where, they hoped, Azim's treasure chamber lay, Morgan peered ahead into the gloom. If this had been his palace, he'd have posted guards there, despite all the traps and snares they'd encountered thus far. A good thief—and Toniq was very good, he allowed—could simply avoid or disable them. Morgan didn't think Azim the type who'd leave things like this to chance.

So, at the least, there ought to be something else in store for them. Something not on the plans, to deal with clever intruders. Barzak had said as much, and Morgan had made his own plans to counteract what he anticipated Azim's surprise to be. He hoped...

Ahead, Toniq halted again. He was barely visible now, merely a slightly lighter shadow among the other inky shadows in the passageway. Morgan could just make him out, scanning the corridor ahead for unseen dangers.

Toniq, evidently satisfied, waved his hand in a "come ahead" motion. As he did, dim lights flickered in the corridor ahead, winking in and out of sight. He stood rooted to the spot. The rest of the party, a bit behind him, edged back to where Morgan stood.

"W-what's happening?" Alain cried.

"Shhh!" cautioned Nardis, as he raised his staff. Toniq, backing slowly away from the increasingly visible lights, was breathing hard.

"It felt like something pressing against me," he reported. "Like—"

A low wail cut off his words. Morgan herded his team behind him, against the corridor's wall. The wails grew louder as the flickering lights increased in intensity. Morgan could glimpse, if only barely, forms in the lights, dim and spectral. The wails changed to moans as the forms coalesced into recognizable shapes.

"The ghost knights," Morgan breathed. "He was right."

"Who was right?" Marissa asked, as she stared up at the ghostly figures now ranged before them. She shuddered, and Morgan put an arm around her. The ghost knights blocked the entrance to Azim's treasure chamber.

"Barzak," Morgan muttered, as a voice boomed out.

"Who dares? Who dares defile these sacred halls?"

Nardis leveled his staff at the spectral guards. "*Vanisti!*" he cried. A burst of white light erupted from it, lancing into the spirits.

Instead of scattering, the ghostly knights seemed to absorb the power Nardis hurled at them. They swelled larger than before, and a mocking laugh rang out to fill the passageway.

"A paltry effort, wizard," boomed one of the specters. "Canst thou not do better than this? 'Twas only a tickle."

Nardis's eyes were wide in shock. "It should have destroyed them," he said through clenched teeth. Morgan could hear a tremor of fear in his voice.

Marissa stepped forward. "Let me try," she said, and before he could protest, she lifted her hand, crying "*Luminas acciato!*" The fiery sword he'd seen her wield against Augustus Rhenn blossomed into being.

The ghost knights, wary at this new threat, floated back slightly. She advanced on them, her mystic weapon held high. "Begone from here," she ordered, "lest I smite thee."

A hissing sound filled the corridor, echoing off the walls. Marissa took another step toward the spectral guards. Most edged back further but one, larger than his companions, stood his ground. Contempt was plain to see on his ghostly visage.

"So, witch," he thundered. "Thou wouldst smite me, eh? Very well. Smite, then, and have done."

"Don't!" Morgan called. He was too late.

Goaded thus, she swung her flame-tipped blade. The ghost knight raised his own spectral weapon, a curved scimitar that shone with a silvery glow. The two blades met, warm gold and cold silver, in a crashing shower of sparks.

Marissa gave a surprised grunt as the ghost knight's sword parried her attack. She swung her golden sword again. Her adversary blocked the blow with a casual flick of his own weapon.

"Oh," she said weakly. The ghost knight regarded her with distain.

"A puny bit of smiting," he observed, snapping his fingers at her in contempt. "Here, I will show you some true smiting." He hefted his silvery scimitar. It gleamed with cold, terrible fire.

The ghost knight advanced on Marissa. She retreated, scuttling back before his advance. The spirit laughed, an ugly mocking sound that reverberated off the stone walls in a cacophony of contempt.

Nardis moved forward to stand by Marissa and pointed his staff towards the ghost knights. Though it was his own place by right, Morgan kept behind them. His more earthly weapon would be no use against the spirit's.

"Take him," Morgan urged Nardis from between teeth clenched in frustration.

"*Varistas!*" The wizard cried, and once more power lanced from his staff toward the spectral guard.

The scimitar, cleaving through the air, was deflected by the force of Nardis's strike. It turned just enough to miss Marissa where she stood, transfixed.

Morgan darted forward. He grabbed her and dragged her out of range of the ghostly weapon. "Down!" he shouted to the others as he and Marissa tumbled painfully to the stone floor.

"Now!" he cried. "Sir Jamie, to me!"

A sound like a rushing wind filled the passageway. Then the thud of marching feet manifested, and the forms of men, translucent at first, materialized before them. They shimmered and flickered, as the ghostly guards had done, rapidly gaining solidity. A full dozen strong, garbed in translucent crimson tunics blazoned with the Kilbourne emblem, ranged themselves about Morgan and his companions. Each bore a sword or pike, and the corridor was filled with their voices.

"Aye, lads, to me. Let's rout these fellers," cried their leader. He charged the ghostly defenders, with his company close behind.

Sparks flared like fireflies in the dark as spectral sword met sword. The defenders, also a dozen strong, met the attack. They maintained their line at first. Snarls and curses echoed around the hallway. Morgan held his bride tightly, away from the spectral combatants, as the battle grew heated.

"Where did they come from?" Marissa's eyes were wide as she watched the melee. "How—?

"I thought we might need some reinforcements," Morgan said, as he edged them away from a pair of spectral boots.

"Who are they? What are they?" Her gaze shifted between him and the spectral knights, with dawning comprehension. "Is one, um, our ghost?"

"Well, yes, now you mention it." He grinned. "Since we were taking over the house, I felt it only proper to introduce myself. As Sir Jamie seemed a decent sort, when Rhys and Foxwent dumped this mess in our laps, I asked if he might like to round up a few friends and accompany us on this little venture."

"And you never told me?" Her voice was thick with accusation.

Sparks flared above their heads. Sir Jamie and his squad, Morgan observed, appeared to have the upper hand against Azim's ghost knights. "I wasn't sure you'd believe me," Morgan told her as Sir Jamie's sword cleaved the captain of the ghost guards in twain. "I wasn't sure I believed it myself. Plus, I didn't want you to worry they might be watching us at night on the voyage here."

"Oh," was her only response. Morgan was fairly certain he caught her blush a fierce red.

"Sir Jamie assured me they'd keep well clear," he went on. He wasn't sure she was convinced. Honestly, he wasn't sure he was convinced himself. But there was no help for it now.

Sir Jamie and his squad mopped things up. As Morgan watched them, the spirits of Kilbourne dispatched the last of the ghostly guards, who faded slowly from sight with moans and sighs. Sir Jamie sheathed his sword and floated over to Morgan, who stood and helped Marissa to rise.

Bowing to the ghost, Morgan said, "Sir Jamie. Well done indeed."

"'Twas naught," replied the ghost with a satisfied grin. "Most excitement the lot of us have had in a century or so." He sketched an elegant bow to Marissa. "My lady."

"Sir Jamie, allow me to present Marissa duB—um, McRobbie, Duchess Westdale. She is the new mistress of McRobbie House."

Marissa presented a perfect curtsey to the ghost. "Well met, Sir Jamie. I am charmed to make your acquaintance. Your timely intervention was most welcome. You have my heartfelt thanks."

"It was our pleasure to lend aid in your time of need," replied the ghost. Morgan was sure the specter's eyes twinkled.

"Did you slay those other ghosts?" Marissa asked.

"I'm afraid not," Sir Jamie replied. "Only inconvenienced them for a bit, you might say. They'll pull themselves together again. Don't know how long it'll take 'em, though. Whatever you're doing, you might best get on with it before they do."

"Your point is well taken," Morgan said. We'll get right to it. Thank you for your assistance. We couldn't have managed without you."

"Well," the ghost said, swelling a bit with obvious pride. "Hem, yes, guess we'll be off then, eh?"

"An excellent plan. Back to the ship, if you please." Morgan gave the ghost a crisp salute.

Sir Jamie returned it, although his hand went through his head slightly. Then he waved to his squad. They formed up in precise, if wavy, ranks, then swiftly faded from sight.

"Why back to the ship?" Marissa asked.

"They evidently can't travel over water on their own," Morgan replied. "At least, not very far. Now, where's Toniq?"

The thief, who had watched the vanishing specters with unveiled interest, turned at the sound of his name. "I'm ready," he said.

Nardis provided more light, and Alain directed them into the corridor where the treasure chamber lay.

"I'd say this was familiar," Morgan muttered, "except one corridor is just like every other in this blasted place."

Marissa patted his shoulder. Toniq examined a section of the wood-paneled wall closely. Drawing a roll of cloth from his pack, he unfurled it to reveal an assortment of steel implements.

Toniq directed Nardis to hold the light where he wanted it. A tiny keyhole was revealed. The thief deftly probed the opening with one, then another of his tools. When he inserted the third one, he gave a satisfied nod.

As he twisted, it. something sizzled and hissed. Toniq jerked his hand away, wringing it in pain. The steel sliver glowed red, and wisps of smoke rose from the keyhole.

"Warded," Toniq growled. He wrapped the hem of his tunic around his hand, then grabbed the lockpick and yanked it free. It dropped to the stone floor, where it landed with a "plink."

Nardis passed his hand over the lock. "A simple ward, though none the less effective for it. If any except the correct key is inserted, it triggers the ward. You're lucky you got away as easy as you did."

The thief, blowing on his singed fingers, scowled. "I didn't sign on to get my hand scorched off," he said. "I shan't try that again."

"Alain, is this the only way in?" Morgan asked

"To the best of my knowledge. I've never heard of a second entrance, but that's not to say the prince didn't add something later. I'm afraid I'd have no idea where to even begin to look."

"No, of course not," Marissa said. "Nardis, is there any way you can deactivate or counter the spell on the lock?"

"Exactly what I've been trying to work out," replied the wizard. "It should be possible." He closed his eyes in concentration, then passed his hand over the lock once again. "If I can feed enough power into the lock, it should overwhelm the ward, and—"

Toniq shook his head. "No, you can't. You'll turn the lock into a useless lump of melted slag. I've heard about this problem before. We need the lock to be able to open, or we might as well go home now."

"We also need it to close again," Morgan put in. "We're supposed to do this undetected. Leaving a burnt-out lock behind doesn't exactly say undetected."

"What if," Marissa said, "we don't worry about the lock at all?"

"There's not another way in," Alain protested. "At least not one we know of."

"No, I don't mean another way in. What if, instead of mucking about with the lock, we counter-warded the lockpick?"

"M'yes, I see." Nardis brightened. "It should be fairly simple. I think. Toniq, let me see the pick, will you?"

The thief retrieved the bit of steel from where he'd let it drop to the floor. "It's cool enough now," he reported. He handed it over.

Nardis took it, turning it over and over in his hand. He stroked the pick with his long fingers, then uttered a spell in a low voice. When he opened his hands, the pick glowed with a faint silver light.

He handed the pick back to Toniq. "The spell should prevent the pick from absorbing any more heat from the ward on the lock. But don't dawdle. I'm not sure how long it will last."

"I won't need long," Toniq replied.

He probed the lock; in moments there was a sharp click. A door, cleverly concealed in the wall, opened a scant few inches, allowing a faint light from within to limn the edges. Toniq pulled his pick free and pulled the door fully open.

Marissa started forward, but the thief held up a hand to forestall her. "Wait," he said. "There still may be more traps inside. Let me go first."

She moved back to rejoin Morgan, then gestured for Toniq to precede her into the treasure room. To keep her from darting in before Toniq ensured the room was safe to enter, Morgan grasped her hand in his.

With an insouciant wave, the thief dived headlong through the opening. He rolled and came up quickly on his feet. From inside the room came an ominous rumble. A large chunk of stone, studded with deadly spikes, dropped sharply to the floor.

Chapter Thirty-Five

"Ugh." Marissa shivered. "If I'd walked through the door..."

"You'd have been quite well ventilated," Morgan finished. He pulled her close, squeezing her tightly. "Well, so much for undetected. Even if we didn't have those chaps locked up in our rooms, Azim would certainly realize someone has been here."

"Nothing to be done about it now," Marissa said.

She watched as Toniq inspected the room. He gave the all-clear sign, and Morgan led his band of thieves into Azim's treasure room. He hadn't had much chance to do more than take a quick glance around in his previous brief visit. While Marissa conferred quietly with Nardis, Morgan took time to survey the chamber now.

Gold glittered and sparkled from every visible surface. Crowns, goblets, coins, and daggers, all made from gold, many encrusted with precious jewels, were displayed along the walls. In the room's center, glinting evilly in the flicker of torchlight, rested the Demon's Fire ruby.

Morgan stepped toward the jewel. It was, as he'd been told, about the half the size of his closed fist. Considering it only as a jewel, it was enormous. And enormously valuable in and of itself.

Not to mention exceedingly dangerous. Simply for its monetary value, there were far too many men who wouldn't hesitate to kill to obtain such a prize. It was also dangerous, even more so, in light of what it contained. A thousand or more demons?

He looked at the jewel again and shuddered at the thought. Truth be told, he didn't want Marissa anywhere near the blasted thing. Or himself, for that matter. With a fierce scowl he gave his attention back to Marissa and Nardis.

She had begun to chant. Her face was lined with concentration, and her nose was scrunched up in the adorable way it often did when she was under stress. Arcane words, unfamiliar to Morgan, fell from her lips. Words taught her by Wyvrndell: the spell she'd need to create the required illusion.

In her cupped hands rested a small ruby, winking red in the light. Compared to the one they'd come to retrieve, it was so tiny as to be nonexistent. She spoke, and Morgan observed a vague haze form around her, power gathered to her in a barely visible shimmer. Nardis waited close by, watching, ready to lend his own power should Marissa falter.

She didn't falter. As she chanted the words of the dragon-wrought spell, the ruby in her hand began to glow. Softly at first, then brighter, its intensity increased, and the gem grew steadily larger. What began as little more than a tiny pebble soon swelled to double its size. It continued to expand, until it almost filled her cupped hands.

Her face tight, eyes squeezed closed, she poured more power into the spell. The ruby she held was huge now, nearly the size of its mate which rested on the plinth nearby.

"Easy now, you're close," Nardis cautioned.

Marissa opened her eyes, blinking in apparent surprise at the size of the stone in her hands. She breathed heavily for a moment as she centered herself for the last of her task. Resting the jewel in one hand, she passed her other hand over its top.

"*Fini*," she said. The ruby glowed again, in a brilliant crimson flash. It subsided, and she sagged.

Morgan hastened to her side, taking her arm to steady her.

"Thanks," she murmured. She straightened her shoulders and held up the ersatz ruby to compare it with the original.

"It's not identical," Toniq critiqued. "But close enough to pass a cursory examination. Unless someone looked very carefully, they'd likely never notice it wasn't the same stone. Handy trick, I have to say. Have you ever considered..." He noted Morgan's glower and grinned. "Well, it was just a thought."

"Have you checked the plinth for traps?" Morgan asked him. "Is it safe to switch the jewels?"

Toniq shrugged. "As far as I can tell, yes. Perhaps your tame wizard there might want to give it a go."

Nardis bared his teeth. He stepped to the plinth and circled round it, palms outstretched, as if feeling for an invisible barrier. He moved closer and passed right over the Demon's Fire.

The wizard froze, panic flashing across his dark face. "The ruby," he whispered. "It's warded."

Toniq was at his side in an instant, eyes gleaming. "Tell me," he ordered. "Anything you can sense. Any detail might be important."

He was now truly engaged, for the first time since they'd begun this venture. This, Morgan realized, was what the thief lived for: the sheer thrill of outwitting his adversaries. The attraction wasn't so much the things he stole. It was more the desire to win. This was why they'd included Toniq on the team.

Nardis frowned. "It seems to be—" he passed a hand over the ruby again, then furrowed his brow. "No, I'm wrong. The jewel itself isn't warded. I think it's the plinth. I think as long as the weight on the plinth remains constant, nothing happens. If the weight is removed...Well, I'm not exactly sure what will happen. I don't think we really want to find out."

"So, nothing should happen if the jewel is touched?" Toniq pressed.

"I don't think so." Nardis blinked rapidly. "I—"

"I think you're right," he said. "I've run across something like this before. Devious, but not unbeatable. If the jewel itself was the trigger, then we'd have a problem."

"How long will it take?" Morgan asked. "We don't have a lot of time here."

"Not long." Toniq grinned. He was in his element, Morgan realized, and they were merely onlookers who needed to let him do the job he was trained for, and not joggle his elbow.

A rumble of thunder shook the room. Toniq's grin broadened. "Perfect," he said. "Timing is everything."

He rummaged through his pack and produced a coil of fine cord, gossamer thin, more like spider's silk than woven material. More thunder sounded, louder this time. Several of the objects in the room shook slightly on their display stands.

Including the ruby. The plinth was tall and slim, about four feet in height, its supporting column of serpents no more than five or six inches in diameter. Only the base of lions' claws, and the top on which the jewel rested, were larger.

"Is this thing solid?" Toniq asked Marissa. He pointed to the duplicate ruby in her hands.

"Yes, of course." She offered him the jewel.

Toniq tossed it in his hand appraisingly to judge its heft, then nodded once. He eyed the Demon's Fire, comparing the two.

"The ward on the plinth can't be very exact," he said, "or all the rattling around the jewel does in a storm like this would trigger it. So..." He handed the fake ruby back to Marissa, then scanned overhead. High above, long beams ran across the chamber's width, supporting the rafters. "Ah, better and better," he crowed. "They've practically made this just for me."

Uncoiling his cord, he tied a small weight to one end. Morgan comprehended what he was about to do as Toniq whirled the weight around in a quick circle and let it fly.

The weight, with the cord trailing behind, soared up. It struck a beam and didn't quite make it over. Toniq caught the weight one-handed as it fell and sent it twirling round and round again in an instant. This time it sailed up and over the beam. Keeping a grip on the loose end, Toniq stepped over to catch the weight.

"Now what?" Marissa asked, intrigued.

"Now comes the fun part," Toniq replied, his eyes dancing with glee. "Bring the ruby you made over here, please."

The room shook once more as thunder rent the night. The ruby trembled slightly on its perch. Toniq untied the weight from his cord and slipped it back into his pack. He withdrew two small nets, each made of even finer material than the cord. The plinth rocked again as thunder rolled.

Toniq pointed to Morgan and Nardis. "I need you two," he said. The wizard raised his brows in Morgan's direction. He gave a decisive nod.

"What you're going you need to do," the thief told them, "is to gently—very gently, mind—rock this plinth, like the thunder has been doing. Not enough the shake the jewel off, just enough to move it around a bit."

Morgan saw where he was headed. "Got it." To Nardis, he said, "He wants to slip his little net under the jewel while we rock the plinth."

"Right." Nardis nodded his understanding. Together they crouched next to the plinth. Each placed his hands on it.

"Now," Toniq directed. The two men gently rocked the plinth.

Above their heads, the jewel trembled slightly. Though Toniq's hands weren't visible to him, Morgan was pretty certain he could envision what was happening.

"A bit more," Toniq directed. "Um, not quite so hard, we don't want the damned thing to roll right off."

A bead of sweat rolled down Nardis's face, ending up on the tip of his nose. Morgan could feel his own perspiration forming on his neck and forehead. Not from exertion, but from the tension of the moment, as they attempted to rock the stand just the right amount to give Toniq what he needed.

"Got it," Toniq said.

Morgan's hands dropped from the plinth an instant before Nardis's did. Carefully they stood to see what the thief had done.

The gossamer netting rested under the Demon's Fire. It weighed less than nothing, a mere whisper of breath. Not enough to trigger the trap. Toniq laced more fine cord through the net's ends, then drew it gently upwards to form a pouch around the gem.

When he was done, he tied one end of the cord stretched over the rafter to the pouch. With the other piece of webbing, he formed another pouch around the fake ruby Marissa created. He pulled the long cord snug, though not tight enough to shift the Demon's Fire. He ran the other end through the ersatz ruby's pouch. He didn't tie off the end yet. A bit of judicious measurement ensued. Toniq's bottom lip was caught in his teeth as he eyed the two gems and calculated.

"How are your hands?" he asked Morgan.

"You're mad," Morgan said. "Brilliant, but mad." He grimaced. "I reckon they're not bad."

"All right, then, you get to play catcher," the thief told him. "Move about two feet to the left..." He pointed, and Morgan stepped into position, stopping where Toniq told him to.

"It's going to come fast. Whatever you do, don't drop it."

"Right." Morgan readied himself, hands outstretched.

Toniq moved directly opposite him, holding the fake ruby in its webbed cradle.

"Test run," he said. He moved the jewel in his hand on its string toward the one on the plinth. He frowned, adjusted the length a fraction, then repeated his movements. This attempt elicited a fierce smile.

"We're ready to play skittles," he announced. To Morgan, he said, "When you catch it—not if, when—raise the jewel up a bit. There can't be any tension at all on your end. Got it?"

"Right."

"Good. Here we go, on three. One. Two. Three!" Toniq sent his jewel-laden pouch sailing on its string, toward where the Demon's Fire rested on the plinth. The fast-moving jewel collided with its stationary twin with a sharp crack and sent the Demon's Fire flying toward Morgan.

A momentary panic seized him. If he missed... Toniq's aim was true, and the ruby flew straight at Morgan. He fielded the jewel perfectly, raising it slightly, as Toniq had directed.

The fake jewel, when it collided with the real one, stopped dead, to rest on the plinth right where the original had been.

No one moved. They all waited for the ward to activate, for all hell to break loose. For Azim and his guards to swoop down and seize them.

Thunder rumbled. Someone heaved out a breath. Morgan was pretty certain it wasn't him. He wasn't about to breathe until the Demon's Fire was secured and the replacement firmly in its place.

Toniq was a blur as he untied the cord and whisked the little net from beneath the fake ruby resting on the plinth.

"Much easier off than on," he commented cheerfully.

Taking the real jewel from Morgan, he untied the cord. Then he pulled on the cord until the other end was over the rafter and slithered down to the floor. Toniq had it coiled and stowed away in his pack in seconds. He handed the jewel to Marissa.

"All right, let's get out of here," he said.

"Not so fast," said a voice from the door.

Chapter Thirty-Six

Everyone froze.

"What are you doing here?" Princess Saia stepped into the treasure chamber's dim light. Her eyes were wide with a combination of fear and fury.

"Saia," Marissa said, moving toward the princess. "It's not..." She halted as the princess's fierce gaze came to rest on the ruby clutched in Marissa's hand.

"But...you have Azim's ruby," she squeaked. "What are you doing with it? I must summon the guards." She took a deep breath.

In an instant, Morgan clapped a hand over her mouth. Saia's intended shriek emerged instead as a muffled grunt and gasp. She writhed in his grip like a serpent. He managed, barely, to hold her tight.

Marissa kept her voice measured. "Princess Saia, listen to me."

The princess halted in mid-struggle. She'd been focused on an attempt to kick Morgan's shins; a rather futile effort, since he was clad in sturdy boots, while she wore soft slippers. Marissa fixed her gaze on the princess and repeated, "Listen to me."

He had never heard this tone in her voice before. She spoke, not in entreaty, but with authority. A command, rather than a request. With the force of her will behind it, perhaps? He supposed he shouldn't be surprised. Still, he wondered for a wild instant what this might portend later, for him, as her husband. Well, this wasn't the time to worry about it.

Saia was stilled now, her gaze locked on Marissa, who said, "Morgan, you may release Her Highness. She will not do anything rash. Will you, Princess? You will listen to me, won't you? We are, after all, sisters, after a fashion."

Morgan raised a brow. Marissa shot him a quick nod. He released Saia. The diminutive princess took in a lungful of air, choked on it, then straightened to glare at Marissa.

"Sisters?" she snapped. "I think not. But I will listen to your explanation of this... this travesty. You can tell me why you've done this. Did you come all the way to Arvindir simply to steal Azim's prized jewel?"

Marissa smiled. "Azim's ruby? Hardly, Saia. This jewel belongs to Kilbourne's wizards. Your brother came to Caerfaen, on the day of my nuptials, to steal it from them. We were sent to retrieve it."

"No!" Saia recoiled. "He would never..."

Marissa let loose a bitter laugh. "Wouldn't he? You know full well Azim takes what he desires. Don't you, Princess? You told me yourself. Like he attempted to steal my power from me. He would have succeeded and left me an empty shell. Only your intervention forestalled his designs, Saia. You know this is true."

The princess shrank at Marissa's words, and her gaze turned inward. Her voice was small, almost childlike, as she said, "He wants power. Always, more magic, more power." She focused her stare on Marissa once more. "This thing, this jewel. It contains much power?"

"Unimaginable," she said. "In the wrong hands, extraordinarily dangerous power. This is why we were sent to retrieve it. I don't know if your brother quite understands exactly what he's got here. If not, well, best he not muck about with it and unleash something dreadful."

"And if he does know?" Saia asked.

Marissa folded her arms across her chest. "If he does know? Then not only is he a fool and a scoundrel, he's also a monster, bent on destruction. It doesn't matter right now. Either way, he can't be allowed to keep this." She held up the jewel. "And we have to go now, before anyone discovers us. Before anyone else discovers us," she amended with a smile.

Now it was Saia who folded her arms, a sullen expression tinging her face. "No!" she snapped.

Marissa paused, the ruby halfway into her pack. "No? So, you would summon the guards after all? Subject us to your brother's wrath? Allow him to unleash this thing upon the world?"

The princess's eyes shone with a fey light. "My brother? Pah? Azim gives himself airs. This will show him he is not so great, not so powerful, as he imagines himself."

Marissa's face was a mask of confusion. Morgan didn't blame her. "Should I grab her again?" he asked quietly.

She ignored him. "What, then?" she asked the princess.

"I will allow you to leave this room, unchallenged, on one condition." Saia set her head at a cocky angle.

"What condition?"

Morgan interrupted. "Marissa, we don't have a lot of time here…"

She shushed him with a distracted wave. "What condition?" she repeated.

"You must take me with you."

"Of course," Marissa replied instantly.

"Absolutely not!" growled Morgan. "Marissa…"

"Don't mind him, he gets grumpy," she said, throwing a fond glance his way even as she hurried to Saia. As she took the princess into her embrace, she said, "We do need to get away from here quickly. How soon can you be ready?"

Saia hugged her back. "Thank you. There is nothing for me here, sister. I can leave at once."

"I've got a really bad feeling about this," Morgan muttered. Nardis grinned broadly. Toniq merely rolled his eyes.

"Nonsense," Marissa said. "What could possibly go---"

"Don't say it!" All three men spoke in chorus. Alain's gaze shifted back and forth between them as if they were mad.

"All right, all right." She flapped a hand at them. "What are you lot standing about for? Let's go." Hand in hand with Saia, she led the way toward the door.

From out in the corridor, Morgan heard the sound of booted feet. A small squad, in a hurry. "Company," he announced. "Alain, which way out?"

"Uh. Through that door. It's the only way out." He pointed in the direction of the hurrying boots.

"No," Saia said. "Close the door. Quickly!"

"We'll be trapped in here," Morgan protested.

"Close the door," she insisted. "There is another way out. A secret way. Azim had it put in. He thinks he is the only one who knows about it." Her smile was grim.

He slammed the door and bolted the latch. "Lead on, Princess. We're in your hands." *And I hope to God Marissa knows what she's about.*

"This way." Saia hastened toward the dimly lit rear of the chamber. "If I can just find the latch…"

"Um," he swallowed a curse. "If?"

"It's here somewhere," she said. "I only found it by accident. Azim left it ajar one day, and I saw." She fumbled at the wall's panels, hands scrabbling desperately.

"Would some light help things any?" asked Nardis. He held up his hand and summoned the now familiar ball of light to chase away the shadows.

Saia nodded her thanks as she continued her tactile search along the wall. "I know it was... ah, here." She pressed an inconspicuous knothole. With a little creak, a section of the wall inched open.

"There are guards in the corridor," Toniq said quietly. "Three. I can hear them breathing."

Morgan placed his hand on his sword. "Well, I guess there's nothing for it. We'll have to fight our way out."

"No," Saia said. "Leave this thing to me." Without waiting for an acknowledgement, she pushed open the secret door and stepped through, closing it firmly behind her.

"Princess?" Morgan heard a guard say, bewilderment evident in his tone.

"I have checked this chamber thoroughly." The princess's voice was clear and strong. "There is no one in there. If there was anyone, they must have already gotten away. You may go now."

"But our orders—" stammered the guard.

"Your orders," Saia snapped, "which you have received from me, are to rejoin your squad in the other corridor. You may go now."

"Your Highness..."

"Do you like your head attached the way it is?" The princess's voice was as cold and hard as the corridor's stones. "Because if you aren't gone by the time I count to two, we can see how you manage without it. One..."

Morgan grinned at the sound of a mad scramble as the guards hustled double-time down the corridor. After a few moments, a quick knock on the panel sounded the all clear. Toniq, who'd evidently been using his eyes when the princess opened the panel earlier, pressed the knothole. The door inched open once more.

"Hurry," Saia urged. "They've listened for now. Their captain is no fool, though; he may become suspicious. We need to be gone by then." She grabbed Marissa's hand and led her along.

"Princess," Morgan said urgently as he dashed after them. "We need to get to the tower. The one where Azim and you took us, when we flew on the carpets."

Saia stopped so suddenly Marissa caromed into here. "The...the tower?" She stared in astonishment at him. "Not to the docks, to your ship?"

"Already sailed," Marissa said cheerfully. "We've, um, arranged other means of transport."

"You plan to use Azim's carpets?" Saia demanded, incredulously. "You can't. Azim is the only one who can make them fly."

Marissa shuddered. "No, not the carpets. We have…other plans. But we must get to that tower."

The princess shook her head bemusedly. "Very well, the tower it shall be. I certainly hope you know what you're about."

"So do I," Morgan muttered darkly. "So do I."

Candles in sconces illuminated this section of the palace. Nardis extinguished his spell to conserve energy. Soon they reached a junction, where hallways branched dimly left and right. Saia headed left without hesitation. Halfway down the passage, a stairway led upwards. Morgan stayed back as the others hurried up, following the princess's lead. He held his breath as he strained to catch the sounds of pursuit.

Silence reigned. With a satisfied nod, he trotted up the stairs.

Saia led them up, and up, and up. "I've got to get back into training," Morgan groused to himself as his legs began to burn from the climb.

He didn't dare think how the others fared. Right now, it really didn't matter. They had no choice. To stop now would mean capture and imminent death. At best, a quick death. Somehow, Morgan didn't think Azim was the type to allow quick deaths. No, they would be prolonged, painful, and dreadfully messy. Silently, Morgan vowed to do everything in his power to prevent their capture. He had weapons, and skill at arms. And a witch and a wizard, he reminded himself with a grim smile. Potent weapons indeed. In the meantime, they needed to continue to the tower. Their only means of escape from Arvindir lay at its pinnacle.

"How much further?" gasped Marissa.

"Down this next passage," Saia said. "The entrance to the tower is there. Then we must climb to the top." She broke off, panting, and halted to stare into Marissa's eyes. "I suppose you do want to all the way to the top, don't you?"

"Not want to. Must. It's the only way we can get out of Arvindir."

"And we'd best hurry," Morgan interjected. "I think I hear the guards after us."

"They're not close yet," Toniq put in. "They probably won't be long. They can move much faster than we can."

Saia huffed out a sigh and led them down the corridor. At the end a door, closed and foreboding, blocked their exit. She tried the latch, but the door remained shut. The way was barred.

"This door is never locked," she protested. "I've come here a thousand times."

Toniq unrolled his little pouch and selected a tool. "Allow me," he said as he brushed past the princess.

Morgan kept an eye to their rear while the thief worked. Toniq discarded the first bit of steel, selected another, and probed the lock again. In the distance, booted feet pounded on stone cobbles.

"Nardis," he called quietly. "Is there any way you can create a veil here to make it appear the corridor is empty?"

"Nice." The wizard flashed him a grin.

He stared at the door for a moment as if to fix the details of it in his mind. He stepped next to Morgan and spread his hands wide. Speaking softly, he uttered the words of his spell. Morgan's view down the passageway shimmered and blurred.

"It's not perfect," Nardis said. "And it won't last long. If they come close, they'll manage to see through it. From a distance, it should suffice."

"Perfect. Quiet, everyone," Morgan hissed.

Toniq continued to attack the lock, his face a mask of concentration. Alain stood near the princess now, an expression of adoration on his face. Saia flashed him a brief smile.

From the passage's far end, a voice called, "Looks empty down here."

Morgan breathed a sigh of relief. It was short lived; another voice said, "That way leads to the tower. Best go check it out. Make sure the door is secured."

"Damn their efficiency." Morgan peered over Toniq's shoulder. "Not to rush you or anything, but now would be a really good time…"

"Got it!" crowed the thief. He yanked open the door.

"Go!" urged Morgan, shooing his little band into the stairwell. He held Toniq back. "Lock it again," he whispered.

The thief looked startled at first, then nodded in comprehension.

"I've killed the veil," Nardis muttered in Morgan's ear.

Toniq eyed the lock, inserted his slim strip of steel, and twisted. The lock snicked quietly closed. Morgan urged him and Nardis upward as the door rattled.

"It's locked tight, sir," the guard called.

"All right, good," came the reply. "I didn't really fancy climbing all the way up the blasted tower. Let's go."

Morgan held his breath until he heard their boots in retreat down the passage before he fled quietly up the stairs. "Now," he muttered under his breath, "would be an excellent time to arrive."

"We're on the way," came a mental reply.

Morgan allowed a grim smile to play across his mouth. With a little more luck, they might make it out with their skins intact.

And with the ruby, he added. Then his treacherous mind

amended, *and with the princess*. Morgan winced. Rhys would not be one little bit happy about this development. It was, politically speaking, a nightmare in the making.

It didn't matter. There was no chance Morgan could dissuade Marissa. If Saia wanted to come with them, then come with them she would. He was forced to admit, she'd been much more help than hindrance thus far. They wouldn't have even escaped the treasure room without her knowledge—and her courage.

He quickened his pace, hurrying to catch up with the others. The climb felt endless. He recalled their previous visit with Azim and how high they'd been as they'd gazed down over the city. Part way up was no good; it was the top, or nothing. He slogged on, step after endless step.

He smelled fresh air before he caught sight of the rest of the group. Saia had opened the door to the parapet, and she and Marissa were just outside, under the inky, rain-spattered darkness. Alain and Nardis followed. As Morgan came up the last couple of stairs, Toniq waited just outside the door.

"Go on," Morgan urged.

Toniq shook his head. "I'm not coming with you, Commander."

"What?" Morgan jerked to a halt and stared at the thief. "Why ever not?"

"There's nothing for me back in Caerfaen." Toniq shrugged. "Anyway, I rather like it here. Think I'll take a little holiday."

"Toniq, they'll find you up here."

Toniq grinned as he hauled a rope from his pack. "No, they won't. I'll be fine. Trust me, I'll be long gone before any guards show up." He quickly tied grappling hooks to the rope's end, then attached the hooks firmly on one of the pillars lining the tower's edge. He tossed the other end over the parapet. "Thanks for a most interesting experience, Commander. Farewell." With a jaunty wave, the thief launched himself over the side.

Morgan stared after him for a moment, then shrugged. It wasn't his problem. If Toniq fell, or was captured, it would be his own lookout. Morgan needed to get his team out of Arvindir, right now. He hurried to where Marissa waited.

"He says they'll be here in a few moments," she reported as she scanned the sky. "Where's Toniq?"

"Gone." He also turned his eyes to the inky, cloud-strewn sky. The rain had stopped momentarily, but the moon and stars were completely blocked from view. Only a faint light from the city below gave a tiny bit of illumination.

"What on earth do you mean, gone?" She stared, incredulous, hands on her hips.

"Later," he said. "Not our concern. We've got other things to worry about."

"Like getting off this tower?"

"Exactly." He cast his gaze skyward again.

He blinked to clear his vision against the jagged streak of lightning that left a bright scar across the night. Thunder rumbled in the near distance, and then a huge dark shape swirled out of the clouds. A second joined it, and then a third.

"Dragons!" cried Alain, falling to his knees. His eyes were wide with terror.

"Yes, dragons, thank God," Morgan breathed. "They made it." To Wyvrndell, he said, "You might want to know these stones are supposedly enchanted to keep dragons away."

"I sense no danger, Morgan McRobbie," the dragon replied. *"Any enchantments on these stones have long since faded away."*

He breathed a sigh of relief. "I was a bit worried," he admitted.

"Even if the enchantment still held, we would have found a way," Wyvrndell replied. An unfamiliar dragon hovered over the tower for a moment then landed as Wyvrndell told Morgan, *"The storm will not hold off much longer. Make haste. Wyzandar can bear two of your party."*

"Wyzandar?"

"My sire," Wyvrndell said, a hint of pride in his voice. *"Now, hurry."*

"Nardis," Morgan called. "You and Alain on Wyzandar, who has landed for you." The dragon turned a curious eye on them. Nardis clutched the cowering archivist's arm and dragged him forward.

"He'll eat us," protested Alain.

Wyzandar eyed him up and down, his great eyes blinking. *"You would not even make a good mouthful,"* he said. Alain's eyes went wide. *"Come, I will not hurt you. I am here to bear you away from this place to safety."*

"Do as he says, Alain," called Princess Saia. She hurried over to take the archivist's arm. "Do not worry. These people are not fools. They planned this, don't you see?"

"But…"

"Come on, my friend," Nardis said. "We'll go for a jolly little ride, eh? We really don't want to stay around here, now do we? I don't think those guards would be friendly in the least. You like your head, don't you?" He shoved and prodded the unresisting, still trembling archivist up onto the dragon's back, then scrambled up to sit behind him. "We're ready," he said to Wyzandar.

The dragon leapt gracefully into the sky. His wings snapped out to catch the air and lift his burden up, in order for Aireantha to land. Wyzandar circled the tower while Marissa and Saia clambered up onto her back. A flash of lightning split the sky as she leapt up and took wing. Rain began to fall in earnest as Wyvrndell finally descended to land on the tower's turret.

"Thank you," Morgan said, and meant it. He scrambled up.

The dragon didn't wait for him to get a firm seat, leaping into the sky, practically right into another bolt of lightning. Morgan winced as the air sizzled around them. Wyvrndell's great wings clawed at the air as he sought to rise upwards. To get above the storm, Morgan wondered?

"This sky is nothing but storm," the dragon said, in answer to his thoughts. *"We shall have to endure it, I'm afraid. Hold firm to my scales, for the wind is fierce."*

With this, he banked, soared over the harbor and headed west, leading the way toward the open sea. Below, through another flash of lightning, Morgan saw several of Azim's naval vessels. They were headed back toward the harbor's shelter. *Given up the chase?* Morgan hoped the pirate—former pirate, he amended—was well under way and headed safely back to Caerfaen.

He glanced back to see Marissa on Aireantha, with Saia's arms clutched around her waist. Next to them, Alain and Nardis came on Wyzandar. Even from here, and through the rain, Morgan could see the archivist's eyes stretched wide and white with trepidation.

"I didn't expect your sire to accompany you on this journey," he said to Wyvrndell.

"Neither did I, However, he insisted. He said if I was to risk my neck on some fool's errand, he had better come along to make sure I did not make a mess of it." The dragon chuckled. *"In truth, I think he was less concerned about me and more interested in a bit of excitement."*

Morgan was still scanning to their rear. Was that—no, it couldn't be, could it? He blinked and craned his neck as he waited for the next flash of static to light the sky and confirm his fear.

"I think he's about to get all the excitement he might wish for," Morgan said. "Damn it!"

In the distance but closing rapidly, Azim charged after them on a magic flying carpet. "We have a problem," he told the dragon. "The mage is in hot pursuit."

"I have alerted the others," Wyvrndell reported a moment later. *"Fortunately, he cannot cast any spells to harm us."*

"Um." Morgan glanced back over his shoulder at Azim. "He can't cast a spell to harm you dragons. I don't think the restriction on dragons includes passengers, does it?"

"Oh. Well, yes, there is that." Wyvrndell sounded a bit nonplussed, something Morgan had never before encountered. *"I suppose it doesn't."*

"Can we outfly him?"

"Unburdened by passengers, likely so. In this instance, I fear not."

"Well then. This presents an interesting problem, eh?" Morgan looked back toward Azim. A beam of greenish light lanced from the mage's hand toward Aireantha.

Chapter Thirty-Seven

Aartis eyed his visitor askance. In the distance, the cathedral's bells tolled the hour: half one in the morning. He made no attempt to hide a capacious yawn and scrubbed a hand across his face. "Of course, I'm always delighted to see you, but couldn't it have waited until a more suitable hour? Like lunchtime?"

Bishop Randolph MacFarlane removed his battered pirate's hat, shaking raindrops off onto the entryway rug. "No," he snapped. His expression was grim. "It couldn't."

Aartis huffed out a breath. "As bad as that, eh? All right, you'd best come in." He led the way to his study, ushered Randolph into a comfortable chair, and held up a decanter. The bishop, surprisingly, waved the spirits away.

"No drink?" Aartis's brows rose to unprecedented heights. "My God, it must be a calamity."

"You've no idea," muttered the bishop darkly.

"Hmmm." Aartis considered the bishop's words, then poured himself a generous tot. "I think I'd best fortify myself." He took a sip and set the glass down on a table. "Now... what the hell, if you'll pardon the expression, is wrong?"

Randolph leaned back with a huge sigh and closed his eyes. Aartis took another sip of the claret and waited.

Eyes still squeezed shut, Randolph spoke. "There are days," he said, "when I feel there might be hope for us." He opened his eyes and pointed an accusing finger at Aartis. "This ain't one of them."

Aartis blinked. "What did I do?"

Randolph regarded his finger. He lowered it with a somewhat sheepish expression. "Sorry, I didn't mean you."

"Well, I suppose it's somewhat a relief. I was picturing sudden hellfire, or worse." He considered for a moment. "Is there worse?"

"Don't ask. That's not in my job description. I leave the hellfire and such to a higher power. My task is simply to point in the opposite direction, if you get my meaning."

Aartis emptied his glass and went to refill it. He waved the decanter in the bishop's direction. This time, Randolph nodded. "Perhaps it'll calm me a bit. Right now, I'm so angry I could spit."

Aartis poured, then handed him the glass. "And the cause of this most un-bishop-like anger is…"

"A cadre of my fellow bishops, if you must know."

"Well," Aartis mused. "I suppose I must, since you showed up on my doorstep at this ungodly hour—pardon the expression again—specifically to tell me about it."

"They're all godly," Randolph said. "The hours, I mean."

"And these bishops of yours?"

"They ain't so godly. At least, on the available evidence."

"Randolph, I'm losing valuable sleep here. Get on, will you?"

Randolph emptied his glass. "They have decided," he said, "they don't like witches."

Aartis stared. "I don't— Oh. Right. The Royal Enchantress."

"Exactly. The Royal Enchantress." He held out his glass. "Perhaps another wee drop?"

Aartis obliged. Randolph was a large man, and evidently his notion of what comprised a wee drop was correspondingly large. He only said "stop" when the glass was nearly filled to the brim. Glass in hand, the bishop leaned back again, took a sip, and nodded once. "Not bad. The '03?"

"If you say so. I don't ask, I'm not particular. Now, would you care to elaborate?"

"Very well. It has come to my attention that several of my fellow bishops recently gathered themselves in a rather clandestine convocation. A meeting I, and several others, were most noticeably not invited to."

"Yes, all right. And?"

"After some rudimentary discussion, they evidently took a vote, in companionable unanimity. They determined the practice of witchcraft was henceforth to be deemed anathema to the Church. Any practitioners of these so-called dark arts would be immediately excommunicated. In addition, they might, subject to the decisions of said august body, be brought to trial."

"Randolph, is that legal?"

The bishop shrugged one massive shoulder. "Who would dare to gainsay a gaggle of bishops?"

"Surely the king wouldn't allow such a travesty. Would he?"

"Well, there's a bit more to it, you see. Because these chaps have also decided anyone who consorts with or harbors said witches would also be subject to excommunication. Myself included."

"Even Rhys?" Aartis shook his head in disbelief.

"Potentially, if they decided to push things that far. Which I wouldn't put past them."

Aartis closed his eyes. When he opened them again, Randolph was still there, so this wasn't simply a bad dream. "Why? Who's behind this? Because there must be someone instigating things. Your fellow bishops didn't suddenly up and decide to rid Kilbourne of any witches they could find. I don't believe it."

Randolph gave him a wan smile but said nothing. Aartis went on. "Tell me, how did you learn about their plans? And why come to me?"

"Good questions, every one of 'em," Randolph said approvingly.

"I'll add one more. Why witches, not wizards?"

"Ah, very good. I'd wondered if you'd notice the little discrepancy there. I was right—you've more going on in this artfully tousled head than you let on."

"When I decide on an appropriate cutting remark, I'll let you know. In the meantime, enlighten me."

Randolph grinned. "All right. As to how I learned about their little conspiracy, I have a spy."

"One of the bishops?"

"Them? Bah. Nope. But you can't expect a lot like this, such important men, to run their own errands or take their own notes, can you? One of my old clerks is embedded with one of the fellers I felt needed some minding. 'Twas he who tipped me the wink."

Aartis nodded. "Well done."

"As to the who and the why? Those questions, I think, are rather tied together, along with your concern about witches but not wizards."

"You think the wizards are behind it?"

"Well, not 'the wizards,' as such. Just one. Chief Wizard Foxwent."

"What—I mean, how could he possibly have influence over these bishops? And why would he care about the witches? It doesn't make any sense."

Randolph drank some more claret. "I'm only theorizing here, understand. Still, I'd be pretty surprised if I'm far wrong. It's the old story, Aartis. Those in power seek to stay in power and to gather more and more to themselves. The wizards, as a whole, and Foxwent in particular, have also managed to amass a sizeable bit of gold along the way. And you know the golden rule, m'boy."

"Do unto others?" Aartis offered.

"Nope." Randolph waved this away. "Them who have the gold, make the rules."

"Oh." There was really little more to say with regards to this cynical outlook.

Randolph went on, "I think this whole debacle has less to do with witches in general, than with one witch in particular."

"Lady Mar—I mean, Duchess Marissa."

"Got it in one. The Royal College of Wizards, and the chief wizard in particular, have for ages served in an informal advisory capacity to Kilbourne's kings. Now, out of the blue, their role has been supplanted by the new Royal Enchantress."

"Who also happens to be a close friend of the queen," Aartis noted.

"Exactly. Not to mention, she's the wife of the Knight-Commander, who also happens to be one of the most powerful men in the kingdom and a close confident of King Rhys."

"Mmm, I see where you're going with this," Aartis said.

Randolph gave a disdainful sniff. "I don't think the chief wizard would have minded one bit if Augustus Rhenn and Kiara Northram had succeeded in doing away with Morgan and Lady Marissa. Since they failed, I think Foxwent has decided to take matters into his own hands. Albeit indirectly, pulling the strings for this renegade group of bishops."

"They've gone along with him for the money? What about those vows of poverty and such?"

"Oh, I think it's less about the gold—although I'm sure a bit of extra gold doesn't hurt their feelings any—than about the ability to exert control over these women. Again, it's all about power. About whom calls the tune for whom."

"Doesn't sound particularly holy," Aartis observed.

"Ah, holy. Now, there's a topic for you. There's many who would argue quite forcefully that these witches are the ones who are unholy. Don't ya see?"

"Even when, like the Royal Enchantress, they've pledged to use their powers for good? After all, aren't those very powers a gift from God?"

"Well now, pledges, like vows, can be broken, eh? There's some might say the witches' magic comes not from God in his heaven, but rather straight from hell itself."

"Oh, bosh!"

"So you say. To the ignorant and the easily swayed, it makes all kinds of sense."

"Dancing around in the moonlight with no clothes on?"

"Less dancing, I reckon, and more in the lines of sacrificial rites and summoning of dark things," Randolph said. "Demons and such."

"Randolph, no one does that kind of thing. Do they? I'm certain Lady Marissa doesn't."

"No, I know she don't. Although, besides her, I'll be forced to admit I'm not on what you might call social terms with anyone, um, of the witchy persuasion. So, while I have strong doubts about it, I can't actually prove it."

"And, for sure, there's some old crone back in the hills, who's done something suspect enough to get a bad reputation."

"Yep. She'd be the exception which proves the rule, don't ya see?"

"Yes, I do." Aartis frowned. "All right, Randolph, you've made a good case. At least, as you say, in theory. Why bring this information to me? Why not directly to Rhys?"

"Two reasons." Randolph held up a beefy finger. "First, Rhys doesn't really have any direct action he can take. At least, not at this point." He raised a second finger. "Second, because you are acting Knight-Commander while Morgan's off gallivanting around the countryside with his new bride. There's going to be a schism soon, Aartis. I want to make certain the Legion is on the right side."

"Damn it, Randolph, are you serious? You really believe they'd take that risk?"

"There's no accounting for what stupid, rapacious, arrogant men will do. So yes, I'm afraid. Very afraid."

Without a word, Aartis refilled both their glasses. He raised his. "To the resistance?" he said, a bit weakly.

Randolph gave him a fierce grin. "Good man!"

"Randolph, you've got to tell the king about this. He needs to know, even if he can't take action yet."

"Oh, I suppose you're right. I reckon he'll hear about it soon enough, even if I didn't. I don't think this lot will sit on their hands for long. I'd be surprised if there wasn't an announcement—a proclamation, if you will—forthcoming in the next few days."

"Speaking of which, don't you find the timing of this whole thing a tiny bit suspicious?"

Randolph lowered his glass and regarded Aartis with a curious gaze. "How d'ya mean?"

"Well, consider this. Both the Knight-Commander and the Royal Enchantress happen to be in two other places entirely at the moment.

While they're away, the bishops decide to act. Doesn't that strike you as a bit dodgy?"

"Hmm, yes, I see what you mean. I hadn't taken that into consideration. You may have something there. Definitely an odor of dead rat lingering about, isn't there?"

"Especially when you consider they're gone at the chief wizard's behest on some super-secret mission."

"What?" Randolph roared.

Aartis nodded. "Morgan told me himself when he left me in charge of the Legion. He didn't go into any details, but evidently the wizards have lost some artifact or another. Morgan and Lady M—oh, I'm not used to this yet..."

"Honestly, I find it easier to refer to her as Lady Marissa myself," Randolph admitted.

"Well, anyhow, they were dispatched to retrieve the whatsis."

"Hmph. You're right. As coincidence goes, it does seem a bit much to swallow."

"If you think that's hard to swallow, wait till you hear my next brainstorm."

The bishop cocked a brow. "I'm simply agog."

"Your concern is the religious implications and the effects on those everyday women who happen to practice a bit of magic here and there. I'm thinking in terms of tactics. I'm a soldier, after all."

"All right." He sipped his drink. "Go on. Give me your notions on tactics."

Aartis paced about the room. "If I, God forbid, were to attempt to topple a kingdom, what simpler way is there than to enlist the religious establishment to help me? Present company excluded, of course."

Randolph remained silent. Aartis continued to pace as he warmed to his theme. "By contriving this nonsense about witches, I manage to have the kingdom's military leader, the king's new magical advisor—and emissary to the dragons, by the way—and even the king himself, declared anathema. With the church's support, because no one argues with the church unless they want to be condemned as well, I, a wizard of no little power, might manage to have myself declared the kingdom's de-facto ruler."

Randolph's horrified gaze faded away, and he gave a slow nod. "It's absolutely insane. And monstrous. Even worse, it might work."

"The question becomes," Aartis said, "what do we do about it? I can see how it might work. How to counter such a move is a different animal altogether. This is much more political than military, I'm afraid. I'm a bit out of my depth."

"Oh." The bishop's face fell. "I'd rather hoped you'd come up with some brilliant solution."

Aartis shrugged. "Unless it involves calling up the Legion and attacking your rogue bishops…"

"Probably not. At least, not at this juncture. They haven't actually done anything, not yet."

"No pre-emptive strike? It would make things much easier."

"Yes, wouldn't it? Hmm, wait a moment. You've given me the glimmer of an idea. Pour me a bit more claret, will you? Perhaps it'll lubricate my brain a bit more."

"Much more lubrication and I'll have to roll you home in a barrow," Aartis muttered. "A very large barrow." Nonetheless, he poured. He said, "So, do I need to rouse the Legion after all?"

It was one thing to engage in idle speculation, but something entirely more serious—dire, even—to contemplate rounding up bishops of the church, no matter how misguided, at sword's point.

"No, not the Legion," Randolph reassured him. "Let your lads sleep. We are about to rouse the king."

"Oh." Aartis's voice didn't quite crack, though it was a near thing. "Couldn't we skip this part, and get straight to the hellfire and damnation? It's bound to be much more pleasant."

~ * ~

"Randolph," Rhys said sternly, "this is getting to be a habit."

The bishop assumed an air of innocence. "Why, whatever do you mean, Your Majesty?"

Rhys tugged his brocade dressing gown more snugly around his spare frame. Elegant and ornate the palace might be—warm, not so much. He pulled on a tasseled bell cord. When a servant appeared, Rhys requested tea. Then he sat, waved his confessor and his acting Knight-Commander to chairs, and regarded them intently.

"Captain Poldane, does your presence at this hour mean we face imminent invasion? Because it's the only reason I can see…"

Randolph saw Aartis swallow nervously, and jumped in. "My fault entirely, Your Majesty. In answer to your question, yes, we do. Face an invasion, I mean. Well, of a sort. Not a foreign power, however. I—"

A soft knock on the door heralded the return of the servant, pushing a loaded tea trolley. Once steaming cups, along with biscuits, had been dispensed, Rhys nodded to Randolph. "Go on. You have my attention."

As Randolph explained what he'd learned, and the issues he and Aartis had discussed, Rhys methodically munched ginger biscuits. Each was dispatched with precision and, if Randolph was any judge, with a rising tide of fury.

When he'd finished his precis, Randolph sat back and sipped his tea. Not nearly as bracing as Aartis's claret, though probably a more sensible option at the moment. Rhys uttered a low growl and smacked a fist into his other hand.

"Priests and wizards," he muttered. "Who would have ever thought such would come to pass? It doesn't seem possible."

"I highly doubt the wizards, as a collective body, are involved," Randolph said. "I imagine the chief wizard is playing a lone hand."

Rhys should his head in disgust. "And I abetted his scheme. I encouraged—no, ordered—Morgan and Marissa off to Parthane on his behalf. I feel like such a fool. Foxwent seemed genuinely appalled at Prince Azim's theft of the ruby."

"I really don't think it would have mattered," Randolph consoled. "It you hadn't, Foxwent would have found some other way to get them out of Caerfaen."

"I suppose." Rhys sounded dubious. "Still, there's no help for it now. Very well, now I know what's happened, or is about to happen, what do we do about it?"

"Your Majesty, not all of the bishops are involved in this scheme. There are five who are: MacAdoo of Cormaine; Quaraltus from Drysllywn; Cardine of Westdale; Llachnahn of Dunstanshire; and Farriday in Vynfold. Four of us were not invited to their convocation. Presumably since we would be likely to object to the scheme."

"Well, I suppose it's something," Rhys allowed. "Although the opposition still has a majority."

"In terms of numbers, yes," Randolph agreed. "But Bishop Donnelly, who was not invited to their meeting, is our Primate. Chief among equals, if you will. He holds a great deal of influence, not only over our curia, but also over the priests at large. This could make a huge difference."

"Fine, fine." Rhys took a sip of tea. "What do you suggest I do, under the authority of the monarchy? Because I'm certain you have some scheme in mind."

"Captain Poldane's the one who gave me the idea, if a bit indirectly. He viewed the whole thing in more military terms, naturally, and mentioned a pre-emptive strike. This is what needs to happen. But without any Legion involvement."

"You'd best explain, Randolph. It's late—or early—and I'm not following you."

"Your Majesty, I believe your best course is to steal a march on the rogue bishops. A royal proclamation, as early as can be managed."

Rhys rubbed the stubble on his chin. "And this proclamation would say what, exactly? 'Hear ye, hear ye, these bishops are fools and knaves?'"

Randolph chuckled. "No, although such a proclamation might be interesting. No, you simply announce how the witches of Kilbourne are blessed by God with their powers. For all gifts come from a benevolent God, do they not? Thus any so-called witches who pledge to use to their gifts for the good of others will be under the Crown's protection. Under the auspices of the Royal Enchantress, if you will. Also, any who use God's gifts for evil will be dealt with by your magistrates, and punished accordingly, the same as any who flaunt Kilbourne's laws."

"Mmm, yes, I see. Do you think this will forestall your brethren?"

"Oh, no, I'm certain they'll go right on. Here's the important bit, though: we'll have gotten in first. The renegade bishops will be seen to be in direct opposition to your established decree. They would be, in fact, renegades, acting against Kilbourne citizens specifically under the Crown's protection. You would be well within your rights to request Bishop Donnelly to remove them from their positions of authority within the church."

Rhys nodded. "Well, it seems simple enough. At least, in theory."

Aartis spoke up. "Your Majesty, with all due respect, it will not be simple. The bishops may well refuse to stand down. They may, in fact, strengthen their call for ecclesiastical punishment for those they deem anathema. That would include any who associate with or succor them. This would naturally include yourself. There are, unfortunately, many who will rally to their cause. People who are ill informed, or simply envious, or those who don't want women to have any sway."

"Such a shame to think something like this might come to pass in this day and age," Rhys said.

"You will need to direct the Legion, along with the various city watches and rural constabulary, to protect these women, sire. Some will, no doubt, defect to the renegades' cause. Most will uphold your commands."

"You've obviously given this a good deal of consideration, Captain," Rhys said.

Randolph felt, more than saw, the dark look Aartis shot him. Aartis replied, "I've only had a little time to consider, Your Majesty. Other ideas may come to me when I've a bit more time to sleep on it. To me, the upshot is, we need to protect these innocent citizens of

Kilbourne."

Rhys nodded. "You're absolutely right, Captain." To Randolph, he said, "I'll prepare a statement first thing in the morning. These conniving clergymen won't know which way is up when I'm done with them."

Randolph smiled to himself. Captain Poldane, for all his earthly passions, was an excellent advocate. He'd been right in his selection of co-conspirators.

Chapter Thirty-Eight

Marissa's eyes widened as Aireantha reported Azim was in pursuit on his enchanted carpet. It was, she had determined earlier, a rather silly and awkward mode of transport. No less speedy, for being silly.

Marissa whipped her head round. Good heavens, he was close. Only a few furlongs distant. As she watched in dismay, Azim lifted his right hand, palm extended toward her. She could see his mouth move, no doubt to utter some dire and deadly spell. Why, oh why, did she always end up on the receiving end of wizards casting nasty spells intended to kill her? It was really a bit tiresome.

A green beam of magic energy came streaking toward them. "We're under attack," she told Aireantha. The dragon didn't acknowledge verbally, but instead sideslipped suddenly. Azim's spell passed harmlessly by to their left.

The mage sent another bolt of what Marissa presumed to be killing energy toward Wyzandar. The older dragon evidently wasn't as nimble as his younger companions, for the spell stuck him across his haunch. Azim, however, must not have been well versed in dragon lore and did not realize any spell used against a dragon would reflect back on the caster. The spell rebounded off Wyzandar, straight back toward the enraged mage. She had the satisfaction of seeing his eyes widen in shock. His expression changed quickly to fury as he took evasive maneuvers to avoid his own spell.

"What happened?" cried Saia.

"Your brother has learned dragons are impervious to magic," Marissa shouted. "Although he won't make the same mistake again. He'll aim right for one of us."

"Of course he will," Saia replied, her voice bitter. "What can we do? We're easy targets, and we can't get away from him. He'll kill us all. And enjoy it."

"Well, if he does, at least he won't get the ruby back. It'll drop right down into the Thundermist Sea. I don't imagine his carpet will carry him to the bottom to retrieve it."

"Tell me," Saia said, as Aireantha dodged left this time to avoid another of Azim's strikes. "What in the name of all the devils is so special about this blasted jewel to make everyone want it so?"

"Oh, nothing much. It's merely a repository for about a thousand captive demons," Marissa said. "If someone—urp, duck!—if someone, like Azim, wasn't careful, the whole lot of them might get released from their prison."

"But—" Saia swallowed. Hard. Her face wore a mask of anguish.

"Yes," Marissa said. "If the demons were released, it would likely not end well. We humans wouldn't stand a chance against such a force. A legion of angry demons, all on the rampage at once? It would be...bad."

Saia bent low over Aireantha's neck as Azim sent another bolt of energy toward them. "You make it sound so prosaic when you say it. 'Oh, we'll all just die.' It's what you meant, though, when you said if Azim knew, he was a monster."

"Yes." Marissa squirmed around, craning to see his position. Drat! He was uncomfortably close. At this range, he couldn't miss them much longer.

"Aireantha," she called. "Do you think there's any chance you can lose him in the clouds?"

"I suppose we can try." The dragon plowed the wind and rain, gaining altitude as she headed up into the storm-tossed clouds.

Lightning sizzled ominously around them, while the pelting rain stung Marissa's face and made it almost impossible for her to see.

Hopefully, it would present the same challenges to Azim. With any luck, it would be more a liability for him than for them, since the dragons were the ones doing the flying.

"I'm going to try something," Marissa called to Saia above a crack of thunder which threatened to jar them right off the dragon's back.

"Well, do it soon," Saia shouted back. "He's too close!"

Marissa concentrated in a desperate attempt to dredge up a half-remembered spell Wyvrndell explained to her once, what seemed like ages ago. They were in the thick of the clouds now, perfect for what she had in mind. Praying she recalled correctly, she spoke the spell's words and gathered power into her cupped hands.

With a wild cry, she released the spell into the roiling clouds. For a long, fretful moment, nothing happened. She sagged with disappointment. Then the spell blossomed out like a flower. Behind them, the rain suddenly froze into ice pellets, right in Azim's path.

It wouldn't stop him, she knew. It certainly might slow him down a bit. It also might serve to spoil his aim as well. The dragons were each in the cover of the clouds now, flying in formation, with Wyvrndell in the lead. Aireantha was slightly behind and to his right, while Wyzandar matched her, wing-beat for beat, on the left.

As Marissa glanced over toward the older dragon, she saw Nardis focus on Azim. He gestured, and a large sphere of blue light launched from his hands. It expanded rapidly across Azim's course. The mage, his beard coated in ice and an expression of killing fury in his eyes, sent his carpet into a steep dive in an effort to get under whatever trap Nardis had set for him.

He wasn't quite quick enough. His shoulder brushed against the blue screen. A roar mimicking thunder and a sizzle like concentrated lightning nearly sent the mage tumbling from his enchanted carpet. He clutched at the edges with icy hands and strength born of sheer rage and managed to hang on.

"He's still coming!" Saia yelled.

Indeed he was. Azim's face was twisted with hate and fury now. Power exploded from his hands, directed toward Nardis. Wyzandar dove, managing to keep his riders safe. Then Azim sent another burst of power at Aireantha. Or rather, at the women perched precariously on her back. The dragon swerved, but Azim must have anticipated her move. The bolt of magical energy grazed Marissa across her shoulder.

With a gasp, she felt her body go numb. The spell's force sent a dreadful chill through her core, even as it sent her flying off the dragon's back, spinning out into the lightning-filled night.

Marissa screamed.

Chapter Thirty-Nine

Wyvrndell banked so sharply, Morgan was caught unaware and nearly lost his seat. He managed to grab onto one of the dragon's scales with one hand, while he clenched his legs together, just managing to keep himself from toppling off into space.

The dragon dived now, down through the dense, rain-swollen clouds at a mind-numbingly steep angle. "What's happened?" Morgan managed to ask. He wondered if his stomach, which felt quite some distance behind and above their current position, had any hope of catching them up.

"Lady Marissa," Wyvrndell replied tersely. *"Falling. Hit by the wizard."*

Morgan's blood turned instantly to ice. He tried to speak but couldn't even form a coherent mental sentence.

"I am tracking her, by her thoughts," went on Wyvrndell.

The dragon plummeted, his wings pulled in tight to give him maximum velocity. He didn't fall like a stone, Morgan thought, but more like a stone fired from a trebuchet. Except straight down. He peered ahead, scanning for any sign of Marissa.

This was, he realized with mounting anger, next to impossible. The clouds hemmed them in from every side. The only light came from sinister sizzles of lightning. "Faster!" he urged. "We've got to find her."

"Almost there," Wyvrndell growled.

Their precipitous drop through the clouds continued apace. Morgan was forced to content himself with the dragon's assurance. There wasn't a damned thing he could do to help matters in the slightest. While he didn't generally like to rely on anyone else, in this case there was no better ally than Wyvrndell.

At that moment, the cloud cover lessened, then they were out of the clouds entirely. All in all, this didn't feel to Morgan much improvement. The rain lashed in torrents, driven almost sideways by a fearsome wind. Morgan shielded his eyes against both wind and rain, scanning the surrounding sky.

"*Get ready,*" Wyvrndell ordered. *"She is above us, falling fast. I will attempt to match her descent. You will have to try to grab her."*

Morgan cursed. The rain, the wind, the lightning, the wizard, the ruby. He cursed them all, and...

There she was! Her cloak billowed out, whether by accident or design, he didn't know. Either way, it caught the air, slowing her descent. Not by much, but perhaps enough. Wyvrndell slid like an eel through the air, undulating to match her fall, moving himself so Morgan was situated directly under her.

He stretched from his tenuous mount on Wyvrndell's back. Reaching out, he called to her as he tried to grasp her flailing hand. "I've got you!" he shouted. He had her cold, icy, slippery fingers in his. Now to pull her in to safety...

A gust of wind chose that moment to blast across the sky, driven by a frenetic flash of lightning that practically seared Morgan's vision. His hand closed on empty air and rain. Marissa was yards away now, carried by that bitter, merciless wind toward the roiling, crushing waves below.

"Go!" he screamed. Wyvrndell folded his wings again and dove like a falcon. Morgan clenched his legs around the dragon's neck to keep himself from joining Marissa in midair.

The sea churned beneath them, much too close now. They'd only have one more chance, even assuming Wyvrndell could catch up to her and maneuver into position again. Another slip and she'd be lost in the terrible troughs of the sea, with no possible hope of rescue. Wyvrndell slithered through the night, serpentine, straining to reach her in time.

"*Get ready,*" the dragon ordered again. *"Almost there..."*

He'd somehow managed to get directly into the path of her descent. Morgan could just see Marissa, not far above their position. He locked his legs tight as he could around the dragon's torso, readying himself.

"*Hang on...*" muttered the dragon, more to himself than to Morgan. Perhaps to Marissa? *"Almost... Now!"*

Wyvrndell's great wings snapped out. They caught air much as Marissa's cloak had, nearly halting their descent altogether. Which meant Marissa, still tumbling through the air, landed directly on Morgan. He scrabbled blindly for whatever he could find: a hand, a piece of clothing, it didn't matter. The only thing that mattered was to hold her, keep her there with him, never let go, not let her fall again.

Marissa bounced once, twice. Her hands scrabbled for any

purchase. Through rain-lashed eyes—those certainly weren't tears, of course not—Morgan latched onto her flailing arm with every bit of strength he could muster. He pulled her into a more secure position, locking her in a fierce embrace.

Wyvrndell drove upwards again, away from the grasping, deadly clutches of the Thundermist Sea. Marissa opened her eyes. Blinking owlishly, she gave Morgan a weak smile. "Well," she said. "I shouldn't like to do that again anytime soon."

He gaped at her. "You...you can joke about it? You almost died!"

"I'm still here, aren't I? Thanks to you and to Wyvrndell." She snuggled closer to him. "So... yes."

It was too much. Morgan bellowed a laugh, but it caught in his throat and emerged as a gasping sob. He steadied himself. "I was sure I'd lost you for good this time."

"Mmm. I was sure you'd lost me too. Pretty rotten for both of us, I'd say. Thank you, Wyvrndell. Once again, you've managed to save me from disaster. This is getting to be a habit. Rather a bore for you, I'm sure. I appreciate it none the less."

"Think nothing of it. It was... exciting. And it worked."

Morgan wasn't sure if dragons could grin. If they could, he was certain Wyvrndell would be doing so.

"You were brilliant," she said. "I'm glad I could provide you with some entertainment to lighten the journey. Death-defying leaps performed nightly for the crowd's pleasure. See the mad flying lady and her amazing dragon."

Morgan heard what might have been a draconic chuckle. Then the dragon's voice became grim. *"Hold on. We're headed back up. Your dratted wizard is still up there, wreaking havoc with the others."*

"Oooh, let me at him," she said, as she tried to sit up. "I've got a score to settle with him."

Wyvrndell's wings beat the air. He climbed through the storm and toward the clouds again. To Morgan, it seemed like the storm had dissipated some, the clouds thinned. A few clear patches of sky were visible. He even caught a quick glimpse of a gibbous moon floating across the night.

A roar resounded through the air. Wyvrndell's pace quickened, something Morgan hadn't thought possible. *"Aireantha!"* the dragon bugled, streaking higher.

Through the last of the storm clouds, Aireantha appeared. A sizzling fireball followed her. Even as the dragon dodged and jinked to avoid it, the sphere of magical flame continued to close in on Saia.

As Wyvrndell approached Aireantha and Saia, Wyzandar swooped toward the mage. He sent a searing gout of flame after the flying carpet. Azim flicked a finger to produce a barely visible shield which neatly blocked the dragon's fire.

Nardis sent a spell hurtling after Azim's fireball. Moments before it overtook Saia, Nardis's counter-spell struck it. Azim's deadly spell vanished in a shower of sparks.

Aireantha wheeled back toward Azim, bellowing fire and fury. Wyzandar continued his assault on the mage's defenses, as Wyvrndell arrived to add his own flame to the battle. Beset from three sides, still Azim did not appear concerned.

To Morgan's amazement, his expression evidenced not worry, but contempt for the dragons' effort. He could see the mage's mouth move as he prepared to launch another spell. This one, he was certain, would be something devastating and deadly.

"Morgan!" Marissa cried. She tugged on his arm and pointed toward Aireantha. "Look at Saia."

Morgan, who'd been watching Wyzandar's attempt to flank Azim, jerked his head around. Saia sat straight and stiff on Aireantha's back. When she spoke, her voice rang through the sky like thunder.

"Enough, Azim!" she cried. "I am sick of you. You steal, you bully, and now you even try to kill me and my friends."

Azim sneered as he prepared to launch another fireball toward his sister.

"Not again, Azim!" she screamed, her voice louder still.

As Morgan watched in wonder, Saia raised her arms and uttered strange words in a long-forgotten tongue.

From above, lightning crackled, then descended upon the princess. From far below, a greenish mist rose up, spiraling, swirling, its tendrils grasping, until the mist engulfed Saia, and she was almost lost in the green glow of it.

"Thundermist," breathed Marissa. "It's… it's infusing Saia, just like it did me. Oh…"

Wyvrndell and Wyzandar hovered in midair, transfixed. Suddenly Saia emerged from the mist and lightning, her expression ferocious. Astride the dragon, she soared toward her brother like some avenging fury from ancient legend.

"Be gone!" she bellowed, and the wind roared down, buffeting Azim on his carpet. Saia pointed both her hands toward her brother. Green fire leapt from her fingertips to beat mercilessly against Azim's shielding spell.

"No woman can hold power, eh?" she snarled. She leveled

another, even stronger blast toward her brother. "What do you call this, then?"

Doubt flickered through the mage's eyes. It was quickly replaced by fear. His defenses appeared nearly breached, and still Saia continued to pour an unrelenting stream of power toward him. Her face was a mask of deadly concentration now, her focus the single objective of overwhelming Azim and besting him. Destroying him.

He attempted first to bolster his defensive spell. It didn't have much effect, as far as Morgan could see. Then the mage sent another spell hurtling toward his sister. In his haste, however, his aim was thrown off, and the spell struck Aireantha instead. It rebounded, returning straight for Azim.

Eyes wide in terror, Azim sent his carpet into a swift dive to avoid his own killing spell. His effort was futile, for the fireball he'd created pursued him, edging ever closer even as Saia's green fire followed him.

Aireantha swooped in pursuit. Saia clenched her fists and screamed curses at her brother as the lightning crackled around her.

"She's drawing on the power of the mist," Marissa breathed, as the princess strained to pour more and more power into the fire she sent toward her brother.

The other dragons followed in the chase. Finally Saia's fire broke through Azim's shield and shattered it. Her spell took him in a glowing embrace, even as the mage's own fireball caught up with him. Fingers of green flame tightened around Azim's throat at the same time the fireball caromed into him.

"Saia, no!" Azim cried. It was too late. The princess closed her hands into tight fists. The green flames wrought of her spell cut off his entreaties as they tightened like a hangman's noose.

He slumped sideways onto his carpet and slid off the side. Silently, robes billowing, he plunged toward the churning waves far below.

All three dragons hovered now, uncertain what to do next. Morgan exchanged a glance with Nardis, who shrugged.

Cold drops of rain, hard and stinging, pelted them again. *"Shall we go?"* suggested Wyzandar to the group at large. *"The storm has caught up to us again. We will need to fly fast to outrun it."*

"Yes, let's," replied Marissa. "There is nothing more to be done here."

"There is one more thing," Wyvrndell said.

He flew close to Azim's magical carpet, which still hovered, sodden and tattered. Opening his massive jaws, he sent one fiery breath at the carpet. It exploded instantly into flames. In moments, all that was left were a few smoldering fibers, drifting down toward the sea and oblivion. Morgan watched until the last ember winked out under the fury of the waves.

"*Now, it is finished,*" Wyvrndell said. He banked toward the west, wings beating quickly to outrace the storm as the dragons carried them home.

Chapter Forty

The dragons delivered them to Caerfaen as the sun hoisted itself up over the horizon.

Marissa felt, more than saw, Morgan pry himself wearily off Wyvrndell's back. He stretched, groaned softly, and reached up to help her dismount. She looked down at the ground, glared at Morgan, and made a face.

"I'm not sure I can move," she muttered.

He flashed her a wan smile. "Believe me, even days at a time on Arnicus doesn't prepare one for this. Stay there until you feel ready, then I'll help you down."

Aireantha swooped into the square to land gracefully nearby. Saia, Marissa noted, appeared positively wretched. Her light garments were soaked through from the storm. The princess shivered, half frozen and in urgent need of dry clothing, a warm fire, and a stiff brandy. All in all, this prospect didn't sound half bad to Marissa, either. She glanced down at her own woolen traveling cloak. Shrugging it off, she tossed it down to Morgan.

"Wha—?" He caught it, but his eyes were filled with confusion.

"Take it to Saia," she directed. "Quickly. The poor girl's nearly done in. And she definitely wasn't dressed for travel, especially a-dragonback." As the chatter from hurriedly gathering spectators came to their ears, she flapped a chivying hand. "Go. She doesn't need to be on display like this for the entire city to gape at."

As Morgan hastened toward the princess, Marissa swung her leg up over Wyvrndell's back. "Ugh," she muttered. It was an awfully long way down from up here, and her legs and feet burned as blood flowed to them again.

"One moment, Lady Marissa," Wyvrndell murmured in her mind. He settled himself lower to the ground and swept his tail around. *"Perhaps this will be of some assistance?"*

"Perfect, thank you." She stepped gingerly onto his tail, wincing at the pins and needles sensation in her limbs. "As long as it doesn't hurt you."

"Not at all. Now, you might be able to walk down my tail, if you balance yourself on my side."

She did so, but noticed his scales felt much cooler than she remembered from previous encounters. "Are you all right?" she inquired. "You seem quite cold."

"A bit tired, perhaps," the dragon admitted. *"It was a long flight and a rather busy night."*

"Yes, I suppose you could say so." Marissa laughed. Once her feet were on solid ground again, she patted Wyvrndell's neck. "Thank you. Again. For saving my life once more."

"It was my pleasure. Not only," he added, *"because I have a vested interest in your continued survival."*

She locked her gaze upon Wyvrndell's huge, green, faceted eyes. "I will help you if I am able," she said. "And not merely because you keep rescuing me."

"Then we understand each other." A rumble that might have been a chuckle came from the dragon's superstructure.

Morgan arrived with Princess Saia, who was now swathed in Marissa's cloak. Even so, the princess shivered uncontrollably. Wyzandar landed, and Alain scrambled hastily from the dragon's back.

Sketching a quick bow to Wyzandar, he trotted over to the princess. "Your Highness," he cried. "You saved us all. You were magnificent!"

"T-thank you," she replied through chattering teeth.

"Princess, you are so cold," the archivist said, catching her hands in his. "Please, allow me to warm you."

A brief smile tinged Saia's nearly blue lips. "That would be…welcome, Alain." He folded her into his arms and wrapped his cloak about the trembling princess.

The sound of boots on the cobbled courtyard heralded the arrival of a guard detail. The soldiers eyed the dragons warily. Marissa was more than happy to let Morgan deal with this lot. She had other things to worry about right now.

Like the ruby.

She could feel its dark, angry weight tucked away in her pack. How she'd managed to hang onto the jewel, when she'd been nearly catapulted into the Thundermist Sea, was anyone's guess. Perhaps the jewel, like the grimoire, preferred her company to the alternative of spending eternity at the bottom of the sea. The two magical items together in her pack had probably not been such a good idea. She shivered at the thought of what they might conspire together.

Well, it didn't matter now. What mattered was what she needed to do with the blasted ruby. She focused her attention back on Morgan, who was staring down the guard captain.

"Yes, Captain," Morgan said in a commanding voice, "I do indeed expect you to summon His Majesty at the crack of dawn. The Royal Enchantress has just now returned from a vital mission, one the king himself set her. He will, I'm quite certain, wish to be informed of her safe arrival and of the status of her mission. Do it, Captain. Now."

Morgan's voice remained calm—he didn't even use what he liked to call his "parade ground" bellow—but his tone carried the authority of command. Under its force, the guard captain saluted, spun neatly on his heel, and sprinted toward the palace.

"Well done," she murmured.

He quirked a grin at her. Then, evidently recalling the stress of their flight from Arvindir, he asked, "Are you all right?"

She shrugged. "Not really. I need a hot bath, a very, very large cup of tea, and about three days' sleep. None of which I foresee in any possible future. Instead, we have to wait for Rhys. Then, wait even more for Foxwent. Oh, Morgan, I just want this to be over."

He heaved a sigh. "I know, I know. Well, it should be over soon enough, eh? One way or the other."

He took her hand in his, then pulled her close. The warmth of his body felt exquisite. For a brief instant Marissa was ready to chuck the ruby into the midden and go home. Home, with Morgan. To spend eternity together, only the two of them. No more dragons. No more wizards. No more magic. Except the kind they'd make together.

A cock crowed, loud and raucous and utterly prosaic. Marissa shook herself, as if released from a spell. She grimaced. "I suppose we'd better send for the Chief Wizard."

"Don't sound quite so excited about the idea," Morgan said. "But you're right. I'll send one of this lot," he gestured toward the guardsmen, "to present the Royal Enchantress's compliments and fetch him hither."

"My, he even talks like a duke. 'Fetch him hither,' indeed. Well, while you're at it, perhaps you can send someone for Master Sebastien. He ought to be here for this."

Morgan trotted over to where the guardsmen stood at attention. Marissa closed her eyes for a moment.

"I hope you won't mind," Wyvrndell put in, *"I anticipated you might wish Sebastien's presence. I have already notified him of your*

return. He is on his way."

"Brilliant," she told him. "Thank you. I suppose you could have told King Rhys too, couldn't you?"

"I could have done," Wyvrndell replied. *"But I would not have ventured to do so. He is your king, after all. It might have seemed presumptuous on my part."*

"No, you're right. One moment, I need to tell Morgan not to bother about Sebastien." She hastened over and filled him in.

"Fine. Only one wizard to corral instead of a pair." Morgan nodded, tossing a half salute to the dragon. "Should save some time. I hope they can track down Foxwent. I don't know if he lives at the Royal College of Wizards, but it's where I've sent our messenger. If he's not there, hopefully someone will send him on in the right direction."

"I'm surprised he's not already here," Marissa mused. "I'd rather assumed he'd sense the Demon's Fire's presence."

He nodded slowly. "Yes, I see what you mean. I—ah, here's Sebastien. Good."

The old wizard strode up the street toward them. His hat was askew, its feather bobbed, and his robes flapped round his legs. "So, you're back in one piece, eh?" he said as he approached. "Well done. Did you get it?"

Marissa nodded. "We did. And almost lost it again. That's a tale for another day. We're waiting for Rhys and for the Chief Wizard."

"You feel the king should be present?" Sebastien's eyes were alight with interest. "Simply to return the purloined jewel to the Chief Wizard?"

"Yes, as we've discussed—courtesy of Wyvrndell—at some length. Morgan agrees."

Sebastien gave her a tight smile. "Yes, of course. Well, I must say, I'm sorry you've been put into such an awkward position by all this."

"By the Chief Wizard, you mean."

"Well, yes." Sebastien's expression was a cross between amused and grim. "I suppose he thought he was being quite clever."

"By sending Marissa and not a wizard?" Morgan put in.

"Yes, exactly." Sebastien gave a slight grin. "Unfortunately, he underestimated his opponent, as he's soon to learn. Well, here comes the king. I suppose I should fix my hat, eh, and straighten my robes? I'd hate to look like something the cat dragged in when His Majesty joins us."

Marissa saw Rhys emerge from the palace. He was dressed casually, rather like he'd been the night he, Barzak, and Foxwent had interrupted a long-anticipated evening. Well, Marissa supposed he'd been woken from a sound sleep and hadn't wanted to bother with any formal regalia. She couldn't blame him even a little bit.

Although, she reflected with a tinge of bitterness, at least Rhys had in all likelihood seen his bed. Something neither she nor her companions had managed. Sleeping on a dragon's back just didn't bear contemplation, even in one's wildest fantasies. One simply held on and hoped for the best.

"Good morning, Your Majesty," she called as Rhys came near enough not to have to shout. "Thank you for coming."

Striding along, his boots beating a tattoo on the cobbles and his retinue of guards on double-time march to keep pace, the king exuded an aura of...eagerness, perhaps? Did he have some sense of what was about to happen? Marissa didn't see how, but with Rhys, one never knew. He just...knew things.

"Well met, Royal Enchantress," he said, halting before their little group. Well, not really little, when one added in three very large dragons. "Duke Morgan. Master Sebastien." Rhys returned his attention to Marissa. "I am glad to see you back safe and sound. Was your mission successful?"

"In a manner of speaking," Marissa replied enigmatically. "While we await the arrival of Wizard Foxwent, there's something else we've brought you."

"Indeed?" Rhys's brows went up. "What? Something exotic from Parthane?"

Marissa smiled. "You might say so. Please, come with me." She led Rhys to where Alain and Saia were still huddled together. "Your Majesty, please allow me to present Princess Saia, of Arvindir. And this is Alain, formerly the head underarchivist in Arvindir. Alain was—is— one of Lord Holman's agents. He was extremely helpful in our quest to retrieve the ruby. As for the princess, well, her brother, Prince Azim, tried to murder us when we fled Arvindir last night. It was only thanks to Saia we were able to make good our escape."

Saia unfolded herself from Alain's arms and faced the king. Alain gave a low bow. Saia said, "I am sorry to intrude upon you like this, Your Majesty." She shrugged. "I'm not sorry I killed my pig of a brother. Not a bit. Arvindir will be much better without him."

"I...see..." Rhys said, his brow furrowed. Then he rallied. "Welcome to Kilbourne, Princess Saia. Please accept our hospitality while you are here."

"Thank you," she replied. "Although, I must warn you. I'm not going back."

"It's a long story," Marissa muttered in Rhys's ear. "We'll get it sorted out, don't worry."

"As you say," he replied, bemused. "Although I hope her father doesn't cause trouble over this."

Saia snorted. "My father? He will be glad to see me gone, I imagine. And since no one in Arvindir can possibly know what happened to Azim, well, he'll simply have to wonder."

Rhys turned to his Royal Enchantress. "What did happen to the prince?"

"Later, if you don't mind, Your Majesty? Right now, I have yet another very powerful wizard to deal with, and I need to prepare myself. This will not be pleasant."

Rhys's brows shot up. "But... you retrieved the ruby, didn't you? Isn't it just a matter of handing it over to the Chief Wizard?"

Morgan put a hand on the king's arm. "Rhys, it's not quite that simple. There are ...complications."

"Complications, eh?" echoed the king. "Morgan, this doesn't bode well. Are there demons involved?"

Marissa gave him a tight smile, all teeth and no humor. "In a manner of speaking, Your Majesty. Please, just watch, and you'll see. I'd rather not say any more beforehand."

"She's right, Rhys," Morgan said. "Trust us, will you?"

Rhys's gaze shifted from Morgan to Marissa, then back again. He cocked his head, then nodded once. "Very well, Duke Morgan, Royal Enchantress. Please proceed as you see fit."

"Thank you," Marissa said. "Can we get the princess some place where she can a hot bath and a change of clothes? And Alain too. I'm sure he would like to make his report to Lord Holman."

"Yes, indeed," Rhys replied. "Sergeant!" he called to one of the guardsmen.

When the guard had gotten his orders and taken the Parthanians in charge, Marissa breathed a small sigh of relief. At least one hurdle was cleared. A relatively minor one, in the grand scheme of things. Still if Rhys had balked, it might have made what she needed to do that much more difficult. Now, there was only Foxwent left to deal with.

She extracted the ruby from her pack and walked slowly back to the square where the dragons waited. They huddled—well, as much as three enormous dragons could huddle—against a building in a rather futile attempt to remain unobtrusive.

"Wyvrndell?" she called. "I think it's time we prepare for the Chief Wizard. I imagine he'll make his appearance quite soon."

"Very well," the dragon replied.

He, Aireantha, and Wyzandar moved back into the square to

flank Marissa. As they did, she weighed the Demon's Fire ruby in her hand. Hopefully she wasn't making a grave mistake in what she was about to attempt.

"Lady Marissa, I believe you are correct in your assumptions," Wyvrndell murmured. *"We will help you, as you have requested. Do not be afraid. You have a dragon's heart."*

She took a deep breath, then let it out slowly in order to center herself. Very carefully, she placed the ruby on the ground, then stepped back from it several paces until she was practically up against Wyvrndell's chest. Morgan came to stand with her. Sebastien took up a post to their right. His eyes were bright, and he flashed her a quick smile of encouragement. Next to him, Nardis waited, his face impassive.

Scanning the square, she saw movement. The guardsman who had been dispatched to fetch Chief Wizard Foxwent was on his way back. In his wake, the wizard stalked. His face was creased in a scowl, his hat was askew, and he thumped his staff down at every step.

"What is the meaning of this?" Foxwent demanded as he entered the square.

"Why, Chief Wizard," Marissa said. "You ordered me to retrieve the Demon's Fire ruby. I have done so and have brought it here for you."

"Yes, well… well done, I suppose. You could have waited until after breakfast, couldn't you?"

Morgan stiffened at his words and seemed ready to retort. She squeezed his hand, and he settled. "Why, you were so eager to have the ruby back in your possession, Chief Wizard, I feared to delay, even for a moment. Though we rode through night and storm, at great peril to ourselves, with no rest at all, my first thought was to bring you the ruby you so greatly desired."

"All right, very well, give it to me." The wizard sounded peevish.

Marissa supposed he had sufficient reason. As she was about to demonstrate. "It is here, Master Foxwent. I have placed it on the ground. You have only to take it."

Foxwent spied the ruby and stepped forward, an eager expression lighting his face.

She said quickly, "Before you take it, there is one thing I would like to ask you."

He halted. "Well?"

"Tell me again, Chief Wizard, why it was you wanted me specifically to go retrieve the ruby? Not some powerful wizard. Me, an untried, very inexperienced witch."

His eyes narrowed. "I thought I explained it quite clearly. Prince

Azim would have known why a wizard was there and dealt with him accordingly."

Marissa cocked her head. "Not, then, because I would not have been able to sense the ruby's true nature? And your connection to it?"

"True nature? Connection?" Foxwent scowled ferociously. "Duke Morgan, what nonsense are you allowing your wife to speak?"

"Nonsense, Chief Wizard?" Morgan bared his teeth. "I don't think so. Let us see, shall we?"

She sent a command to the dragons. Each craned their neck over the humans, focused intently on the ruby. It lay, winking darkly crimson, in the morning sunlight. Then, as one, they began to breathe their combined fire upon the jewel.

Foxwent opened his mouth to protest as their fire hit the ruby. Then, soundlessly, he began to twitch and writhe. The dragons increased the intensity of their flame, and he whimpered softly.

"I questioned all along," she said, "why you chose me, of all people, for this task. You certainly held me in no regard as a practitioner of magic. Not that there was any reason you should, but it seemed odd. So I began to wonder if there was something about the ruby requiring you to keep it away from the other wizards. I discussed this idea it at length with Wyvrndell, my tutor, and through him with Master Sebastien. Both agreed it was unusual. Still, it wasn't conclusive. Not by itself."

She raised a hand, and the dragons ceased aiming their fire at the ruby. Foxwent passed a hand over his face, more himself again. A restorative spell, no doubt. Marissa smiled grimly. He would need more than restoratives, soon enough.

"Then I got to thinking about demons," said. "My family has somewhat of a history with them, you know. My father was expelled from the Academy because he was unjustly accused of summoning one. I wondered, Chief Wizard, if perhaps you hadn't somehow managed to summon a demon yourself. From his imprisonment in the ruby." She raised her hand again, and the dragons resumed their assault on the jewel.

Foxwent screamed as their combined fire engulfed the ruby. Marissa watched him, even as her stomach churned. "Our research revealed your rise to power within the Wizard's Council began about the time the ruby was found," she went on. "This was an interesting coincidence. Unfortunately, I don't really believe in coincidence. Was it, perhaps, the source of your power, Chief Wizard? We wondered. Oh yes, we wondered. In fact," and here she gave a sign to the dragons, who redoubled their assault on the ruby, "we wondered if you were really less Chief Wizard Foxwent and more a demon, taken over his form, in order to gain control over the wizards. With plans to wreak who knows what havoc in the world."

It was horrible to watch. As the dragons continued to sear the ruby with their flames, the wizard's skin began to slough off. Writhing, squirming, Foxwent seemed to shrug off the remnants of his human coverings. As he gibbered and steamed and cursed, Marissa saw revealed the red, scaly skin of a demon.

"Enough," screamed the creature that had once been Foxwent. He swelled now, rising to twice the height of a man. He stalked forward, toward the ruby.

"Your prison awaits you," Marissa said. "Return to it, now."

The demon laughed, and it was terrible. The onlookers held their ears and quaked. All except Marissa. Resolute, she faced the demon.

"If your dragons destroy the ruby, what then?" demanded the abomination from the netherworlds. "I will be free to ravage your world as I have long desired."

"Oh, that was merely a trial, to confirm my theory was correct," Marissa said. She drew in a deep breath, let it out again, and asked, "Will you go willingly back to your prison? Or do I have to destroy you, here and now?"

"You, destroy me? You puny mortal! You could not even tickle me, not with your measly powers. It is I who shall destroy you. All of you!" The demon gazed around at the gathered humans, who cowered in horror at his aspect, and then at the dragons. "Even these, I shall devour," he cried.

Marissa had shrugged off her pack, and now she withdrew something from it. "No," she said quietly. "You shall devour none here, demon spawn of the netherworlds. You shall be banished, back to prison again." She flung the object she held to the ground before the demon. *"Aviasti, enzunati, makelmin!"* she cried.

The grimoire, lying on the ground, opened suddenly. From it a golden light flowed upwards to engulf the demon. The light swirled, like a dust devil in a breeze. The demon raged and struggled, but the light bound him and held fast. It dragged him slowly but inexorably toward the grimoire.

"Enzunati!" she repeated. "Be gone, foul creature of darkness. You are not welcome in this world."

She gestured, and power surged from her hands. The demon, still caught in the throes of the golden light, grew rapidly smaller. It ranted and sizzled, screaming with rage as it shrank, struggling desperately to break free. Marissa's spell, wrought from the grimoire's dark pages, pulled the demon toward the book. The swirling light faded as it receded back toward the grimoire, and it dragged the cursing demon along with it.

She stood impassive now, summoning up the strength to do what had to be done. In a low, harsh voice, she chanted ancient words of power, aimed at cleansing the world of the demon who had become Foxwent. The swirling light, bearing the still raging monster, flowed back into the book.

And then, the demon was gone. The golden light winked out. The book slammed closed. She sagged.

Morgan caught her in his arms before she could fall to the ground. To Wyvrndell, he growled, "Destroy it. Destroy it with fire. Now."

All three dragons trained their flames upon the grimoire. More and more, hotter and hotter, their combined fire scorched the little book. Together, they accomplished what Morgan's small fire, back at Marissa's townhouse, could never have done.

The grimoire smoked, curled, then burst into flames. In moments, the dragons reduced it to a mere heap of ashes. Still more superheated flame they directed upon it, even the ashes, until at last, there was nothing left at all, save for a single flake that floated skywards, was caught in a sunbeam, and winked into nothingness.

Chapter Forty-One

Morgan shook his head, like a dog attempting to dislodge a pesky fly, in an effort to banish the overwhelming combination of weariness and horror he felt. He'd seen many awful things in his career as a soldier, but nothing to equal this. He uttered a silent prayer Marissa would be able to sleep at night after what she'd been required to do. He held her tightly, and she gave him a wan smile.

"My God," breathed Rhys, his eyes wide and staring. "I...I can't believe it. Poor Foxwent."

Sebastien stepped forward. "Have no sympathy for Master Foxwent, Your Majesty," he said. "He crafted his own fate when he attempted to bargain with that monster from the nether hells. His lust for position, for absolute power, became his ultimate downfall. He was subsumed by the very horror he tried to control for his own ends."

"How could he have continued to function as Foxwent?" Rhys demanded. "I don't understand it. He seemed...well, human."

"I'm sure a part of the creature was still Foxwent," Sebastien said. "He was, after all, an extremely powerful wizard. He couldn't control it, I imagine. Still, he could continue to play the part of Chief Wizard, even as he laid his plans to overrun the world with his fellow demons."

"What?" Rhys's mouth gaped open. "You think he would have done such a thing?"

"Foxwent himself, no. But he was fading. The demon possessed Foxwent's knowledge and his cunning. The ruby was central to his scheme for annihilation. When it was stolen, he knew he needed to act quickly. He couldn't send another wizard to retrieve it. Any wizard worth his salt would have recognized the connection between Foxwent and the jewel. Even in the short time it was gone, my sources tell me the Chief Wizard reported he was unwell and took to his chambers. He needed the ruby's presence, for it was the source of his power, and the connection was strong. When it was stolen, he began to fade. So, he contrived the admittedly brilliant scheme of sending Lady Marissa to retrieve the jewel he desperately needed. He assumed she would never even contemplate any connection or his true nature. That was his mistake, for Lady Marissa is not only a powerful witch, but an intelligent and curious woman as well."

She flashed the old wizard a fond smile. "As I told Foxwent— well, what used to be Foxwent— it was hard not to wonder about his motives. Both for wanting the jewel back so desperately and for his insistence on dispatching me to retrieve it. Fortunately, I had Wyvrndell's assistance, and through him, Sebastien, to try to determine between us what it was all about. Or at least what we thought the Chief Wizard might be up to."

"Simply incredible," Rhys murmured,. "Now, what do I do about the Wizards Council, I wonder? With both Foxwent and Rhenn gone…"

"Your Majesty, if I might make a suggestion?" Marissa said.

"Please, do," the king replied.

"Why not place Master Sebastien as head of the Wizards Council," she said, even as Sebastien waved his hands wildly in negation. "Only temporarily, of course, in an effort to smooth the way. Until the Council can come together to determine how best to proceed. Sebastien has proven himself a most capable and honorable wizard and unswervingly loyal to Kilbourne. I believe he would be an excellent choice."

"I don't know," Rhys said. "I'm not sure I have the authority to do such a thing, The wizards will be—"

"The wizards," Morgan interrupted, "are likely to be in a complete dither after they learn what has happened. Remind them they've allowed themselves to be ruled over by a demon. And keep in mind, it is after all the 'Royal College of Wizards', isn't it? I believe this might give you some leeway to pose such a solution."

"Mmm," the king mused. "Perhaps you're right. Master Sebastien? Would you be disposed to take on this challenge, as a personal favor to the Crown?"

The wizard grimaced, glared for a moment at Marissa, then nodded. "When you put it that way, Your Majesty, I can hardly refuse, now can I?"

"Good man," said Rhys. "Hopefully, it will not be for too long."

"And we," Morgan said, keeping a firm hold on his bride, "are headed home. My lady is exhausted from her labors these past few days and today especially. I fear it's taken its toll upon her."

"Of course," Rhys said. "We owe you a great debt. Both of you. But it may wait upon the morrow. Sleep well, duchess. You have earned it. Just a moment, though. I need to speak to you about another matter, but first…"

He turned now to the dragons, Morgan was glad to see. To them, the king said, "Please, Wyvrndell, introduce me to your companions."

The dragon stretched his neck toward the white dragon. *"This is Aireantha, my dearest friend. And this elderly dragon,"* he nodded toward the other, *"is my sire, Wyzandar."*

"Elderly dragon, indeed," grumbled the older dragon, but Morgan could tell his heart wasn't in it. His attitude, if such could be countenanced, seemed one of tremendous pride in his offspring.

Rhys bowed to each dragon in turn. "Wyvrndell. Aireantha. Wyzandar. I bid you welcome. Indeed, you may consider yourselves always welcome here in Caerfaen. We owe you a great debt as well. First, for aiding our agents in their flight from Arvindir. And especially, for your service here today to help us rid the kingdom of the monster who lurked unbeknownst among us. Please convey my compliments to King Petrandius. Urge him to craft an agreement of mutual cooperation at his earliest convenience, as we have discussed. And," he said to Wyvrndell, "I shall encourage the Royal Enchantress, as soon as she feels able, to assist you in your quest to obtain magic."

"Thank you, King Rhys," Wyvrndell replied, speaking so everyone could hear. *"We will return to our home now, to do as you ask. And to prepare for Lady Marissa, when she is ready."*

The dragons stretched their wings, then leapt into the air and took flight, toward the north. Rhys turned to back to Morgan and Marissa. "Before you go, there is one bit of news I need to tell you."

"From your expression, I'm pretty certain isn't good news, is it?" Morgan said.

"I'm afraid not. Although, with Foxwent gone now, perhaps it won't be quite as bad. Anyway, here's the nub. A group of bishops of the church have declared witches, and anyone who associates with them, anathema. There are rumblings about excommunication and worse."

"Worse?" Marissa stared, horrified. "What could be worse?"

"There have been ecclesiastical trials of witches before, Enchantress." The king's face was grim. "They are long in the past, fortunately. But they were…well, brutal, to be honest."

She clung to Morgan's arm and squeezed her eyes closed for a moment. "Damn. It's the prophecy, after all," she muttered.

Morgan stared at her. "Prophecy? What are you babbling about?"

"Oh, I never told, you, did I? I'm sorry, Morgan, what with one thing and another, it completely slipped my mind. I met Miss Alford, who is the head of the Witches' Council. She told me about a prophecy, which I have to confess I scoffed at. It said the witch who was foretold, whom she claimed was me, would rise to save her sisters from their oppressors. Or something to that effect. I told her it was nonsense. Now, I'm not so sure. Damn! I really didn't want her to be right about this. I reckon she was."

Rhys patted her arm. "Duchess, I hated to even mention it, but I wanted you to know what's happened while you were away. I've been working with Bishop MacFarlane to do what I can to circumvent these blasted renegades. It was he who alerted me to what they were about. He, and Captain Poldane, have both been very helpful"

"What have you managed?" Morgan asked.

"Well," Rhys said hesitantly. "At Bishop MacFarlane's suggestion, later this morning I will be issuing a proclamation, which places any witches who pledge to use their powers for good under the Crown's protection. To be overseen," here he glanced warily at Marissa, "by the Royal Enchantress."

"Oh." She sighed. "Of course. It would have to be, wouldn't it? The prophecy."

He held up his hands, as if to ward off a blow.

She shook her head. "Don't worry, I'm not angry. What I am right now is tired. I want to go home." She snuggled a bit deeper into the security of Morgan's embrace, then regarded Rhys thoughtfully. "Which isn't to say I shan't be angry once I've had a bath and a rest and a decent meal," she warned. "We'll see."

The king chuckled. "By all means, get along home. You've earned it. Both of you. I'd best go see to our, um, unexpected guest. I'm sure Gwyn thinks I've lost my mind, sending her a bedraggled Parthanian princess."

Morgan gave his liege a curt nod and led Marissa away. He'd spotted a sedan chair not far away and decided it an ideal means to transport them back to McRobbie House. As they walked, albeit unsteadily, toward the chair men, Morgan, as unobtrusively as he could manage, ground a stray piece of ash beneath the sole of his boot. No sense, he rationalized, in allowing it to wander about and somehow cause trouble.

"Morgan," Marissa said as he handed her into the sedan chair. "I don't like this."

"Much better than walking, don't you think?" He clambered in beside her, pulled the door closed, and rapped on the front of the box.

The chair men hoisted up their cargo and headed down the street.

"Not what I meant, and you know it. I meant I don't like this whole thing about the church causing problems for witches."

"No, no more do I," he replied. He'd closed his eyes. The gentle rocking motion of the chair threatened to put him to sleep. He straightened, opened his eyes again, and said, "Still, it sounds like Rhys has the situation at least somewhat under control."

"Perhaps."

Morgan glanced sharply at her. "You have doubts?"

Marissa nodded. "There have been stories from long past, of the persecution of witches by the church. I've read about them, although at the time, not knowing I was one, I didn't really give them much more than passing pity. I never realized I might one day be placed in the same situation. As will you, Morgan, if these bishops get their way."

"Me? I'm not the one with... Oh. Because I am 'consorting' with a witch, you mean?"

"Yes, oh consort," she replied. "That's exactly what I mean. I suppose we'd best talk to Randolph as soon as possible, hadn't we?"

"Not," Morgan replied, "until tomorrow. Whatever lies ahead, it'll keep until then. You've been through enough for one day. One lifetime, if you want the gospel truth. You—well, both of us—need food, rest, and that hot bath you've been dreaming about. Not necessarily in that order."

She gave him a tired smile. "You make a darned nice consort," she said, and hunkered down, with her head on his shoulder. Moments later, he heard her breathing deepen, and she was asleep.

Chapter Forty-Two

Marissa yawned so widely she felt her face would crack in half. Sebastien chuckled. "Serves you right," he said.

She clung to Morgan's arm to keep from toppling right over there in the morning room. She regarded the wizard with bleary eyes. "Serves me right, how?" she demanded.

Even though she'd gotten a partial night's sleep, she wasn't at her most coherent. She'd not even had her morning coffee yet, and here Sebastien was, expecting her to think.

"It was you who told the king to make me Chief Wizard. What do I know about running things, I ask you? Here I was, all prepared to take life easy. Now I'm in the soup, for sure."

"It's only temporary, Sebastien," she said. "Just until they can sort things out."

"Hmph!" he replied. Glaring at her, he tugged on his beard. "Wizards, sort anything out? They'll still be arguing at the last trump. I'll be trapped there for years."

She drew herself up and stared the old wizard in the eye. "Well, I'm sorry, I'm sure. I thought Rhys needed someone on the Wizards' Council he could trust. Since you're the only trustworthy wizard I know—well, there's Nardis, of course, though he's much too young. I'm afraid you were the only logical choice."

"I suppose." He sounded far from convinced. "I do have a couple of ideas, mind you."

"See, I knew it." She beamed at him. "Oh. I suppose you'd better have this." She pulled the ruby from her reticule and held it out. "I've had quite enough of magical artifacts to last me several lifetimes, thank you very much."

"Amen," Morgan muttered.

Sebastien took the ruby and weighed it thoughtfully in his hand. "What you did yesterday could have gone wrong in about a thousand different ways."

She shivered and felt Morgan's arm tighten around her. "I know. It needed to be done, didn't it?"

"Oh, absolutely," the wizard agreed. "And no one else could have managed it. You did well, m'lady. Very well, indeed. We wizards—the entire kingdom, perhaps even the world—owe you a great debt."

"Well, you can repay it, at least in part, by securing the blasted ruby away some place where no one will ever mess with it again. Perhaps the dragons would agree to guard it."

"Hmm. I don't know. I'll consider it. In the meantime, I'll figure some way to keep the thing safe. Both from thieves and from wizards with more ambition and less sense than is good for them. At least we don't have to worry about the grimoire any more. That's a relief, I must say. Well, I'd best be going, I reckon. I shall have a lot of explanations to make soon, once the Council realizes what has happened."

"Be sure to remind them," Morgan suggested, "what happened is only because they let themselves be taken in by a demon, who basically was in charge of their Council. Might give them some food for thought, eh?"

"Ha! It might. It's worth a try, anyhow."

A tap sounded at the door. Briana entered to say, "My lady? There's a young woman at the door. She said you invited her to call. A Miss Taggart?"

"Good heavens," Marissa said. "I'd completely forgotten about her."

"And you're surprised by this how?" Morgan asked.

She could see the lines in his face and knew her own probably mirrored it perfectly. A night's sleep hadn't really begun to make inroads in the exhaustion she felt.

"Well, I can't send her away," she said. She flapped a hand at the maid. "Please show Miss Taggart in, Briana. Oh, please see if Cook can provide tea and cakes, if there are any."

"Very good, m'lady." Briana scurried off. Marissa heaved a sigh.

"Sorry, Morgan. If I cry off now, the poor girl will likely never trust me."

Sebastien spoke up. "Well, since you have another guest, I'd best take my leave. Where the deuce is my hat?" He scanned around the room, then peered suspiciously at Morgan and Marissa, as if they might have taken it upon themselves to hide it.

Marissa felt Morgan stifle a chuckle. She wasn't as successful.

"Umm. It might serve to check your head, Sebastien."

Reaching up slowly, the wizard's fingers found the missing hat. "Well, bless my soul," he declared. "Who would have ever thought to look for it there? I'll lose my head, next."

"If you do," Morgan suggested, "you might consider searching under your hat."

Sebastien gave him a baleful glare, spoiled somewhat by the lines of mirth crinkling his face. "All right, I'm a doddering old idiot," he agreed. "Still, it has been a rather stressful few days. And yes, I know for you two even more so. I'll leave you and see what I can do with this passel of wizards. Not that I'm sanguine in the least about the prospect, mind you." Tucking the ruby away in a pocket, he headed toward the door as Briana ushered in Kate Taggart.

"Good day, my lady witch," Sebastien said to her as he passed, touching his hand to his hat.

Marissa stared after him, her mouth opening in surprise.

"What?" demanded Kate, rounding on him. "What did you call me? Wait a minute, you. You can't just go on your merry way! Come back here."

He paused in the doorway. "Yes, I can," he said. "Witch I said, and witch I meant. I'm sure Lady Marissa will be happy to explain. She's all up on unbeknownst witches, as you might say. Now, good day to you all." And, swirling his cloak around him, he departed at speed.

"But I—" Kate stared at his retreating form, then turned to Marissa, her face a mask of bewilderment. "What on earth was he on about?"

Marissa, having put the clues together, gave her a wan smile. "It's a rather long story, I'm afraid," she replied. "And unless I miss my guess, it'll go down much better with a round of tea and cakes. Please come in sit down, and I'll try to explain it to you." She moved forward to take the other woman's arm. "Sebastien is a good friend, and a good judge of...well, witches, I suppose you could say. He's the one who discovered I'm a witch. Although here, I think, he was simply showing off, since I've put him a rather awkward position, and he's not best pleased with me. Please, won't you have a seat?"

Kate stared blankly at her for a moment. Then she shook her head as if to clear it. "I'm sorry, but I just don't understand."

Marissa smiled in sympathy as she led her to a comfortable chair.

"Morgan," she said, "why don't you go off somewhere and do duke-like things? I don't need you hovering while I explain things to Miss Taggart. Oh, see if you can hurry along the bloody tea, I'm dying here."

"Yes, my love." He planted a kiss on Marissa's cheek, sketched a bow to Kate, and left them.

Kate choked back a laugh. "Good heavens, you have him well trained, don't you? How do you do it?"

"Witchcraft," Marissa said and grinned. Before she could continue, Briana appeared with the tea trolley, loaded with a welcome cargo of iced cakes, cups, and a steaming pot of tea. "Thank you, Briana, I can pour," she said.

Once Briana departed, Marissa poured strong tea and divvied up the cakes. Taking the first, marvelously restorative sip, she felt it warm her down to her toes. "My, I needed that," she breathed.

Kate blew on her cup. Gazing over the rim, she said, "I must apologize for showing up on your doorstep like this. I suppose I should have sent a message round first. You did say to call, and…"

"I'm delighted you took me at my word. I'm just afraid I'm not quite at my best at the moment. We've only recently returned from a long journey, via dragon, and destroyed a particularly nasty demon yesterday. I'm afraid I'm a bit the worse for wear."

Kate stared at her. "My word. Well, I can come another time." She started to rise.

Marissa waved her back. "No, please, stay. We need to talk."

"About…what that man said?"

"Yes, about what he said. His name is Sebastien, and he is a wizard. The king has just appointed him as Chief Wizard, temporarily, at my suggestion. Which is why he's a bit put out with me. It was Sebastien, as I said, who discovered I'm a witch. He was able to sense the magic dormant in me. I think he did the same thing with you."

"I'm not a witch! I mean, wouldn't I know?"

"I didn't," Marissa said. "Hadn't the faintest idea. I inherited power from my parents. Both were very talented magically, although they never bothered to mention the fact to me, since I didn't display any potential. So, I suppose the question becomes, do either of your parents have magic?"

"I've never seen my father do anything the least bit magical. My mother, I couldn't say. She died when I was very young."

"Oh, I'm sorry," Marissa said, and meant it. She couldn't imagine what it must have been like to have grown up without a mother. "How rotten for you."

Kate shrugged. "My dad took good care of me, at least as much as he was able. I suppose my mother might have been a witch. It seems so crazy."

Marissa poured more tea for herself, then held up the pot toward Kate, who nodded. When she'd filled the other cup, Marissa said, "I'm not qualified to say whether or not you have magic in you. But if Sebastien said so, I'm pretty certain it's true. He'd have no reason to make up such a thing, for one. He's very sensitive to magical talent, for another."

Kate took a bite of an iced cake. She swallowed, then asked, "So, what should I do?"

"We'll have to find someone to train you in the arts of magic," Marissa said. "Um, wait. Perhaps, not now."

"Why, 'not now'?"

"Because I've just learned the Church—or at least a faction—is about to declare a war on witches," Marissa told her. "If no one knows you're a witch, you're safer for the moment. At least until I can get things sorted somehow."

"The Church? That's dreadful. How could they do such a thing?"

"Yes, it is, isn't it? King Rhys is doing his best to circumvent these rogue bishops who have created all the bother. I'm sure Bishop Randolph has his own schemes in motion. In the meantime, you're much better off being plain, untalented Katherine Taggart."

Kate snorted. "Enough of a burden in itself, you know."

"I'm afraid I've never met your father," Marissa said. "I've heard stories, of course, but they're—well, only stories. However, I know Morgan has dealt with him on several occasions, and he has a good deal of respect for your father. That's good enough for me."

Kate sipped tea thoughtfully. "So, I simply need to lie low until this business with the Church is sorted out?"

"Lie low? No, not at all. I simply wouldn't spread it around about your potential magical powers. Once things are resolved, then we can see about some training for you. If you want it, of course. If you'd like my opinion, I would recommend it. You don't want to suddenly find yourself casting random spells or something."

Kate choked on a laugh. "No, I suppose not."

"Captain Poldane might look askance?" Marissa asked.

The other woman's mouth curved into a fond smile. "Yes, he might. Although it might serve him right, for being such a nuisance."

"Even if he is an extremely attractive nuisance?"

"Well, yes, he is, for certain." Kate grinned. "And now, I'll thank you for the tea and cakes. And counsel. I shall take my leave. You're done in, and you don't need me here to keep you from your bed."

"I could use a good nap," Marissa admitted.

"More like two solid days in bed."

"I wouldn't say no. I do want you to come again, Kate, and soon. For lunch next time, if you will."

"I'd—I'd like to, Your Grace."

"Bah. No 'Your Grace', please. If we're to be friends, and I sincerely hope we are, please call me Marissa. I'm only a duchess by accident of marriage. I don't think it's really sunk in yet anyway. You can help to keep me from getting a swelled head."

"You're really too kind...um...Marissa," Kate replied.

"See, it wasn't difficult, now was it? All right, plan to come by next Tuesday?"

"I'd like to." Kate gave a shy smile. "Thanks awfully. For everything. For...for being nice, when most people would have taken the opportunity to be horrible."

"The world needs more nice, don't you think? And I see nothing in you to be horrible about. Mind when you open the door," Marissa warned. "Briana likes to listen at the keyhole."

An indignant hiss from the hallway greeted this remark. Kate grinned, rose, said, "Thank you," again and departed.

Morgan came into the room. "I've had a bath drawn for you," he said.

"You," she replied, flowing into his arms, "are all I could have ever desired in a husband."

Chapter Forty-Three

Morgan woke the next morning to find sunlight streaming through the window, casting shadows across the bed, where Marissa lay snuggled under a light quilt. Rubbing his eyes to rid them of sleep, he slipped from the bed and tiptoed to the garderobe.

When he returned, she was hunkered under the covers. He sat in a wing chair, watching the rise and fall of her breast while she slept and counting his blessings. How had he been this lucky, to have won this woman? Their beginning hadn't been especially auspicious, although he supposed he was mostly to blame. He'd kidnapped her, gotten her tangled up with spies and assassins, and nearly gotten her killed. And, at least for a while, it seemed like she'd slapped him at every opportunity. Unbidden, his hand went to the spot where she'd first kissed him, on a night an age ago. The same spot where she'd managed to land a good number of those slaps.

Marissa stirred restlessly. He smiled fondly in her direction. He counted himself most fortunate to have managed, more by luck than by any of his own devising, to have secured the affections of such a formidable, indomitable, beautiful woman. He grinned as he noticed her blinking at him owlishly.

"I love you," he said.

"Well. What a nice sentiment to wake up to." She tossed aside the covers and stretched languorously. "Mmm, it's a bit chilly in here. Why don't you come back to keep me warm?"

"It would be my pleasure, my love," he said.

Sometime later, the warming process having been completed to the satisfaction of both parties, she retired to her bath. A gentle knock at the door heralded the advent of Kevin Jacoby with a large tray of coffee, fresh scones with jam and cream, a large wedge of cheese, and a pile of sausages.

"Thank you, Kevin," Morgan said. He took his first sip of

steaming coffee. "Your timing is excellent."

"Thank you, Your Grace. I thought you'd want to know, a boy arrived with a message for you. I've left it on the tray."

Morgan, who'd been too engrossed in his coffee to notice the note, picked it up curiously. "Who—ah, from Captain Poldane." He cracked the seal and unfolded the paper. Scrawled on it were the words, "I need to see you soonest. Ten o' clock. Aartis."

Morgan glanced at the clock. Half nine already. Here he was, sleeping or lazing, half the morning away. Was this what it was like to be a duke? He'd better not get used to it if he planned to maintain his position as Knight-Commander.

He gave instructions to Kevin to admit Captain Poldane when he arrived and set about getting dressed. Morgan's own bath and shave would have to wait since his bride was still splashing happily in the tub.

He was moving a bit slower than normal. The last several days had taken their toll. Vowing to get back into training, he. slipped his feet into his boots just as the clock struck the hour. Marissa came into the room, clad in a fluffy robe, her hair still damp. She looked delectable, and he was more than half tempted to ignore his imminent caller.

"You're dressed," she observed.

"Well spotted. Aartis sent a note round to say he needs to see me. He should be here any moment, so I'm headed downstairs. I hope you don't mind."

"Not at all," she replied. "I'm tired, sore, and in desperate need of breakfast. I see you've already made inroads on it."

"I left you a substantial share," he assured her. "I knew you'd be famished. See, I even left you some of the sausages."

"You're bearing up nobly under the strain," she teased.

"It was one of the more difficult things I've ever done," he replied gravely. At the sound of the front door knocker being vigorously banged, he said, "There's Aartis now, I imagine. If you'll excuse me?" He stepped over and planted a kiss on her lips. She tried to ensnare him in her arms, but he managed to slip free—albeit with reluctance—and hastened downstairs.

"Good morn, Commander," Aartis said when Morgan entered the morning room where Kevin had led him. "Thank you for seeing me."

"I'm not really sure I had a choice, did I?" Morgan replied.

"Well, I don't know I'd have gone so far as to drag you from your bed. I am glad to find you up and about."

"It's only temporary, I'm afraid. So, what's on your mind, Captain?"

Aartis grimaced. "I know you've been off somewhere on a

mission for the king. I don't know how much you've heard about what a bunch of the bishops are up to."

Morgan nodded. "Rhys mentioned it briefly yesterday. In all honestly, I really haven't had much chance to find out any more."

"Allow me to fill you in." Aartis clasped his hands behind his back like a schoolboy ready for his recitation.

He paced as he made his report. He led with his visit from Bishop Randolph, outlined their meeting with the king, and the plans they had made to attempt to circumvent the bishops' campaign against the witches.

"So," Morgan asked when he'd finished, "you think this was instigated by Chief Wizard Foxwent?"

"Bishop Randolph thinks so. Personally, I've no idea."

"Hmmm. Well, since Foxwent has been, shall we say, dealt with, I wonder…"

"Wonder what?"

"If his demise will have any impact on this whole mess."

Aartis shrugged. "Commander, I wouldn't count on it. I think these chaps were simply itching for an opportunity to do something like this. The fact Foxwent isn't in charge any more won't matter. By now, their scheme has likely taken on a life of its own. What's worse, I think many people—ignorant, uneducated, superstitious people, granted, but there are a lot of them, more's the pity—will be quite happy to rally to the bishops' cause."

"Unfortunately, you're probably right." Morgan scowled. "And it will create real problems for a lot of innocent women."

"Aye, it certainly will." Aartis's expression hardened. "You know, Commander, when Randolph came to me in the first place, this was simply an exercise to me. Now…"

"Now, it's personal?" Morgan suggested. "Because of Miss Taggart?"

"Aye, it's personal. I'll be the first to admit, I'm still a bit in shock to learn she might be a witch."

"Believe me, it takes a lot of getting used to," Morgan assured him. "I speak from experience. Not to mention, persecution like this, under the auspices of the church, is a real danger. Not only for our loved ones, but for so many women who have done nothing to warrant such reprisals. Oh, I'm sure there are a small number who misuse their powers. The vast majority? They've done nothing except use the talents God gave them."

"Very true." Aartis ran a hand through his hair, flipping it out of his eyes.

"So the question becomes, what do we do about it?"

"I bloody well wish I knew. I mean, the simple solution would be to detail a couple of companies of the Legion to round them up…"

Morgan said, "Unfortunately, the simple solution would create even more problems in the long run."

"Oh, I know." Aartis heaved a sigh. "Don't mind me, it was mere wishful thinking. If we did go after them, we'd no doubt make martyrs of them. It would rally even more people to their cause. I don't think there's any hope of convincing the bishops of the error of their ways, either. The whole thing's rather at an impasse."

Morgan grimaced. "It is, damn it. All right, let's take it one step at a time. Have they issued any decree yet? Or is it merely a whispering campaign to begin with?"

"No decree thus far. Randolph thinks they'll try to get the archbishop on their side before they take the next step. He doesn't think that's likely, though."

"Well, perhaps that will buy us some time before they do anything drastic."

"I hope so. Do you know Rhys has already issued his own proclamation? He wanted to get ahead of things. This should provide some measure of protection. For any of the witches who care to avail themselves of it, that is. Not all of them will, I imagine."

"Can't say I know enough witches to have any sense how this might play out," Morgan admitted. "Still, it gains us a little time to come up with a solution."

"I suppose." Aartis shrugged. "You're sure you're dead set against the whole 'march in with the Legion' thing? It would make it much easier."

Morgan snorted. "Let's table it for the moment, shall we? If nothing better presents itself, perhaps we'll reconsider. Anyway, it's a decision Rhys would have to approve. I've got a strong hunch he'd never countenance such a plan unless there was no other option."

"No, I suppose not. Hmm. What about magic?"

Morgan paused in his pacing. "What about it?"

"Well, here we are, with all these witches. Witches have magic… I— No, forget I even spoke, it's daft."

"No, go on, Aartis. It might be daft. Even so, it might spark an idea."

"I don't know, I suppose I just wondered if there was any way their magic might help in some way. I mean, I know they can't use it against the bishops, to change their minds, but…" He shrugged.

"Yes, I see." Morgan nodded. "Perhaps there's something in it.

I honestly don't know. At any rate, there's nothing we can do right here and now. Besides, Marissa is about to undertake a rather daunting task for the dragons, about which least said the better." His eyes narrowed at the prospect. "So, these pesky bishops will simply have to get along without us for a few days." He turned back to Aartis. "In the meantime, let me mull things over a bit. I want to talk to Randolph and Master Sebastien. Then we'll reconvene, after this whole dragon business is done, to see what we can figure to do."

"Very well, Commander." Aartis tossed off a casual salute. "Good luck with the dragons, whatever it may be."

"Go take care of your lady, Captain," Morgan suggested. "That's what I plan to do."

Chapter Forty-Four

Wyvrndell hesitated before he entered the king's council chamber. Upon his return to Ervantium, after rescuing his friends from Arvindir, he'd been met with a summons to attend Petrandius. The messenger had stressed Wyvrndell should make haste, as the king was eager to see him. Which, by and large, meant one of two things: either Wyvrndell done something to earn the king's displeasure or else something to garner his accolades. While he hoped it was the latter, he wasn't really certain.

"Go on," he chided. "Either way, get it over with." With this, he steeled himself and made his way down the short passageway to the chamber where the king awaited him.

The hoary black dragon was not alone. He was engrossed in conversation with Wyzandar and another dragon. Wyvrndell wasn't sure if this was reassuring or even more reason for concern. Composing himself, he bowed before Petrandius. When the king turned to acknowledge him, Wyvrndell spoke deferentially.

"Your Majesty," he said. "You wished to speak with me?"

"Ah, Wyvrndell," Petrandius said. "Thank you for coming so promptly. I know you must be tired after your recent endeavors."

"Perhaps a little," Wyvrndell admitted.

The third dragon emerged from the cavern's shadows, and Wyvrndell's spirits plummeted. It was Jakarian, one of Petrandius's counselors, and a fierce opponent of what he considered Wyvrndell's heretical views. He'd called for banishment (and, in private, even worse) when Wyvrndell had confessed to "consorting" with humans.

Jakarian had railed mightily against the recently signed accord with the Dwarf nation, which had been facilitated through Wyvrndell's friendship with the Dwarf Prince R'gm'l. He'd labeled the younger dragon a traitor to dragonkind and attempted to have him declared anathema. His presence in the king's chamber filled Wyvrndell with a sudden, terrible foreboding.

Petrandius said, "Your sire has just been regaling us with tales of your exploits. He says you planned the extraction of the enchantress and her companions from Arvindir. And you managed to rescue the human enchantress from almost certain death, in what he described as a most spectacular fashion."

Wyvrndell said nothing. He wasn't sure where this would lead. Jakarian stared ferociously at Wyvrndell and steamed silently.

"Finally, he tells me you assisted the enchantress in exposing and destroying an extremely powerful demon which threatened the humans."

"Yes, Your Majesty. I—"

Jakarian spoke at last, his voice tinged with fury. "Peace with Dwarves. Serving as steed to humans! By the Elders, what are we becoming, Petrandius? If this whelp has his way, we'll soon see dragonkind in complete ruin. This cannot continue."

Wyzandar growled, deep in his throat, and Jakarian rounded on him. "I don't care if you are his sire. He is no true dragon, Wyzandar, and you know this to be true."

Before his sire could reply, Wyvrndell said, "Lord Jakarian, would you then have us go back to the old ways?"

His voice filled with contempt, Jakarian replied, "I would indeed. This reckless—"

Wyvrndell cut him off. "So, we should be reduced to hiding in our caverns, to emerge only to steal gold when we can find it? To do battle with Dwarves and men, instead of working with them? You can do so if you wish, Lord Jakarian, but I say the world is moving. If dragons do not move with it, do not take advantage of the opportunities given us, we might as well go into our caverns and never come out again."

Jakarian sputtered in indignation at what Wyvrndell was certain he considered supreme insolence. Wyvrndell pressed on, even as his mind urged him to be silent. It was too late for silence.

"Lord Jakarian, fate has put me where I am. It was fate which led me to encounter Lady Marissa and Sir Morgan. It was this same fate which brought me together with the Dwarf, R'gm'l."

He paused for a moment, to see if Petrandius would order him to silence. The king merely watched, so Wyvrndell continued, "Yes, I consort with Dwarves, which I know disturbs you greatly. By doing so, I have helped facilitate an accord which will let our nations exist in peace and perhaps even, one day, in cooperation. Rather than steal and slaughter as you would have us do. And yes, I even dare to consort with humans. By doing so, I may help us gain something which has eluded dragonkind for our entire existence—magic. I believe fate has directed me toward this end and toward a new place in the world for dragons."

Jakarian stood speechless, and Wyvrndell could sense his silent fury. He had known, even when he first spoke, he would never convince Jakarian to accept his views, to see the world in a new light. He hadn't realized, however, just how adamant the old counselor was, how determined he was to undermine the course Wyvrndell was on.

Glaring at Wyvrndell and his sire, Jakarian nodded brusquely to the king and stalked from the chamber.

Wyvrndell hung his head. "I am sorry, Your Majesty," he said. "I should not have spoken."

Petrandius shook his hoary old head. "That is where you are mistaken. I summoned you here for the express purpose of hearing you speak. So I might understand just how committed you are to the course you fly. I summoned Lord Jakarian for the same reason. I wished him to see how the world is changing."

"Yet all I've done is earn his enmity," Wyvrndell said. "I am sorry. You have supported me, and now Jakarian will be opposed to you as well."

Petrandius shook his head again. "Wyvrndell, there is no law which says we must please everyone else. There will always be differing opinions. Sometimes those differences can be resolved. Sometimes, when a dragon has his head stuck so firmly in his cave, as does Jakarian, there can be no resolution. I, as king of dragons, must act as I see fit to benefit the majority of dragonkind. I believe your actions have helped to lead us to such an outcome. I have done my best to show Jakarian; alas, he refuses to see."

Wyvrndell swallowed hard. "Thank you, Your Majesty. Your words mean a great deal to me."

The king nodded. "Yet even if I opposed your views, I would still expect you to do nothing differently. Well done, young Wyvrndell. Well done indeed."

Wyvrndell stared, unable to speak. Petrandius was never overly generous with praise. This was practically effusive. Finally, he roused himself enough to say, "Thank you, Your Majesty. I have acted in what I deemed the best course both for dragonkind and my human friends. I am glad my actions meet with your approval."

Petrandius nodded graciously. Wyvrndell said, "Your Majesty, when I spoke with King Rhys, he instructed me to tell you to prepare an agreement of mutual cooperation between dragons and humans for him to review."

"Excellent. Yet another feat accomplished," the king said.

"What will you attempt next, I wonder?"

"Your Majesty, if I have overstepped…"

The king cocked his huge head. He regarded Wyvrndell through large faceted eyes. Eyes which, the younger dragon realized in a moment of shock, were cloudy with age. *He is old,* Wyvrndell said to himself. *So very old. Yet what will become of us dragons, if something were to happen to Petrandius?*

"No, young one, you have not overstepped," the king said. "At least, not yet. You have acted in a manner befitting a dragon. A bit impetuous, perhaps, but nonetheless appropriate for that. No, Wyvrndell, what I meant was, it is time for you to undertake to your final task."

Wyvrndell's head jerked up. "Erkarna is ready?" he breathed.

"So he tells me."

Petrandius sounded a bit uncertain of the endeavor. "Is something wrong, Your Majesty?" Wyvrndell asked. "Is Erkarna concerned the ritual might not work?"

"No, not to my knowledge. Erkarna," Petrandius replied, "maintains a perfect confidence." He exchanged a glance with Wyzandar. "Perhaps too much so."

"I—I don't understand," Wyvrndell said.

Wyzandar said, "We have spoken with Erkarna. Suggested to him perhaps some additional dragons, to aid in his endeavor, would be sensible. We asked him share with us some of the secrets of his research. Share just how he expects to accomplish this task."

"He refused," Petrandius said shortly. The old king heaved a steam-laden sigh.

Wyvrndell stared. No dragon simply refused a request from the king himself. It was…inconceivable.

"He said," Wyzandar continued, "he only required one assistant. You, Wyvrndell."

"Oh." There was not much else he could say.

"And so, young one," Petrandius said, "I now ask you. Can you tell us any details of what Erkarna expects to do?"

"I cannot, Your Majesty." At a combined stony glare from his elders, he hastened to say, "Not because I refuse to tell you, but because I honestly do not know. Erkarna has not confided any details to me. My role in this endeavor has been solely to act as liaison to Lady Marissa. To help convince her, if she would, to aid us in gaining the gift of magic we have long sought. Erkarna says he has devised the ritual but has not told me anything about how it works."

"No, he wouldn't," Wyzandar said. "He has always been extremely secretive."

Petrandius shrugged. "Such is his way. Yet if he succeeds, it will be a triumph for the ages, will it not? And much of the credit will go to Wyvrndell, who will have made it possible through his connection with the humans."

"And if he fails?" Wyzandar asked, his tone acerbic.

"He will not fail," Wyvrndell replied. "He has dedicated his life's work to gaining magic for us dragons. I have studied long under his tutelage. I am certain he will accomplish it."

"The enchantress? She will cooperate with Erkarna?" Petrandius, despite his earlier enthusiasm, now seemed dubious.

"Yes, Your Majesty. She has assured me she will."

Wyzandar said, "Wyvrndell, from what I saw on the flight back from Arvindir, and when she faced the demon, she may be willing, but not necessarily capable. She has power, certainly, but no notion how to utilize it."

"From what little Erkarna has told me," Wyvrndell said, "Lady Marissa will not be required to do more than activate the spell Erkarna has devised. It will require magical energy in massive amounts, but little in the way of actual skill to wield it. Erkarna has assured me of this and that it will be safe for her."

Wyzandar and Petrandius glanced at each other. "So, you do know something about what Erkarna intends," the king stated.

"Only what I've just told you," Wyvrndell said. "Truly, I know nothing else. As for massive amounts of magic being required? How could one assume anything else? It is simple logic."

"Simple logic." Petrandius nodded. "Very well, young one. Alert your human friend, this Lady Marissa. I suppose, when this is over, for good or ill, I should stir myself from my own cavern and meet her."

"Your Majesty, I believe you would like her. She has the heart of a dragon."

"Indeed? Where does she keep it?" At Wyvrndell's astonished expression, he said, "No, never mind, it was mere persiflage on my part. I must be getting old. Off you go, then. Hopefully to move us a bit further on in the world. To gain us magic."

"I, along with Erkarna, will do my best, Your Majesty," Wyvrndell replied, bowing low before the king.

"If you succeed, you will usher in a new age for dragons," the king replied. "Go now, and may the Elders smile upon you."

Wyvrndell bowed again and left the chamber. Wyzandar followed after him. "Wait a moment," the older dragon said.

Wyvrndell turned to face his sire. Was this to be another upbraiding? Wyzandar was not as hidebound as Jakarian, but he still viewed his offspring's activities with a jaundiced eye. Mentally preparing himself for another argument, he was shocked when Wyzandar said, "Wyvrndell, I am proud of you."

"I—" For once, Wyvrndell was at a loss for words.

"Jakarian is a fool," Wyzandar went on. "Oh, I know I have sometimes been narrow-minded myself, with regards to your 'consorting' with humans and Dwarves. Petrandius is right, though, when he says you will drag dragonkind kicking and flaming into a new world. A better world. I spoke with the humans I brought back from Arvindir. Actually talked to them. Well, after the fight with the mage, that is. I found them...interesting. I am glad I went with you on this adventure."

"As am I, Father," Wyvrndell said truthfully. "It meant a great deal to me, to have you by my side."

"You comported yourself well. Very well indeed. And I must confess, I now feel if anyone can succeed in bringing magic to us, it is you."

"Thank you, Father."

"Which is why," Wyzandar said, "it grieves me to have to say what I am about to."

Wyvrndell's heart sank. Here it came... Had his sire merely been softening him up to deliver the final blow?

"Beware Jakarian," Wyzandar said. Wyvrndell started in surprise. "He has long been a friend to me, though no longer. He is dangerous to you and your cause. He will do you harm if he can manage it. If you fail, you and Erkarna, in your quest to bring magic to dragons, Jakarian will use it against you. He will be merciless, for you have made him look the fool he truly is. I do not think even I will be able to protect you from him. Only Petrandius might. Yet the king grows old, and weary. If you fail, I fear Jakarian might even use this as an excuse to attempt his overthrow."

"Then we must not fail." Wyvrndell. "We will not fail."

"May the Elders be with you, my son," Wyzandar said. "Go now. This is your time, for good or ill. Use it."

With a conflicted heart, Wyvrndell departed the dragon kingdom of Ervantium to meet his destiny.

Chapter Forty-Five

Aartis followed Jameson, Ian Taggart's factotum and bodyguard, into the crowded sitting room. Ian reclined in an armchair, a sheaf of documents in his hand. He put down the papers when Aartis entered the room, and a welcoming smile spread across his face.

"Aartis, m'boy," he said. "It's been too long since ye've come to call."

Aartis gave his host a glum nod. "Ian," he said.

"Why, what on earth's wrong, boyo? Here I was thinkin' you was here for a glad reason. Instead, you look like someone killed your best hound. Sit down, sit down, and tell me your troubles."

Aartis flopped into a chair. Jameson, at a sign from Taggart, poured two snifters of brandy and handed them round. Taking a restorative sip, Aartis sighed, drank a bit more, then sat up straighter.

"Ian, I have to ask you a few questions. Personal questions." He glanced meaningfully at Jameson. Taggart gave a brief smile, then shook his head in negation. Aartis said firmly, "Extremely personal questions, Ian."

"Indeed? Well, then. All right, Jamie, that'll be it for now. Wait outside, if ye please."

Jameson gave Aartis a searching gaze, as if to say, "Don't upset Mr. Taggart, or you'll have me to answer to." Aartis ignored him, waiting until he had closed the door with an acerbic thump, and faced Ian.

"All right, laddie, what's eatin' ye?" Ian asked.

"Tell me about Kate's mother, Ian."

"What? Her mother. Nae, Aartis, 'tis too much yer askin'. Ye don't need to know such."

"Damn it, Ian, don't you think I realize it? I wouldn't ask if it wasn't important. Perhaps vitally so."

Ian regarded him thoughtfully over the rim of the brandy snifter. He gave a slight nod. "Perhaps," he said, "you might explain just why it's so all-fired important."

Aartis took in a deep breath, releasing it slowly. "Because yesterday, when she went to call on Duchess McRobbie, Kate was informed she has witch blood. The wizard, Sebastien, was on his way out when she entered the house. He sensed it in her."

Ian's eyes were wide. "Nae, it's not possible. Not my Margaret. She was no witch. This wizard, he must be mistaken. Tha's it, he's made a mistake is all."

Aartis shook his head. "I don't think he made a mistake, Ian. He's the same wizard who discovered the magic in Lady Marissa. She inherited it through both her parents. Now, though you're one of the luckiest men I've ever known, I don't think you have any magic in you. So, it must have been passed down from Kate's mother. Your wife."

Ian's eyes squeezed closed. "Aartis, as God's my witness, I don't know. Sure, an' she bewitched me, I reckon. Though I never saw a shred of evidence to suggest Margaret had any magic in her. If she did, she never told me. She never used it, to my knowledge.. If she did have it, perhaps she could have cured herself..." He opened his eyes again, and Aartis saw pain and loss in them.

"I'm sorry, Ian," Aartis said, and meant it. He swallowed hard. "The last thing I ever wanted to do was to dredge up old memories like this for you. Cause you any grief. But if you know anything at all, Kate needs to know it too."

"Why's it important to you, Aartis? Are you telling me you'd not love my Katie if she was a witch?"

Aartis stared, thunderstruck. "What? No, Ian, no! Don't you see? If Kate has witch blood, she'll be subject to all this nonsense those renegade bishops are stirring up. They want to cast witches as evil, cut them off from the sacraments. Maybe even put them on trial. It's happened before, Ian, long ago. From everything I've heard, it was really, really bad. This time, it'll likely be even worse. I need to know, so I can protect her."

"I've heard some whispers about this, Aartis. I really didn't pay much heed. I—well, you know, I've had other matters on my mind. What with one thing an' another..."

"I know." Aartis smiled. "I just thought Kate should know, if you had any notion her mother possessed magical powers."

"Not that I was ever aware of. But, Aartis, Katie's never shown any inkling of having magic in her either."

"No, of course not. Lady Marissa didn't know she had magic in her until a few months ago. From what Morgan's told me, her parents were both extremely talented. They never saw any evidence the talent was passed on when she was young and never mentioned it. She didn't even know her parents had magic until she met this wizard, Sebastien, who was an old friend of her parents. They'd sworn off using it, I guess. The point is, this wizard says Kate has magic. She got it from someone, and you say it wasn't you, so it must have been on her mother's side."

"I suppose so." Ian shrugged. "Although I don't reckon it makes any difference how she got it. The point is, if she's a witch, she'll be in danger from these damned bishops and their obsession. All right, laddie, what do we do about it?"

"Exactly the question I rather hoped you might have an answer for."

Ian's face sagged. "I wish I did, Aartis. See here, this is more political, m'boy, and outside my area of expertise. Even worse, it's church politics to boot. You don't think the king's proclamation will put a stop to it?"

Aartis shook his head. "It may slow them down a little. I hope so. But stopping them? I doubt it. Things like this simply take on a life of their own. A bit like an avalanche—once those first few pebbles start to fall, the only thing you can do is get out of the way and hope to God you don't get caught in it. But there's no way on earth, short of a miracle, to stop it."

Ian grinned. "So, you're saying we need a miracle? What about this bishop who came to see ye? A bit more in his line, ain't it?"

"If only it was that easy. I'm sure Bishop Randolph would have settled the whole mess already, if he were able. He's extremely indignant about the whole thing and calling down thunderbolts from the heavens on his fellow bishops. To no avail, I'm afraid. I've wracked my brain to figure some way to counter this. I've got nothing. I've talked to Commander McRobbie to see if he can come up with anything…"

"An excellent idea. McRobbie's a canny feller; he might see a way through."

"I hope so. Oh, by the way, changing the subject entirely, may I have your blessing to marry your daughter?"

"E'en though she's a witch?"

Aartis grinned. "Even though she's a witch. Well, might be. Probably is. Whatever, it doesn't matter a whit to me."

Taggart sipped his brandy. "Aartis, me lad, it's not me you should be askin', y'know. Have you asked Katie herself?"

"Of course I have. Many times. Finally, she said yes." Aartis grinned again. "I think I wore her down. Plus, I am rather irresistible." He struck a dashing pose.

Ian chuckled as he raised his glass. "Well now, Captain

Irresistible, if you've gotten Katie's consent, I reckon tha's all right, then. I wouldn't care to stand in her way when she's made up her mind on something. Be a bit like yon avalanche ye were goin' on about. So yes, for what it's worth, ye have my blessing. You take good care of her, y'hear? Otherwise, I might have to forget I'm about to become some kind of gentry."

"You've no worries on that score. Thank you. It means a lot to me, to have your approval."

"Ach, get on wit' ye. Perhaps I'll even come to the wedding. I wouldn't want you to get a swelled head."

"You'd jolly well better come. You have to give the bride away, you know."

"Oh." Suddenly, Ian looked a bit unsure of himself.

"Don't worry, it won't be so bad. Now, let's have another round to celebrate. Think of it this way: you're not losing a daughter; you're gaining a son. A... well, you're gaining me, at any rate, and what could be better, eh?"

"Ach, ye young idiot, pour the drinks already, and stop quacking. I hope you know what you've let yourself in for."

"The ride of a lifetime," Aartis murmured as he poured. "The ride of a lifetime. Oh, by the way, apropos of nothing at all, Kate told me you were thinking about selling your house in town."

Ian's brows rose. "Aye, I am," he said. "What—"

"If you are, I'd like to make you an offer for it."

"Aartis, m'lad, you don't need to. I'll sell it just fine."

Aartis nodded. "I've no doubt. This is for me, not you, Ian. Remember, I'm in bachelor officer's quarters. I plan to wed your daughter. I need a place to bring my new bride. What could be better than the home she has such fond memories of? Not to mention, you'd be keeping it in the family."

Silent, Ian sipped his drink. Aartis tossed one last enticement. "Plus, you'd be able to come visit and see your grandchildren there."

Ian's eyes lit with a keen fire. "Grandchildren, ye say? Now there's a thing I'd never thought to hear in all me life, and that's the gospel truth. All right, we'll talk about it further. Pour us another, laddie, and we'll toast to your happiness. And Katie's."

Aartis poured.

Chapter Forty-Six

Randolph pushed open the door to the Knight-Commander's outer office and stepped inside. Morgan's clerk, Arthur, stood to greet him. "Good afternoon, Your Excellency," he said, shedding documents as he rose from behind his desk.

"Hello, Arthur. Good to see you." Randolph inclined his head toward the inner office. "Is he in?"

"Aye, he is. Actin' more like an ol' bear roused from his slumber than commander of the Legion. You're welcome to him."

Randolph grimaced. "You've been giving him paperwork again, haven't you, Arthur?"

"Well, certainly I have. It's me bloody job, ain't it? Beggin' your pardon, of course."

Randolph waved his apology away. "It's all right, Arthur. I'll soon put any thoughts of paperwork out of his head anyway. He'll have bigger problems when I'm done with him."

The clerk rolled his eyes heavenward. "Saints preserve us then. I'll let him know you're here."

"We can only hope. And don't bother, I'll show myself in." Randolph stepped toward the inner door, raised his hand to knock, then dropped it again. Instead, he reached for the knob, turned it, and entered unannounced.

"No more files, Art— Oh, it's you." Morgan's scowl lessened minutely, and he leaned back in his chair.

"You really need to stop bullyragging poor Arthur," Randolph advised. "He's only doin' his job, ya know. It ain't his fault you hate all this paperwork."

Morgan opened his mouth to dispute this, then closed it again, waving away Arthur and his files. "What's wrong?" he asked. "You didn't come here simply to berate me for how I treat my staff."

"No, that was merely an added benefit. You're correct, though, this is not a casual visit. I have news."

Morgan snorted. "I get the distinct impression I'm not going to like this news."

"No, you're not. Actually, you're going to hate it." Randolph pulled over a chair; it was, if not quite suitable for his large frame, at least marginally adequate. Plopping himself onto it, he regarded Morgan. "Before I give you my news, tell me what you've been up to these last several days. You rather vanished off the face of the earth."

"Well, I did get married, you know. I was…occupied."

"Yes, I know. I was there, remember? But 'occupied', eh? Hmph. Not in Caerfaen, you weren't. I heard you left by schooner, returned a-dragonback, and did something pretty drastic to the chief wizard. C'mon, m'boy, tell Uncle Randolph."

"Uncle Randolph, indeed." Morgan snorted. "Very well, you asked for it."

Randolph listened as Morgan recounted the visit from Rhys and company, the trip to Arvindir, the theft of the Demon's Fire, their escape through the storm, the battle with Azim, and the final confrontation with Foxwent—or rather, the thing Foxwent had become.

When Morgan finished, he gave a thoughtful nod. "Well, I reckon you and your lady have had a time, haven't you? I'm surprised you're even here."

"Marissa made me," Morgan admitted sheepishly. "She said I was moping around underfoot and to go do something useful."

Randolph hooted. "Good for her."

Morgan grinned momentarily, then his face grew grim again. "All right, now you're up to date. Give me the worst. I guess I'm as ready as I'll ever be."

It was Randolph's turn to scowl. "Very well." He pulled a paper from the pocket of his robe and passed it to Morgan. "I received this message this morning from the feller I've got keeping an eye on those upstart clergy who want to cause problems for the witches. Read it."

Morgan unfolded the note. A moment later he exploded from his seat, the parchment crumpling into a ball in his hand." "I'll kill them," he growled. "I'll kill them all." His eyes were wide and blazed with fury, his nostrils flaring dangerously. "Where are they, Randolph? I'll go now."

Randolph snapped, "Morgan! Sit down, man. Take a breath. You can't, and you know it. Going crazy won't to do anyone any good. Neither you, nor your bride."

"Oh, no?" Morgan loomed over Randolph, his smile more wolf than man. "Randolph, they want to kill Marissa. I think it might be a most satisfactory way to solve the problem. For everyone concerned."

"And get yourself hanged for murder? Don't be an idiot."

"Damn it, Randolph, they want to kill my wife!"

Randolph sagged in his chair. "Yass, I know, th' bloody great fools. Doesn't mean you can simply hare off and decimate the lot of 'em."

"The hell I can't." Morgan stood there, breathing hard, his hands clenched into fists. "This is your doing."

"My doing?" Keeping a wary eye on his oldest friend, Randolph levered himself out of the chair.

"Yes, you! This whole mess is your fault, Randolph. You convinced Rhys to make Marissa the Royal Enchantress. If not for you, she wouldn't have this target on her back. Maybe I can't kill them right now. But I can start with you!" Morgan pulled back his arm and let fly a wide, roundhouse punch.

Randolph jerked his head aside, a leftover instinct from his long-ago days boxing for the Battling Brothers of St. Mark's Seminary. The blow went harmlessly by, and Morgan staggered in its wake. Then he righted and came at Randolph again, eyes narrowed in fury.

"Get hold of yourself, man," Randolph urged. "You don't want to do this."

"Your fault," Morgan shouted.

Randolph backed away, keeping his chair between them. Morgan lunged again. Randolph managed to edge away once more. He wouldn't be able to keep it up for long, he knew full well. Morgan was a trained fighter. Randolph had boxed, many years ago, and hadn't been bad at it, all in all. This was a totally different kettle of fish. He wasn't dealing with an opponent in a judged competition. Here and now, he was fending off a man beside himself with anger, fear, and frustration, and maybe a touch of madness.

Morgan eliminated the problem of the chair by hurling it out from between them. Randolph swallowed hard. That was an extremely heavy oak chair, and Morgan tossed it aside like a matchstick. He closed now, eyes narrowed, arms raised, ready to strike.

As he let fly another punch, the door flew open. Marissa stepped into the room, Arthur at her heel. Randolph saw her mouth form a shocked "O" even as he ducked Morgan's blow. Arthur's brows rose to unprecedented heights.

"Morgan McRobbie, stop it this instant. Have you gone mad?" she demanded. "What on earth do you think you're doing, you great idiot?"

Taken completely unawares, Morgan staggered when his blow

missed its mark. His boot caught on a footstool, and he careened into the wall. Randolph reached to steady him.

"My fault entirely, Duchess," Randolph said. "I was regaling Morgan with tales of my old boxing bouts. I'm afraid in the reenactment, we might have gotten a bit carried away. No harm done." He cast a gaze around the room. "Well, except perhaps to the furniture."

Morgan hung his head. "Sorry, Randolph," he muttered. "I— I'm sorry. Truly."

"Don't worry, my friend," Randolph boomed, keeping his tone light. "I reckon I've still got a bit of the old footwork left in me, even after all these years. Well, I'd best be going, eh? I suppose I've caused enough chaos for one day. G'day, Duchess, Arthur."

Gathering his robes around him, Randolph swept out of the room with what few shreds of dignity he could muster.

~ * ~

Marissa eyed her husband dubiously. "A reenactment of one of Randolph's boxing matches? Really, Morgan."

"Well…"

"You could have hurt the poor man," she went on, not waiting for him to answer. "You idiot, you're a trained soldier, and he's an out-of-shape priest, for heaven's sake. Which, I suppose, it is," she observed, with a chuckle at her own joke. Well, someone had to. Morgan appeared ready to eat his boots.

"Well, don't just stand there," she said. "Come along. We've got to get going."

"Umm. Going?" He shook his head bemusedly.

"Yes, going. Wyvrndell is on his way. He says the preparations for the ritual are completed, and Erkarna is eager to begin. I might as well get this over with. I thought you might want to come watch."

"The…the ritual? Already?"

She moved toward the door. "Wyvrndell will be here soon. We need to go."

"I—they—"

She glanced back over her shoulder. He seemed to be a bit unsteady from his mock fight with Randolph. A bit strange, but perhaps he was still feeling the effects of their adventure in Arvindir and its aftermath. She was too, heaven knew. Still, after the dragons had been so very accommodating, extracting them from Arvindir and helping to deal with the Foxwent-demon, she wasn't about to tell Wyvrndell no.

She flapped a hand at Morgan. "Of course, if you don't want to accompany me, I don't suppose you really need to."

"All right, I'm coming," he grumbled. "Arthur, let Captain

Poldane know I'll be gone for the rest of today will you? Likely tomorrow too."

"Of course, Commander," the clerk replied.

"Thank you, Arthur," Marissa said. Taking Morgan's hand in hers, she led him from the office. "We'll have just time enough to get back to the house before Wyvrndell arrives," she told Morgan. "I want to change into something a bit warmer to travel. These flights on dragon-back get a bit nippy."

This got a laugh, at least. She led Morgan though a side door of the palace, to where the coachman waited. Dawkes leapt down to open the coach door. Marissa allowed Morgan to help her in and scramble in beside her. Dawkes was already back up on his high seat, and he set the horses in motion before they were even settled.

"You have things well under control," Morgan muttered. "Especially me."

"Well, I did think you'd want to be there. I didn't want to keep Wyvrndell waiting about, after he and the other dragons have been so helpful. We'd have never made our escape from Arvindir without them, would we?"

"No, true enough."

"And Wyvrndell has saved my life more than once now. I do rather feel an obligation, even if I hadn't already said I'd do this."

"Point well taken," he replied. "We both owe the dragons a great deal. I guess I really didn't think it would happen quite this soon. Are you sure you're not too tired to attempt it?"

"Oh, I'm fine," she said. "Always fine, you know me."

Morgan took her hand in his. "Yes, I do," he said. "And I'm worried you aren't up to this yet. You—we—have been through a lot in the last few days."

"Nothing another cup of strong tea won't fix," she said cheerfully. Since this statement put paid to any further objections, Morgan simply stared at her, shook his head, and kept silent.

Chapter Forty-Seven

Morgan leaned against the hard back of the coach seat and took a deep, silent breath. Then another. This attempt at calm did little to settle his frazzled nerves. Damn it, what was happening to him? He was normally cool and collected under pressure. No anxiety, merely an urgency to get the job done. When the job was killing enemies invading Kilbourne, so be it.

Now, he realized, things were different. While he felt no less loyalty to king and country, Morgan now had an additional layer of loyalty and obligation to his duchess.

The renegade bishops were a direct threat to Kilbourne. They could easily divide the kingdom into factions: those supportive of Kilbourne's witches and those who feared them. Morgan would oppose the bishops' treachery with every ounce of his resolve. With his steel, if necessary, to keep the kingdom at peace.

More than this, though, the bishops made a grave tactical error. They'd deemed Marissa a target. Their prime target, in fact, and this made their machinations personal. He'd vowed to Randolph he would kill them all. Yes, he'd said it in the heat of anger, but he'd meant it. If the need arose, he'd do it with no more remorse than a butcher slaughtering a cockerel. His mouth twisted into a tight, fierce smile.

"Morgan?"

He jerked his attention back to the woman he'd do anything to protect. "Yes?"

"Why were you about to pummel poor Randolph? And please don't feed me some cock-and-bull story about rehashing old sparring matches," she added, before he could do so.

Morgan's mouth snapped closed. She eyed him with a speculative gaze. "I think," she mused, "if I hadn't arrived when I did, you would have injured him. Why?"

"It's—" He fumbled to find the words. He already felt awful

enough about letting his anger get the best of him, taking it out on his closest friend. This didn't help in the least. He finally said, "I guess I lost my temper. Poor Randolph happened to be in the wrong place at the wrong time and nearly bore the brunt."

She frowned. "That's not like you, Morgan. What on earth prompted such behavior?"

How could he even begin to tell her? He set his jaw, then leaned back against the hard seat and stared straight ahead. "I'd rather not discuss it," he finally muttered.

"Oh, no you don't. I am your lawfully wedded wife now. Courtesy of Bishop Randolph, I'll remind you. There will be no secrets. You listen to me, Morgan James McRobbie. I'll—I'll use my witchcraft on you if you don't tell me what's wrong. See if I don't."

A strangled laugh escaped him. Morgan tried to call it back, but it was no use. "All right, your witchiness," he said. "You really want to know?"

"Yes, I really want to know."

He sighed. "All right, I'll tell you." He took a steadying breath, then blurted out, "I lost control when Randolph informed me the renegade bishops have put a price on your head. They want you dead."

She stared at him, her mouth opening and closing soundlessly. Finally, she managed a small, "Oh."

"Exactly." He exhaled. At least she wasn't going to break down in terror at the prospect. "I was an idiot, through and through," he went on. "I told Randolph it was his fault and went after him."

"His fault?" Marissa stared at him in bewilderment. "How in the names of all the saints did you arrive at such an outlandish conclusion?"

He shrugged. "He's the one who convinced Rhys to name you the Royal Enchantress. If not for your new title, and the fact you're now responsible for the kingdom's witches, you wouldn't be in danger from those—" He bit off the word he'd been about to use.

"And you forgot, in your wroth, the reason Randolph did it was to safeguard me? That it placed me under the Crown's protection? In the same way Rhys is for the witches at large?"

Morgan slouched further down into his seat. "Yes, blast it, I know. I'm afraid I just—well, went a bit berserk when he told me, if you want the truth. Logical thought went right out the window, and…"

"…and you attacked your friend. Who, you might have noted, still held you in high enough regard to lie for you when I asked him about it. I saw his face. He was ready for the lightning bolts to strike and saying penance under his breath even while he tried to shield you." She glared at him. "I'm ashamed of you, Morgan. That's not the man I fell in love with. Not the man I married."

He buried his face in his hands. She went on, relentless. "I know, you wanted to protect me. You always have. It's sweet, if unnecessary. Lashing out at your best friend, and best ally as well, is a rather silly way to go about it."

"Don't you think I know?" He groaned.

"I think perhaps it's started to seep into your thick head—which normally is fairly intelligent, for a man—at least a little bit. When we get back to the house, you should dash off a note of apology to Randolph."

I—" Morgan stopped. A good soldier knew when he was outflanked and outmaneuvered. "Yes, of course. You're right."

"How much?"

It was his turn to stare. "How much, what? How much are you right? Completely."

"No, silly I meant how much of a price did they place on my head?"

"Oh." He paused to remember. "A hundred crowns, I believe."

"What?" Her eyes flashed with fire. "Why, I've never been so insulted in all my life. A hundred crowns? How dare they? I'm worth a thousand, at the very least. Maybe five!" She slammed back in her seat, nostrils flared in righteous indignation. "Hmph!"

Suddenly, he couldn't help himself. A giddy laughter bubbled up from inside himself, and in a moment it burst forth like a geyser. He laughed until the tears rolled down his cheeks.

"Hmph," she said again. Then her own mouth crinkled, good humor getting the better of her, and she laughed with him. "Oh, Morgan, what are we going to do?"

He quirked a grin. "Well, evidently I'm going to beg Randolph's forgiveness, while you prepare yourself for whatever the dragons have in store. I don't suppose you could be anywhere any safer, at least from homicidal clergymen, than locked away in a dragon's den, eh?"

She wrinkled her nose at him.

Sliding over toward her, Morgan slipped an arm around her and held her close. "I'm sorry," he said softly. "I just couldn't bear it if anything were to happen to you."

"I'm not wild about the notion either," she said, snuggling closer into his embrace.

Morgan silenced this persiflage in the only manner possible, by kissing her. This pleasant activity was cut short when the coach halted. Through the blood pounding in his ears, Morgan heard Henry Dawkes leap from his seat and kick down the steps, preparatory to opening the door for them.

"Shall we?" Morgan asked, offering his arm.

"Thank you, darling," she replied, giving him a dazzling smile.

Morgan breathed a silent prayer of thanks. He was forgiven—at least for now. He helped her to alight, and they made for the house.

"Don't worry about the bishops and their lunacy right now," she ordered. "We can deal with them later. At the moment, I've got enough to keep me occupied for a while. One thing at a time, right?"

"Do the job before you," he agreed. "You have the right of it. Well done, you." They walked together up the stairs, and he opened the front door.

While he rounded up quill and parchment and wrote his note to Randolph, Marissa went upstairs to change. As he folded the note and sealed it, Morgan heard the soft patter of paws.

"I take it the dragons are ready to begin the ritual?" Francesca asked.

"So it would seem." Morgan was still having a bit of difficulty holding conversations with the cat. At least now he was able to not leap like a started deer whenever the beast spoke to him.

"I'm coming with you."

"No, you'll do no such thing," said Marissa, as she walked into Morgan's study.

"Mrowr," said the cat.

Morgan said, "For once, odd as it may sound, I have to agree with Lady Francesca."

Both cat and duchess regarded him with surprise. "What?" he said. "It couldn't hurt anything. Besides, it'll give me some company while you're off doing—well, whatever it is you'll be doing."

Marissa shifted her gaze from Morgan to her familiar and back. "Oh, very well," she said at last. "But both of you, keep quiet and stay out of the way."

A shadow crossed the window, and the rustle of giant wings heralded Wyvrndell's arrival.

Chapter Forty-Eight

"Morgan, I'll be fine," Marissa said for the umpteenth time. "Truly. Wyvrndell wouldn't do anything to hurt me."

Morgan didn't bother to reply. It wouldn't have made any difference; she was set on this course, and nothing he could say would sway her from it.

Francesca, however, was evidently not so stoic. "Perhaps he wouldn't," she muttered. "What about this other lizard?"

Morgan glanced over to where Erkarna, the other dragon, waited. With a decided air of impatience, it seemed to Morgan.

Marissa glanced at her familiar. "Erkarna is the one who taught Wyvrndell everything he knows about magical theory," she said. "I should imagine he knows what he's about. Anyhow, he's not going to hurt me. He needs my help."

"Even though you still don't really know what this help entails, do you?" the cat pointed out.

"Well, no, not exactly. Not the details. I'm sure he'll explain it soon."

"*I shall indeed.*" Erkarna's voice rang in their heads. He inclined his huge head to Marissa. "*Thank you for coming. Enchantress. All your questions shall be answered. And my hopes realized at last, if the ritual goes as I anticipate.*"

She nodded to the dragon. "I am honored to be able to assist dragonkind in such a great work. Erkarna, please, tell us about this ritual."

"Yes, let's hear this," Francesca muttered. "I can't wait."

Marissa made a shushing motion The dragon appeared to take no notice. Instead, he began to lay out, in very basic terms, what they would attempt. He only spoke to Marissa, so all Morgan could do was watch as she nodded at the dragon's explanation.

"All right," she said when he'd finished. "It sounds simple

enough."

"*Simple, it will not be. It will be extremely difficult,*" Erkarna said. "*It will tax your powers to the utmost. However, Wyvrndell has assured me you are up to the task.*"

"I'll do my best," she replied. "When shall we begin?"

"*If you are agreed, we can begin at once.*"

"Oh." She took a step back.

Morgan grasped her hand in his, to offer what little reassurance he could manage. She looked a bit less certain, now they'd come to the crux.

Wyvrndell said, "*Lady Marissa, if you need more time to decide what to do, we can wait.*"

The other dragon rumbled but said nothing. Morgan got the impression he wasn't necessarily in agreement with Wyvrndell's sentiment. What would happen if Marissa changed her mind?

She wouldn't. He understood how her mind worked. If she could help, she would, in spite of any danger to herself. He'd seen her put herself in harm's way too many times already. This really shouldn't be dangerous, should it? *Keep telling yourself that, Morgan.*

"Nooo, we can do it now," she said. "The sooner the better, eh?" She smiled up at her friend. Wyvrndell nodded slightly.

"*Excellent,*" said Erkarna. "*Then let us begin. First, your companions should wait outside.*"

"What?" Morgan sputtered.

"Not a chance," snarled Francesca.

Marissa spread her hands placatingly. "I'll be fine," she said.

Morgan shook his head. "I won't interfere, but I'm not leaving," he told the dragons. "I'll stand over here in the corner, out of the way."

"I'll be right there beside him," Francesca added.

Erkarna scrutinized Morgan, who held his ground under the dragon's gaze. He nodded, then bent, his huge faceted eyes fixed on Francesca. "*You are adamant, little one?*" he inquired.

"She is my witch," Francesca replied, as if this explained everything.

The dragon heaved a steam-laden sigh. "*Very well. You may remain. I must caution you not to speak or move about. This exercise will be arduous enough, both for the enchantress and for me. Any distraction could prove disastrous. Do you understand?*"

"Understood," the cat said.

The dragon turned his attention back to Morgan. "*And you?*"

"I understand," Morgan replied.

Marissa faced him. Her eyes were a bit misted, but she smiled at him. "Give me a kiss, and let's get this over and done with."

He obliged, taking her into a close embrace. Finally, he released her. "Be careful," he said.

"Oh, don't worry. I'll be fine." She hurried toward where Erkarna waited. "I'm ready."

Erkarna said, *"Wyvrndell, I trust you will keep these two in charge. There can be no interference in the ritual, else it may come undone. This could prove disastrous."*

"Of course," Wyvrndell replied. He turned to Marissa. *"Good luck, Lady Marissa,"* he said. Then, with a wave of his talon, he guided— no, herded, Morgan realized—him and Francesca to a spot near the cavern's wall.

"You will be able to observe from here," Wyvrndell said. *"I will wait here with you."*

"Won't you be needed for the ritual?" Morgan asked.

"Erkarna will let me know if he needs my assistance," Wyvrndell replied. *"I believe he has everything well under control."*

"I hope like hell he does," Morgan muttered. He folded his arms and leaned against the wall. Francesca sat by his boots, her attention focused on Marissa and the dragon.

Wyvrndell stared directly at Morgan. *"You are concerned?"*

"I—yes, I am worried." Morgan shrugged. "I don't want anything to happen to Marissa."

"Nooo," Wyvrndell said slowly. *"Of course not. But, Morgan McRobbie, this is merely a usage of her magic. A massive use, granted. It will not put her at risk. I would not allow it. She is my friend."*

Morgan scrubbed a hand across his face, even as he kept his gaze on Marissa and Erkarna. The huge dragon was now evidently speaking only to her, since Morgan could no longer hear his words.

"I imagine Erkarna is explaining the ritual in more detail," Wyvrndell said.

Marissa watched the dragon, nodding. She appeared calm and confident now. Morgan wished he felt the same way. He glanced at Francesca. "What do you think?" he muttered. "Will this be all right?"

The cat paced in a circle for a moment, then sat again and curled her tail around her feet. She gazed intently at Marissa and Erkarna. "I don't know. This is one of those theoretical things. Either it will work perfectly or a hundred things could go wrong. No way to know which. And yes, I know this isn't what you wanted to hear. I would much prefer to say, yes, it will be fine."

Marissa moved to stand in the cavern's center. Morgan saw she held a staff. "Where did she get the staff?" he asked, of no one in particular.

"Erkarna captured it from a wizard, many, many ages ago," Wyvrndell said.

As they watched, Marissa used the staff to scratch a large circle in the dirt floor of the cavern. "A protective circle," Francesca observed. "That's good, at least."

Erkarna approached as she finished the circle. When the ends met and the circle was completed, she uttered a word of power. Morgan heard a sharp click, and the circle around Marissa shimmered slightly, like heat off the ground on a summer's day.

To his surprise, Erkarna began to create another circle with a talon. This one encompassed both himself and Marissa's circle. Morgan turned to Wyvrndell. "I thought dragons had no magic," he barked. "Isn't he creating a magic circle? What's going on?"

"I-I'm not exactly sure," Wyvrndell said. *"Erkarna has not explained the ritual to me, so…"*

Erkarna closed the circle. There was no corresponding flash of completion as there had been when Marissa finished hers. "Maybe it didn't work," Morgan said under his breath.

Then Marissa rubbed out part of her circle with the toe of her boot. She strode to the circle Erkarna had made and touched it with the staff. Instantly, the shimmer Morgan saw before coalesced in the larger circle, encompassing both Marissa and the dragon. They were still visible, though their figures were unclear.

"She built up a power reserve within her own circle," Francesca explained. "Then she was able to flood Erkarna's circle with power to protect them both."

"Wouldn't it have been easier for her to simply create the larger one first?" Morgan asked.

"No, she did well. Taking small steps at a time, to conserve her energy for the larger task to come. A smart way to begin." The cat sounded impressed.

"Now what?" he asked.

"They will begin the ritual," Wyvrndell said. *"I wish I could hear what they are saying, but the ward does not allow the passage of their thoughts."*

Morgan stared as dragon and woman stood facing each other within the protection of the circle. Marissa was still holding the staff in one hand. She extended her other hand to touch Erkarna's outstretched talon. She closed her eyes, her face scrunching up in fierce concentration, summoning power from the depths of her being. The shimmer of the circle around them seemed to grow more intense.

Francesca watched, swishing her tail furiously. "I wish I knew more about this blasted ritual," she muttered. "I have a bad feeling about this."

"Do not worry, little one," said Wyvrndell. *"Erkarna has prepared for this moment for centuries. He will not fail, nor let any harm come to the enchantress."*

The cat sniffed. "If he's been after magic for this long, do you really think he'll give any consideration to what happens to my witch?"

Morgan heard the dragon start to answer, then stop as the impact of Francesca's words percolated into his brain. *"No,"* Wyvrndell said. *"He wouldn't. He promised me…"*

A series of flashes, each one brighter than the one before, issued from the warded circle. To Morgan, Erkarna seemed to be growing larger. The dragon's wings were outspread, so Marissa was nearly hidden from view. He could barely see her, arms upraised, mouth moving as she spoke the ritual devised by the dragon.

Morgan squinted. "What the hell? It looks like she's…she's…fading? This can't be right! Wyvrndell, what's going on?" he demanded, craning his head to see better. He moved forward, closer to the protective circle.

No, do not approach them," protested Wyvrndell. *"You will disturb the ritual."*

"What? Fading?" Francesca raised her head, then leapt into Morgan's arms. "Hold me up. We need to get closer. Let me see."

Wyvrndell's warning came too late, for Morgan was already on the move, the cat on his shoulder.

"You're right," Francesca said. "The damned dragon is draining her power. She's started to shrink in on herself. If he keeps up—"

Wyvrndell's gaze jerked from the circle to Francesca and Morgan. *"Are you sure?"*

"We… we've got to stop them," Morgan breathed. "How do we stop them?"

"I—I don't know," Francesca said, uttering a low growl.

"Come on, you're the witch," Morgan said. "Or were, or whatever. Think, damn it! How do we stop this, before it's too late? I know what happens if she's drained of all her power. We've got to stop them!" He shifted his gaze frantically between the cat and Marissa.

Francesca seemed to come to a decision. "All right, got it," she said. "Do you see the plinth? Over on the other side?"

"Yes. What about it?"

"You need to make it fall across the circle. That will break the ward. Go!"

"Will that stop—"

"Don't ask questions, just do it!" the cat ordered, jumping down from his shoulder. "I'll take it from there."

Morgan sprinted across the cavern floor. Looking over his shoulder, he could barely perceive Marissa's form in the warded circle. She was still…fading. Diminishing, somehow. Adrenaline kicked in as he ran. Blood sang through his veins in the familiar rush he often felt before engaging in battle. When he reached the stone plinth, he grabbed it and heaved, in a desperate endeavor to drag it across the circle and break the ward.

He yanked too hard. The blasted plinth almost toppled over on him. With a grunt of effort, Morgan managed to stop it from falling completely over. He heaved again, and this time managed to drag the stone a few feet toward his objective.

"Come on, damn you!" he growled, as his muscles strained to their utmost.

One agonizing foot at a time, he hauled the plinth across the floor and toward the circle. Morgan grunted, every muscle taut with effort, and moved it inch by agonizing inch.

Marissa's eyes were wide, her mouth open in a scream.

"No!" Morgan cried. With a final desperate heave that threatened to wrench every sinew of his being, he hurled the stone plinth across the ward.

The energy from within exploded into the cavern with a deafening roar. He was flung across the cavern, to land against the stone wall with a bone-wrenching thud. Sparks sizzled from every stone. Francesca's fur stood on end.

"No! You fools!" thundered Erkarna. He swelled up in wrath, power emanating from him in waves.

Had the ritual succeeded? Given the old dragon magic after all? Morgan, his breath coming in heaving gasps, stared wildly. If so, what would he do with it?

Something flashed by his boots. Morgan looked on in stunned disbelief as Francesca launched herself into the middle of the circle. Not at the dragon, as he'd assumed, but at Marissa. The cat, all four feet outstretched, with claws extended, struck on her right side. Marissa cried out in shock and pain, stumbling away as Francesca executed a neat flip to land upright on the stone floor before the dragon.

Erkarna was focused on drawing the last reserves of power from his unwitting victim. Now the cat stood in Marissa's place, though the dragon was too caught up in the heady throes of his ritual to notice. Francesca stood her ground as the dragon spread his wings, now nearly twice his normal size.

His eyes glowed with a fey light. *"Mine!"* roared Erkarna. *"The power is mine! Magic is mine!"*

Morgan stumbled to his feet and scrambled to where Marissa had fallen, just outside the limits of the circle she'd crafted. Erkarna raised his head and howled in triumph. Wyvrndell watched in shock and horror, seemingly rooted to the cavern floor, unable to move.

Morgan reached Marissa. Ignoring Erkarna, he grabbed her shoulders, dragging her farther from the maddened dragon. Erkarna was growing larger still, as the magic he'd absorbed infused him.

"Give it to me, witch! All of it!" he cried, folding his wings around the spot where Marissa only recently stood.

Francesca snarled in reply. "Too late, lizard," she taunted. "You cannot have her, nor her magic!"

Erkarna reared up in dismay, now realizing Marissa no longer stood before him to be stripped of her remaining magic. Yet the power drain he'd set in motion was still working for Francesca was diminishing before their eyes. Her life force, and her residual magic, were absorbed by the dragon. Frozen in place, Morgan stared in horror as Francesca faded from sight with a sigh like a soft "Mwrow."

"Fran—Francesca," Marissa moaned, covering her eyes with her hands. "Oh, Francesca…" Then she roused, a look of fury in her eyes. "Damn you, dragon!" she screamed.

Jerking out of Morgan's grasp, she raised her arms to cast a spell. Before she could complete it, Wyvrndell thundered across the cavern.

"Nooo!" cried Wyvrndell as he hurtled toward his mentor.

Erkarna's head jerked around, and he brought up a talon toward the younger dragon Before he could complete the gesture and cast a spell, Wyvrndell attacked.

Morgan dragged Marissa behind the marginal safety of a rock pillar. Wyvrndell's flame washed over Erkarna, and the heat of it, even from where they stood, made Morgan's skin prickle. The old dragon stood erect, as it bathed him in crimson fury.

"You cannot stop me, Wyvrndell," Erkarna sneered. *"Thanks to you, I now have magic. Power beyond measure, taken from your witch. She will be a useless husk. I have taken all her power for myself."*

"You—you lied to me," Wyvrndell replied, his voice near to a sob. *"You said we would gain magic for all dragons…"*

"What do I care about all dragons, you fool? The power is mine now. I will rule, and all will bow to me. Dragons. Humans. Dwarves. No, not Dwarves. I will destroy them instead! It is only right."

"No," Wyvrndell said again. *"Erkarna, you cannot do this. It is*

madness. You've hurt Lady Marissa. You've killed Francesca. You must stop this, now!"

"Stop? No, little one, you are the one who is mad, to think you can stop me. No one can!" Erkarna reared up to send a gout of magic-laced flame toward his apprentice.

Wyvrndell dodged the flames. *"You hurt my friends."*

"Fool! They are merely for our use."

"You hurt my friends," Wyvrndell repeated, shaking his massive head.

"Bah. Dragons do not have friends."

"You are wrong, Erkarna. Dragons do indeed have friends. It is monsters who do not have friends." With a roar, Wyvrndell launched himself across the expanse of the cavern. He hit his mentor with teeth and talons, ripping at him. What he lacked in comparable size and strength, he more than made up for in fury. He ripped scales from Erkarna's hide and managed to shred one of his wings before the older dragon could react.

Morgan watched, stunned, as the younger dragon bit and ripped at his mentor. He shredded his second wing and managed to bite a large gash in Erkarna's neck. Erkarna roared in defiance but was unable to halt Wyvrndell's frenzied onslaught. Finally, Erkarna managed to break free for a moment. Rather than physically attack the younger dragon, he uttered an audible word of power. A brilliant shaft of green flame lanced toward his foe.

Wyvrndell skipped sideways with the agility of a young goat, then whirled and advanced on his mentor once more, to rip and tear at whatever he could manage. Erkarna growled in rage and leveled another gout of magical flame toward Wyvrndell.

This time the attack struck the younger dragon full force. Caught in the magical onslaught, Wyvrndell screamed and writhed. As Morgan watched in horror, Wyvrndell seemed to diminish and wither under the force of Erkarna's spell.

"He's fading," Morgan breathed. "Like Francesca did."

Marissa hauled herself upright. "No," she breathed. Her voice broke into a sob. "No!"

As Erkarna prepared to unleash yet another blast of magic-laced flame at his opponent, Marissa staggered toward the dragons. Her voice, when she spoke, was low and harsh. "I've got to help him."

Morgan started after her. What did she think she could do against this monster? Still, she was the only one who might have any hope of opposing him. He had no weapons. Even if he did, they'd be less than useless against Erkarna and his newly acquired magic. Wyvrndell had failed and would soon be consumed by the older dragon's onslaught.

"Do it!" Morgan urged as he took his place beside her. "Whatever you're going to try, do it now."

Erkarna, his attention still focused completely on Wyvrndell, never even glanced at Marissa as she called up the remains of her magic. Morgan put his arm around her waist, to steady her. He knew what this might cost. And what it would cost her—and himself—if she didn't at least make the attempt.

With a will born of desperation, she drew on her remaining well of power, focusing whatever magic she still possessed. She leveled her arms at the rampaging dragon and uttered a harsh cry: "*Nazantim argonist!*" She hurled the spell at Erkarna.

The magical blow struck the ancient dragon amidships, blooming out all around him. It sizzled and sparked, not unlike the way Marissa had described her venture through the Thundermist with Toby Fanshawe. She'd received something from that encounter. It had infused her own magic with whatever strange properties the Mist possessed, enhancing her powers. The Mist-laden power had enabled her to defeat Rhenn in the desolate tower, as Morgan's fate hung in the balance. Perhaps, he prayed, it might somehow help her to best Erkarna. If not, the fate of the world might well hang in the balance.

As the spell left her, Morgan wrapped Marissa in his arms to keep her from toppling over. Her efforts had been too much, and she could barely remain upright. He feared this was what Nardis had spoken of, back in Arvindir: the loss of her magic would leave naught but an empty shell. He couldn't bear the notion.

"Don't leave me," he begged. "I need you, Marissa. I love you!"

At his words, he felt some small semblance of strength return to her. Enough, at least, for him to hope she'd manage to hang on. She straightened and flung her arms around him, as a swimmer clings to any scrap of flotsam to keep from drowning. The spell she'd cast did its deadly work on the dragon. Erkarna was momentarily stunned and appeared less enormous than he'd grown when he first absorbed Marissa's magic. No, Morgan corrected himself. Not absorbed—stolen.

Wyvrndell, too, was now no longer shrinking under Erkarna's spell. He was almost back to his normal size, though he appeared dazed, shaking his head muzzily. "Whatever you did, it I think it worked," he said. "Well done."

Her voice was raspy, but she managed to croak, "No. It's not over yet."

Morgan stared at her, his eyes wide with dread. "What...what must you do?"

"Finish it. Finish him," she said. "Retrieve my stolen power, before he can use it again, against us. Or against anyone, humans or dragons." She loosened her embrace, and he reluctantly let her go. "I have to do it now, quickly, before he can recover. If I can."

"You are," he told her honestly, "the strongest person I know. If anyone can do this, it's you."

She gave him a quick, wan smile. "Flatterer," she said. Then she narrowed her gaze and turned to face Erkarna.

The dragon shook his head, like a fighter trying to recover from the effects of a particularly strong blow. Marissa's spell had not simply stopped him in his tracks. It had dazed him as well. He tried to raise a talon, presumably to cast another spell, but couldn't seem to manage it.

A grim smile crossed her face. She took a deep breath, readying herself to hurl another spell at the dragon. Suddenly she stopped.

"What's wrong?" Morgan asked.

"I-I should create a circle, a ward..." she said haltingly. "I—oh, there's no time!" She drew herself up once more and reached out, taking his hand in hers. "I need your strength," she said quietly. "Help me?"

"Take whatever you need," he said. He moved to stand close to her and gave her hand an encouraging squeeze.

She squeezed it, closed her eyes, and began to chant. The words were none he ever heard before, nor was he likely to ever again. Ancient words, filled with power which few mortals knew. Where Marissa had learned them, he could only guess. The grimoire, perhaps? The thought chilled him, even while he mentally urged her to get on with it. It damned well didn't matter. This was no time for half measures.

Her words rose in pitch and volume, echoing now around the cavern, to reach a final, hideous crescendo. She extended one arm toward the still bemused dragon. "*Avantil! Urganas!*" she cried.

Instead of power lancing toward the dragon from her outstretched hand, the reverse seemed to occur. An essence, barely visible, flowed out of Erkarna's huge, battered, scaly body. It writhed and twisted in the air, like some monstrous, tentacled thing. Morgan gaped. Was this Marissa's magic, in tangible form?

The effort must have cost her dearly, for she slumped and would have fallen if not for Morgan's support. He steadied her once more, and together they watched the scene play out before them.

Instead of returning to its source, the magical essence now circled around the cavern, like a dust storm caused by a sudden wind. It hovered over Wyvrndell's swaying form. Slowly, tentatively, as if it had reached some momentous decision, it descended upon the dragon. It swirled and pulsed and flickered with an ominous light. Then it slowly disappeared, and Wyvrndell seemed to glow, infused with the strange, greenish light.

"It's almost like what happened in the Thundermist," Marissa breathed.

"Um," Morgan muttered. "That wasn't supposed to happen. Was it?"

Her eyes were wide as she turned to stare at him. "Not exactly. Well, I-I don't know. It certainly wasn't what I'd intended, no."

"Are you all right? I mean…without your power?"

She took a deep breath. "I suppose I'll have to be, won't I? I mean, the magic chose where it wanted to go. And where it wanted to go was…to Wyvrndell."

Chapter Forty-Nine

"It was not supposed to be like this."

Morgan looked up. Wyvrndell lay sprawled on the stone floor of Erkarna's chamber. Slowly, the dragon dragged himself partially upright. He swayed, as if a good breeze would topple him back over again.

"It was not supposed to be like this," he repeated, shaking his great head. He stared to where Erkarna's body lay, battered and still. Erkarna was dead. With a groan, Wyvrndell sank to the ground again.

"No," Morgan growled, unable to conjure up any sympathy at this point. "I don't imagine it was." He wrapped his arm more tightly around Marissa's shoulders. He'd failed. Failed to keep her safe during this debacle, and he needed an outlet for his anger and frustration. "Damn it, Wyvrndell, you could have gotten Marissa killed. Nearly did. What were—"

Marissa sat up and pulled away from his protective arm. A trace of her old fire lit her eyes for a moment. "Don't blame Wyvrndell," she said. "He was merely trying to do his best for the dragons. He couldn't have known what Erkarna had planned."

"No, Lady Marissa," the dragon said. *"Morgan McRobbie has the right of it."* Wyvrndell straightened again, bit by bit. Even as he stood at least somewhat erect, his head sagged low, in an air of exhaustion and defeat. *"I failed you in this. Both of you. You trusted me."*

Morgan remained silent. Wyvrndell gazed around the chamber. *"Your trust in me was not misplaced. I had no intent to deceive you. My fault was my trust in Erkarna, my teacher. My friend, or so I thought. I did not see how deep his lust for power had gone. Did not realize the depths it had driven him to."*

Wyvrndell turned to regard them now. His faceted eyes weren't filled with their normal spark of intelligence and curiosity. No, what Morgan perceived in the dragon's eyes was sorrow and a knowledge of his own abject failure.

"I am truly sorry," Wyvrndell said. He turned away, no longer able to face them.

"Wyvrndell," Morgan said. To his own surprise, he added, "my friend." The dragon looked up sharply.

Morgan went on, "Those who would do evil are the canniest folk among us. It makes no matter whether they be human, or Dwarf, or dragon. Something eats away at them, from the inside, where none can perceive it. Many times in this world has it happened before. Many times in the future, I have no doubt, it will happen again. And good men, and dragons, and Dwarves as well, will look back in sorrow as you do today. They will wonder, in anguish and in anger, how they failed to see, or what they could have done to prevent such events."

Wyvrndell's huge head dropped at his words. Morgan said, "Such is the problem with those of good will: they believe the best of others. Especially those they hold in regard or in friendship. Most often, this belief is justified. Sometimes it may even cause those of doubtful character to alter their actions, so they might live up to those expectations."

"Not in this instance." Wyvrndell's voice was low, filled with regret and sorrow.

"No," Morgan agreed. "Not in this case." He rose now and helped Marissa to stand.

Slowly, he led her to where Wyvrndell crouched, wretched and alone. Morgan reached out his hand to place it on the dragon's side.

"In this case, what gnawed at Erkarna was too ancient, too hidden. Too much a part of him, deep down. He hid it where none could discern. In spite of your trust in him, in spite of your own good will and intentions, he deceived you. You saw what you expected to see: another dragon, eager to bring a new age to dragonkind, as you were. You saw exactly what he wanted you to see. He was a master of deception. Even your king, old and wise as he must be, had no inkling of Erkarna's treachery. How, then, could you?"

"I should have," protested the dragon. *"I should have known. My sire was concerned about Erkarna and his secrecy. I reassured him, told him Erkarna was about to perform a great service for dragonkind. I was blind and a fool."*

"No, my friend. Do not fault yourself for not seeing what Erkarna planned. Instead, reflect on this: you put yourself at risk to protect Marissa. You fought the monster Erkarna had become, in hopes your friend might be spared. And you prevailed. No one could have asked more of you."

The dragon sat a bit straighter now. He stared at Morgan, his eyes wide with astonishment. *"But—"* he protested.

Morgan patted his side again. "When it counted, Wyvrndell, you did the right and noble thing. You acted against one of your own kind, when you could have easily joined in his scheme. I heard what you said to him: 'Monsters do not have friends, but dragons do.' You turned against the monster within Erkarna for the sake of your friends. If you had not, neither Marissa nor I would be here right now. This thought will help get you through the long, sleepless nights, when you relive all this and question your very existence. You acted decisively, in defense of friends over kin."

Wyvrndell bowed his head. *"Thank you, Morgan McRobbie,"* he said softly.

"I should like to say something," Marissa said. The dragon nodded, his expression wary. Morgan couldn't really blame him.

"Say what you will," Wyvrndell said.

"I will simply say this," she said. She stepped forward to wrap her arms around the dragon's long neck. "Thank you, once again, for saving my life. Morgan is right. There was no way you could have known what Erkarna meant to do. When it came to the pinch, you chose your friends—me and Morgan—over your own kind. A terrible decision for you. I am glad you chose as you did, and I am proud and honored to call you my friend."

Wyvrndell transferred his gaze from Marissa to Morgan, his eyes now filled with wonder. *"Humans are amazing creatures,"* he said. *"Thank you, my friends. Thank you."*

He glanced around the chamber again. *"As are cats. Francesca did not like me, I know. And I held no great affection for her. But she was indeed a great spirit. I wish I could have saved her as well."*

Morgan noticed Marissa blink back a tear. "Like you," she said, "at the crux, she did what needed to be done, even though it cost her own life."

Wyvrndell nodded. *"Once we leave this place, I will seal the chamber. It will remain here, as a monument to the evil that almost was and to the bravery which overcame it. To Francesca."*

"To Francesca," they both echoed.

"Now," Wyvrndell said, *"I will summon Aireantha. She will bear you back home again. I am certain you want to leave this place. I don't know if I could manage it at the moment."*

"Wait," Marissa said. She stepped back to take Morgan's hand. "Before you do, there is one more thing we must discuss."

If the dragon had been wary before, his expression now was

almost stricken. *"What is it?"* he asked dully.

"Hold out your—well, talons, I suppose."

Slowly, obviously confused, the dragon did as she instructed.

She smiled. "Now, envision a ball of light. Command it to be. If it helps, you may say the words. *Lluminas accacio.*"

Wyvrndell stared at her. His great jaws dropped open in shock. *"No,"* he said. *"No, it cannot be. Impossible."*

"Do it," she urged. "At least, try. For me?"

Wyvrndell looked from her to his outstretched talons. He glanced at Morgan, who gave him an encouraging nod.

"Lluminas accacio," he said. Then, *"You see. Nothing."*

"Pooh. You didn't even half try. You merely muttered the words. Put some purpose into it, Wyvrndell. Imagine that ball of light. Make it so. Trust me, as I have trusted you. You can do this."

He gazed at her for a long moment. *"Very well,"* he said.

Morgan and Marissa watched, hand in hand, as he regarded his talon. Focusing on it, he narrowed his huge green eyes. *"Lluminas accacio."*

Nothing happened. At first. Then, suddenly, a faint bloom of light took form in the dragon's claws. It was tiny, a mere spark, and the surprise caused Wyvrndell to rear back. The light winked out again.

The dragon's face was a mix of awe and hope. *"I-I did it."* His voice trembled with emotion.

"Again," Marissa ordered. "Do it again."

Giving his head a shake, as if to bring himself to his senses, Wyvrndell extended his talons once more. *"Lluminas accacio,"* he said.

His voice held a tone of command now. The light blossomed again, brighter this time to chase the shadows from the corners of the chamber.

"Magic," he said, eyes wide with wonder. *"I have magic?"*

"It would seem," Marissa said, smiling up at him, "you do."

Chapter Fifty

Aireantha made a gentle landing on the front lawn of McRobbie House. The trip back from Erkarna's cavern workshop hadn't taken more than a couple of hours, but Morgan was certain Marissa was near the breaking point. He steadied her as she descended from the dragon's back. Who was going to steady him was another question entirely, one he wasn't quite prepared to answer.

They'd both been silent on the journey home, each lost in their own contemplations. Once they were home, cleaned up, rested, and perhaps fed, they could begin to process the day's events. Morgan scowled at the thought of "the day's events." An awfully prosaic term for something this devastating. This earth-shattering.

Once he and Marissa were both on solid ground again, he bowed to the dragon. "Thank you for bearing us home safely."

Aireantha regarded them, her eyes tinged with sadness. *"I am sorry for all that has happened today. I hope you can forgive Wyvrndell for dragging you into this mess."*

"Of course," Marissa said. "Though things didn't go as he'd hoped and planned, he did accomplish what he set out to do. At least somewhat."

Aireantha cocked her head. *"Yes, I suppose he did. I wonder if he will find the result worth the cost."*

Morgan noted a knot of people who'd stopped to stare in their direction from along the street. "Perhaps you'd better go now," he told Aireantha. "Before we draw more of a crowd than I really care to deal with at the moment."

"As you wish." Inclining her head toward them, the dragon spread her wings and leapt into the sky.

She caught air and soared upwards. An audible gasp came from the onlookers. Morgan and Marissa watched her until she was nearly out of sight.

Then Morgan took her hand, saying, "Come on, let's get inside."

He led her toward the house. "Worried someone might try to claim the hundred crowns?" she asked.

Even though her tone was light, Morgan knew she didn't feel the least bit playful. It was a bitter reminder of the evil pervading the world. Of Erkarna. Of Azim. The renegade bishops. Foxwent. So much evil. And so few men—and women, he added resolutely—willing to make the sacrifices necessary to battle that evil, for the sake of the rest. Right now, though, he didn't want to contemplate the nature of evil. He just wanted to go home.

"A bit," he admitted. "I know you scoffed at the amount. Remember, to some people, a hundred crowns is nothing less than a fortune. Someone might well decide to try to claim it. Right now, in the shape I'm in, I wouldn't care to chance it."

"I don't want to have to look over my shoulder for the rest of my life, Morgan. We've got to do something."

"I know." he heaved a sigh. "I just really don't know what."

She gazed up at him. "Do you think Rhys has any chance? To convince them to stop? The bishops, I mean."

"Honestly, I'm not—" The sound of boots pounding on pavement brought his words to a sudden halt.

He whirled and pushed Marissa into a place of relative shelter behind him. A man ran headlong toward them. In his hand Morgan glimpsed a flash of steel. "Stay behind me," he instructed Marissa.

The attacker's legs pumped furiously as he closed the distance to his prey. "Death to witches!" he cried and raised the knife. His eyes were wild and unfocused, as if gripped by some inner madness which drove him.

People on the street stopped again, to point and stare at the spectacle. Some evinced shock or disgust, others eager anticipation of a rousing entertainment. Several fled the scene, although Morgan doubted any of them were off to summon the Watch. No one seemed inclined to lend any assistance, either to the man with the knife or to his potential victims. Morgan, still weary from the debacle with Erkarna, knew he was on his own. Unless Marissa could summon up a bit of magic.

"Be careful, Morgan," she called.

Morgan rolled his eyes at this. He bloody well didn't have the luxury of being careful. With no weapon, not even the dagger normally secreted in his boot, he'd have to rely on his own skills in close-quarter combat, against an opponent with a knife and an air that indicated it didn't matter if he lived or died, so long as he achieved his aim. Morgan bared his teeth and swore a silent vow to keep this man from coming anywhere near his objective. As he kept a close eye on the assailant, he bent for a moment to scoop something from the ground.

The attacker didn't slow as he reached them. He waved the knife wildly and shouted incoherent oaths as he came like a whirlwind. Morgan smiled grimly. This was to his own benefit, as long as Marissa stayed behind him and out of reach. The man might score Morgan with the knife, but he'd not be able to injure his real target.

"Move back when I do," he muttered to Marissa.

The man was only steps away. "Now!" Morgan said and stepped out of the line of the man's charge.

At the same time, he flung the handful of dirt he'd scooped up into the attacker's eyes. Blinded, the fellow windmilled his arms as he passed harmlessly by them, cursing wildly.

"Oh, well done," she cheered.

"Don't get cocky," Morgan said. "He's not done yet."

Indeed, he wasn't. The assailant managed to halt his mad dash, wipe the dirt from his eyes, and gave every indication of being ready to make another foray. At least this time, Morgan hoped, he wouldn't have to deal with quite such a headlong rush. The man approached more slowly now, an evil grimace on his face and murder in his eyes.

"Morgan?" Marissa's voice quavered slightly. He glanced over his shoulder for an instant, then returned his attention to the man with the knife.

"I'm a bit busy here," he replied. "Trying to keep us alive."

"Trying to keep me alive, you mean. But…Morgan, there's another one. From the other direction."

"Damn." He spared another glance over his shoulder.

Sure enough, another knife-wielding man bore down on them, from a position behind Marissa. He was going to have to deal with the first chap quickly in order to keep her protected from the second. He had no idea how he was going to manage it.

"Any chance you can cast a spell on him? Like you did with Nadiz's guards in Arvindir?"

"I'll try. I wouldn't count on it."

Morgan heard her mutter the words to a spell, while he kept a wary eye on the first assailant. Who, sensing victory by means of this flanking attack, stayed out of Morgan's reach, seemed satisfied to wave his knife jauntily. He presented just enough threat to keep Morgan's attention occupied, while his accomplice would be able to deal with the hated witch.

"Any luck?" he called over his shoulder.

He wasn't sure how much power she still had, after the disaster with the dragons only a few short hours before. Even if she did have anything left, would she have the strength to wield it?

As the man before him slashed with his knife again, Morgan heard Marissa mutter "Drat."

Which didn't bode well, even if it was unsurprising. As he contemplated this dilemma, an odd shimmer grew between himself and the first attacker. Both Morgan and the man with the knife reared back, startled. A loud wailing noise rent the air, and the shimmer grew in substance, to near full solidity. Morgan beheld the spectral figure of Sir Jamie before him. Arrayed around him were several ghost knights, their swords drawn.

Sir Jamie, flanked by three of his ghostly companions, interposed themselves between Marissa and the second attacker, while two other wraithlike figures stood shoulder to shoulder with Morgan. Both attackers wailed in terror as the specters approached them.

"Witchcraft," one yelped, making the horns sign with his hand, ostensibly to ward off evil.

Morgan thought they might reasonably debate the issue of who bore the greater evil: the witch they cried death to or the men with bloodlust in their hearts. But at the moment, all he wanted was to be rid of these two would-be assassins.

"Be gone from here," boomed Sir Jamie. "These good folk are under our protection. Any who assail them will face our wrath."

Grim-faced, the spectral soldiers bore down on the two assassins. Moaning in terror, both men flung down their weapons and bolted. As Sir Jamie and his comrades pursued them across the lawn, Morgan heard whistles in the distance. Thank God. Someone had finally summoned the Watch.

Loathe to leave Marissa, in case there was yet another assassin nearby, Morgan stayed put instead of giving chase. The spectral soldiers herded the two assassins like exuberant sheepdogs with their flock and sent them into the arms of a knot of Watchmen. Onlookers called to the constables that these were the fellows who'd attempted murder upon the duke and his lady.

Well, at least they were good for something, Morgan groused silently. A little tangible help would have been more appreciated. He growled under his breath.

Their work accomplished, the ghost knights drifted back toward Morgan and Marissa. "My heartiest thanks," Morgan said. "Once again, you have come in our hour of need."

"Noble spirits," Marissa said, "you shall have songs sung of your mighty deeds."

"Ah, 'twas near to nothing," replied Sir Jamie. Yet Morgan could see the ghost puffed up with pride at her words. "No way could I allow those ruffians to attack you here on this very land, once mine, and now belonging to you. Consider yourselves under our protection here. And now…" A pair of constables approached, and the spectral knights faded from view.

"Your Grace, are you and the duchess all right?" asked one of the Watchmen, even as he stared in wonder at the vanishing specters.

"No thanks to those two, we are," Morgan replied. "Take them into custody. Tell Captain Jenks I'll be down to see him tomorrow to present formal charges against those men."

"Very good." The Watchmen bowed to Marissa and trotted off to lead the two assassins to the cells.

Despite the day's warmth, Marissa gave a little shiver. "Let's get inside," she said.

Morgan was more than happy to concur. Together, hand in hand, they walked up the front steps. Rather than ring the bell for someone to open the door, Morgan used his key and pushed it open. Marissa stumbled a bit, and he put a protective arm around her waist.

"Food, bath, or sleep?" he asked.

"Bath first," she said. "If I don't fall asleep in it, then perhaps a bite of something to eat. Then sleep. For at least a week. This all took more out of me than I thought. Morgan, help me upstairs, will you? I want to shed these clothes and sink into some hot water."

He held her hands in his. He pulled her upright and into his arms. "I love you," he said softly and kissed her.

"Even though I stink like dragons?" She wrinkled her nose. "Get Briana to attend to my bath?"

"Briana!" Morgan bawled.

Marissa sent a weary half-glare in his direction.

"I could have done that," she chided, but spoiled the effect by laughing. "I love you too, Morgan."

Briana hurried into the room, sucked in a breath at her mistress' appearance, and scurried off to carry out Morgan's orders. Morgan helped Marissa up the stairs.

"I hate this," she said. "All this nonsense with the renegade bishops. If today was any example of things to come, we'll be up against it. Not only you and me. There are so many women out there, who've done nothing to warrant it, who are going to be in danger from madmen like those we encountered today. They won't have the same protections, of station, or power, or friendly specters. We've got to do something. Got to save them."

"You're right, of course." Morgan gave her an affectionate squeeze. "Rhys was right to make you their protector. We'll figure something out. Tomorrow."

Chapter Fifty-One

Marissa took a final sip of coffee. Last night's bath, a good dinner, and a night's sleep—albeit one interrupted by dreams about rampaging dragons and madmen with knives—had contrived to make her feel at least almost human again. Still sore and drawn, stretched near to the breaking point, she had yet to assess how much magic she still possessed. If any. She didn't think she was quite up to the task yet.

Right now, she decided, she would mourn. For Wyvrndell, betrayed by his mentor. For the witches of Kilbourne, betrayed by the church, even if most didn't yet realize their peril

Most of all, for Francesca, who made the ultimate sacrifice to save Marissa from Erkarna. She blinked back sudden tears, laid her head down on her folded hands, and gave a little sob. For all the cat's irascible ways, she'd been an excellent companion. Not to mention, she added, managing a wan smile, an excellent mouser.

She glanced up as Morgan strolled in with something cradled in his hands. She couldn't really see just what he held. When he approached, she saw it was a tiny black kitten.

"Morgan? What on earth?" she demanded, even as she cooed at the kitten, which blinked up at her sleepily.

He grinned. "I went out for a stroll in the back garden. Wanted to get a bit of air and clear my head. When I came back to the kitchen door, I looked down. Lo and behold, here was this kitten. I scooped her up and brought her in. Couldn't just leave the poor thing outside, could I?"

"No, of course not."

"I asked Cook, but she said she'd never seen it before. Cute little beast, isn't it?"

"She's lovely," Marissa cooed, taking the kitten into her arms and snuggling it gently. "Simply lovely." She stroked the kitten's soft fur. It purred happily under her touch, one paw reaching up to rest on her hand. Staring into its deep green eyes was like gazing into pools of eternity.

"Kind of reminds me of someone," Morgan observed.

"Yes, she does," Marissa agreed. She chucked the kitten under the chin. Quietly, so only the kitten could hear, she said, "So you were right, eh? You did have a couple of extra lives left?"

Other Books by Author

Knights of Kilbourne
Stolen Knight
Enchanted Knight
Desperate Knight
Traitor Knight

Acknowledgements

Conventional wisdom and popular memes dictate that "One does simply walk into Mordor". Similarly, one does not simply write a book. Every writer I know struggles with the process: uncommunicative characters, plot holes, writer's block, the dreaded "How do I end this thing?" Crafting a novel is not a task to be undertaken lightly, and we only do it at peril of our sanity. And I wouldn't change a thing.

But, as it takes a village to raise a child, so it takes a team to craft a novel. Here's my opportunity to thank mine.

My amazing editor, Nikki Andrews, who put off her retirement solely so she would work on *Stolen Knight* with me. We have made a great team over these last four outings, and I'm so grateful for her insights and guidance (and her dreaded red pen). She has made me a much better writer and helped me tell much better stories than they were when they started out.

My publisher, Cassie Knight, and her terrific team (especially Kelli Keith and Kat Hall), who take my words and actually turn them into the book you're holding, either digitally or in paperback.

My cover artist, Melody Pond, who consistently delivers amazing artwork. Because, despite what they say, we all do judge a book by its cover—and mine are pretty darned amazing.

To all the readers who took a chance, and especially those of you who came back for more. Thank you so much for investing your time and money into my stories.

And especially, to the person who keeps me inspired, motivated, and on track—my wonderful wife, Patty. I couldn't do this without her support and encouragement.

About the Author

Keith W. Willis graduated (long ago) with a degree in English Lit from Berry College, which has the distinction of being the world's largest college campus. He now lives in the scenic Hudson Valley/Adirondack region of NY with his wife Patty. Keith is certain those rumbling noises attributed to Henry Hudson's crew are really just the dragons grumbling.

Keith's interests include reading classic fantasy, sci-fi, and mysteries; camping and canoeing; and cutthroat games of Scrabble. He began writing seriously in 2008, when the voices in his head got too annoying to ignore. When he's not making up stories he manages a group of database content editors at a global information technology firm.

Stolen Knight is his fourth venture into the magical kingdom of Kilbourne.

Keith loves to hear from his readers. You can find and connect with him at the links below.

Website/Blog: http://www.keithwillisauthor.com/
Twitter: https://twitter.com/kilbourneknight or @kilbourneknight
Facebook: https://www.facebook.com/TRAITOR-KNIGHT-191368320972613/

~~~

If you enjoyed *Stolen Knight* and want to see how Morgan and Marissa met, their adventures being in *Traitor Knight*, book 1 of the *Knights of Kilbourne* series. Just turn the page.

SWASHBUCKLING ACTION
A CENTURIES-OLD FEUD
DANGEROUS AFFAIRS OF THE HEART

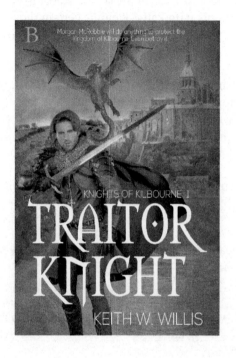

TURN THE PAGE
FOR A PEEK!

Chapter One

A clamor of rooks exploded through the trees, nearly drowning out the woman's scream.

Morgan straightened in the saddle. Trouble, at last. The patrol had been boring up 'til now. He set his heels to Arnicus's flanks and the big gray gelding quickened his pace along the narrow trail. The birds flapped off, their raucous calls fading in the distance. A watchful silence overtook the woods, broken only by the thud of Arnicus's hooves on the summer-dry earth.

Morgan peered through the trees, searching for the source of the cry. He knew no good reason why a woman, screaming or otherwise, should be in the middle of the King's forest. But no matter the reason, he had to find her. Help her, if possible. He'd never been one to shy away from trouble. No soldier was, or he didn't remain a soldier for long. He loosened his sword in its well-worn sheath.

Another shriek split the air. Arnicus leapt forward, nostrils flared and ears laid back. Morgan bent low over the horse's neck, scanning ahead for danger. It might be a trap. The trees thinned slightly, the mottled light of the forest replaced by brighter sunshine that heralded a clearing. Suddenly Morgan jerked hard on the reins, causing Arnicus to toss his head in equine complaint. He paid little heed.

Just ahead, the trail opened out onto a serene sun-dappled clearing. The little meadow, dotted with bright patches of wildflowers, would have been charming if not for the hulking blue dragon crouched in its center.

"My God!" Morgan whispered, half curse and half prayer. Arnicus pawed the ground nervously, suggesting a strategic retreat might not be such a bad idea. Morgan didn't blame him in the least. "Steady on, fellow," he whispered, as much to himself as to the horse.

Despite the generally accepted notion that dragons had been extinct for centuries, this one looked pretty damned corporeal. Iridescent azure scales covered the creature's enormous body. Huge green eyes gleamed with an alien intelligence from beneath bony brow-like ridges. Vast leathery wings rested on the creature's back, twitching slightly as if eager to lift off into flight. Curls of steam vented from its snout, forming delicate patterns in the air.

Blast! The standard-issue dragons had been bad enough. This was one of the fire-breathing ones. And he didn't have time to call up reinforcements from the Legion garrison at Caerfaen. This was his problem.

The dragon held a dark-haired girl in its talons, and its attention was focused exclusively on her. Which was both good and bad. Good, in that it hadn't noticed him yet, giving Morgan a brief moment to reclaim his scattered wits. Bad, in that its attention was focused on the girl in its talons. He was going to have to act at once to have any hope of saving her.

Morgan swung down from the saddle and drew his sword. The steaming nightmare inspected the girl much as a cook might a particularly savory delicacy. She strained to free herself, wriggling and even managing to land a fierce kick on its snout. The dragon didn't deign to notice. A surge of adrenaline fizzed through Morgan, familiar as the hilt of the sword in his hand. Well, he'd been looking for excitement, and he was about to get it. Likely a lot more than he could handle.

"Unhand that maiden!" he shouted, storming toward the monster and probable death. "Release her and prepare to meet your doom!"

The dragon, hissing like a brace of tea kettles, turned to face this interruption of its mid-morning snack of maiden flambé. Ominous rumblings sounded in the beast's superstructure. The girl struggled harder now, a wild hope lighting her eyes.

If nothing else, perhaps he could force the dragon to drop her. Then she might have a chance to escape while Morgan kept it occupied with killing him. He heard the deep rumbling again, herald of his own doom. With a wild yell he darted forward to strike the first blow.

The sword ricocheted back off the protective scales, nearly cleaving Morgan's head in two. His hand throbbed as if he'd just launched an attack at an anvil. *Curse it, that just wasn't fair!* Fire and armor, against his insignificant sword and a worse than useless shield. Definitely not fair. He stubbornly hacked again with roughly the same effect as the girl's kick.

The dragon tracked his progress, taking careful aim like an archer sighting on a target. Well, if he had to die, Morgan thought, it might as well be in combat with a dragon. Perhaps after he went up in flames he might go down in song. Assuming anyone found enough in the charred remains to tell who he had been. But without a doubt his death was going to be quicker and messier than it was glorious. From what he'd seen on battlefields over the years, death usually was.

The dragon opened its mouth to flame. Like a fighter desperate to get inside his opponent's reach, Morgan flung himself directly toward the beast, clutching at its haunch. He scrabbled one-handed for purchase on the smooth scales, using the dragon's body as a shelter against the fiery death intended for him. A roar like a thousand forges being lit at once nearly deafened him. Then the flames came, passing just overhead. The heat slammed into him like a blow from a giant, sending him reeling.

Quitting his refuge before the dragon decided to squash him, Morgan dodged around the massive hindquarters. He spared a glance up at the girl. At least the fire hadn't harmed her. Yet. She was still trying to break free. He made another quick foray with the sword, but it was like trying to drive a butter knife into a boulder. Then a huge clawed foot lashed out, catching him in the chest. Morgan went flying.

He hit the ground with a wrenching thud, skidding on his back until he crashed against a large rock. He fumbled around for the sword. It lay halfway between him and a very smug-looking dragon. When he reached for the weapon, blinding pain shot up his arm, exploding in his scrambled brain. It didn't seem to really matter. He was going to die, with or without the sword. Morgan swore like the Legion soldier he was.

He spared a quick glance at the girl. She watched his imminent demise with an air of resignation. Her expression almost seemed aggrieved, as if she resented having her hopes raised only to see them dashed again so quickly. The dragon took careful aim once more, opening its jaws to deliver the *coup de grace*. Morgan struggled to his feet and raised his shield. It was pointless, he knew, but instinct was driving him now. He stared into the gaping maw and waited for death to overtake him.

But instead of deadly fire, what emerged was a little plume of steam and a loud "Urp!"

Morgan stared. The dragon stared back, as if daring him to snicker. It took another sulphur-laden breath and gave forth what was probably intended to be a mighty roar. The effort was punctuated with another series of hiccoughs and a large wisp of acrid blue smoke.

The dragon tossed its head in a gesture of what Morgan could only interpret as frustration. It made a final effort to produce a flame, but more spasms shook the massive body. Shaking off his trancelike state, Morgan made a dash for the sword. Not that it was going to do him any good, but at least he'd have made the effort.

Looking rather sheepish, the dragon hiccoughed twice more, dropped the girl, and unfolded its wings. With two flaps it began to rise, the ascent marred by its ongoing hiccoughs. Morgan grabbed his sword in his left hand—his right still felt useless—and slashed savagely at the dragon as it gained altitude. The blade bounced off its scales again, and

Morgan growled in frustration.

The spiked tail lashed almost idly in his direction. Another shudder spoiled the dragon's aim, and what should have been a killing blow flashed harmlessly by. Morgan stood captivated as the dragon winged drunkenly away over the treetops. One final "Urp!" echoed back to him.

Good God, I'm still alive! And still had all the important bits attached.

A feminine voice broke in on his reverie. "Don't just stand there gawking," it commanded. "Help me up!"

Chapter Two

The girl lay sprawled in a tangled heap. Morgan sheathed his sword and extended his hands, wincing at the pain throbbing through his right arm. He ignored it and when she took his offered hands he pulled her upright.

She swayed for a moment, as if she might topple into his arms. A little part of Morgan's brain, one he had thought well suppressed, suggested this might not be such a bad prospect. He slammed the door on this notion. He didn't have time for such distractions, no matter how pleasant they might be.

Anyhow the girl either regained her balance or thought better of the falling-into-his-arms motif. She made a rather futile attempt to smooth out her tattered, mud-stained dress. Morgan noted a telltale trembling in her hands, but when she finally spoke her voice seemed calm, betraying no hint of her recent horror.

"Thanks," she said. "I really didn't think anyone would hear me scream. I figured I was going to end up as the dragon's breakfast."

"My lady," said Morgan formally, "I'm happy to have been of service. Did you take any injury from your... from the..." His voice trailed off, his brain refusing to allow the word past his lips.

"Dragon," the girl finished for him briskly. "Most definitely a dragon. I've seen drawings in the old storybooks, and in history texts as well. Rather a magnificent creature, wasn't it? And no, thank you, I don't seem to be at all hurt. Are you? He caught you a pretty good kick there. But we're both still alive, so I guess things could have been worse, eh?"

Morgan gaped.

"You did cut it a bit fine though, didn't you?" she went on, as calm as if she was commenting on the weather. "Another few seconds, and I would have been part of the history texts myself. First girl eaten by a dragon in three centuries. My claim to fame."

She laughed at Morgan's startled expression. "Don't worry, I'll be fine. Although in about five minutes, I'm probably going to have screaming hysterics. You won't mind too much, will you?"

"I...what?" Morgan opened and closed his mouth like a gaffed fish. She should have been quivering in horror, not bantering like this. She had as much self-control as any battle-hardened veteran. Most women—men as well, he conceded—would have already succumbed to those screaming hysterics. He was having a hard time suppressing them himself. But if she could manage it, so could he. "No, of course not," he said. "Who could blame you?"

But as the tension of the moment drained away, it was being replaced with a strong curiosity, itching to be satisfied. "At the risk of being thought rude, who are you?" he asked. "And what are you doing out here? The forest is no place for a girl!" He looked around, but no one else emerged from the safety of the trees. "And you're all alone, aren't you? No escort?"

"No, no escort," she replied with a shake of her head, the gesture a mixture of defiance and wariness. Subtle golden flecks in her brown eyes gave her a slightly exotic look at odds with the plain sensibility of her green walking dress and sturdy boots. Morgan wrested his attention back to her words as she added, "I've never needed one before."

Interesting. This girl was no delicate flower if she traipsed about the forest on her own. As far as Morgan could tell, most of the ladies at court felt quite daring if they chanced to stroll through the palace gardens. A tramp through the woods? Not likely.

Which made her an object of suspicion. Because this would be an excellent place for a clandestine rendezvous. Well, except for the dragon, of course. But all in all, this secluded clearing, far from prying eyes, would be an ideal meeting place for someone with treason in mind. Someone passing sensitive information to agents of King Varsil, monarch of Kilbourne's aggressive neighbor to the north, Rhuddlan.

Someone was doing just that, as Morgan knew all too well. There was a traitor in their midst, someone highly placed. In all likelihood one of the men on the Royal Council, of which Morgan was a member. That person was funneling political and military intelligence to the Rhuddlanis. Information that would make it much easier for them to mount another invasion attempt into Kilbourne territory. One Morgan and the Legion he commanded would find hard to halt this time.

Morgan's current assignment, known to only two other men, was to determine the source of the leak and stop it. Was it possible this girl was a courier, acting for the traitor? Had he unwittingly stumbled on a lead to his quarry? He scanned her face for some trace of duplicity but found none. Actually, all he could see were those fascinating gold-flecked eyes.

She regarded him in turn with less enthusiasm than might have been expected from someone who'd just been rescued from certain death. Of course, Morgan temporized, her reaction might be due to the realization that her rescuer wasn't the typical knight in shining armor.

His unusual heritage was writ plain to see in his features. They didn't call him the Dark Knight for nothing. Although not to his face, at least not anymore. He thrust this thought away and resumed his scrutiny. Their eyes met for a brief moment and Morgan felt a sudden chill course through him, as if the sun had passed behind a cloud. Odd. Perhaps she was up to something.

Yet his instincts told him she was more likely just an innocent victim of circumstance, in the wrong place at the wrong time. He'd long since learned to trust those instincts. Still...

"You're a frequent visitor to the forest?" Morgan kept his tone mild but added just a touch of steel. He needed answers. Needed to be sure she wasn't linked to the traitor he was supposed to uncover. The traitor most people assumed was Morgan McRobbie, Knight-Commander of the King's Legion. The Dark Knight.

"Actually, yes," she replied.

He couldn't decide if she looked guilty, or merely annoyed at being challenged. But he pressed on. "All right, I'll ask again—who are you, and what are you doing out here?"

Morgan found himself on the receiving end of a fierce glare. "If you were going to be beastly," she said, biting off each word, "perhaps you should have just left me to my dragon."

As Morgan choked on this, her belligerent expression softened. She gave what might under other circumstances have almost been a faint smile. "Oh, very well. I suppose, since you rescued me, you have the right," she conceded. "My name is Marissa duBerry. I'm lady-in-waiting to Queen Gwyndolyn. I'm here because I came to collect flowers for the queen's boudoir." She indicated with a gesture what once might have been a basket, now trampled flat under the dragon's weight. "Oh, look, the foul creature sat on them!"

Either she was an excellent actress, or her story was true. To his surprise Morgan found his credulity still intact. *Trust your instincts.*

She continued, "I often walk in the forest, gathering flowers for the queen's pleasure. The day was so pleasant that I went a bit farther afield than normal. But bandits and ogres wouldn't dare come around here. And I certainly never thought to encounter a dragon." She shivered at the memory. "I didn't think dragons even existed anymore."

"Neither did I," Morgan admitted, relaxing his own guard a little. "If I hadn't seen it with my own eyes, I wouldn't have believed it." He rubbed his aching arm. It wasn't broken, by some miracle, although he was going to have a marvelous batch of bruises to show for this little escapade. If he hadn't been wearing a mail shirt, the dragon's kick would have likely torn him in two. As it was, it just felt like it had.

"You should be safe now," he said. "I don't think it will be back, now it knows there's a knight here to challenge it."

"Let's hope so." Her voice was dubious, and she glanced up toward the sky. "Although," she murmured, "it didn't seem so much concerned as indisposed. Ah well..." She cocked her head, reminding Morgan of a pert and inquisitive sparrow. "And so, bold knight," she went on, "having saved me from the dragon, what reward would you claim?"

Morgan bowed. "None at all," he said. "Your thanks are payment enough. It's my oath-bound duty to see justice done and evil banished from the kingdom."

Her eyes narrowed. "My word! Did they teach you that in knight school?" The sarcasm dripped from her voice like honey from a hive. "A pretty speech and a most noble sentiment. It does you credit, I'm sure. But you shall have some reward. I won't have it said any man had a claim on me."

Morgan shook his head. "Nay, m'lady. You have thanked me, and that will suffice."

Her eyes flashed dangerously and her voice was filled with agitation as she demanded, "Would you deny me?" Her hands began to tremble again. She quickly clasped them together and smiled up at him. It was a bright and brittle smile which looked as if it could dissolve into either sobs or hysterical laughter without warning. "I wish to grant you a boon. Are you churlish enough to refuse a lady so?"

Hmm. Was her offer intended to distract him from asking more questions? He mentally tossed a coin, which came up on the side of *no*. "As you wish," he replied. "I will accept your gracious offer, since you insist. You may satisfy your obligation by having dinner with me this evening."

Morgan blinked in surprise. *Good lord, why had he made such a request?* His dratted instincts taking over again, no doubt. With all the concerns he had to juggle at the moment, he couldn't afford the distraction a girl would present. No matter how interesting her eyes might be.

"Have dinner with you?" she repeated slowly, as if the concept were completely alien to her.

Morgan nodded, not trusting himself to speak. Having made his request, he was not about to go back on it now. *Instincts, trust your instincts.* The refrain rang through him almost like the toll of a bell.

"Why?" she demanded, hands on her hips. She brought to mind a stern schoolmistress from his distant past, challenging why a certain young boy didn't have his sums completed. It was rather daunting. Under the force of her glare Morgan grasped desperately for explanations. Unfortunately the only thing he could come up with was the truth, and it was something less than diplomatic.

"You're... different..." He trailed off, a flush rising to his hairline. Damn it, he wasn't good with words. Give him a sword any day. Although right now he just wanted to fall on one.

She grimaced. "Not exactly a courtier, are you? If that was intended as a compliment, I think I should return it for repairs. It seems to lack a certain something."

Morgan groaned to himself; she must think him a babbling idiot. That impertinent part of his brain piped up again, wondering just why he cared. He ignored it.

"I'm sorry, I'm not putting it well," he said, scrambling to think how to explain without offending her any further. "All right, look. Ninety-nine girls out of a hundred, having been snatched up by a dragon and rescued in the nick of time, would have murmured 'My hero!' and swooned at her rescuer's feet."

"A bit hard, all that murmuring and swooning," Marissa observed.

"That's exactly what I mean! You have a different outlook on things. No swooning, no murmuring. Instead, you calmly dust yourself off and start in by berating me for my tardiness. I've never met a woman—anyone—like you, and..." He looked at her helplessly. "Dinner?"

Chapter Three

Marissa regarded her rescuer with a mixture of curiosity and suspicion. He'd been so bold as he had faced the dragon. Now he just looked nervous. As if he was unsure of himself? Or of her?

Well, it didn't matter, did it? If a dinner together was the worst she had to endure, so be it. After all, he *had* rescued her. She had a good idea what reward most of the so-called "gentlemen" of her acquaintance would have exacted. On the whole, the attentions of the dragon would be preferable. One evening in this knight's company should be tolerable in exchange for her life.

Decision made, she replied, "Very well, Sir Knight, I will accept your invitation." She narrowed her eyes again. "Peculiar though it and your explanation both seem. But first, tell me your name. You seem to have neglected to do so."

Her champion hesitated. Finally he said, "I do beg your pardon, m'lady. Sir Morgan McRobbie, of the King's Legion. At your service." He made an elegant bow.

"Morgan Mc…" She recoiled as if another dragon had suddenly hoven into view. "Oh! That…" She couldn't stop the look of burgeoning horror she knew must be spreading across her face.

She should have recognized him before. If only because of his dark complexion, so different from almost every other man in Caerfaen. In the excitement of the moment she'd just chalked it up to a man who lived his life outdoors, exposed to the sun and weather. But no, this was Morgan McRobbie all right. Morgan the half-breed, some called him. And worse. Although not within his hearing.

And he wasn't just "of the King's Legion"—he *was* the King's Legion. Knight-Commander, in fact, and dashing hero of the wars against the Rhuddlani invaders. Of all the people who could have come to her rescue. Morgan McRobbie. The man everyone whispered had turned traitor against Kilbourne.

Was he out here to meet an enemy agent? To hand over information the Rhuddlanis could use to try and invade Kilbourne again? Had she—and the dragon—interrupted something sinister?

Her expression must have given her away. Sir Morgan heaved a sigh. "Aye, m'lady, that one," he acknowledged. "And now, should you wish to decline my invitation I will certainly understand. There are few enough who wish to be seen with the likes of me."

She'd been about to do just that. Then Marissa caught an unexpected flash of despair in Morgan's eyes, so overwhelming as to crumble her resolve under the weight of it. *Does he suffer so because he's a traitor? Or because he isn't?* Well, it didn't matter. It wasn't in her to refuse him.

"I have already accepted your invitation," she told him. "I would not be counted false. Even if you are as black as is rumored..." she trailed off as he grimaced. Marisa flushed, realizing the statement cut two ways. She gathered herself and soldiered on. "Still and all you did save my life, and I'm in your debt. I suppose my reputation can stand a wee bit of tarnish."

"Lady Marissa, you don't have to..."

She cut him off with a raised hand. "Sir Morgan, I have given you my answer. Shall we stand here and debate it until the dragon returns?" She glowered. "At what hour shall I expect you?"

It looked like he was about to choke, although whether from annoyance or amusement, it was difficult to tell. He finally seemed to regain control enough to reply, "Half past seven, if it suits your convenience."

"I shall await..." A shadow fell across them, nearly blotting out the sun. Looking skyward Marissa spied the dragon, high overhead.

Its great wings were outstretched and it rode a current of air in an aspect of silent menace. Then it wobbled slightly. Another hiccough? If the dratted thing regained its ability to flame, it likely would be on them again, looking to continue the fight. Looking to gobble them both down. As they watched, the dragon roared, and then produced a spectacular gout of flame. *Drat!*

It began a lazy descent.

Marissa tore her gaze from the dragon and back to Sir Morgan. "I think," she observed, "it knows there is a knight here who would challenge it. Do dragons, I wonder, *enjoy* a challenge?"

He ignored this well-aimed barb, changing from nervous to confident again in an instant. It was an amazing transformation. A fierce gleam lit his eye as he scanned the terrain, no doubt picking a spot from which to make a stand. He exuded a palpable air of confidence and competence. Indeed, even of nobility.

It was a little disconcerting. Rather like watching a rabbit suddenly turn about and begin to hunt a fox. This was definitely a man to be reckoned with, she realized with a little frisson. If he was a traitor to Kilbourne, he would be a most dangerous one.

"M'lady," he said, "I should get you back to Caerfaen at once. If the dragon returns you'll be in grave danger while I fight him. Having managed by sheer luck to rescue you once, I wouldn't wish to tempt fate a second time."

She wasn't about to let him get the last word in. "You mean he'd swoop down here and char both of us on the spot, don't you?" she observed. "Very well, let us away. I wouldn't want to be roasted and eaten quite yet. You've promised to stand me a dinner."

Morgan stared at her, his mouth opening and closing, but no words emerged. Finally, shaking his head he said, "So I have." He turned and gave a sharp whistle.

An answering whinny and the pounding of hooves heralded the appearance of a huge gray horse at the edge of the clearing. It galloped toward them, stopping in a cloud of dust and rearing to paw the air with steel-shod hooves.

Marissa eyed the stallion in awe. "He's magnificent!" she exclaimed.

"This is Arnicus," Morgan informed her proudly. In an undertone, he muttered, "He's rather a show-off when he's got an audience." The horse nickered and regarded Morgan with an air of reproach. Marissa stifled a chuckle as Morgan continued, "He's served me well over the years and has gotten me out of several tight spots in our time together."

"Good, he can get us out of this one. Less talk and more leaving, Sir Morgan. The dragon's on his way. I don't know about you, but I don't relish the thought of a second engagement."

Marissa found herself practically tossed up onto the horse's back. Morgan mounted in front of her. "You heard the lady," he told the horse. Marissa grabbed at Morgan's waist for support as he shook the reins. "Now, Arnicus!" he cried, and the great horse leapt forward at a speed which was almost dizzying.

Marissa had not been on a horse in years, and never one as fast, or as enormous, as Arnicus. Corded muscles like steel bands rippled beneath her legs as the great gray ran through the trees. She looked down. It was a long way to the ground from up here!

She clutched at Morgan in a determined effort to maintain her seat as they crashed through the forest, stifling a wild laugh. Had she been saved from the clutches of a fearsome dragon only to be killed by falling off a speeding warhorse ridden by a traitorous knight?

Behind them, the dragon roared. In frustration at their escape? Or in triumph at having driven them off? She decided she didn't really care to find out which.

"Can't this nag go any faster?" she yelled into Morgan's ear.

He spared a quick glance back at her, shrugged, and kicked the horse's flanks. Arnicus shot through the forest paths like he had been hurled from a catapult. The dragon roared again.

Out Now!

What's next on your reading list?

Champagne Book Group promises to bring to readers fiction at its finest.

Discover your next
fine read!
http://www.champagnebooks.com/

We are delighted to invite you to receive exclusive rewards. Join our Facebook group for VIP savings, bonus content, early access to new ideas we've cooked up, learn about special events for our readers, and sneak peeks at our fabulous titles.

Join now.
https://www.facebook.com/groups/ChampagneBookClub/

Made in the USA
Middletown, DE
23 February 2023

25423672R00179